Love Nor Money

Brandy Jones

To Jenneviere Villegas and C. Mac Donoghue,
I couldn't have done this without you.

1

There was a sex swing in her bedroom.

Maya narrowed her eyes, head pounding, staring at the object in front of her. When had she gotten a sex swing? *Why* had she gotten a sex swing? And the sheets, these were some kind of satin. Slick against her skin in a way she found disconcerting. It was astonishingly bright, sunlight pouring in from larger windows than she could recall having.

Sitting up so fast she got dizzy, Maya bit back a scream. This was not her room. This was someone else's room. Someone else's *sex* room.

The room was... she searched for a word before settling on *hedonistic*. The bed was the center of attention, pressed up against a wall made entirely of windows. It had to be at least eight by ten. Who needed *eighty square feet* of bed? To her right was another full wall of windows, the sex swing hanging sedately between her and it as though it weren't the most ridiculous thing she'd ever seen. The other wall had chains and some brackets that she could only venture a guess to their use.

Okay. *Okay*. The only logical conclusion was that she had wandered into a brothel. That was... fixable. Surely. And she wasn't attached to any of the chains on the wall, so that was encouraging.

Chains. *On the wall.*

First step, get out of the bed. Maya opted for going over the foot, ignoring the sneaking suspicion that something on the walls might reach out and grab her if she got too close to them. She crawled over the bench that stretched the width of the mattress, trying her best not to touch it. It looked clean but she had a fairly good idea what activities it had seen. There was a door directly in front of her and she opened it cautiously, finding an all marble bathroom on the other side.

She ducked into it quickly, shutting the door and leaning back against it with a sigh of relief. It wasn't *out* but at least she felt moderately safer. She met her eyes in the mirror and choked back a laugh. No need to worry that she'd been sold into the life of a sex slave, she looked *awful*. Last night hadn't started the best and from the looks of it had gone downhill from there. Her brown hair was an absolute rat's nest, what little eyeliner she'd managed to put on smudged back to her ear.

The water from the tap was instantly hot, a far cry from the several minutes it would have taken at her apartment. A few quick scrubs with a washcloth and she at least looked a little less like something a cat dragged in. Tossing the cloth into the sink she took in the gold fixtures - what she had originally thought was an oddly oblong spout were in fact a pair of lips. The handles looked like women's legs, toes pointed to each side. She blinked, wondering if they would turn into something less hideous, but no amount of study made them better.

She glanced through the cabinets, searching for something that might identify where she was. A hotel logo maybe? A hotel that catered to a *very* specific clientele? She found a random assortment of items, but nothing that seemed personal, nothing to give any clues to who usually occupied the room.

Cautiously, she opened the door, peering around it to see if anyone had entered while she was in the bathroom. It was blessedly empty, although just as freaky as she had remembered. She scooted up close to the window, glancing down.

It was far. Very *very* far. Enough that she took a step back before she got dizzy. Okay, she was in a brothel - maybe sex club? - at least twenty stories up. Despite the restraints she hadn't been tied down and she was still wearing all her clothes from the night before. Some of that was good news.

There were two doors remaining, one on the same wall as the bathroom and one on the far wall. The one with the chains. She was pretty sure she knew which was the exit but her curiosity was getting the better of her and she crossed to the nearest doors instead, flipping the light switch with one hand.

She blinked. Then blinked again. Nothing changed from one to the next. Well, she was right about one thing, it *was* a closet. Roughly the size of the bedroom in her last apartment. And it was stuffed full of clothes.

A dark blue outfit that might charitably be called a dress swung gently from a padded hanger - a cheesy plastic badge was pinned to the chest, a pair of silver handcuffs attached to the shiny patent leather belt. Behind it was a white nurse's outfit, complete with stitched red cross. The next outfit looked more like real clothes, a full length bodysuit, but further examination revealed it to be a crotchless astronaut flight suit.

That was the naughty Halloween side of the closet. Noted.

The other side and back wall had waist high dressers lining the walls, above them a jaw-dropping amount of shoes. Boots, pumps, sandals... each with a minimum of four inch heels. None of them useful for running away.

Surely, *surely*, somewhere in this den of smut there had to be normal clothes. What kind of person kept a closet devoted to nothing but fetish wear?

The first dresser she checked was full of perfectly normal lingerie. Lacy thongs at the top, peekaboo bras the next drawer down, stockings and garter belts. All of it made to fit someone who lived a life on a treadmill and had never been in the same room as a cheesecake, let alone eaten one for breakfast. Maya cautiously picked up one of the more substantial pieces. She *might* be able to get it up to her thigh. Maybe.

The next dresser was animal themed. Printed fabric and soft ears in the top drawer. The one below held tails attached to - she slammed the drawer shut and cautiously opened the next to reveal a truly startling amount of whips.

Maya was blushing to the tips of her ears and didn't bother looking in the last one. Curiosity was one thing but she did *not* need to know what other kinky fashion was hidden in there. She backed out of the closet, closing the doors softly behind her. Taking in the room again, from the too large bed to the BDSM gear she felt fear rising in her throat.

What the hell had happened last night?

It had started at a bar.

Well, not really, it had started when she got evicted. Then it had moved to the bar while she tried to decide what to do with herself and a Honda Civic's worth of belongings. But she was relatively certain her eviction wasn't related to her present circumstances so it seemed best to start at the bar.

It wasn't a nice place, but not a dump either. Just nice enough to attract an after work crowd with a pool table in one corner and a menu of "cocktails" that made her snort. Its best perk, however, was that it *wasn't* part of any syndicate, as

4

far as she knew. Too close to the nicer suburbs to be involved in seedier activities.

"ID?"

Sighing Maya pulled her wallet, thumbing the card loose and handing it over. "Do I look *that* young?"

"If you look under thirty-" he started to say then paused, staring at the card. His eyes flicked up to her face and then back to the name. "You're-"

"Nope," she cut him off quickly, snatching the ID back. "No I'm not. And even if I was, I don't know what you're talking about."

He eyed her dubiously. "Okay," he drawled slowly, "what'll it be?"

"Vodka cranberry, whatever is cheapest."

Maya watched him move behind the bar, grabbing a bottle of what was most definitely *not* their cheapest vodka. When he came back she pulled out cash, slipping her ID in her wallet. "How much?"

"On the house."

"Oh for goodness-" Maya pulled a twenty, shoving it his direction. "I swear, he's not going to cover my tab. Take the money."

The bartender shook his head, backing away with his hands raised. "Do you know what would happen to me if my boss found out I charged you?"

With a small sigh she took the drink, leaving the money between them. "Look, I'm leaving this twenty no matter what. However many drinks it buys me is up to you, the rest is your tip."

He considered that for a moment and nodded, taking the twenty and putting it in a jar back by the register. Maya sighed as she watched him go.

"Hey, if I end up catching a cab later, is my car good here overnight?"

"We won't tow it," he tossed over his shoulder. "But I can't guarantee no one will break into it."

She nodded to herself. It would have to do. If she called around she might be able to find a cheap motel. That would be one night down at least. And tomorrow...

She tossed the drink back in one slug. Tomorrow could be tomorrow's problem. Looking up to signal for another drink she saw that he was on the phone. For a moment she debated serving herself, but a decade of work in customer service kept her hands on her side of the bar.

Instead she swiped a pen and napkin, neatly writing out her prospects. She had three hundred or so in cash, both a big and a small number. Not enough to *fix* her life, but enough to keep her alive for a few days. Next she put her car, it was over a decade old and needed a new transmission but she would drive it into the ground if she had to. A few books. Her clothes. A pillow.

Maya stopped herself before she could put her pasta strainer down. It wasn't important, and made not a dent in her net worth. All together it wasn't much, in fact it was very, very little. She needed a job. And not one that shorted her hours and pay every other week. And an apartment that had reliable water pressure. Maybe a pet as well, while she was wishing.

The bar was picking up, a rowdy group by the pool table, a few men in a booth nursing beers. She was no longer sitting alone at the bar, a couple a few stools down was snuggled up and giggling. Good for them.

Crossing her arms on the wood she settled her chin onto her wrists. What she needed to do was get out of town entirely, go somewhere her name didn't mean anything and she might actually be able to build a career. Tapping the edge of her glass she signaled the bartender for another, watching as he poured the reddish liquid. She should *definitely* not be

6

drinking.

"Hey beautiful."

Maya sighed, barely glancing as the man sidled up next to her. "I'm not what you're looking for."

A long pause, in the mirror behind the bar she could barely make him out around the bottles. He seemed confused, staring at her while she looked straight ahead. "And what do you think I'm looking for?"

With an even heavier sigh she sat up, turning to him. He was handsome, nearly black hair neatly styled without a strand out of place, a perfectly trimmed goatee hugging his mouth, and far overdressed for this dive bar. A dark gray suit and black shirt, loafers so polished she could see her reflection in them.

"A good time," she responded.

She wasn't what he expected, she could see that. The way his dark eyebrows drew down and he frowned at her. He was leaning on one arm, practiced nonchalance - his sleeve pulled up enough that she could see his expensive watch.

Great, she could be some guy's 'slumming it' catch.

"You're not a good time?" he asked, taking his drink from the bartender and slipping cash into the man's hand. Maya's eyes narrowed, that definitely looked like a hundred dollar bill. A generous tipper? Showing off?

"I'm a *great* time," she corrected, weighing her options. The door was on the other side of him, the bathroom behind her. Was there a back door? And if there wasn't she'd be leaving him alone with her drink which was number one on the 'Things Single Ladies at Bars Shouldn't Do' list. "I'm just not going to be *your* great time."

"Maybe I could be *your* good time?" Great, her forced abrasiveness had caught his interest. And his continued presence didn't bode well for him taking no for an answer. She'd all but written him a thesis on 'no' and he was refusing to take it. And then he smiled and he had a *dimple* and Maya needed to end this fast, before she made a *very* bad decision.

"Six minutes bent over the back of your couch?" she turned fully to him, arching an eyebrow and channeling her mother. "A cab ride home? Please, forgive me, but *no thank you*." Draining her glass she gestured for another. "You seem like… well you seem like a person. And you're not *not* attractive. I'm sure one of the nice ladies over at the pool table would love to give your couch a try. But I just want to drink my cocktail in peace." She hesitated before adding, "Please."

The air stood still, he looked like maybe he wasn't even breathing. Then he nodded, "Fair enough," and left.

The bartender brought her another glass and she took it with a sigh. She'd hoped to have an excuse to leave but he swiped the old one before she could stop him. What was this, her third? Fourth? She felt fine but also knew the moment she stood up she was going to have a problem. She tossed half back immediately, trying to get it over with.

"You drink it like you got a grudge against it."

Maya choked, pressing a hand to her chest and looking up through teary eyes. "What?"

The man gestured at her glass, "The whiskey, you're drinking like someone on a mission."

Was she wearing a 'Try your luck' sign? What the hell was going on tonight? He, at least, seemed more relaxed. Black polo and dark gray pants, a thick black beard and shaved head. She glanced quickly to see if it was to cover that he was going bald but couldn't see any evidence. He smirked at her, eye twinkling from behind wire-rimmed glasses.

"You done eye-fucking me?"

"*I was not*-" she began quickly and caught the twitch of his lips. She glared, "I wasn't eyeballing you, I was checking for male-pattern baldness."

It was his turn to glare, opening his mouth to retort but she cut him off.

"Please don't. I'm sure whatever you're about to say will be charming and probably flirtatious and then I'm going to have to spend the next ten minutes letting you down and I'm having a really bad day so can we just... not?"

He pursed his lips and nodded, knocking one hand against the bar before leaving. What an utterly odd-

"Hey can I-"

"Is there some kind of freaking *bet*? What is-" she burst out, rounding on the newest man before swallowing the words back at his stunned expression. "Sorry, sorry, but seriously?" Her eyes roved the bar and sure enough the first two men were leaning against a table nearby, heads together and watching the newest sacrifice with barely disguised glee.

"How much?"

His tongue darted out to wet his lips, one eyebrow arching. "Pardon?"

"What's the bet for? How much?"

He blinked at her and then tilted his head. "Hundred bucks."

A hundred... Jesus Christ, they were probably from one of those financial firms downtown. Just what she needed. "Hundred for what?" He seemed confused so she started counting possibilities off on one hand. "Buying me a drink? My number? A kiss? Taking me home? Be more specific."

"Taking you home," he answered without missing a beat.

"No."

"Worth a shot," he said with a grin. "Actually it was only getting your number... and a kiss."

Maya hummed, trailing a finger around the rim of her glass. He was cute, all three of them were. But he seemed softer than the other two, his smile coming more easily. His brown hair looked soft, and his scruffy beard had the beginning of some gray in it.

"Okay."

He blinked at her. "What?"

"Okay," she turned on the barstool, shielding herself from the other's views. "But you split it with me."

"Fifty, fifty?"

"Yes, and I get mine upfront. Now."

A wide grin split his face as he pulled a bill out, tucking it under the edge of her glass - for all the world like he was paying for the next round. She scribbled a random set of digits on the back of a bar napkin and tucked it into his shirt pocket.

"No tongue," she warned him and he pouted.

"Take *all* the fun out of it why don't you," he muttered, sliding a hand behind her neck and pulling her into him. His lips were softer than she expected, the hairs of his mustache tickling under her nose. When she pulled away he nipped at her lower lip, tugging it softly and giving her a devilish grin when she jerked backwards.

Holding his hands up he tried to look contrite, "That was teeth, not tongue."

A technicality. She glared and he laughed, chucking her lightly under the chin. "A pleasure meeting you, Maya."

"You too," she said automatically, purposefully not watching him go. She needed to start thinking of how she was going to get to her next stop. Driving was out of the question, and she had a feeling walking might be as well with as much as she'd had to drink. She searched her pockets for her phone, there was enough money on her debit card to front a ride... wherever.

And she had fifty extra bucks. Hooray for her.

She tossed the last of her drink back, pushing away from the bar. When she stood the room tilted precariously and she put a hand out to steady herself. Someone caught it, wrapping an arm around her waist.

"I'm fine," she slurred, knees crumpling. "Really I'm-"

It was the last thing she remembered before the world had gone dark and she'd woken up with the sex swing. A quick pat down showed her clothing still all in correct place and fit so whoever it was - despite the terrible taste - was at least gentleman enough not to do anything while she was out cold.

Low bar, but amazing how hard it was for some people to clear.

The only question was… who? Her kissing partner? The abrupt one who looked bored? Expensive watch?

She supposed she should feel a little more shame at the thought. Waking up in some stranger's sex dungeon - could it really be a dungeon with such big windows? But it wasn't her first drunken hookup and likely not her last. The key was to get out fast, without seeing anyone. Get back to her car, make a plan…

Pressing her ear to the last door she held her breath, listening. There was a vague murmur of voices but they weren't nearby. If she moved quickly enough, with enough confidence, she could be out within two minutes.

Easy peasy.

2

"Good morning."

Maya froze. Maybe if she didn't move the owner of the voice wouldn't see her.

"I can see you."

She eyed the man a few feet away dubiously, it was the guy she'd kissed, with the scruffy beard. So not the *worst* possible scenario. But as she got closer she saw it wasn't just him, but all three men who had tried their shot.

All three, Maya? Really? she thought, trying not to blush. That was... new. For her. Even if they hadn't actually done anything the idea that she *might* have sent a thrill down her spine. She wouldn't, of course, she wasn't the type. But it *was* an electrifying possibility to ponder.

They were just as handsome in the daylight, posing in various positions around the kitchen. She'd like to give them the benefit of the doubt but who read their tablet with their butt stuck out like *that*? Posing, definitely.

"Hi."

"Bagel?" Butt-out stood up, running a hand down his chin and reaching for a plate, sliding it her direction. In the light of day her kissing partner had tattoos, a lot of them. Wrapping up his arms and barely visible at the base of his neck. Maybe other places? She wracked her mind, trying to remember if she'd seen his other places.

"No thank you," she declined politely, edging towards the door. "I think I'll just… go. It's been great, I'm sure."

"Stay," the order came from the man who had approached her first. Had he given her a name? At the bar or while they… *had* they? He looked almost exactly the same as at the bar, perfectly put together in a slightly different suit, expensive wrist watch catching the light. How could he look so good this early in the morning?

"No, really," she demurred, holding her hands up and backing away. "It's all good. Thank you for what was probably a good time and-"

"You're not going anywhere," the last man said, the one sitting at the table with his feet propped up. It was shaved head, looking nearly as smug in the kitchen as he had at the bar. "We kidnapped you."

Maya blinked.

"For fuck's sake Daniel," Beard groaned, pushing away from the kitchen island. "We've gotta teach you some tact."

"What for?" the man, Daniel, asked with a scowl. "She's gonna figure it out eventually. What's the point in fucking about?"

"We agreed to present it gently," Beard retorted, knocking the man's feet off the table with one hand and settling into the chair across from him. "Do *you* want to deal with some hysterical girl in the apartment?"

"*I'm* not dealing with shit," Daniel grunted, dropping his eyes to his phone.

Expensive watch ignored them, watching her as she struggled to process what was going on.

"Excuse me?" The two at the table went silent, both looking up at her. "Can you say that again?"

"Think of it as an involuntary vacation," Watch said in complete seriousness.

"An involun-" Maya trailed off, darting her eyes between each of them. She could run. The door was right there, only twenty feet away. She might make it before they caught her. But what if it was locked? And this was not a small building, there'd probably be an elevator to wait for or stairs to find. That would take time.

And not for nothing, she *was* technically homeless right now. Kidnapping wasn't the best solution to her problems, but it was *a* solution. And it *was* a nice apartment. Certainly nicer than the last place she'd been kidnapped to. Fourteen years old and a day into her first period. She'd have personally given her captors anything they wanted for ten minutes indoors with an A/C unit and a tampon. Compared to it this place felt like a vacation.

"Okay." All three gaped when she slid onto a bar stool, reaching for the plate of bagels Beard had offered her. She carefully spread cream cheese across it before looking up to meet Watch's eyes. "For how long?"

His eyes narrowed in suspicion. "At least a couple of weeks."

Shrugging, she took a bite of the bagel, humming softly. It was good. "Do you have tea?"

Beard responded, walking to a cabinet and pulling down a box, setting it in front of her cautiously. With one hand he flipped the button on an electric kettle. "You're taking this better than I thought you would."

Maya shrugged again. "It's not the first time. You're looking for money I assume? I hate to tell you, it won't be a lot."

The corner of Watch's lips quirked and he studied her with something new in his eyes. "For his only daughter? I think Alvani will find some cash."

She laughed, she couldn't help it, then choked when a piece of bagel went wrong. Pressing the heel of one hand to her chest she coughed until she could breathe again, tears welling in her eyes. "That's… that's funny. You might be able to get a couple grand out of my brother, as long as Dad doesn't find out. But Eric Alvani himself?" She snorted, pulling an empty mug towards her and dropping the tea bag into it, "Not a chance."

"Sounds like something a kidnap victim would say," Daniel pointed out, teeth flashing white when he gave her a shark-like smile.

Pouring the hot water Maya smiled back at him. "Just don't take it out on me when it goes sideways. Do you have any milk?"

She sipped her tea and watched them exchange glances. Expensive Watch pulled a small pitcher out and handed it to her, studying her face.

"What if something happened to you?"

"If you killed me, you mean?" Maya snorted. "He'd be mad, for sure, and there would be retaliation. But short of that…" Sighing, she deepened her voice, "*You're not my problem anymore.*"

"Sounds like a peach."

A shrug. "He's who he is. I haven't spoken to him in over a decade. If you wanted a hostage you'd have been better off with Nico." Maya cocked her head and laughed, "Not sure he'd have gone for that whole kissing ruse though."

"You *barely* did," Goatee pointed out, "I was nearly offended."

"Needed the money," Maya didn't look at him as she said it, stirring her tea absently. "Sounds like we've got the same problem."

"We're not looking for money, we just need him distracted," Goatee corrected.

She stared at him, pursing her lips. "Who *are* you?"

"Stefan," Beard pointed at himself. He glanced to the right and Expensive Watch lifted an eyebrow. "Diego. Short, dark, and scowly over there is Daniel."

She smiled back and frowned when Daniel only stared and then turned his nose up at her. "You can call me sir."

Maya rolled her eyes, "Stefan, Diego and Dorkus, got it."

Stefan laughed and even Diego's lips twitched into half a smile while Daniel glared.

"I'm… well I guess you know who I am." She narrowed her eyes at Stefan, "That's your names, but who *are* you?"

"The Kings."

Oh, she'd been hoping they would say anything but that. Even as far as she'd removed herself from her old life, she'd heard the name. They'd risen in the area a few years back and quickly become major players in the underground. She thought they mainly dealt in weapons, but maybe drugs too? Human trafficking?

Suddenly she didn't feel quite so amused at the situation.

"You've heard of us?" Diego asked, face carefully neutral.

Maya nodded slowly. "I have."

"Then you know we're going to do whatever it takes to get what we want."

Maya nodded again.

Someone touched her hand and she jerked away, staring at Stefan in shock while he held his palms up and out in a universal sign of 'no harm meant.' "We've got a job coming up and we need to do it without interference from the Alvani cartel. Our plan was to keep you locked up here for a couple weeks. Let him stew a bit, then let you go." His brows drew together, "But if you're telling the truth-"

"I am."

Stefan frowned. "Then we need a new distraction."

"What if we fucked you?" Daniel asked, strangely calm as

though he hadn't lobbed a verbal grenade at her.

"No thanks," Maya gave him a tight smile. "I'm not that desperate."

"Aren't you?" Diego asked with a raised eyebrow.

"Hey," she scowled back.

Stefan pulled his wallet, thumbing loose a piece of paper. "Forty dollars, cash. Two hundred fifty, bank. Honda Civic, 2004. Table lamp, broken. First edition *The Great Train Robbery*-"

"What are you doing?"

He held it up between two fingers, "Looks to me like a list of assets. A *short* list of assets."

"Give that back, it's private," she snatched at it but he pulled away.

"You gave it to me," he held it up so she could see the fake number she'd scribbled on the back. "So it's fair game."

"Sounds like you need some money," Diego drawled.

"I'm not going to sleep with you for fifty bucks, I'll crawl into the river looking for pocket change before I do that." She didn't add *again*. There was no reason for them to know and she had only needed once to learn her lesson there.

"I think we can offer a bit more than fifty."

Maya gaped at him, then looked between them. "You're serious?"

"We need him distracted," Diego shrugged. "And it sounds like there's no love lost between you. So how about you spend a couple of weeks here with us? We've got people, can cater to your every desire."

A shiver ran down her spine at 'every desire', one she tried very hard to ignore. "I'm not... I mean, that's not something I-"

Stefan slid the napkin towards her, holding it in place with one finger when she tried to take it. "It's only got to be real enough that he'll believe it."

17

"How long?" It wasn't a concession, it *wasn't*.

"Two weeks?" Stefan shot Diego a glance and the other man nodded. "Maybe three."

"And we don't actually have to... you know," Maya couldn't bring herself to put the word to it.

"Not if you don't want to." Stefan looked like he was sure she would want to. And he wasn't wrong, *per se*.

"To be clear, you're offering to give me money to pretend to be your... what? Mistress? For a few weeks?" Maya said slowly.

"Wait," Daniel spluttered, "when did we go from kidnapping her to paying her?"

"When you needed me to pretend to be in love with you. If you want me to cooperate I need incentive," Maya snapped back.

"Love is optional," Stefan drawled, "we'll settle for lust."

Well *that* wouldn't be hard. Whatever pheromones they were giving off had her head spinning. "Fine, lust then. That's actually harder."

"It is?" Stefan asked, pouring himself another coffee.

"With love I can bat my eyelashes, moon about. Sigh when you're nearby," Maya pointed out. "But lust, it's more physical. Probably more touching."

"Twenty grand," Diego offered without hesitation. She gaped at him, at his fingers drumming against the island. "Twenty grand to be our mistress."

Twenty grand. That was the down payment on a new place. Furniture. Food and rent until she could find another job. Getting her car fixed. It was a life-changing amount of money.

"Twenty-five," she countered.

Diego smiled. "I'd have gone to thirty."

"A week."

Diego blinked, a grin breaking out across his face. The

dimple on his right cheek made him look younger, boyish. "For that much money I'd expect some actual services in return."

"Services?" she squeaked.

Across the island Daniel grinned, teeth flashing. "You wouldn't be the first girl we paid for sex." He paused, a thoughtful look on his face, "Maybe the most expensive though."

"No," Maya shook her head, hair falling in front of her face which she brushed aside. "I'm not… I'm *not* that girl. But I'll *fake* it."

"Wouldn't be the first to do that either," Daniel sighed.

She glared. "I'll *pretend* to be your mistress. And even be all touchy feely with you - *within reason* - when there's other people around."

"It will need to look real," Diego pointed out. "It's more than hugs and a few kisses on the cheek."

"Why?" This was quickly becoming more complicated than she wanted.

"Because no one would believe it otherwise, kitten," Daniel told her with a smirk. "Not with us being who we are, or you looking like that."

Looking like what? she wanted to ask but bit it back. She was in way over her head as it was. "I accept that there will need to be *some* touching. But nothing… X-rated." They laughed. All three of them laughed at her and she didn't like it one bit, glaring at each of them in turn. "That's the agreement. Pretend and minimal touching."

"I'll pay you," Diego purred, crowding into her space. "We can come to an agreement on that, because it's easier than the alternative. But part of that is that it's going to look real." He stroked a finger down her cheek, down her neck, tickling the swell of her breast. "And that means we are going to be all over you. *That's* the agreement."

Maya mulled it over. Her father would kill her, that was a certainty. But she wasn't sure what had been holding him back all these years anyway so it didn't feel like that was much of a change. It was a bridge she'd burned ages ago. Her concern was more local - with the three men in front of her. Did she trust them to do what was best for her? Absolutely not. She did, however, trust them to do what was best for themselves - and assuming they were telling the truth she was useful to them. Like a car you bought to drive around for a couple of weeks to impress your friends.

"And if I say no?"

"We go back to the kidnapping plan," Diego shrugged, dropping his hand.

And Maya would get nothing. "Fine. Just, nothing down there."

Daniel snorted. "Down there?"

She tossed a glare his direction. "You know where."

"No, tell us, where?" It was Stefan's turn to tease her, apparently.

Crossing her arms she frowned at all of them.

"No one will touch your pussy," Diego promised. His serious face turned into a sly smile, "Not unless you want us to."

"That won't happen."

They were laughing at her. Again.

"Well," Diego said, an amused grin tugging his lips. "We have a deal?"

When Maya was eight she'd jumped off the roof of their lake house, sure that the sheet she was holding would break her fall. It hadn't, although the rhododendron bushes had done an admirable job of it. She'd walked away with a sprained ankle and enough scratches her mom was convinced she'd gotten into a fight with a neighborhood cat.

At thirteen she'd followed an older boy behind the school

bleachers after a high school football game. She'd been lucky to leave that situation with bruised knuckles and a new appreciation for why her father told her to stay away from boys.

And at sixteen she'd left her entire life and family behind.

But in all of that, all of her life's lessons and conflicts, Maya was sure she'd never done anything as stupid as what she was about to.

"It's a deal."

The shower pressure in the bathroom was outstanding.

The tiled stall was, no surprise, built large enough for four people to wash their hair and not bump elbows. A startling array of knobs and levers lined three walls. Maya spent a good five minutes adjusting temperature, pressure, angle, and spout. One set turned the entire ceiling into a shower head, gently cascading down like rain. Another lit the room up in brightly changing colors. She was pretty sure it was bluetooth enabled.

A quick scout around in the cabinets had amassed a variety of hotel sized soaps and moisturizers. She had her choice of scents, settling on something vaguely orange blossom. The towels were fluffy, thickly woven, and felt like they'd recently been washed.

Thankfully.

There were hair curlers and straighteners, a box of bobby pins, hair ties, clips in every size she could imagine, and even makeup. It really was a full service sex room, no poor woman needed to limp home after a night in this apartment with smeared makeup or lopsided hair.

Wrapped in a towel Maya stared at the closet. She studied the layout, mentally cataloging what she wouldn't consider, even if it *did* fit. There was a whole drawer she knew of that she wouldn't bother opening again. And her gut said the back half of the closet was best left untouched. She'd rather leave the whole thing untouched but that had been quickly nixed by all three of them at once.

"Can you have someone go get my car? It's parked out by the bar. I've got a couple of suitcases of stuff that I can-"

"Pull something out of the room," Daniel said with a hand wave, already brushing by her with his nose buried in his phone.

Maya stared at him. "You mean the closet of lingerie? In the sex dungeon? Whose room is that anyway?"

"Yours, now."

He left before she could say another word, leaving her to turn her attention to the other two. "You can't really expect me to-"

"For that money," Diego gave her a dispassionate assessment, "you can wear what we want you to."

Stefan gave her a commiserating look but had been no help either, leaving her standing in the kitchen by herself. She had two options: continue wearing the one outfit she had on or find something in that closet. Or go naked.

So three choices.

One by one, she started with the costumes. Half of them were immediate no's, based on size alone, thrown into a pile outside the door. The other half she stretched and poked at, discarding another dozen. Then she dove into the drawers with the same methodicalness. When she finished she had a small pile of six items. Of the pile, most of it was string. Presumably held on by dark magic and wishful thinking.

It was not, perhaps, the *best* start to a two week wardrobe but it was something.

And a robe. Thank god for a bathrobe. Large and fluffy and big enough to fit two fully grown humans inside of it, not that she could imagine any of the men participating in after shower cuddles.

Tying the robe tightly closed she regarded the shoes. There were a variety of sizes and she found hers quickly, pulling the options off the rack and lining them in a neat row on the dresser. Three pairs of four-inch stilettos, one pair of clear platforms that were at least six inches tall, and a pair of thigh high patent leather boots that would not in a million years zip up over her calves.

So that would be a no on shoes then.

Barefoot, robe swishing around her heels, she strode back to the living room, intent on finding more caffeine and someone to talk to about the state of her wardrobe. It was, not surprisingly, empty - so she continued on through the apartment, pressing her ear to the first door she found. There were voices she didn't recognize so she continued on to the second, swinging it open when she heard silence.

Daniel looked up at her, eyebrow cocked, eyes raking down her swaddled form. "Not what I had in mind."

"Have you ever had anyone in this house bigger than a size four?" The office was cramped, cabinets and what looked like a server rack taking up the majority of the space. Daniel sat at the only desk, but Stefan was there too, lounging in a dark leather armchair.

Daniel's expression didn't change at her question. "What's that have to do with anything?"

Maya blinked and saw Stefan hide a smile from the corner of her eye. She made a mental note, at least one man in this house wasn't an idiot. "Nothing back there fits."

Daniel rolled his eyes. "It doesn't need to look tailored, kitten. Just find something."

"Just…? I look like a stuffed sausage."

"It can't be that bad."

Maya dropped the robe, tossing it over the couch edge and putting her hands on her hips as she stared at Daniel. "No one, in a million years, is going to believe I put this on me willingly in an attempt to look sexy."

Next to her Stefan choked, but she didn't bother to turn to him. She knew what she looked like. 'Deranged burlesque performer' was probably the best name for her aesthetic. The corset back was pulled apart as far as she could get the laces to go, showing several inches of bare skin between the eyelets. She'd found a wrap mini skirt that was probably meant to go around twice on someone else but on her went one and a half and left one leg exposed in a strip from ankle to hip.

Daniel didn't say anything, raking his gaze down her body. He pursed his lips, studying the outfit before meeting her eyes. "Well first of all it doesn't match."

Stefan guffawed and Maya rounded on him, pointing a finger. "Hush."

"You're just spilling out of that thing aren't you?" Daniel muttered, his voice moving behind her.

One of his fingers traced the laces and she shivered, stepping away before looking back at him. "It doesn't *fit*."

"I'll have some bigger stuff sent up," Daniel shrugged.

Maya tried hard not to take it personally. *Bigger*. She knew she wasn't supermodel thin - she was *average*. A fact she constantly reminded herself of. Average was not some waif-like double zero … she took a deep breath, forcing a smile. "In the meantime, my suitcases-"

He cut her off with an abrupt motion. "I've seen what you wear. No."

The sound of her teeth snapping together filled the silence in the room as she growled, "Fine." Swiping the robe from the couch she stalked out, trying to ignore the heat of their eyes following her.

Twenty-five grand. She could do it for twenty-five grand. Twenty-five grand could replace every t-shirt she owned and then some. Maya repeated the mantra to herself as she left, shutting the bedroom door softly behind her.

3

"You think this is a good idea?"

Diego poured himself a drink, frowning down at the amber liquid. No, in fact, he didn't. He didn't like someone else in their home, didn't like the idea that she would be in their lives. But he had more information this morning than he'd had last night when he'd acted.

The girl hadn't been lying - she *was* estranged. As near as Daniel could find out for them she hadn't had contact with the Alvani family in over a decade, living paycheck to paycheck in a neighborhood on just the wrong side of respectable. No sudden deposits in her bank accounts, no gifts appearing out of the blue from daddy.

It put a snare in Diego's plans.

"I think it's the best one we've got." He poured two more glasses and handed them off, settling behind his desk and relaxing back into the soft leather. Daniel and Stefan sat in chairs across from him, the former looking uncomfortable as usual and the latter like he owned the place.

"We can always put her back where we found her," Stefan offered, swirling the liquid but not taking a drink.

"And risk her running to dad?" Daniel scoffed. "Why not

hand her all our security codes as well? We should get rid of her."

Diego knew what that meant, knew someone in the room had to say it. It *would* be easiest. If she wasn't going to be useful it was the smartest thing to do. But he hadn't given up the idea that she might be useful yet.

"What's the harm?" he said, rifling through the papers on his desk. "If it works we get what we want, and if it doesn't we've got some easy pussy in the house."

Stefan snorted. "I don't think she's going to be that easy for *you*."

"And you think she will for you?"

"She likes me," Stefan preened. "I'm not the one who kidnapped her nor am I the asshole who called her fat."

"Wait," Daniel jerked his head towards the other man, "when did I call her fat?"

"I believe the term you used was *bigger*," Stefan made air quotes with his hands, holding his glass carefully.

"How can I be an asshole for being accurate?" Daniel countered.

Stefan snorted. "It's shocking to me you've never had a girlfriend."

"Do I even want to know?" Diego sighed, eyeing the decanter across the room.

"I had to order more clothes," the words were defensive, Daniel sinking back into his chair. "The stuff we had didn't fit."

"*Jesus fucking,*" the words left him in a rush and he groaned, rubbing the bridge of his nose. "Are you fucking serious? Since when do you fucking care?"

"It was pretty bad," Stefan smirked. "I mean… even I was a little less ready to fuck her."

"A little?" Diego raised an eyebrow.

A hand went up across from him, finger and thumb a

hairsbreadth apart. "A touch."

"So you got her clothes?" Diego asked.

"I ordered some new stuff, should have gotten here an hour or two ago, she knows to come here when she gets changed."

Movement caught his eye and Diego glanced up, blinking slightly. It was the girl, wearing a gray slip of some kind that seemed to have a life of its own. Clinging to all her curves, moving in a myriad of ways every time she breathed. It was fascinating to watch and Diego realized he was staring when Stefan gave a slight cough.

"Fuck, get in here." He motioned at her and she approached, eyeing the three of them warily and stopping partway to his desk.

"Nice," Stefan hummed, running a hand along his beard. Diego would need to watch that. The man had always liked the soft girls, the ones he could pretend were his girlfriend until he inevitably grew bored.

"Better?"

The girl's eyes shot to Daniel, her lips pursing. "Better is really relative. It *fits* though."

"Good."

They glared at each other and Diego sighed. "You are not doing a good job at this so far."

Instantly she smiled, batting her eyelashes at him. "Oh, like this?"

Stefan snorted and Diego rolled his eyes. "Fucking hell. Don't make me reconsider just killing you." The girl jerked away from him, eyes wide and mouth dropping open. Diego sighed again, "I'm joking, we don't kill people randomly. Bad for business."

Her eyes narrowed but she kept her mouth firmly shut crossing her arms and pushing up a pair of very nice breasts. The action also pulled the hem of her skirt high enough he thought he could catch a glimpse of her panties. He wanted to squeeze his hand in there, feel how warm she was.

"Speaking of," Stefan butted in, "we should really get down to it don't you think?"

"I prefer direct deposit."

Diego glared, watching Stefan bite back a chuckle. "I'm sure we can manage that."

"Daily," she pushed. Daniel nodded in return and she relaxed. "And can someone reassure me my car is safe?"

"Had it towed to our garage," Daniel mumbled.

Something loosened in her shoulders and she took a deep breath. "Okay, well… that's something. My phone?"

"Come over here," Diego gestured at the desk in front of him and she stopped at the edge, looking down at him cautiously. "I want to control the narrative. Leak information in drips that *I* control. So no outside communication from you princess, not until I can trust you."

A frown pulled her lips down but she nodded. "That doesn't *not* make sense."

"Glad you agree." He pushed away from his desk, splaying his legs wide and crooking a finger her direction. "Now, on your knees."

"*What*?"

Daniel's shoulders shook and Diego bit back a smirk. "I said on your knees."

"No," she backed away, "we said-"

"We said we were going to *fake* it." Diego shook out his wrist, glancing at his watch. "I've got another meeting in ten so no time like the present."

She'd paused a few steps away, glancing between the three of them. "No time like the present *to do what*?"

"You get down here," he pointed at the rug for good measure, "I'll undo my pants, and when they get here they can think what they want to think."

Her eyes darted to the side, "And they...?"

"We're not shy, sweetheart," Stefan smiled, leaning back and stacking his hands behind his head. "But if you want involvement all you have to-"

"*No*," she shook her head vehemently, dropping to her knees in front of Diego with a huff. "Now what?"

"Take it out."

Glaring up at him she sat back on her heels. "This isn't... I wouldn't do this."

"Give head?" Daniel asked. "Shame."

She couldn't see him from where she was but Diego watched her shoot a glare his direction. "I mean - I wouldn't do it *like this*. With you like that."

Rolling his eyes, Diego glanced at his watch again. "You're going to have to be more explicit, princess."

"I wouldn't let you *use* me," she gritted out. "If we're going to do this, it's one thing to pretend to be," she gestured vaguely, "to all of you. It's another to be..."

This was taking more effort than it was worth and Diego opened his mouth to tell her to leave. They could go back to the original plan. But Stefan beat him to it, getting up and crouching beside the desk to look her in the eye. "Say what you mean."

Her eyelashes were fluttering and Diego realized she was blinking back tears. "If I'm going to be labeled your whore can I at least be one you pretend to like?"

She wasn't looking at them, staring at a point somewhere in the mid distance and taking deep deliberate breaths. Diego met Daniel's eyes and the other man shrugged, clearly not caring one way or the other. Looking down at Stefan, Diego could see he was already a little gone - the girl's request had probably made him hard as a rock, the sap.

"So like this?" Stefan moved behind her, taking a knee and wrapping an arm over her chest, his other hand slipping down to her thigh. "If you wanted to be *liked* you should have been more clear."

She opened her mouth and Diego leaned forward, cupping her jaw in his hand and pressing his thumb to her lower lip til she opened for him. "Tell me, what kind of blowjob *do* you like to give?"

Hot air shuddered over his finger and he pushed hard, wondering if that was really half a moan he heard from her. Stefan snickered, running the back of his fingers up where her thighs were pressed together tightly.

"You can't ask her to talk while her mouth is occupied, that's just not fair," he teased.

Diego shifted closer, positioning her between his spread legs so his knees touched the outside of her shoulders. She looked good like this, looking up with some emotion he couldn't quite place. He fumbled with his belt with one hand, shoving his hand beneath the fabric of his pants when a soft cough jerked his eyes to the door.

"Sorry boss, we-"

Fuck. He had a meeting. He knew that. Removing his hands he patted her on the cheek. "We'll have to finish this another time, princess. Why don't you go find something else to do?"

Blinking she shook her head, scrambling to her feet and dodging around Stefan. She paused and took a deep breath, giving him a smile that sent blood straight to his cock.

"But what if I get lonely?"

Diego palmed himself roughly as he did up his pants, motioning Stefan away with a jerk of his head. "Don't you *dare*, that pussy is *ours*."

She nodded, biting her lip and backing away, scooting past the men in the doorway and disappearing out of sight. Everyone watched her leave, Diego's fingers tapping on his desk as he considered his decision. This was going to be complicated, for sure, but it also was shaping up to be a bit of fun too.

And he'd been missing a bit of fun.

4

Maya didn't quite *run* away, but an outside observer would be forgiven for thinking it. She *hurried*, feet skidding along the floor until she was back in the kitchen, pouring herself a large glass of water and guzzling it down in seconds.

"What are you *doing*," she questioned her reflection in the stainless steel refrigerator.

It took another glass of water and a wet dishtowel before Maya felt ready to face her situation again. It was her fault, really, for asking for something different. It would have been easy to throw herself across the nearest piece of furniture whenever they liked and let them mime whatever depraved sexual acts they wanted. It would have been *simple*.

But no, she had to reach for more, something more genuine. *Gah,* why was she always like this? Trying to find some kind of connection in places where there couldn't possibly be one?

Well, she'd found a connection alright. She was *throbbing* with the 'connection' she'd found.

Shaking herself she took a step back, hip hitting the island behind her. They were all in a meeting, probably for at least a while. This would be a perfect opportunity to explore her cage, snoop around a little.

The kitchen was an obvious first choice and Maya threw open cabinets and drawers one after the other. Each one held pristine pots and pans, a bevy of kitchen gadgets that had never seen use. The fridge was devoid of food, the door was filled with condiments and half the remaining space to alcohol. There was an entire shelf in the freezer devoted specifically to gin.

"What do you guys eat?" Maya muttered, crossing past the dining table to peer out the large glass walls. The terrace looked nice, a fire pit, comfy chairs - but there was no way she was going out there without more clothes so she moved on, ducking under a set of open stairs and into the living room.

Chrome. Chrome and glass and black leather as far as the eye could see - or at least the thirty feet to the far wall. A fireplace that looked like it had never been used sat across from an expansive two-story window that overlooked the north side of the city and the water beyond. A gray rug framed the furniture, looking far too thin over the stone floors.

It was the most beautiful and yet devoid of personality room she had ever seen. People *lived* here?

Maya poked around a little, finding a magazine, a small shelf of hardback books, and a remote - for what she had no idea, there was no television in sight. Behind the wall that held the fireplace, a hallway connected the kitchen and the far side of the house, the surface dotted with precisely framed photographs.

And a door. A big double door.

An *exit*.

It was curiosity, she told herself, turning the handle and ducking her head out. Best to know what the building looked like in case she ever needed to go somewhere.

"Oh," she jerked backwards, accidentally opening the door wider. "Hi."

A man lounged in a chair by a set of elevator doors, his coat pushed back and a gun rather obviously tucked under his arm. "You need something?"

"No I-" His eyes were somewhere south of her eyes and Maya realized she'd opened the door far enough for him to see everything she *wasn't* wearing. She closed the door abruptly and winced, slowly cracking it open again. "Sorry, I was just… checking."

The man looked amused, giving her a nod and she shut the door with a gentle click.

Now what?

Grabbing a book she settled on the uncomfortable couch, glaring at the glass coffee table as she bumped her shin on it. After a few chapters there was noise, the sounds of people out of sight and the door opening and closing. But no one came to talk to her. Was it possible they had all left?

Dinner arrived promptly at eight without, as far as she could tell, any discussion. A neat row of white take out boxes appearing between one moment and the next.

And there it sat, growing cold on the white marble counter while Maya paced around trying to decide if she was supposed to wait on them. After an hour passed she finally grabbed a carton of glass noddles and debated whether or not she wanted to go back to the sex dungeon.

On the pro side, it was private. It was likely intended to be where she slept. It definitely *wasn't* where any of them slept full time. And it had a door she could shut.

On the cons… it didn't have a lock.

Also, it was a sex dungeon.

Privacy won out in the end, and it took Maya a solid five minutes to move the deceptively heavy bench in front of the door before she settled into the center of the bed. She would have changed but her clothes had disappeared. The real ones. The ones made of cotton with pockets. The kind you bought at a store that didn't also have a curtained 'specialty' section. Instead she pulled on the fluffy robe, crossed her legs and let the Thai food rest in her lap.

What a weird day - and for someone who had first seen her house raided by the D.E.A. when she was six, that was saying a lot.

She needed a game plan. And some ground rules.

One, she was *not* going to have sex with them. Even if it seemed like a good idea. Even if it seemed like a *great* idea. It would only make things far more complicated than they needed to be.

Two, she was not going to let them see her stumble. Whatever games they wanted to play she would do, short of point one, as long as she kept her dignity. They didn't deserve the satisfaction of seeing her riled.

And three, they were not going to get away with treating her like an object. They'd already tried, Daniel treating her like some kind of doll, Stefan and his touches, Diego and his...

Maya shivered. Best not to think about Diego and his dark eyes and whatever cologne he wore that made her stomach flip over. That was dangerous territory. Instead she should think about the money. She'd always wanted to live in the mountains, near a lake maybe. Somewhere that got a little snow but not so much she'd get snowed in. She could barely drive on dry streets, no need to add black ice to the equation.

If this went on long enough she could have fifty, even a hundred grand. That'd be enough for at minimum the down payment on a place of her own - somewhere she could paint the walls and hang pictures without worrying about her security deposit. Buy new furniture for the first time in her adult life. Maybe even get a cat.

Maya lost herself in her home decorating fantasy, mentally picking colors and backsplash tile. It soothed her, made her think of a real future for the first time in years.

All she had to do was remember the plan.

Any hope she had that her hormones were through going haywire were dashed when Daniel strode in while she was having breakfast the next day - snapping his fingers, issuing a curt and rather particular command, and then disappearing.

"Good morning to you too," she muttered, carrying her tea back to the dungeon and pulling the closet doors open, staring at the racks of new clothes that had been sent up. It was almost exactly what had filled the closet previously, only in her size. "Why yes my day is going swell, thank you for asking."

She continued her mutterings as she changed, and while she tiptoed through to the other side of the apartment. She bypassed Diego's office and opened the next door to an empty room, packed full of books. Making a mental note to come back she went to the last, opening it to find Daniel hunched in the near dark, a mess of monitors nearly blocking him from view.

"This is ridiculous."

Daniel barely looked up from his computer, "Get over here."

Rolling her eyes, Maya crossed the bare floor, stopping near him and folding her arms. He looked up then, eyes widening slightly as he took in the pleated mini-skirt, the short-sleeved white button-down with no buttons, ends tied together under her breasts. She'd put her hair in pigtails to complete the picture as requested - full on naughty school girl.

At least she had socks, thigh high white ones with a stripe around the top.

"This is demeaning."

Daniel was already looking back at the computer, reaching a hand out and pressing her hip, motioning for her to spin around. She did it reluctantly, noticing how his eyes darted from the screens to her and he wet his lower lip as she turned back.

"Nice."

"Pedophile," she retorted.

Daniel snorted in response, patting his thigh. "No harm in fantasy, kitten. Hop on."

Maya eyed his lap with trepidation. "I don't think-"

With a tug Daniel tumbled her into his lap, spreading his thighs to hold her steady as she sat sideways, curling her hands into his shirt to keep herself from falling. "Stop, I'm too heavy."

He ignored her, shifting her until her back was pressed to his chest, her legs spread wide over his knees. It was a startlingly vulnerable position, her thighs held open by his. He huffed a short laugh, gently pressing on her forehead and laying her back against his shoulder. He smelled warm, something almost like honey where her nose was practically nuzzling into his neck. He wrapped an arm around her middle, splaying one hand wide on the bare flesh of her stomach.

"You're light as a kitten."

Well that was a blatant lie but she could barely concentrate with his warm breath tickling her temple. Was she supposed to just sit there? She had to be in his way but he didn't seem to mind it, shifting her slightly until he had her in a position where he could type comfortably around her.

"What are you-"

He shushed her, elbowing her slightly, fingers not stopping. With a huff she settled her hands on her stomach, turning her head and closing her eyes. Fine, he wanted to be like that? She could be like that too. Longer even. He'd see who gave in first.

The first thing she'd do at her new place was take down any blinds. She hated them, too hard to clean and ugly to boot. Long gauzy curtains would be the thing. Maybe she could manage a little piece of land, so she wouldn't need to worry about her neighbors seeing in. She'd never mowed a lawn in her life but she could learn, surely.

Yeah, a yard of some kind seemed nice. A hammock to nap in, maybe a little table to drink her tea at in the morning and watch the sunrise. In her mind the cat morphed into a dog, a big black lab that chased butterflies while she sat and watched the world go by.

And maybe someday she'd find someone to share it with.

In her mind the hammock expanded, a warm body joining hers. Legs tangled together, their hands gently stroking her hair while she snuggled into their shoulder. Low murmurs and soft kisses, fingers skating up and down the skin of her thighs, a hand cupping her breast and slowly thumbing her nipple.

"Horny?"

Maya's eyes flew open, the drowsy feeling that had overtaken her disappearing in a flash. She wasn't in a hammock next to a lake. She was in a chair, with *Daniel*. The furthest thing from her mystery lover as possible. "What? No."

Daniel hummed, thumb brushing under her breast. "Are you sure? I could get you off real quick if you wanted." His hand slipped down, over the fabric of the skirt before toying with the edge. He was so close, would only need to move the skirt an inch or two up to expose her panties. And with her legs spread wide like this there was no way he *wouldn't* see the dark spot of arousal staining them.

"Quick isn't exactly a selling point," she said instead of

giving a straight answer.

Both hands were on her now and she was going to melt into a puddle of want on the floor. A hand cupped beneath her breast, not quite touching - while the fingers of the other slipped under the hem of the skirt, tracing light patterns on the sensitive skin of her inner thigh.

"You're right," he whispered into her ear, his low baritone rumbling through her. "I should take my time. Stroke your pussy until you're squirming, dripping all over my chair." A light flick of his tongue made her jerk, and he pulled her closer in response. His hand was splayed across her thigh, one finger so close to her center she could barely think straight.

"I could do that for you, stroke you until you purred for me, kitten. Make you come until you begged me to stop." His teeth caught her earlobe and she moaned. "Then I'd bend you over this desk and have you screaming for me."

His thumb had slipped beneath the edge of her panties, brushing the cap of curls. She couldn't remember why this was a bad idea. What was her list again? Don't be an object? She could fix that though, turn around and straddle his lap and-

"Hey boss I got a-" the door opened and the man cut himself off, staring at her. Or maybe at Daniel. Maya couldn't tell, didn't want to know. She knew exactly what he was seeing, exactly what was about to happen if he hadn't walked in.

"Take care of it," Daniel called out, not moving his hands, barely acknowledging the intrusion at all.

The man nodded, eyeing her a moment longer before shutting the door.

"Where were we?"

Maya sprung away, moving to put his desk between the two of them. "I said no touching down there!"

Daniel grinned, stacking his hands behind his head and leaning back in his chair. "Not unless you want us to. Was I reading you wrong? Seemed like you wanted it."

"I said not X-rated!"

"Pfft," Daniel made a dismissive sound, waving a hand, "that was PG-13 at worst."

Maya gaped, mouth opening and closing like a fish out of water. "What kind of movies have you been *watching*?" A devilish glint entered his eye and she took a step back, holding both hands up. "You know what? Never mind. Don't answer that."

"Get back here," Daniel held a hand out to her, eyes already refocusing on the screen. "I wasn't done with you."

"Yes you were," Maya countered, eyeing him suspiciously.

Daniel rolled his eyes. "Fine, no more touching," he pointed at her with a frown, "but then you have to stop squirming and making those little whimpers-"

"I was *not*!" Maya protested.

"- and be a good girl for Daddy."

Maya blinked. "No."

"No?" An interested look crossed his face. "You want to be naughty?"

"I don't-" Maya faltered, hands in the air, "I am *not* calling you Daddy."

"Aw come on," he wheedled. "Come back and sit on Daddy's lap."

She shook her head, backing up a step. "I have enough father issues without adding you to them, thank you very much."

Daniel seemed to consider that, shrugging and turning his full attention back to the computers. "Fine, but I still want you over here."

Steeling herself Maya went back, perching primly on one of his knees. She didn't protest when he pulled her closer, but she kept her thighs firmly closed, turned sideways and leaning into his chest.

"Brat," he grunted, adjusting so he could reach the keyboard.

"Jerk."

"Am I interrupting something?"

Daniel ignored him and she shifted to look at Stefan, leaning in the doorway and grinning widely at the two of them.

"Please tell me you have something you'd like me to do," she was almost begging and Daniel's body turned tense under her. "Something that doesn't involve canoodling."

"Canoodling?" Daniel murmured into her ear.

"I think I can think of something," Stefan held his hand out and Maya slid out of Daniel's lap, noting that he didn't make a move to keep her there. He didn't argue, just pulled his chair back tight to the desk and went back to his typing.

Taking Stefan's hand she followed him to the office with all the books, definitely his, and gestured towards a large couch against one wall.

Maya eyed it dubiously.

"It's not going to bite you," Stefan assured her, leaning one hip on his desk.

"Not the couch I was worried about."

"What was that?"

"Nothing," she settled onto the cushion, turning slightly and trying to keep the short skirt from showing anything. "How do you want me? Shirt ripped open? Panties around my ankle?"

As she spoke Stefan's eyes got wider until he barked a laugh. "The fuck did Daniel do to you while I was out?"

Maya shrugged, "Playing pretend."

He hummed thoughtfully, pulling his phone and checking something on it. "Well I just wanted your company."

Suspicious, Maya watched him for signs of some shiftier plan. "*Just* my company?"

"You're also nice to look at," he shrugged. "I've got someone coming in in a bit and I'm kind of hoping you'll throw him off his game."

"Oh," she cast her eyes around, "so you just want me to sit here?"

"And be beautiful." He thumbed through a stack of papers. "Maybe lose the braids though."

Without a moment's hesitation Maya pulled the elastic off the ends, combing her fingers through the pigtails and letting her hair fall into loose waves. "Not a fan?"

"The role-play is Daniel's thing - be glad he went easy on you."

What does that mean, she thought with a frown before giving herself a mental shake. But apparently she didn't shake hard enough because she immediately blurted out, "So what's your thing?"

He eyed her curiously, "I like people." Shrugging nonchalantly he crossed his arms, "All kinds. As they are."

Oh. Okay. That wasn't charming *at all*. Nope.

"If I thought I had time I'd tell you to go change, but you'll have to make do." He gestured and Maya saw a blanket thrown over the end of the couch. She grabbed it and covered her legs quickly, snuggling under its softness and feeling warm for the first time since she'd left bed that morning. Well, warm in a way that didn't involve a heavy pulse point between her thighs. Watching him from the corner of her eye she pulled a magazine off the side table, some weekly news thing, and thumbed through it as casually as possible.

When the knock came Stefan didn't hesitate to invite them in, gesturing at an armchair and keeping his position leaning against the desk. The man was dressed nicer than anyone she'd seen so far other than Diego - a full suit and tie, glasses perched on his nose. He was also sweating profusely, a drop sliding behind his ear to touch his collar.

Stefan didn't introduce her and she didn't say anything, watching them from her peripheral and pretending to read the text in front of her.

"I assume you're here because you've fixed your little problem?"

The man's eyes darted to her but Maya studiously ignored him.

"Yes, well, I mean, no, I mean..." he tried to open his briefcase but fumbled with the locks. "Mr. Contreras it's not as simple as-"

Stefan took the briefcase, setting it deliberately on the table next to him. "Then explain it to me."

"Once the shipment is in the customs database we can't just erase it. I don't have that kind of access and it's the federal government, they have firewalls and-"

"We've never had a problem before now."

"If you'll let me show you the documents I can show that-"

"I've seen the documents," Stefan cut him off with an abrupt motion. "What I'm hearing you say is that you're incompetent."

Maya choked back a snort of laughter. That poor man was going to pass out and she would bet all of her money - what was twenty-five grand divided by seven anyhow - that Stefan was messing with him. Flipping a page in the magazine she let her eyes dart to the tableau.

Yeah, that guy was going to pass out soon.

"Not only that," Stefan continued, "but you have the audacity to come here and make *me* look incompetent in front of my friend."

Wait, did he mean her?

"I don't like to be embarrassed, Peter."

Peter was giving her a pleading look but she wasn't sure

what she was supposed to do. Ignore it? Shake her head disapprovingly? Intervene to give Stefan an excuse to be nice?

"You are aware what happens next, yes?"

That was a chilling tone. Her certainties about Stefan were dissolving away under his cold friendliness. There was an edge to it, a razor hidden inside the gentle words.

"Yes," Peter sounded like he might cry.

"Fix it. Don't let me see it again until you do. And if you don't..." she felt his eyes land on her. "Well I can't have my baby thinking I let people get away with this shit."

"Of course," Peter jumped to his feet, grabbing his briefcase and backing away. "Of course Mr. Contreras, of course. I won't fail. I-"

"Get out."

Maya shivered at the tone, sliding deeper into the warmth of the couch, magazine forgotten in her hands. She didn't move when Stefan sat on the other end, tugging her feet into his lap.

"Heavy reading," he gestured at the magazine, warm smile settling on her. "I've got some novels if you'd prefer. I'm partial to sci-fi but there's a bit of everything lying around."

"I have one." Her voice sounded dry, crackly. "It's in the living room."

He was wrapping her feet up in the blanket, carefully tucking the ends under and patting them softly. "Bring it with you next time, you're always welcome to read in here. I know how fucking uncomfortable those damn couches are."

Maya nodded, barely breathing as he pulled his phone out and scrolled through it. She stared blankly at the pages in her hands, concentrating on calming her heartbeat. It wasn't that she hadn't known they were dangerous, but the reminder was good all the same.

5

The rhythm of the apartment was easy to fall into.

On nights they didn't go out, dinner came from a local place. They never seemed to actually order anything, Maya certainly had never been asked, food just appeared at the apartment. On nights they were gone, food appeared as well - still without Maya's input. Someone showed to clean around eleven in the morning, an older lady who spoke what was maybe Romanian. One of the Romance languages but far enough removed for Maya's high school Spanish to be no help at all.

Through hand signals and interpretive dance Maya managed to ask the woman where cleaning supplies were, including the laundry. But her hopes that she might find the clothes she'd shown up in were dashed quickly among the stacks of men's briefs and hanging plastic bags full of dry cleaning. She *did* swipe some t-shirts, however, certain they wouldn't miss them.

The only place in the apartment she hadn't been to was the second floor.

No one ever specifically told her *not* to go there. It was just... that was *their* floor. Where their bedrooms were. And

Lord only knew what else. Going up there felt like it would be an invitation, or an announcement of some kind. That she *wanted* to be in their bedrooms.

She was curious, but not *that* curious.

Four days in and a routine had developed. A couple of times a day someone would grab her, usually Daniel or Diego, and set up a little scene for their henchmen to walk in on. Maya would play coy and sad that they'd been interrupted, whoever's turn it was would say something dirty, and Maya would be dismissed back to her own devices. In the afternoon she read on Stefan's couch. Sometimes he was there too, making phone calls about business deals she couldn't make out - others he would settle her into his side while he talked to someone. But more often he would gesture her back there and then disappear, leaving Maya to wonder if he was watching her somehow to see what she'd do.

She kept to the couch when in his office, not even poking through his shelves but restraining herself to the books she'd found in the living room. What if she went to take a book and found a hidden door to some kind of even *more* secret sex dungeon? No thank you.

No one had ever told her how *boring* it would be to be a mobster's mistress. Or even *three* mobsters' mistress. She was starting to go stir crazy. And pants, she craved pants. A quick walk outside in pants, it didn't seem like too much to ask.

"No."

Maya pouted, sitting on a barstool and watching Diego shrug into his jacket. "If I were *really* your mistress I'd make you take me," Maya pointed out. Closer to the door Daniel tapped fingers restlessly against his thigh.

"If you were *really* our mistress," Diego smirked at her, "you'd be too tired to go anywhere."

"People are going to think you don't like me," she crossed her arms, moving them when she realized they pressed her breasts up for his appreciative gaze. "Or you're hiding me."

"We *are* hiding you," Daniel grunted, motioning Diego with a sarcastic wave. "We're not announcing until next week."

"*Announcing*?" Maya scoffed. "What am I having some kind of debutante ball?"

"Something like that."

They left without a backwards glance, leaving Maya to stew with a mountain of dumplings. *Apparently* no one had told whoever did the ordering that they weren't staying in. She felt an overwhelming desire to toss them up the stairs, see if she could get them over the railing up top and into whatever room lay beyond. It was either that or more reading, she'd found the TV but it was behind a large framed piece of art she hadn't been able to figure out how to move. She supposed she could *listen* to a show, maybe see if she could blindly navigate to a stand-up special or something.

Settling onto the couch she tried to remember what the screen *should* look like. She'd tried three different combinations, nothing was playing, and she was about to give up when the front door slammed.

"*Fuck*."

Stefan stalked out and into the kitchen, grumbling to himself the entire way. He spotted her in the corner of his eye and turned slightly, giving her a curt nod. There was a splatter of something dark red on his shirt - blood unless she was wildly off the mark.

Cautiously she moved from the couch, going the long way around the island to stay in his line of sight. Stefan sighed, thrusting his hand beneath the tap. The water tinged pink as it fell to the sink below, a low hiss coming from between his teeth.

"You're hurt."

"You noticed," he snapped back, switching to the other hand.

"Let me help?" she said softly, reaching out and examining the cuts on his knuckles. "You should put something on these so they don't get infected. Where's the first aid kit?"

"Third drawer," he gestured behind himself and she squatted down to look in it.

"Jesus Christ," she breathed softly, "you've got half an O.R. in here."

"Well, we're not always the safest bunch."

Yeah, she knew that. Pushing back a smile she pulled out what she needed, closing the drawer firmly and noting there wasn't anything as simple as a bandaid in it. Hip-checking him slightly, she pushed him over so she could stand with him at the sink.

"I can see gravel, Stefan," she chided, "did you punch a wall?"

He shrugged, some of the tenseness flowing out of him, letting her take his hand again. "I might have, in the ruckus."

"I'd have thought you had better aim than that." She shot him a grin as she said it, watched him settle his raised hackles when he realized she was teasing.

"It came out of nowhere."

"The wall?"

"Yeah," he nodded, a smile tugging his lips. "Just jumped me."

Once the water was the temperature she wanted she stepped closer, bracketing his forearm with her own and gently massaging his wounds with her fingers. He didn't make a sound, shifting his body until his chest was pressed to her back, trapping her between him and the sink.

"I like this," his free hand smoothed over the lacy nightdress, playing with the small bow at the hem. "I notice you wear a lot of things I like." His lips brushed her hair, "You doing that on purpose?"

Oh, the honeymoon looking stuff was for him. She should

have guessed that. Daniel was into the role-play, Diego the nasty stuff, but Stefan would like it sweeter - the girlfriend experience.

"It's not as raunchy as the other stuff," she told him, examining what medical supplies she had at her disposal. He stayed silent while she shifted through the various bandages and creams, setting out what she was going to need.

"You don't have to do this."

"I know," she lathered his hand, letting the water pour over it, turning it over and checking for anything she missed.

"You bandage up this minor shit and the guys will think I'm getting soft."

"Tell them I didn't want you to get blood on me."

"Would you mind?" His breath was hot on her neck, his lips barely touching her skin. "If I got a little blood on you?"

Biting her lip she repressed a shiver. "I didn't figure you for the type, Stefan."

"Mmm," he made a contented noise, rocking his hips against her back. "Let me get my hands on you and I'll show you."

"Too bad you hurt them," she averred, lightly massaging a speck of sand from his wound and resisting the urge to trail her fingers up the black lines of his tattoos. "You won't be getting your hands on me for a while now."

His lips caressed her shoulder, "Guess I'll just have to use my mouth."

An unsteady breath left her and she braced her hands on the sink. "Stefan, please."

"Please what?" He nibbled softly and she shuddered. "Please kiss you?"

"Let me finish."

"I'm not stopping you."

She bent over slightly, reaching for the paper towels, and Stefan pressed closer. She had to catch herself on the counter to keep from collapsing. A hand moved her hair off her neck, pushing it over one shoulder.

"Don't get distracted, sweetheart," his lips warm on her spine. "I'm bleeding out here."

That broke her from her trance, making her giggle and stand up straight, leaning slightly sideways to look back at him. "No you're not, you big baby."

He pouted at her, full lip sticking out so far she had the ridiculous urge to bite it. "No no, I can feel the infection setting in. I'm getting gangrene."

Softly patting his hand dry she reached for the antibiotic and smoothed it over the cuts. "Well I'm sorry, we'll have no choice but to amputate." Wrapping gauze around his palm and over the back of his hand she sighed melodramatically. "I'm afraid it's a lost cause."

He chuckled and she smiled, turning her attention to the other hand, giving it the same attention. He was quiet this time, staying close with his chin hooked over her shoulder as he watched her work.

"You're good at that," he commented as she finished, washing her hands for the final time.

"Well, this isn't my first rodeo," she responded, moving sideways and out of his embrace.

"Rodeo, huh?" He grinned at her mischievously and she started to back up a step. "I got a bull you can ride if you're looking for a good time."

Maya shook her head, "Don't you dare."

She turned to run but he caught her around the waist with a bark of laughter, lifting her onto the counter. God, it would be so easy to like Stefan. He was playful, less intense than the others, even if he was just as dangerous.

"Stefan," she whined, pushing lightly on his shoulder, "let me down."

"Not til I get my eight seconds," he protested, eyebrows

waggling.

"You think you could last eight seconds?"

"Could I-" his eyes caught hers, licking his lower lip. "Are you that wild sweetheart?"

"Maybe I just don't have faith in you."

He growled, leaning forward and nipping her chin. "Tease."

His hands were warm on her thighs, slowly massaging the muscles. He didn't slip inwards like Daniel had tried; then again, he had her pulled forward so the bulge of him was situated right at her center. That was worse. That was so much worse. Because she couldn't pretend she was trying to get away from his touch when she rocked against him. Couldn't pretend her body was doing anything other than straining for him even as her mind tried to shut the whole thing down.

"That's it sweetheart," he murmured, skating his lips down her neck. "Show me how you'd ride me." His palms slid up her skin and he swore, leaning back and ripping at the bandages she'd just put on him with his teeth.

"Stefan, wait, *stop*." She grabbed his wrist, meeting his eyes and the almost blank look in them. "We can't."

"We *can*," he used her grip to yank her forward, crashing his mouth over hers. Why did he have to keep *kissing* her? She could resist when it was hands, when it was illicit touching and the certainty that this was all business. But when he had his tongue in her mouth all of that flew out the window and she was back in that bar about to go home with a stranger and it all seemed like a *really good idea*.

"Come on sweetheart," he licked at the shell of her ear, "you've made your point. You're a good girl. We get it. But you don't need to keep playing that you don't want this."

Eyes that had previously drooped closed as he touched her flew open, hands shoving him as hard as she could. "Get *off* me."

His chest heaved, hands clenched into fists by his side, his nostrils flaring as he took in every inch of her body. She watched as his tongue snaked along his teeth, mouth twisting into a mocking smile. "Make up your mind."

Scooting off the counter she ducked away from him, putting distance before turning back and glaring. "You don't know me. You have no idea who I am or what I want."

"Don't I?" He leaned back against the counter, arms crossing. "Seems like you're the one confused."

"Screw you," she snapped, blushing at the curse.

"See?" he grinned. "Mixed messages."

"Why you-" she struggled to find a word, growing angrier by the moment until she saw the way he was pointedly keeping his lips pressed together, his shoulders shuddering slightly. "Are you *laughing* at me?"

Stefan burst with it, his deep bellow filling the apartment, rolling over her down to her toes. Maya didn't know if she wanted to slap him or laugh along with him. She settled for rolling her eyes, crossing her arms and glaring until he finished.

"I am not *playing*," she pointed a finger at him. "You are a bad idea. You *all* are bad ideas. And I'm not desperate enough to sell myself out for a quickie on the kitchen counter."

"What about a long fuck on the-"

"*Stefan*," she scolded and he grinned.

"Let me know when you are."

He was walking away, towards the stairs and Maya gaped after him, trying hard not to take the bait. She failed, of course, self-control had never been her strong suit. "Are what?"

"Desperate enough."

Maya was having an *amazing* dream. There was a bathtub on

a cliff, overlooking a forest. She had no idea how the tub got there, but the water was perfectly warm and there were beautiful pearlescent bubbles covering the surface. A crow was telling her a story, something about tea kettles and spiders and Maya nodded along sagely as the bird went on and on. Someone was kissing her neck, slipping into the tub behind her, their hands cupping her breasts and thumbing her nipples and Maya gasped, the cliff and the forest and the bird disappearing and suddenly she was in bed, stretched out under Stefan.

Someone's hands were on her waist, face tilting up until their glasses caught the light and of course it would be Daniel and his smug smile and the long lick he gave her stomach. Squirming away, she crawled for the edge of the bed, giggling when he flipped her back over, Diego's eyes meeting hers and then the lights changed and she was at a party and all three were there dancing and the pulsing bass beat thrummed through her body and-

Maya jolted awake, eyes wide. The music wasn't a dream. *Someone* was playing music at, she checked the clock by her bed, two o'clock in the freaking morning at an unholy volume and she was out of bed and angrily tying on her robe before good sense could catch up to her.

It was to be expected, given her only semi-alert state, that she wouldn't be paying attention to her surroundings. Or that given that, she might run straight into someone without even noticing they were there.

A naked someone.

A - judging by the feel of him against her stomach - naked *aroused* someone.

He caught her shoulders, grinning as he steadied her. "Well hello there, princess, come to join the fun?"

"What the-?" Maya blinked up at Diego. The smug smile on his face and those deep brown eyes staring down at her.

"Why are you *naked*?"

"Not the only one." He turned her around, guiding her further into the common area so she could see.

There was a lot to see.

Blushing furiously she spun around, staring resolutely over his shoulder. His smirk was still there, leaning in and rubbing his cheek on her temple. Oh, he *wanted* her to throw a fit. To stutter and stammer and lose whatever cool she had. She refused to give him the satisfaction.

"The *living room*, Diego?" she whined instead. "I eat lunch in there."

"Usually we use your room," he whispered into her ear, nuzzling the fine hairs. "But I thought you might object to the company."

"How thoughtful of you." She pushed at his shoulder, "Get out of my way I was just getting something to drink."

"It'll be weird if you don't at least say hi," he murmured, wrapping his arms around her and guiding her towards the living room, "you *are* supposed to be our live-in piece of ass."

"I don't *want* to say hi," she protested through gritted teeth.

He just laughed, the bastard, resolutely backing her towards the living room with an iron grip.

Maya kept her eyes on the windows, admiring the city lights. It really was a nice evening, crescent moon hanging to the east. Did that mean it was waxing or waning? She'd always meant to learn which was which. And maybe that was Venus? To the east? Was that right? That didn't feel right, it was probably a different planet. Or an airplane.

Someone took her hand, pressing a soft kiss to the back. She couldn't help but glance down. Stefan looked up at her, all doe-eyed innocence. A spectacular bit of acting considering there was a woman between his legs with her mouth around his-

"Did you come to join us, sweetheart?"

Was it hot in here? For once? Of course they finally set it to a reasonable temperature when they were wandering around stark naked. Not for her though, half naked and shivering near to death every day.

She stroked his cheek, steadily - and very deliberately - looking only into his eyes. "What could I possibly do for you that isn't already being done?"

He grinned, turning and sucking her thumb into his mouth. A jolt of pleasure shot to her toes and she looked. She couldn't help it. Looked down and saw the way he was disappearing between the woman's lips.

"It's no fun without you baby."

Why was he doing this to her? What had she done in a past life to deserve this? Her cheeks were so warm she wanted to press her hands to them, her heartbeat a staccato she swore everyone could hear. She wasn't cut out for this.

Someone wrapped an arm around her, someone a lot softer than Diego. A feminine giggle tickled her ear and she was pulled backwards, into the arms of another woman.

"And who might you be?"

"M-maya," she stumbled over own name, wondering what she was supposed to do with her hands. "And you?"

"Bambi," the woman giggled, rubbing into her back.

Bambi? Maya shot an incredulous look over her shoulder, expecting to see someone far too young to be here. But the woman who met her eyes gave her a small, secret smile. Not an air-head then, and very likely *not* named Bambi. A hand slid around the woman's neck, Diego's eyes meeting Maya's over her shoulder. And then Bambi gasped, body undulating and was he really having sex with the lady *right here*? With Maya *right there*?

Apparently.

Daniel was on his knees, rocking into someone bent over the glass and chrome coffee table Maya hated so much. There was another woman behind him, pressed to his back, whispering Lord only knew what into his ear. Stefan now had someone in his lap, his hand between her thighs.

This didn't happen in real life. Sleeping in the sex dungeon must have fried her brain and she was having an incredibly graphic dream. That had to be it. There was no reality where she stood in the middle of this giant apartment in a fluffy white bathrobe while these three men did the physically impossible.

Did people actually *bend* like that?

She should go back to bed. Not that this was real, obviously not, but if she could get back into bed maybe her dream would change to the one where she was on a rollercoaster and the seat bar didn't work.

Backing up a step she tried to keep her eyes above shoulder height. For not being real it certainly *sounded* real. And *smelled* real. She wasn't going to leave her room until after the housekeeper came - and she managed to figure out whatever the Romanian word was for 'bleach.'

"Diego said you wanted company?"

"*Jesus.*" Okay, eyes a little lower. The long-haired brunette had scared the crap out of her. "No, thank you. I'm looking forward to a night alone. Thank you for-" she gestured lamely, "taking care of them. For me."

The brunette blinked at her. "Are you sure? He was pretty specific."

Maya did it, she looked down and met Diego's wry grin. Bambi was bent over the couch, Diego barely giving her any attention as he raised an eyebrow.

Jerk.

Turning to the woman she gave her a wide smile, taking her hand and pulling her to the end of the living room furthest from the group.

"I appreciate the thought but I'm not in the mood. You

know how that is." The woman nodded and Maya gave her an awkward pat on the shoulder. "If you just want a break or something you're welcome to-"

"Oh no!" The brunette took a step back quickly. "No, I - this is - I volunteered."

She wasn't going to ask questions. Not a one. Not even, how did the words *volunteer* and *orgy* end up in the same thought. Instead an idea occurred to her and she felt her lips turning up into a grin. Crooking a finger, she beckoned the woman closer.

"Can I tell you a secret? About Diego?" She nodded and Maya continued. "He likes being spanked. *Hard*. He'll protest, but his safe word is 'buttercup.'" Meeting Diego's curious gaze she batted her eyelashes, turning the woman and giving her a small push back to the group. "Have fun."

She wasn't halfway down the hall when she heard a loud *smack* followed by a shouted, belligerent curse from Diego.

6

Maya was bored out of her skull. It shouldn't be boring, living in a mobster's apartment, especially when there were three of them, but if Maya had to read one more mystery novel about a small town she was going to fling something off the terrace.

"Come on, if not my phone then one of your tablets. A smart watch. *Anything*. I am going stir crazy."

Daniel grunted at her, one eyebrow raised as he watched her over the lens of his glasses, his first coffee of the day clutched in his hands. "No."

Maya ignored the plates of pancakes, swiping a cup of strawberries and yogurt and pointing her spoon at him. She tried to keep the whining tone out of her voice when she said, "But *why*?"

"Because I don't trust you."

Maya blinked at his blunt statement. "What?"

He shifted past her while she took in the statement. "I don't trust you and until this is over I'm not going to risk you blowing this for us."

Okay, that made a sort of sense. But she wasn't kidding, if she didn't have some kind of access to the outside world soon she was going to lose her mind.

"I'll put on one of the outfits for you. With the leather."

Daniel froze, cup of coffee barely touching his lower lip. "Which one?"

"Your choice." She knew this was a remarkably bad idea. Knew it in her bones. This relationship didn't need to be any more transactional than it already was. But she *needed* it. "Gotta be something back in that closet of horrors you miss."

He hummed thoughtfully. "Harness, nipple clamps and pony tail."

"Nipple…" Maya tried not to let her shock show. "That's… a lot."

Daniel shrugged. "You offered."

"What about just a ponytail?" she tried, hoping that bargaining was on the table.

"Not *a* ponytail," he corrected her with a smirk. "*The* pony tail. It goes in your-"

"Nope," she cut him off, turning away. "Nope no thank you. I'll find another book."

He snorted behind her, his footsteps receding. She thought he'd gone when he called back, "You know, there's other places to read than Stefan's office."

"He's got the comfy couch," she replied without thinking, glancing back and seeing only his retreating back.

Weirdo.

Maya sighed, she needed a new book. Maybe something dry and boring this time - had she seen an encyclopedia on a shelf somewhere? That would be perfect. She could learn out of date information about bugs and countries that didn't exist anymore and then nap all afternoon.

Halfway down the hall a thought occurred to her and she bypassed Stefan's door and went straight back to Daniel's. He barely looked up when she knocked on the frame.

"When I said there were other places I didn't mean you

should come *here*."

"I want to see my bank accounts."

He looked up, frowning. "What?"

"You said you didn't trust me and it got me thinking, I want to see my bank accounts. I want to see the money I'm supposedly earning."

"You think we'd lie to you?" He didn't seem offended, only curious about her answer.

"Would you?" she countered.

He tilted his head, staring at a spot over her shoulder before shrugging. "Yeah, probably."

Scooting his chair to the side he gestured her over, pulling up her bank's homepage and gesturing at it. She leaned over, trying to ignore the way he watched her breasts move, or the way her hair brushed his forearm, and then hesitated.

"How do I know you won't steal my information?"

"Jesus Christ," he groaned, jerking the keyboard towards himself. "You think I have a key tracker on my own damn computer?"

"Maybe," she countered, standing up and crossing her arms.

"I don't need your money, kitten."

True, he didn't. But she didn't like it. She wrestled the keyboard away from him and opened a private window, ignoring his snort of derision. Yeah, that probably wouldn't stop him if he *was* going to do something, but it made her feel better.

$25,268.34 available.

Maya could barely process the number, blinking at the glowing text in bafflement.

"See?" Daniel growled, already reaching for the system.

She frowned. "That's a week, I've been here ten days."

"Oh for the love of-" he pulled his phone out, tapping a few times and then gesturing for her to refresh.

$25,768.34 available. $10,214.28 pending.

"Did you just do that math in your head?"

Daniel seemed taken aback by the question, logging her out and fidgeting with his screens. "Anything else?"

"No." She gave him a curious look, "That was it."

"Then unless you've changed your mind about the pony tail…"

Maya huffed, stalking out and closing the door firmly behind her. She had *not*.

"What, no orgy tonight?"

They were all home for once. Diego and Stefan shoulder to shoulder at the kitchen island, rummaging through the take-out containers. Daniel had a beer in one hand, his phone in the other, feet propped on the dining table.

"Gotta give the girls a rest," Diego winked at her, pulling a foil wrapped package out of a bag with a triumphant whistle.

"You've worn out every girl in town?" Maya raised an eyebrow at him. "People are going to think I'm not good at my job."

"Do you want to be good at your job?" he retorted with a leer and Maya rolled her eyes. Diego sighed, "You haven't changed your mind then?"

"Nope," she retorted, popping the 'p' and rifling through the bags on the island. "What's tonight?"

"Mexican," Stefan handed her a plate and a beer, one she took and the other she returned. He stared at the bottle in puzzlement. "You don't drink?"

"Not beer."

"We've got wine," he offered.

"No thank you," Maya waved a hand as she fixed a plate. "Wine makes me goofy."

"Oh?" Stefan's interest was piqued, his body sliding over next to hers, hip pressed firmly against her. "What kind of goofy?"

"None of your business goofy," Maya poked a fork his direction. "You'll never see it."

"Wine makes you goofy, vodka makes you rash…" Diego stroked a hand along his jaw. "What else?"

"Vodka does not make me *rash*. My skin is just fine."

"Not *in* a rash," he corrected her with a shake of his head, "*rash*. Risk-taking. Not cautious."

"Oh," Maya mulled that over. "I guess maybe it does."

"What makes you horny?" Stefan whispered in her ear and she spun on him, whacking the back of her hand across his chest.

"Simple, clean-shaven men who don't run criminal empires."

He laughed, rubbing the stubble on his jaw and moving out of her way as she investigated the dinner offerings. There were seven burritos in the bag, two already out on the counter…

"How do four people eat *nine* burritos? And… a quesadilla? Nachos? Are these tacos?" She gave Stefan an incredulous look. "Is there a gym here somewhere I don't know about? There's no way you guys eat like this."

Stefan grinned "What we don't finish goes out to the security guys."

Well that answered one question she had at least. "What if you get snacky?"

"Snacky?" Daniel scoffed from the table and she shot him a glare he didn't bother to look up for.

"You know, you get a craving in the middle of the day…"

"That's what we're supposed to have *you* here for," Diego's voice was so close she jumped, whirling on him with an affronted expression.

"*Stop that*," she pointed a finger, glaring. "I'm going to put bells on you guys."

"Try it," now it was Stefan, pressed to her back and sandwiching her between himself and Diego.

"Maybe we should Stef," Diego's hands cupped her hips, "make music while we're pounding her pussy."

"Ugh," Maya shoved him and he laughed, backing up a step. "Can we not use that word?"

"What?" Diego frowned. "Pussy?"

Maya blushed to the tips of her ears, grabbing her burrito and ducking around them. "Yes, that one."

"You don't like pussy?" Stefan gave her a shocked look. "I thought everyone loved pussy."

"Who doesn't like pussy?" Daniel finally looked up from his phone.

"Maya," Stefan pointed and she groaned.

"No, it's not that I don't… I mean…"

"Look at how red she's turning," Daniel commented casually, leaning back further in his chair.

Maya glared at him, tapping his boots. "Off."

"Excuse me?"

"It's bad manners, off the table."

Daniel stared and a quiet chuckle from behind her was quickly muffled when Daniel shot them a glare. The disgruntled look didn't leave his face as he slowly set his boots on the floor, staring at her as she set her plate near the spot they had occupied.

"The table's eight feet long, why did you have to sit *there*?"

"I like the view."

He preened for a moment until she gestured past him to the city skyline. He grunted, giving her a pointed look, "Why don't you love pussy?"

Maya choked, beating her chest fruitlessly until a glass of water appeared in front of her which she downed gratefully.

"It's fine. As a physical thing I have no objections. I like mine well enough."

"Well enough?"

She ignored Diego. "It's the *word* I don't like."

"Pussy?"

"Can we *not*?"

"Why don't you like the word pussy?" Stefan took the chair next to her.

"It's such a nice word. Pussy." Diego was at the head of the table, passing another beer to Daniel before taking a seat.

"Just rolls off the tongue," Daniel almost sighed as he said it.

"Or on the tongue," Diego pointed out.

This was a mistake, she shouldn't have said anything. "It sounds so juvenile. Like something an eighth grader would say. You're grown men."

Daniel raised an eyebrow. "Would you prefer we say cunt?"

No, no she would not. But she had dug this grave, she was going to have to lie in it. "I would prefer we not talk about it."

"Does it turn you on?" Stefan asked with a leer. She should have sat further down the table, where she could see all three of them and not have to keep turning her head. It felt like she was in a game of ping pong.

Pussy ping pong.

"No."

"No?" Daniel sounded doubtful. "I seem to remember someone getting incredibly wet when I talked about stroking her little pussy."

"Did you?" Diego raised an eyebrow. "I didn't realize you liked the talking. Should we tell you all the things we could do for you?"

"Or maybe you *would* prefer cunt." Stefan's breath flowed over her shoulder and tickled her ear, making her shiver. Making her *wet*. "Oh she liked that. Pussy wasn't dirty enough for you, sweetheart?"

"I hate you," she growled without any heat, picking up her

burrito and water and going to sit at the island instead. Their mocking laughter followed but she ignored it, studying the kitchen backsplash like she was going to be quizzed on it later.

Her attention jumped back to the room when her name popped up.

"We lost our contact in Riga, the Alvani's took the whole gang out."

Maya frowned at Stefan's words. Her father had never been interested in guns - and that was what you pulled out of the former Soviet block. Guns and maybe counterfeiting equipment.

"Shit, I've got a whole order for AR's to send east," Diego grunted, fingers tapping on the table. "Who's our backup?"

"Petrov but he's out of pocket since his son died," Daniel offered.

"Well that doesn't help then, does it?" Diego's fingers tapped faster. "I'm open to suggestions."

"I read this article, about guns." Three sets of eyes turned to her and Maya knew she'd made a mistake. But she was already talking so might as well keep going. "When the militaries were pulling out of-"

"You read an article?" Stefan asked skeptically.

"Yeah." She shouldn't have said anything, shouldn't have butted in.

"What, like in *Vogue* or something?" Daniel asked with a snort.

Maya didn't bother pointing out she could never afford *Vogue*. "No, but it was talking about record-keeping and-"

"Don't you have something else to be doing?" Diego cut her off, annoyance coloring his tone and Maya's mouth snapped shut. No, she didn't actually, but the condescension in the air could be cut with a knife so she left, doing her damnedest not to slam the door to the back bedroom closed behind her.

7

Today was the day. Her big debut. Maya wasn't sure how many people had been invited over for it but there were going to be people, in the apartment. Not only the Kings' men but actual people who were going to *say* things about her. Who were *supposed* to say things. And her job was to give them things to say.

"And you will...?"

Maya sighed at Diego and repeated back, for what felt like the fifth time, "Be the hostess. Gracious. Obviously in love with you."

"Lust," Daniel corrected and she stuck her tongue out at him. "That's the spirit."

"Who is coming?" Diego ignored Daniel's interjection, keeping his eyes steady on her.

"Some of your lieutenants. Gabriel Garcia, who I don't think I've ever met, and some of his guys. Lonny Venturelli, who I *have* met before. I was just a kid but he'll recognize me."

"How do you know he'll recognize you?" Stefan asked curiously.

Maya frowned, pointing at her face, "I got the family nose. And besides that I look just like my mom."

"Your nose is perfect." Even Stefan seemed surprised he'd said it and he coughed before continuing with, "So if someone has met an Alvani they'll recognize you?"

"Yeah," Maya shrugged, "the curse of strong bloodlines."

"But in our favor," Diego leaned his elbows on the desk. "Anyone who sees you will know who you are."

Maya nodded distractedly, trying to cross her legs in a way that didn't make parts of her stand out more than she wanted. "What am I wearing?"

Diego tilted his head, a small smile playing on his lips. "Is what you have on not sufficient?"

What she- it was a teddy. A one piece black lacy thing that originally lived in the 'never in a million years' drawer until she realized it wasn't *quite* as sheer as she thought it was. It was still ridiculous, although only slightly more so than a swimsuit. A swimsuit you could see her nipples through.

"No, it's *not*."

Diego grinned, reaching into a drawer and pulling a box out, coming around and setting it beside him on the desk. It was small, too small to have real clothes in it. Maya couldn't help but look at it like it was a snake, ready to bite.

"Please tell me that isn't more lingerie."

"Do you want more lingerie? That can be arranged." Daniel looked interested in the conversation for the first time.

"That won't be necessary," she quickly averred, pulling the box closer with one finger. How bad could it possibly be?

Bad. Real bad.

"I'm not wearing that."

Diego sighed and Stefan huffed a laugh. "Told you."

Diego leaned back against the desk, crossing his ankles and folding his arms over his chest. "What makes you think you have a choice?"

"I'm not saying you can't brute force me into it, I'm saying that I won't parade around looking like an idiot in it for you."

Maya crossed her arms, "I have to draw a line somewhere."

"Would you rather put on the bustier and the frilly panties?" Daniel asked with an arched eyebrow from by the window.

"*No*," she bit off. "The lingerie, the outfits... that's all well and good when I can just sort of show up and put on my act. But this is an *event*, with *people*."

"We're people," Stefan pointed out, "you've never minded us."

"I *have* minded," she corrected. "But we all have an agreement and as twisted as you are I know you'll honor it."

Diego frowned, standing taller. "No one will touch you. They wouldn't *dare*."

Maya didn't bother pointing out the dozen or so times in her life someone absolutely *had* dared - even when she was under her father's protection. Then again, she felt safer here than she ever had at home.

Life really was strange.

"At least let me pick my own dress," she tried instead. "Something I feel comfortable in."

"Daniel spent time on this," Diego grunted as he walked around the desk. Behind him Daniel shook his head, an incredulous expression on his face. But when Diego glanced back he quickly changed it to a nod.

"I did."

"And I don't want that to have been a waste."

Maya sighed. "It's going to look awful."

"How do you know that?" Diego prodded. "You haven't even tried it on."

"I don't need to," Maya replied. "With that fabric it would need to be made to my exact measurement to not look like a sack on a sausage."

"You think I don't know your exact measurements?" Daniel queried, that damn eyebrow still arching over the lens of his glasses.

"I don't even... *how*?"

He grinned. "Forty-two, thirty-three, forty-three."

Maya gaped. "*How*?"

"Good with numbers," he shrugged. "And a few chances to get some hands-on data."

Maya continued to gape, caught between embarrassment and admiration that he could rattle that off that easily. *She wasn't even one hundred percent sure what her measurements were - but that sounded right. It sounded freakishly* precise in fact.

"Go try it on," Diego gestured to Stefan and the other man scooped up the box, guiding her out of the room.

Maya regained her senses at the bedroom, digging her heels in and yanking the box out of Stefan's hands. "You wait *here*," she pointed at the hallway. "I don't need your help."

"You sure? What if there's a zipper you can't reach?" His smug smile was so smarmy she wanted to slap it off of him. She growled instead, stomping into the room and slamming the door behind her. It made her feel like a petulant child; it also made her feel good.

It *was* a beautiful dress. Slinky silk in a deep blueish color. Simple, with no extra seams or flounces. Thin straps over the shoulders, a thigh-high slit in the floor length skirt, and virtually no back.

And no room for undergarments either.

She did try, but the thin material showed every freckle on her skin, nevertheless panty lines. No chance of any support garments either, even assuming she had some. It would have looked stunning on someone half her size. On her...

"It doesn't *fit*," she finally bit out, glaring at the door.

"Show me."

Maya looked in the mirror, looked at every bulge the dress showed, every place where the fabric tried to stretch too tight across her body. Jesus, she could see the shape of her pubic hair. "Please don't make me. Why can't I wear something else? I'd even go for the bustier right about now."

"I said show me."

His voice brokered no argument and she took a deep breath before opening the door and stepping back so he could see. "See? Daniel was wrong. It doesn't fit."

Stefan motioned her forward and she stepped closer. His eyes roamed over her body, lingering on the swell of her breast and then falling to the long stretch of thigh the slit showed. "You look…"

"Ridiculous," she finished for him, struggling with the urge to cross her arms. Her chest was enough on display already, she didn't need to make it worse.

Stefan shook his head and stepped closer, reaching out until his hand hovered over her collarbone. The heat from it made her shiver and her lips parted as she watched his face. "It's not. It's perfect." He snorted and shot her a grin, "Diego is going to lose his shit when he sees you. Now go find some shoes and do whatever you need to do. Be ready by eight."

"Stefan, please," she caught his arm, felt the ripple of muscle beneath his shirt. "No one is going to believe this. *Look* at me."

"I am." His tongue slid over his lower lip, leaning so close she could feel his breath on her. "And the only thing that would look better on you is absolutely nothing."

She blinked, stunned, barely noticing when he turned her towards the closet, or when he patted her backside softly to send her moving.

Maya took her time getting ready, soaping and plucking and shaving *everything*. Including above her lady parts which she had only done once before, after a night of drinking when she was twenty-one. She wasn't personally a fan of the bald look but with that dress… everything had to go.

Wrapped in a towel she worked on her hair. She needed a trim, had been contemplating cutting it all off for a while. But with the help of the forty-seven different implements tucked in a drawer - including a hair crimper that had to be from 1987 - she had it falling in perfect neat curls.

Makeup was trickier. Her usual 'lips, eyes, blush' wasn't going to cover it but she had limited experience on how to do more. No chance that Daniel would let her use a tablet to watch a tutorial. Whatever, she was a grown woman, she could figure out how to use kohl eyeliner and not the little liquid pen she was used to. And the fourteen different powders and creams probably didn't have a specific order they *had* to go in. And lipstick was lipstick, just put it on your lips. This was easy, fifteen minutes and she'd be done, tops.

An hour later she looked like a raccoon. A raccoon that worked nights in a drag show. What had happened? There was lipstick smudged up to her nose and on her teeth. Her eyebrows were two dark slashes over what might generously be called a shadowy eye - if that eye was shadowed in a dark box on a moonless night.

Maya groaned, leaning into the sink and turning her head this way and that. Was it salvageable? She took a tissue and wiped at her eyebrow but only made it worse. Nope, okay, back into the shower, hair firmly stuck in a bun on top of her head. Not that it mattered because she hit the wrong button and the entire ceiling turned into a waterfall.

Standing under the spray, watching her hazy reflection begin to melt as makeup ran down her face, Maya strongly considered going out like that. What would they do? "Yes, this *is* Alvani's daughter. She's a bit of a mess but we've got incredibly low standards it turns out."

That knocked her into a giggle and with a resolute groan she pulled her hair free. Might as well start from scratch. Knowing she was running out of time, she concentrated on

getting her hair dry and into some semblance of style. Face...
well face would stay what she knew. A basic lip gloss and
mascara - she wasn't about to touch the blush with a ten foot
pole. She didn't know the brand well enough to try *that*
again.

"You ready?" a voice called through the door.

Scrambling, she grabbed for the dress, slipping it over her
head and stumbling towards the closet. "Just a sec." The shoes
were silver, the lowest heel she could find, with straps
crisscrossing her foot and ankle. She threw the door open
with only one on, the other dangling from her fingertips.
Expecting Stefan again she was shocked to see Daniel.

In a suit.

Maya tried not to stare but Lord almighty he looked really
good. All in black, even a black tie, his beard trimmed and
head freshly shaved. His glasses sitting *just so* on the tip of his
nose, his eyes studying her over them.

"How are you not ready yet?"

Rather than go into the whole ordeal Maya waved him off,
putting one hand on the door frame while she tried to pull
the other shoe on. With a grunt, Daniel took a knee in front of
her, pulling the shoe from her fingers and slipping it on her
without a word. His big hand cupped the back of her calf, her
leg bare where the slit in the dress fell away.

"Women," he grunted and Maya's eyes narrowed.

"Didn't know I could get you on your knees so fast."

He glared up at her, finishing the last buckle and starting to
rise. But he kept his hand on her, skimming the back of her
thigh and cupping beneath the globe of her asscheek. "All
you had to do was ask, kitten."

Standing this close, Maya realized she was taller than him.
Maybe the same height ordinarily but in her heels she had a
couple of inches on him. Wasn't that supposed to be a turn
off? Why did it make her want to press her breasts to his face

instead?

"Come on," he spanked her with a sharp slap and she yelped. "Don't want to keep people waiting."

There weren't many, thankfully. A guy she'd seen once before - she'd been perched on the edge of Diego's desk when he'd walked in. Another she thought she knew from passing in the halls. But most she didn't recognize, men in sharp suits and gold chains holding glasses and talking hushed tones. There was an older man with a cigar in one hand, sitting on the world's most uncomfortable couch and chatting amiably with Stefan.

Also in a suit.

She was not going to live through tonight if they insisted on looking like *that*. The gray cloth molded to his body like a glove and was he wearing a *waistcoat*? Had he been reading the diary she didn't keep?

"There she is," Diego's voice flowed over her and she held her head high, meeting his eyes across the room. "Why don't you fix us some drinks, sweet cheeks."

Gracious, she reminded herself, *gracious and loving.*

Lusting, Daniel's voice corrected in her head.

Yeah, lusting was right. Diego was *definitely* wearing a waistcoat *and* a pocket square. He looked good enough to eat. Maya tried to ignore the looks as she poured him a whiskey, doing her best to saunter past the leering eyes when she handed it off to him.

"Anything else, handsome?"

He smiled, leaning down and giving her a soft, casual, kiss on the lips. "See if Stefan needs anything."

"Of course," she gave the man he was talking to a shy smile and turned away. It was to her credit that she didn't jump a mile when Diego pinched her.

"Maya!" Stefan looked elated to see her, pulling her to sit on the arm of his chair. She didn't like that one bit. At least standing she could suck her stomach in, be careful about how she was presenting herself. But Stefan cuddled her hip to his shoulder and her entire leg was sticking out of the skirt and her body bulged against the dress and this was *not* attractive.

"Stefan baby," she cooed, carding her fingers carefully through his hair. "Can I get you something?"

Please let me get up before someone notices I'm not your usual waif-thin supermodel girlfriend. She paused, she wasn't sure they'd ever *had* girlfriends, they certainly didn't act like it.

"Just you sweetheart," his hand dipped between her thighs, the skirt rucking up around his wrist.

"So this is the infamous Maya," the man across from Stefan said. "You know you look just like someone I know."

Pasting on a bright smile, Maya stroked her fingers down Stefan's neck. "You probably met my dad."

"Oh?"

"Eric? Alvani? People have said I look a little like him."

The man nodded, puffing his cigar thoughtfully. Maya tried to cover her disgust, that smell was going to linger for *days*.

You won't be here long enough to notice.

Ignoring the thought, she went back to petting Stefan, half-listening to the conversation they were having about imports. When he told her to get him a refill she jumped up gratefully, grabbing his glass and heading for the bar cart.

"Let me know when they get tired of you."

Maya spun to the voice, feeling her face heat up. "Excuse me?"

The man was in a sharp navy blue suit, waves of brown hair falling perfectly over one eye. He'd probably spent longer with the blowdryer than she had.

"You've got some kind of gold-plated pussy and I've got the money," he shrugged. "Might as well see what the fuss is about."

"I don't-" she started to splutter but the man's eyes darted over her shoulder and he gave a quick nod before leaving. Maya looked back to see Daniel giving her a curious look from a few feet away.

"Did he say something to you?" he asked when he got closer, turning so they were shoulder to shoulder perusing the liquor.

"Nothing," she grunted, yanking the first thing she saw and filling the glass with it.

"Was he rude? We can kill him if he was."

Maya laughed, shooting him an amused look. Except, he wasn't kidding. "Oh, no. Just... you know. Everyone here knows I'm available to three men - not a surprise if they wonder if it could be four."

Daniel snorted, glancing down at the glass in her hand. "Stefan's not going to want a glass of St. Germain, kitten."

"What-?" But Daniel had already gone, leaving Maya to take a sniff of the liquid. The smell of flowers overwhelmed her and she coughed, setting it aside. Stefan would think she'd gone insane if she came back with that.

Glass of whiskey firmly in hand, she crossed back to him, bending over the back of the chair so he couldn't pull her down again. She positioned herself carefully, she was *not* about to give the man with a cigar an eyeful either. "Here you go."

Stefan took it without looking back, fully engrossed in talks of import subsidies and something about taxes she only half followed. She was trying to decide what to do when a voice boomed out across the room, making her turn and smile.

"Maya my girl, you look *ravishing*."

"Hello Lonny," she held a hand out when she got close enough and he kissed the back with a flourish. "How have you been?"

"Same old, same old. But look at you! You were such a little thing last I saw you and now? The spitting image of your mother." His brows drew down and he leaned in closer, voice dropping to what he probably thought was a whisper. "Are these ruffians keeping you against your will? Tell me and I will burn this place to the ground."

Diego met her eyes and she smiled, patting Lonny on the shoulder. "Not at all. I have everything a girl could ask for."

Lonny harrumphed and Diego gave her a nod of approval that absolutely did *not* make her heart flutter. "Well, that's what I told Nico but he insisted on seeing for himself."

"Wait," Maya took a step back, shaking her head. "What do you mean, see for himself-?"

"Hey sis."

8

Oh God they were going to kill him.

"Nico what are you *doing* here?"

Maya's brother stepped forward, dressed in a dark suit and white shirt. His hair was a few shades darker than hers, looking almost black where he'd slicked it back. He looked… older. Authoritative. The last time she'd seen him he was barely twelve, a foot shorter than her and only just starting to hit puberty. Now he was all grown up, looking ready to go toe to toe with anyone in the room.

There was no way she was going to let that happen.

"You need to leave. *Now*." She reached out to turn him around, push him out the door, but Diego was there first, his arm wrapping around her waist and pulling her close.

"What is this, princess? Family reunion?"

"Nope," Maya lied, ignoring the fact that both Lonny and her idiot brother had announced the relationship to the room. And the fact that they looked like two sides of the same coin. "Never seen him before in my life."

"Nicolas," her brother didn't offer a hand to shake. "Nicolas Alvani."

He had a death wish. It was the only explanation.

"Diego Krol." Maya could hear the poison dripping from his voice. "It's not often we get visitors from your side of town."

"All of town is our side of town," her brother said with a tight smile and Maya started searching for a weapon. When this turned sour she was going to need to do *something* to keep him from getting murdered. Even if it was bashing a goon in the head with a vase, like in a cartoon.

"Maybe it used to be," Stefan was on her other side, arm slung around her neck, his fingers tracing over the skin of her chest, all but cupping her breast. "Things change. Maybe you don't own all you think you do."

Nico's nostrils flared and he took a step forward, fist clenching at his side. She couldn't let him do this.

"Nico," she whispered, stepping closer to him, feeling the two men's grip on her tighten before they fell away. "You don't belong here. Please go home."

"You really *want* to be here?" he asked incredulously. "Doing- is it true? All of them?"

This wasn't supposed to happen. She knew they'd find out, but she didn't think she'd have to *see* it. See the betrayal and disappointment on their faces. Especially Nico's. But she couldn't go home, saving face now wouldn't change that. Having him hate her... maybe that was the cleaner break she needed.

"On a stack of *Mr. Popper's Penguins*," she whispered, "it's okay."

He blinked at their old vow, something they'd come up with after hearing someone swear on a stack of Bibles. Maya had decided that she needed to swear on *her* favorite book instead, roping her brother into it. It drove their mother, devout Catholic that she was, up the wall. Swearing, of both kinds, was her nemesis - and the constant scolding when so much as a 'gosh darnit' left her children had settled deep in

80

Maya. It was the only part of her mother she had.

For a moment, as the words settled, Maya thought she'd broken him, that he might cry in front of these men. But it passed quickly and he drew himself up to his full height, looking down that Alvani nose at her. He opened his mouth as though he might say something but spun on his heel instead, stalking out of the apartment without another word.

"Rude," Stefan remarked, sliding an arm around her waist again. "We should go after him."

"Please don't." Maya was tired and she was sure it must be showing on her face. "Just… he'll go tell dad. That's what you wanted right?"

"Right."

Taking a deep breath she found her composure, turning and looking up into his serious face. "Don't let him ruin the fun, baby. Let me get you another drink."

She slipped back into the living room, all eyes on her as she gave them her brightest smile. "This is why you never tell your family about your love life."

A laugh rumbled through the room and Maya relaxed, making her way to the cart and pouring a double, tossing it back without a second thought before refilling and going in search of Diego, two glasses in her hands.

Maya was determined to be the perfect hostess for them, keeping drinks refilled, filling silences where necessary.

"Diego has an idea about that," Maya said when someone mentioned a warehouse issue. She nodded at him and he looked up with a slight frown.

"What was that?"

"You've been dealing with some warehouse issues as well, right baby?" She gave a small giggle, looking at the man sitting next to her with wide eyes. "I don't really pay attention but I remember him saying something about it right before we-"

Biting her lip she turned away, as though she was hiding a blush. Diego watched her with a curious look, settling in next to the man with the warehouse problems while Maya emptied her glass and excused herself for another.

"Daniel can do *anything*," Maya told another man earnestly later, arm on the man in question's shoulder. "I mean he is a *God* at computer things." He puffed a bit, rolling his eyes but nevertheless assuring the man that he could solve the paperwork issue for him for the right price.

Stefan caught her downing another shot, hands sliding around her waist from behind and chin resting on her shoulder. "You're doing fabulous tonight."

"Thank-" she swallowed back a hiccup and tried again. "Thank you. Is it what you wanted?"

"What I wanted…" he hummed thoughtfully, one hand trailing down to rest his fingers at the top of her thighs. "Well that's a loaded question don't you think?"

She couldn't get turned on, not right now, not in this dress. There would be no hiding it if she sat down, the material was too thin and she had *nothing* on beneath it. She needed to think about something else. Radishes. She used to pickle radishes with her grandmother. Smelly vinegar and salt and…

A warm chuckle flowed over her and every thought flew out the window. "Maybe later," he said with a small pat over her mound before leaving her reeling.

She needed another drink. Or several.

The room had started to tilt when she stood up, making her sway slightly while she caught her balance. Other girls had shown up, disappearing out the front door with men one by one. She got into a conversation with one about that kohl eyeliner, gesturing wildly as she complained about how useless the thing was. At some point she noticed Diego next to her, his hand lightly massaging the back of her neck. She leaned into him without thought, resting her hand on his thigh.

"Have you had too much to drink, princess," he whispered, thumb stroking into her hair.

"Dun think so," she slurred back, blinking owlishly. Okay, maybe she had. A little.

"That's a pretty little whore you've got," the man with the cigar commented. Garcia, she thought. The biggest name in the room besides Lonny.

And the Kings of course.

"How much for a taste?"

Diego went stiff beside her. Suddenly he wasn't a convenient pillow but a coiled jungle cat, fingers clenching into a fist.

"What did you say?"

"It's okay," she tried to soothe him but he caught her wrist in a harsh grip, jerking her hand away from him.

"Get her out of here," Diego's voice snapped and she quickly slid away from him, taking Daniel's hand when it was held out to her. Her head spun as she stood, her feet stumbling a little. Daniel caught her easily, sliding an arm around her waist and guiding her out of the room and to the sex dungeon.

Daniel was in the sex dungeon. With her.

She'd done a good job so far of keeping all of them away - not sure if the combination of man and bed was one she would be able to resist. And God did Daniel look good in that black suit with his tie slightly askew.

"You a little drunk, kitten?" His voice slid over her like honey and she bit back a groan. Had he always sounded like that? Like sex and pleasure, the rough rasp counterpointed by his keen eyes.

"Kitten?" She swayed towards him and he caught her arms, his palms warm and solid against her. Her eyes dropped to his lips and she licked her own again, watching as his curled into a smile.

"Does little Maya get horny when she drinks?" His fingers were stroking her bare skin, his body crowding closer until her back pressed against the wall. "Is that it? Tell me what you want."

"You," she breathed and in a flash got her wish.

She had expected him to be scratchy, his beard to feel rough on her skin, but it wasn't. It was soft, tickling across her cheek before his tongue licked out along her bottom lip. She moaned and her hands took on a life of their own. Reaching out, pulling him closer, tangling into the fabric of his shirt. His hands rose to press to each side of her head, palms flat to the wood and then he was *there*. His entire body pressed to every inch of hers. His thigh sliding between her willingly parted legs.

"Fuck I knew you'd taste good," he breathed, nose nudging beneath her jaw so he could press his mouth to the skin of her neck. His tongue snaked out, licking a long stripe across her and she moaned, clutching at his shirt.

If anyone had asked Maya would have guessed Daniel wasn't a kisser. He'd never tried with her, and when she'd seen him with the other women he hadn't even been close to kissing position. But the man kissed like his livelihood depended on it. He kissed like he was experimenting on her. Varying the pressure of his lips, the slide of his tongue, the sharp nip of his teeth. She could barely keep up, letting him take the lead. Take whatever he wanted from her.

He wasn't touching her, why wasn't he touching her? His mouth and his body, but she wanted his hands. Wanted to feel them caress her, feel them slide along her body, on her breasts, between her thighs. She certainly touched *him*. Fingers curling around the base of his skull, clutching his back, trying to get him closer.

"*Ahem.*"

Maya barely heard the soft cough, certainly hadn't heard the door beside her open. But she felt when Daniel moved away from her.

"You've got shit timing."

Stefan grinned, leaning a shoulder against the doorframe. "I think I've got great timing. You get her all warmed up for me?"

Daniel growled, "What do you want?"

"Diego needs you."

A deep groan left Daniel, dropping his head to her shoulder and shifting his knee between her legs. "Why the fuck can't you do it?"

"Something to do with computers, you know we're shit with that."

He was moving, his knee rocking up against her and she couldn't help but move with it, riding his thigh with slow rolls of her hips. Daniel cursed. "It has to be *now*?"

"I'll keep her wet for you," Stefan promised, holding up two fingers. "Scout's honor."

"Other hand asshole," Daniel grunted, finally pulling away, eyes boring into hers when she whined at the loss. "Kitten you gotta stop that or I'm going to fuck you against this wall while Stefan watches."

Maya didn't know why that was a bad idea. "Please?"

He took a step towards her, pupils so wide his eyes looked black, but Stefan pulled him back with a hand on his shoulder.

"Garcia still out there?" Daniel asked, straightening his coat. In the light from the hallway Maya could barely make a shiny patch above his knee. Was that...? Had she...?

"Diego and him had a chat, then he left."

Another nod and Daniel cupped her jaw in his hand, pressing his thumb to her lips. Maya didn't think, pulling it inside and wrapping her tongue around it. Sucking *hard*. He took a step towards her, but Stefan grabbed him, steering him out of the room with a whispered word and a shove.

"You having a good night, sweetheart?" Stefan asked, leaning against the doorframe. The dim light cast his face in shadows, all dips and angles she wanted to lick.

"Yeah," she sighed, slumping into the drywall and shutting her eyes. Just for a moment.

The next thing she knew she was being set down on the bed, someone gently undoing the straps of her shoes and slipping them off. She blinked at the indistinct form. Was it still Stefan?

"Are you coming to bed?"

The man laughed, bending over and brushing a kiss on her mouth. It *was* Stefan. She'd recognize the smell of him anywhere.

"I don't take advantage of drunk girls."

"M'not drunk," she mumbled, already drifting off.

"Good night Maya."

Maya awoke with a splitting headache, dress tangled about her legs and an overwhelming need to use the bathroom. She didn't throw up, but it was a near thing. Splashing water on her face she stared at herself in the mirror. She didn't *look* that bad, a bit of mascara smudged but nothing heinous.

A shower. She needed a shower. And a hot beverage.

Of *course* this would be a morning all three of them were there, sitting around the kitchen with their coffees and crepes, not a hair out of place. Maya pulled the tie of her robe together, not ready to climb into whatever today's lingerie was, and studiously avoided meeting anyone's eyes as she made her tea.

"Good morning." God had Stefan's voice always grated like that?

Maya grumbled a response, nose deep in her mug.

"Here," he slid two pills her way and Maya took them with a grateful smile, tossing them back before suddenly giving him a panicked look. He laughed, "Advil, sweetheart, for your head."

"Thanks."

"No problem."

Silence fell and Maya contemplated going back to the room before anyone could come up with a question for her.

"What do you think he'll do?"

Too late. Maya looked up at Diego, lounging across from her in a pressed white shirt, his jacket slung over the back of the barstool. She didn't ask who he meant. "I don't know."

"Can you guess?"

"I really can't." She shook her head, wincing when the room shifted on her. "I wasn't... Nico coming here changes things. Without him... the not knowing would have killed dad. Was I captured? Was I being raped? Was I just being a whore like-" She cut herself off abruptly and shrugged. "I don't know. I don't even know if Nico will tell him."

"Maybe we should have stuck with the kidnapping plan," Daniel said blandly.

Maya didn't rise to the bait. "Maybe."

"But how much less fun would that have been?" Stefan gave her a wide smile, pinching her side lightly and making her laugh despite herself.

"I'm sorry," she said truthfully. "I hope this doesn't mess up your plans."

Diego gave her a curious look, like someone examining a bug they'd pinned to a board. "What happens, happens."

She nodded. "How much longer do you want me to stay?"

The three men shared a moment before Diego answered. "Til after the job. Few more days."

"And still the lingerie?" she tried to make her tone light.

"Yes," Daniel replied immediately and Maya laughed.

"Of course you would say that."

"You look good in it," Diego said, as though he were announcing the weather. "Take it with you when you go."

When you go. Wherever that might be.

9

Maya couldn't sleep.

The apartment was empty, it had to be after midnight, and she was laying on the eighty square feet of bed with the satin sheets staring at the ceiling. She'd been staring for the better part of an hour. Pillows were strewn every which way, casualties of trying to find a position that she could nod off in. She was convinced that if she only had some curtains, could block the city lights out, that all of her problems would be solved. It helped to have a solution in mind, especially one she couldn't implement.

If she could implement it she'd have to get out of bed instead of just being mad about it.

Instead there she was, staring at the ceiling and trying very hard not to think about what had happened to her life.

Less than a month ago she was homeless, down to her last three hundred bucks, and pretty sure she didn't have any close enough friends to crash with while she got her feet back under her.

Now she was in an apartment the size of a mansion, eating takeout every day, wearing lingerie that cost more than her rent, and trying very hard not to have sex with the men who lived upstairs.

Men. Plural.

It wasn't even just one guy, one she could shrug off as a crush. But three? Had something fundamental changed in her when she'd agreed to this deal. Had she always been the kind of person to do that - only she'd never been given the chance?

Maya turned over, punching the pillow before collapsing face down.

Thinking of them made her think of *all* of them. How their hands felt on her body, the way Daniel had rocked against her or how Diego's naked form had felt wrapped around her. Stefan's smile and those kisses that set her soul on fire.

A few more days, maybe as few as two, and she'd be gone. Out of their hair. But was she really going to leave without even *trying*? Assuming they were interested, that is. It was still possible that all of this was part of the ruse, pretending to be attracted to her the same way she was pretending.

Even though she wasn't.

The click of her door latch made her bolt upright. What a night to forget to put the bench in front of it. Had one of them come home drunk? Was she about to have to fend off a handsy Daniel with the added handicap of being near a bed? Or Stefan, with soft smiles and a come hither glance. If it was Diego he'd probably stand there and stare at her until she invited him over. And who was to say she *wanted* to kick them out. Hadn't she just been considering seducing one or all of them?

Maya opened her mouth to call out - to invite them or tell them to leave, she didn't know - but the shadow in the doorway was wrong. Too short, too stocky. It hadn't occurred to her someone *else* might be there. Might slip inside the door without making a noise.

A stranger was *in the room.*

Maya scrambled off the side of the bed, hitting the floor

beneath the sex swing with a thump. Whoever this was, they didn't knock. They didn't call out to her. There was no way that was a good thing. She needed a weapon. Something she could swing or throw or… she fished inside the nightstand, discovering what she already knew - several boxes of condoms and lube.

Did *none* of these guys have a weapons kink? Really? Even a fake knife might be enough to keep the shadow away from her.

"Come out Maya," the voice called and she blinked. She *knew* that voice.

"Michael?" She popped her head over the side of the bed cautiously, staring across the room at her father's sergeant at arms. "What the hell?"

"C'mere," he gestured to her, glancing furtively back over his shoulder. "I'm here to get you out."

She stood, shaking her head. "Why?"

"Mr. Alvani sent me. Let's go."

"Michael," Maya held a hand up. This was not what she had expected. She hadn't spoken to her dad in over a decade. It wasn't a lie when she'd told the Kings he wouldn't care if she was kidnapped. He *never* had before. Even if Nico had told him about where she was it didn't follow he'd send someone to rescue her. "Wait, which Mr. Alvani?"

"*Mr. Alvani,*" Michael stressed, leaving no doubt he meant her father. "Now come *on.*"

"No," Maya shook her head, hair tumbling around her. Where had her elastic gone? "I'm staying."

He moved closer. "You can't mean that."

"I do," she told him. Leaving wasn't an option. Just like with her brother it wouldn't bring her back into the family fold, it would only mess up everything she'd worked for. "Go Michael, tell Eric I'm where I want to be."

Michael sighed, standing up straighter. "I was afraid you'd

say that." Metal glinted in his hand as he walked towards her with unhurried steps. "I was hoping I wouldn't have to be the one to do this."

"Michael…" Maya held her hands up, backing up until she felt glass behind her. "This isn't… what are you doing?"

"Giving a slut what she deserves."

Maya threw what she had, a box of condoms that hit Michael in the face and exploded into gold foiled packets. He cursed, stepping back and swatting the items away while Maya sprinted across the bed on her hands and knees. She hit the door just as she heard him shout, closing it with a slam and wishing it had a lock on it.

The apartment was dark, she was the only one home. But someone would be on the landing, a guard, *somebody*. There was *always* someone standing guard. She barely registered that the front door was open, not until she skidded up to it, catching herself and choking back a wave of nausea at the body on the other side. Shaking her head she avoided looking at it - she didn't have time to process that right now.

Did she have time to wait for the elevator? Could she outrun him on the stairs? She needed a *weapon*. She was absolutely certain there would be at least one in the offices, but she had no idea *where*. What if it was locked away?

The decision was taken from her when Michael loped into view. Maya waited a beat, until she was sure he was following her down the entryway, then darted into the living room. The kitchen was her best bet, a knife or even a fork would be better than nothing. Michael hadn't shot her so he wanted it to be messy, something she was both grateful for and deeply disturbed by.

It was a straight shot, she could be there in mere seconds, she needed to-

A hand caught in the back of her shirt, pulling her up short and spinning her around. She lost her footing, tumbling sideways into the glass and chrome coffee table she hated so much. She didn't have time to feel joy as it shattered, pieces scratching along her arms, piercing her clothing and slicing down her legs. Michael landed on top of her with a thud, grunting and coming to his knees over her.

"I'm supposed to send a message." The way Michael said it, it was almost conversational, pressing his knife up under her chin. "So you choose how."

"Don't do this," Maya choked, hands scrambling. Her fingers circled his wrist, trying to move him away from her. "Please, Michael. You- you taught me how to swim." There were tears in her voice, "How to ride a bike."

"Shut up," he gritted out, pressing the knife harder and her hands fell to her sides. "If you'd just kept your legs closed we wouldn't be in this situation."

Tears clouded her vision and she shuddered, trying to think. Her grasping fingers wrapped around something sharp, something triangular, and she didn't pause before swinging it up and into his neck.

Pushing herself backwards, she barely felt the sting of the glass shards on her palms. Couldn't take her eyes off him long enough to be careful. He was convulsing, a horrible gurgling noise coming up from his chest. His mouth turned red - brilliant bold red that bubbled from his lips and dripped down his chin.

Cool glass hit her back and she huddled between the couch and the wall, knees pressed to her chest and her arms curled around them. She was protected like this, hidden. The only thing in her sight was Michael.

He didn't go quickly.

Eyes wide, he clutched at his neck, pulling the glass free. Blood poured from the now gaping wound, sliding down his chest and mixing with what had already fallen from his mouth.

He stared at her the entire time, one hand reaching out and scrabbling against the stone floor.

As if from miles away she heard the front door open. Heard the rush of booted feet down the hall. Someone else was coming towards her. Did it matter? She'd gotten lucky once already, she couldn't hope to do it again.

Lucky to kill a man.

Was he dead? He was still making those awful gurgling noises. She wanted to leave, wanted to run, but he was there. Leaving would mean going past him, getting within his reach. The only thing worse than him being dead was if he wasn't.

"Maya?"

Her eyes snapped up to warm brown ones. Like melted chocolate. Diego had a smear of red on his hand. Maybe someone had stabbed him too.

"He got your message."

Diego frowned at her, moving past the body to crouch between her and it. "What message?"

"My dad." She swallowed and felt bile rise in her throat. "He got your message."

Diego inched closer and she flinched back, head hitting the window behind her. He stopped instantly, holding one hand out with his palm open. "Why don't you come out of there, honey? You're safe now."

Slowly she held her hand out, hissing when her palm slid across his. He frowned, turning her wrist so he could see. "You're hurt."

"But alive."

A look of pride flashed over his face, gently pulling her out of the corner and wrapping an arm around her waist. "Let's get you bandaged up, okay?"

Maya stumbled as they passed the body, jerking her head away. But not before seeing Stefan by its side, hands covered in blood as he sank his fist into the gaping wound on the man's neck. His face looked set in stone, his normally kind eyes narrowed to dark points.

"C'mon," Daniel said softly, helping Diego set her up on the marble island. She flinched at their grasp and Daniel gave her a concerned look. "What hurts?"

"Everything," she huffed on a small laugh. "Jesus, everything hurts." She took a gasping breath, feeling her heart speed up. Pressing a hand to her chest she froze when she saw the splatter of blood up her arm. Not hers. It was Michael's, Michael's blood dripping down into the crease of her elbow.

Choking, she twisted as best she could and vomited all over Daniel's very expensive looking loafers.

"It's okay," he soothed, petting a hand down her hair. "You're okay."

"I killed him," she muttered, going to wipe the back of her hand on her mouth and stopping herself. A handkerchief appeared out of nowhere and she looked up into Stefan's eyes.

"No, you didn't." Stefan had as much blood on him as she did, if not more. "You didn't kill him, sweetheart. I did."

"You did?" Her brows drew together as she tried to recall it. "No - his neck…"

"He could have been saved," Stefan told her with a shrug, reaching out with his clean hand and gently cradling her cheek. "What you did was self-defense. And you didn't kill him."

She nodded, blinking at him and giving him a wane smile. Was that inappropriate? Who cared. The faucet behind her turned on and she heard Stefan washing his hands.

Diego stood and she watched Stefan take his place, crouching in front of her and gently turning her foot. There was a bright splash of blood on his sleeve, a few inches where it had been rolled up. She could hear Diego talking to someone in the hallway, felt Daniel's heat over her shoulder as he pressed close and watched Stefan.

"Shit," Stefan cursed, standing up and opening the first aid drawer, "I can't believe he sent someone to kill you."

She arched an eyebrow and watched him rummage through the contents, leaning slightly into Daniel's comforting presence. He wrapped an arm around her shoulder, carefully cuddling her closer. "You told the most dangerous man in the city his daughter was a whore. What did you *think* was going to happen?"

Stefan froze and in the corner of her eye she saw Diego pull up short. "I thought he might try to kill *us*," Diego offered carefully, "not you."

She snorted and blinked back a wave of tears. "Your mistake."

"Give me your foot." Stefan's voice was soothing, the touch of his hand warm on her ankle and she complied without thinking, letting him settle it onto his knee while he inspected the damage again. He worked carefully, warning her before applying pressure anywhere. It was mostly scratches, thankfully, that he bandaged with efficient movements in bright white gauze.

Suddenly Maya laughed. "Guess you owed me this one," she said softly, catching his eyes when they flicked up to hers.

Stefan flashed her a smile, passing the supplies up to Diego when he began to look at her hands.

"These look bad, princess," he muttered, gently tracing one of the deeper cuts. "You might need stitches."

"Tomorrow," she sighed, feeling Daniel's arm tighten. She patted the hand on her shoulder softly, barely noticing the smear of blood she left behind. "Can we deal with that tomorrow?"

Diego nodded and started carefully applying butterfly

bandages across her palm. His hands were gentle, almost delicate, handling her skin like it would shatter if he pressed too hard. Her adrenalin was still high, heart pounding, and she dizzily wondered if anyone had ever treated her with this kind of care.

"Are you wearing my shirt?"

The comment pulled her out of her thoughts and she looked up at Daniel, rubbing the material of her t-shirt between two of his fingers, a quizzical look on his face.

"Is it yours?"

"Mmhmm," he stroked his fingers and she shivered. "I also didn't buy you those briefs." He paused and his eyes hovered at her waist. "Maybe I should have, you look sexy as fuck in them."

"Why are you wearing our clothes?"

She avoided Stefan's eyes as she answered, focusing on his fingers as they wrapped the bandage around her other hand. The rims of his nails were still dark with dried blood. "It was either this or sleep naked."

"Both good choices," Daniel commented and Stefan elbowed him in the side.

"We bought you clothes," Diego pointed out, letting her hand go.

"You ever try to sleep in that stuff?" She flexed her fingers, turning her hands to look at the wrappings. They looked like boxing gloves and she made a fist, glancing up at the man who had bandaged them. She thought she might be able to get a hit in before they could stop her. One solid whack to the nose.

She didn't.

"If you want them back just say so. But at least let me go change into something else."

"No," Daniel quickly answered, rubbing a thumb along the back of her neck. "No, you should… if you like them, keep them, we can buy more."

Maya nodded, weariness overtaking her. Daniel caught her as she slumped against him, Diego's hands darting out as well. "Would it be silly of me to ask if you guys have drugs?"

Stefan laughed, standing up and leaning into her, pressing a kiss to her forehead. "For you? We can find some."

"Good," Maya murmured, sinking into Daniel's embrace. "Give me something I won't wake up from."

10

Every muscle in Daniel's body pulled tight, the fingers he'd barely realized were trying to soothe her clenching against her skin. No, she couldn't - that wasn't an option.

Stefan's eyes met his, the other man's brow creasing in concern. But his hands were moving almost on autopilot, pulling the small syringe and tapping it gently before slipping it under her skin. Daniel felt it hit, felt her relax into him, her body going soft and pliant in his arms. He wanted to bury his face in her hair.

He caught her as she slumped sideways. With utmost care he laid her out on the marble, careful of her bandages. She looked broken, a doll they had played with too hard. And he didn't know what to do about it.

He could crack an encrypted file in hours, get behind a federal firewall in a few days at most - but people, people had always eluded him. Diego and Stefan were easy, his brothers, not of blood but something much closer than that. The men who worked for them were tools, useful but not necessary. His computers were necessary, his brothers were necessary, everything else… expendable.

So where did that leave her?

Maya Alvani. Just another in an endless string of girls through the apartment. It was supposed to be easy - when Diego had struck out at the bar he was certain he'd have better luck. And she'd liked the look of him, he knew the glint in a woman's eye when they found him attractive. It saved him time - hell that was half the battle right there.

But she'd said no to him and yes to Stefan and he had to admit even now he was annoyed by it.

She *liked* Stefan, and it bothered him. Socializing wasn't his strong suit but he didn't think he was a monster either. He was attracted to her but he only moved when she acted interested.

A clear memory formed, her lips parted for him, her cunt riding his thigh while he drank down her little whimpers. Fuck if they hadn't been interrupted he'd have had her up against the wall. Tangled her hands in the chains over her head and shown her exactly what he could do for her.

"I want them destroyed."

Stefan's voice jerked him from his thoughts. Taking off his glasses, Daniel rubbed the bridge of his nose and sighed. "We're not ready."

"*Fuck* being ready," Stefan roared, stilling when the girl mumbled and shifted in her sleep. He petted her thigh in long strokes, waiting until she'd settled. Stefan. Petted her.

What the fuck was happening?

"I want to snap his fucking neck."

"And then what? It will be all out war, blood in the streets," Daniel tried to reason.

"It's *already* war," Stefan was only slightly quieter this time. "They came into our *house*, Daniel. They came in here and killed. We *can't* let this slide."

"Daniel's right." Diego had sunk into one of the dining room chairs, slumped with his head back staring at the ceiling. "We won't win alone. Alvani would destroy us."

Stefan snarled, stalking into the living room and kicking at the body there. He'd lied to Maya, told her that she hadn't killed. And maybe she hadn't. Maybe the man *had* still been alive when Stefan reached into the slit in his throat and pulled his windpipe out.

Daniel rather hoped he had been.

"We do have to respond," he said quietly, slipping his glasses back on. "Stefan's right on that count, we can't let it slide."

"I'm thinking." Diego was studying the girl's face. She wasn't beautiful, not in the way their usuals were, but she was pretty enough. Soft, comfortable - he wanted to curl up in her lap and have her run those long fingers over his skin.

Jesus, the fuck was wrong with *him*?

He shook the thought off. "We've got a body. And tomorrow night we're going to steal half a year's product. The fuck more do you want to do?"

"Kill him."

"I just fucking said," Diego started but Stefan cut him off.

"Not Alvani. The son. I never should have let the bastard leave."

"She asked you to," Diego pointed out. "And if we did that she'd never forgive you."

"The fuck do I care about that?" Stefan snapped and Diego raised an eyebrow.

"Don't you?"

What the *fuck* was happening to them?

"She needs to go." Daniel made the statement calmly. Logically he knew it was right. "We got what we needed, it's time to cut her loose."

"We're not-" Stefan began but Daniel cut him off.

"You really so fucking gone for a piece of ass you'll get her killed? Fucking get a grip."

Stefan's jaw clenched, eyes narrowing. He opened his

mouth but Diego beat him to it. "Make sure she gets paid, figure out where her fucking car keys are. We'll move her to a safe house until she's healed then she's gone." He gave Stefan a long look, "Is that enough?"

Stefan fumed, shoulders heaving, before giving a sharp nod. "Fuck. Fine." He crossed back, lifting the girl in his arms with a slight grunt.

"Not as strong as you used to be, old man," Daniel commented, grinning when Stefan glared.

"I'll still kick your ass."

"Try it."

"Children," Diego sighed, crossing to stand with them. "Save it for tomorrow." He reached out a hand, pushing a lock of hair back from Maya's face. Daniel wasn't sure he was aware he'd done it.

"We should make sure she's got someone there," he said lightly. "She's going to need some help for a bit."

"You volunteering?" Stefan asked with a raised eyebrow.

"Fuck no," Daniel reared back, holding his hands up quickly. The denial came fast to his lips, a sudden need to prove he wasn't invested. "But there's no point in saving her just to let her starve to death in a safe house."

It was rational. Logical. That was what he did. He wasn't good with people like Diego, not good with money or his fists like Stefan. Daniel just wasn't *like* them - hadn't been through the same things they had. What he did was say things no one else would, because it was too harsh or sounded heartless. Daniel could always be counted on to be dispassionate.

That was what he told himself, anyway, as he stared at the limp woman in Stefan's arms. It really would be a waste to go through all this trouble only to let her die because they got lazy.

"Fine," Diego huffed, motioning Stefan away.

Daniel balked when Stefan headed for the back. "Where are

you going?"

"Taking her to bed."

"Back there?"

Stefan paused, looking back at him. "Where else?"

Diego was staring at him too and he grunted, crossing his arms. "I'm not the people person here but even I think laying the injured girl down in the bed she was just attacked in is a bad idea. Remind me to add some money for her therapy later."

"Jesus fucking Christ," Stefan growled, turning back around.

"Put her on the couch upstairs," Diego ordered, pulling his phone out. "We can keep an eye on her there."

Stefan seemed to like that, shifting her in his arms and pressing a quick kiss to her hair he probably thought Daniel couldn't see.

What a pussy.

Can we not? He heard her voice in his head, the flustered blush she got when they had teased her. Biting back a smile he followed Stefan up the stairs. They didn't have room in their lives for little kisses and smiles. Never needed them before, certainly didn't now.

It wouldn't be his problem soon. He'd make sure she woke up in the morning, explain the situation, and bundle her out of the apartment. Then he could go back to his computers and his little room that no one ever bothered him in.

Stefan stopped partway up the stairs, shifting her weight before taking the rest.

"We could have called someone in," Daniel pointed out.

"I wanted to do it, it's fine," Stefan grunted, twisting and setting her down before heaving a heavy sigh of relief. He knuckled the small of his back and stepped away, eyes searching the room. Daniel stepped past him, throwing a blanket over her and making sure she was covered.

Stefan smirked, one eyebrow raised. "Thought you didn't care?"

"I don't," Daniel snapped. "If she wakes up cold she'll start yelling for help and I don't want to be woken up."

"Mmhmm," Stefan sounded like he didn't believe him.

"Fuck you," Daniel snapped without any real bite.

"I don't think I'm who you want to fuck."

Daniel didn't respond, stalking to his bedroom and throwing the door closed, catching it at the last moment to keep it from slamming. Yeah, he wanted to fuck her - he could admit to that. And maybe he wanted her to snap and bicker at him until he put her mouth to other uses. No shame in being a red-blooded man. That wasn't what bothered him.

What bothered him was how much he wanted to go out there and sit with her. Assure her she was safe. See those warm brown eyes light up when they looked at him.

Jesus, he needed to get a goddamn grip.

Tomorrow. Tomorrow they would explain things to her and she would be gone. He could keep himself together for that long, surely.

11

Maya woke in pain. The world swam in front of her and her body throbbed to the pulse of her heartbeat. She tried to make it steady, squeezing her eyes shut then opening them again more carefully. It was bright, brighter than it usually was in her room and it took her a moment to adjust.

She wasn't in her room.

A fireplace was directly in front of her but there were windows behind it. That wasn't…that wasn't right, the living room was the other way. And the furniture was all wrong, not a bit of chrome in sight. She sat up groggily, steadying herself with one hand and then hissing at the pain that shot up her arm.

"Be careful."

Maya whipped her head around, groaning when the action set her throbbing and reeling. When she opened her eyes again there was a hand in front of her face holding a glass of water. She took it carefully, swallowing the entire contents before handing it back.

"How do you feel?" Daniel asked, setting his computer aside and moving to sit on the low ottoman in front of the couch.

"Like I got put through a blender. You?"

He gave her a wide smile, brushing a hand along his beard. "Sounds about right. The Doc is waiting downstairs, we didn't want to wake you up."

"Doc?"

"You may need some stitches, and we want her to check you over for anything we might have missed." His eyes flitted away, "We'll have to talk later."

Maya blinked in confusion, trying to clear her scattered brain. "Why? And where am I?"

Daniel stood, turning his back on her and heading down the stairs. "Second floor."

Well that explained the fireplace at least, it was an extension of the one on the first floor. But it didn't explain how she had gotten up here. Or why. Taking the moment of solitude she studied the room. It was big, probably the biggest single room she'd seen, with doors to what she assumed must be their bedrooms.

Vivid photographs were framed on the wall, and she recognized what looked like Stefan's profile in one. That was... interesting. She couldn't imagine him posing for someone. Mixed in were larger pieces of art, muted colors and simple subjects. A dog, a chair, a storm on the ocean. Some charcoal sketches of things she couldn't make out.

The space was warmer, more inviting than the apartment below. The furniture was still black but it was all larger. Chairs she could imagine curling up in, the couch she was lying on that was nearly as wide as a single bed, decanters of alcohol and whiskey glasses placed at regular intervals.

It was open, welcoming, and distinctly *male*. She could recognize the men's fingerprints over every piece of it.

"How's the patient doing?"

Maya jerked her eyes to the stairs, "What?"

"Disoriented," the woman tutted, crossing and setting a bag

down by the couch. "Possible brain damage."

"No I-"

"I'm joking." The doctor was older, fully gray hair and deep crow's feet from a lifetime of smiling. Maya put her at maybe sixty. "I'm Dr. Paulson, and you are?"

"Maya," she responded, doing her best to sit fully up. The doctor let her, putting out a steadying hand but allowing her to do most of the work herself. "I'm Maya."

"Pleased to meet you Maya. And might I say, I'm happy you're in better shape than my usual patients here."

Maya looked down at her wrapped hands, the scratches that covered her arms and legs, the bandages around her feet. "Really?"

Rolling her eyes Dr. Paulson snapped her case open, pulling out a small zippered pouch. "Oh, those three never call me unless someone is about to die. Gunshots, stabbings, that sort of thing. Too busy being alpha men to worry about their health. Arm."

Maya held it out without question, watching the needle slip into her vein. It wasn't until she felt the rush of warmth and the almost immediate ebbing of her pain that she thought to ask, "What is this?"

"Dilaudid," Paulson replied, carefully tucking the syringe away. "You're going to feel really good for a while. Probably overkill but I was promised dire consequences if you so much as winced during treatment."

"This is good," Maya slurred, leaning back into the couch. She didn't flinch when Paulson started snipping the bandages off her, gently prodding each cut and applying additional dressings as needed. It didn't hurt, nothing hurt in fact. She could have happily floated to the moon if that was an option. It felt like she might.

She watched in mild fascination as Paulson tutted at the state of her feet, but it was only to rewrap them tighter.

"Stefan did this didn't he?"

Maya nodded. Or at least she thought she did. The world moved.

"I figured. He's the best of them at this but that doesn't mean he's good."

"Diego did my hands," Maya stated matter of factly, holding them up. Paulson smiled and Maya smiled back. She liked Dr. Paulson. Dr. Paulson seemed nice.

"I'm saving those for last, I know they're going to annoy me."

Maya tapped her swaddled hands together, grinning at the way they squished. "I don't know, they're kind of fun."

She did need stitches in her right hand, a fact that only barely penetrated the fog she was swimming in. Maya had enough presence of mind not to watch, turning to examine the painting over the fireplace instead.

"Why is that little dog all by itself?" she asked the air. "He seems lonely."

"Maybe he's waiting for somebody to see him."

"That doesn't make him not lonely *now*," Maya countered. "And why is no one *Jesus what are you doing?*"

She'd looked. It was a mistake. Seeing the end of the fishhook needle piercing her palm was enough to make her nauseous, turning and searching for something to throw up in.

"Not my bag," Paulson chided, shifting it away from her with one hand. "Just do it if you need to."

"I can't puke on the rug," Maya argued, glancing around for anything vaguely resembling a container. "They'll kill me."

"Honey, if they were here I think they'd let you puke in their hands."

Maya wasn't listening, contemplating if she could make it to a large vase that stood next to the fireplace. It looked expensive - and old. Maybe the carpet really was a better option.

"Done." Paulson's chipper voice pulled her out of her musings. Maya turned to see her hands once again wrapped, although this time with far more finesse. The doctor was packing her bag, prattling on about water or something before looking at her and saying, "Never mind, I'll let Diego know."

Exhausted, Maya curled down into the couch, tucking her padded hands under her chin and drifting off almost immediately.

The next time she woke was in her own bed. She sat up carefully, using her newly bandaged mittens tenderly. Someone had cleaned up the room, or at least gathered the scattered condoms. Did they also put them back… they were, tucked neatly back into their box in the bedside drawer. But more importantly, there was also a glass of water and a bottle of pills with a note.

"*Take two when you wake up and give a shout.*"

Maya gobbled the pills immediately, there was no indication of what they were but she had high hopes. Then she stared at her door. When she shouted what would happen? Would someone barge in to help her? Would there be questions? She was covered virtually head to toe in bandages and all she wanted was a shower - two things that seemed to be mutually exclusive.

Best to do as the note said. "Hello?"

The door opened immediately, someone with their back turned to her, staring resolutely down the hall as they said, "Yes ma'am?"

"Ma'am?" Maya repeated incredulously before shaking her head. Now wasn't the time. "I need a little help if you-"

"Yes ma'am."

The door shut with a thud and Maya stared at it. Okay, that wasn't what she had expected. What kind of help was that? Grunting with the effort she swung her legs off the bed, gingerly putting weight on one foot. It was too much and she grabbed for the sex swing to steady herself.

"What are you doing?"

Maya barely looked up at the accusing voice, "Going to the bathroom."

"Here," Stefan was at her side in a second, looping an arm around her waist and relieving most of her weight from her feet. "You shouldn't be trying to get around by yourself."

"I didn't realize help was coming," she pointed out, stepping lightly on her toes and leaning heavily on him. "I just need to..." she made a vague gesture and he chuckled, settling her near the sink.

"Call if you need help."

There was no earthly way she would call him. Maneuvering with the bandaged hands was awkward but she managed it, barely. With only her fingertips free she managed to wet a washcloth and rub it over her face, making her feel a little more human. She turned to the door and winced, leaning back against the sink. "Stefan?"

He was there before she got to the second syllable, almost carrying her back to the bed. The room had become occupied while she was gone, both Daniel and Diego looking up as she entered.

"Hey," she said for lack of anything better.

"How are you feeling?" Diego had a concerned frown, watching her limp across the floor.

"Rough," she answered honestly, using Stefan's steadying hand to scoot back onto the bed. He fluffed pillows behind her, setting her to sit up then moving only slightly away, poised and ready to spring back.

"What happened last night," Diego said without preamble,

"was unconscionable."

"You know he's pissed because he's using his big words," Stefan whispered to her conspiratorially and she gave him the smile he was looking for.

Diego shot him a glare before continuing. "You're our guest and you should have been safe here. Under our protection."

"It wasn't your fault," Maya absolved him. "I mean, I knew this was risky when we started."

"Wherever you want to go, tell us and we'll make it happen. Daniel transferred the remainder of the balance this morning. You're free."

"Oh," Maya whispered, "okay."

The room was quiet, Maya staring at her hands and trying to fix the jumbled mess of her brain. The bed dipped and Stefan was next to her, tucking a strand of hair behind her ear.

"We'll make sure you're still protected. Medical care. All of it. We're not just kicking you out."

A small huff of what was almost a laugh escaped her and she gave him a wan smile. "That wasn't... sorry. I'm being ungrateful. Thank you."

"*Fuck*," Daniel spoke for the first time, pushing off the wall to stand on the far side of the bed. "The fuck is it now?"

"Daniel," Diego's warning had an edge to it.

"No," the other man snapped, "agreement over. We all got what we wanted. What the fuck is the problem?"

Stefan's hand curled into a fist and Maya laid her wrapped hand over it, trying to calm him. "It's fine, he's right. I'm not- I mean this isn't-" she sighed softly, trying to swing her legs off the bed, barely fighting off Stefan's hands trying to stop her. "This was all more than fair. If you'll just tell me where my keys are I'll-"

"No," Diego barked, ignoring the glare Daniel shot him. "You're too hurt. Get your ass back in that bed." Maya complied and Diego gave her a short nod. "Where are you going back to? I'll have my guys make sure it's safe."

"Nowhere," she said without thinking, instantly regretting it.

Stefan paused where he was tucking her into the bed. "What do you mean?"

"When you found me… I'd just been evicted. I don't really have anywhere else. I mean, I'm sure I can *find* somewhere. If you give me some time. But…" she trailed off. The pills were starting to kick in. She felt sleepy, and a little fuzzy. "I don't know where I'd go."

The silence that fell over the room was almost palpable. She could hear her own blood rushing in her ears. Could she hear their hearts beating? She swore she could.

"Ah fuck," Daniel murmured.

"Anyone we can reach out to?" Diego's voice was devoid of emotion.

Maya shook her head. "With my dad, the family… I never felt safe." Suddenly realizing how pathetic she sounded she shook her head to clear it, lifting her chin. "I mean of course I have friends," she forced a smile, "it's fine. Just give me a little time to clear my head? Please? The drugs are making me sappy."

Her eyes were watery and she stared at the far wall fighting back tears, keeping her smile glued to her face. This wasn't their problem. She could always find somewhere to go, assuming she had the funds to do so. A moment of panic struck her, a hand reaching out to grasp Stefan's sleeve.

"Wait, do I have… did you pay me?"

He stared back incredulously, looking down at her hand and then her face. "I already told you, of course we did."

"Then I'm fine." She let him go, waving her hand airily. "I'll just stay at the Ritz for a week. It'll be nice. It's fine."

She only choked on the words a little. Stefan scrubbed a hand down his face, shooting a look across her but Maya was already sinking into the pillows, eyelids growing heavy.

Diego sighed, "You can stay here until you figure out where you belong."

The words cut her to the core, a tear slipping out and she hastily scrubbed it away. "I'm tired. Can I just... I just want to sleep if that's okay. Can we talk about this later?" She closed her eyes, willing them to leave.

Something brushed her hair and she heard footsteps, the door closing. She didn't look, sinking down into the pillows and turning her head. Crying for the first time in years.

12

When she came to that afternoon there was food waiting on a tray by the side of the bed. She vaguely remembered telling someone they could come in. How long had it been since she had eaten? As tired as she was she still managed to pull a slice of bread to her, smearing it along the pat of butter and ignoring most of the utensils. The butter knife caught her eye, however, its silver handle shining. It wasn't much of a weapon but it felt like something solid in her hand.

Something better than a box of condoms at least, should the need arise again.

Next to the tray were bottles of pills, a long list of instructions she only barely understood. Thankfully, four pills sat next to a note that said, "Eat me!" and a smiley face. Definitely Stefan's doing.

Drugged and with her hunger sated, Maya fell back against the pillows, watching the afternoon fade into twilight. Taking deep breaths she counted to ten, then back again, steadying her rapidly increasing heartbeat. She was fine. This was fine. Her family was trying to kill her and it was *fine*.

Safe. This was a safe place. She turned the thought over in her mind. It was, it really was. Yesterday's events notwithstanding - Jesus was it only yesterday? - she was safer here than anywhere else she could possibly be. And the Kings were *pissed*. Good for her, bad for anyone else who might try to get in again.

She was safe.

Why didn't she *feel* safe?

The bed which had always felt ridiculous now felt ominous, like a platter waiting to serve her up to someone. She wanted to be somewhere else, anywhere else, somewhere she didn't feel trapped. What would they do if she went upstairs and curled up on the couch again? Or went and bedded down in Stefan's office? She rolled over with a sigh, staring at the swing and the windows beyond. She wouldn't. Those were their spaces, she couldn't intrude in them more than she already was.

The click of the door latch nearly stopped her heart. She turned, eyes adjusting to the dim light, and going to the knife she'd tucked under her pillow. Holding her breath she tried to clench her fingers around it but the bandages were in her way.

"Go back to sleep," the voice rolled over her. Diego. Diego was in her room. *Why was Diego in her room?* And he was… *why was Diego getting into bed with her?* And he was settling. Like nothing was new about this? Like this was a normal thing. Diego in bed with her. Just, laying there. She could reach out and touch him if she…

Well, he was still a good four or five feet away. The bed was *huge*. But he was *there*.

"What are you doing?" She didn't let the knife go, wishing she didn't sound so scared. But she *hurt* and wasn't in any mood to be confused on top of it.

"Sleeping."

"Sleeping?"

"Trying to."

Maya let that sit for a minute.

"Why aren't you in your own bed?"

"The new security measures won't get installed until tomorrow."

That... didn't answer her question. She ventured a guess, "And you're afraid to sleep in your room until then?"

A small huff of laughter broke the stillness and Maya felt herself warm with the knowledge she had amused him. "We all agreed, you shouldn't be alone until we can guarantee your safety."

Maya mulled that over. It made sense. But why *Diego*? He was the last person she would have expected.

"Diego?"

"What?" he sounded tired.

"Is there a reason you're in here with me?"

"Where else would I be?"

Outside, she started to say and then bit her tongue. The idea of Diego standing attention outside her door all night was ludicrous. Finally releasing her grip on the handle she settled back on her side, facing away from him. Now would be a great time for those painkillers to kick in again.

As she drifted away she had the passing thought that the bed didn't feel so scary with two people in it.

Maya woke flat on her stomach, one arm tucked under her pillow and the other stretched out. Fingers intertwined with Diego's.

Fingers intertwined with Diego's.

What?

As quietly as possible, Maya lifted her head, careful not to move her arm. Diego was sprawled on his back, one arm over his stomach and the other stretched out towards her. He didn't look quite so grim asleep, face softened and the deep lines on his face smoothed somewhat. She took a moment to admire him. His lips were fuller than she had thought, and the grays in his goatee caught the silvery moonlight better. He looked peaceful, just another businessman with a too expensive haircut.

Gently, so as not to wake him, she extricated her fingers from his one by one. He held on, for a brief moment, and then she was free.

"Where are you going?"

Maya froze, half out of the bed. "Bathroom."

He grunted and she set her feet on the ground, hissing at the pain the new pressure caused. Diego was at her side like magic, an arm around her waist lifting her nearly off her feet.

"You shouldn't be walking," he said as though that explained it.

"I don't-" she winced when she put her weight down and gave in. "Thank you."

He didn't say anything else as he helped her to the bathroom, but he was there waiting when she came out, gently leading her back to the bed and settling her in before returning to his side. Maya tried not to think about that, about him sliding into bed with her like this wasn't a new and entirely foreign thing to her.

Instead she fumbled at the bedside, pushing aside the glass of water and glancing through the bottles to find something stronger than ibuprofen.

"What now?" Diego's long-suffering sigh made her roll her eyes.

Maya grumbled, pawing at the nightstand. "I'm just trying to find my meds. It's fine." She gave a short happy noise when she found it, fumbling with the lid.

An arm reached past her, warm chest pressing up against her back. "You need to be careful with these."

"I got stabbed *yesterday*," Maya countered. "I get at least one more day of the good stuff."

He snorted and thumbed the cap off, dropping one pill into her palm. The glass front of his watch glinted in the low light when he checked the time. "You can have another at eight."

She nodded, swallowing the pill and setting the water to the side. Diego didn't move when she finished. He was so close she could feel every angle of his body. The warmth of his palm sank through the sheets at her hip, making her all too aware that she was only wearing a thin t-shirt and briefs beneath.

There was *so much bed*. Why was he in her small portion of it? Was he... *cuddling*?

While Maya was still trying to come to terms with his nearness his breaths turned to soft snores. *Lucky*, she thought, turning slightly so the noise wasn't directly in her ear. She waited for the trapped feeling to come again but instead a soft warmth spread from where his hand rested on her waist. She sank into the feeling, letting her eyes drift closed, not bothering to wonder why it would come now, from this man.

The nightmares were familiar. Home. Her father. A boy her age with laughing eyes and a bloody smile. He said he loved her, his hands and feet bloody lumps. There were hands around his neck, holding him up so she could watch him die. Her father laughing and telling her she would never be good enough.

No. Not her father.

Stefan.

Stefan choking the boy with the laughing eyes and gentle, bloody hands. Stefan staring at her as the boy gasped and sank. As blood poured from his mouth and he looked at her with accusing eyes. She reached out, trying to save him, but someone was holding her back. Warmth enclosing around her, a soft voice shushing her and petting her. She turned to it, grasping at it, holding on as tight as she could. And it held back, hands soothing her until she was somewhere else.

Somewhere peaceful. Then the hands receded, the warmth moving away.

They were trying to leave her.

Maya frowned, cuddling closer. She didn't want to be alone, she'd been alone for so long.

"Princess you have to let me go," a voice whispered and she whined.

"Don't wanna."

A soft chuckle, fingertips stroking over her cheek. "Don't tempt me."

She shifted, hitching her thigh higher on their body, warm skin rumbling beneath her. They groaned softly, fingers digging into the meat of her thigh and shifting it slightly. She grumbled, resisting, moving her weight until she felt what they had been trying to avoid. Warm throbbing heat, achingly hard. Without thinking her hand drifted down to it, more wakefulness coming to her when the man caught her wrist in his strong grip.

"You don't want to do that, princess."

He smelled good - like cedar and something expensive. Maya nuzzled into his neck, searching for more while she tried not to wake up. The soft hairs on his chin tickled her lips as she shifted and she licked her lips, stroking her tongue along the curve of his jaw.

"*Fuck.*"

The hand gripping hers changed direction, pulling her further towards him until she was draped over his chest. She moaned and he moved, mouth catching hers, tongue stroking into her. He tasted even better than he smelled, sunshine and warmth and something seductively rich.

This was nice. Her head spun a little, her hand trying to cup his jaw. She opened for him when his tongue traced her bottom lip, sighing into him when he slipped inside and explored her mouth. Then she returned it, slipping along his teeth then further. She wanted to crawl inside of him, have him surround her. He was warm and comforting and something about him made her feel safe.

Wanted.

A hand tangled into her hair, tilting her head so he could trail his tongue down her neck. The other stroked down her back, slipping under the t-shirt to lie warm and solid against her skin before continuing. His fingers dug harshly into her hip and she cried out in sharp pain. The world came into sudden focus, Diego's eyes staring up at her in concern. He looked down at where his hand had settled over the bandage on her hip, the bright red slowly seeping through the white gauze. Cursing he jerked away from her, almost falling out of the bed as he grabbed his shoes and stumbled towards the door.

Maya couldn't take her eyes off the bulge of him, straining against the front of his pants. Or the heaving gasping rise and fall of his chest. Diego *wanted* her. Didn't he? Or had he been half-asleep as well?

"I'll get Doc back," he said without looking at her, door closing with a soft click behind him.

Maya laid in bed til eight, waiting to take her next pill. There was no way she was going to attempt the day drug-free. Not after what had happened the night before. Or what hadn't happened. What *little* had happened.

She groaned, pressing her bandaged hands to her face. Why was she like this? Still hurting, hands and feet throbbing, she managed to limp her way to the closet and pull out a change of clothes. The idea of pulling on lingerie felt ludicrous, what with all the bandages. And hadn't they said the agreement was over?

Shrugging she slipped on another t-shirt, changing her underwear and lamenting a lack of pants. It wasn't like they didn't know she'd stolen them, hadn't Daniel said she looked good in it? Best not to think of that, or his insistence that she needed to get out of the house. She wasn't ready to be an emotional wreck two days in a row. She was going to face today with her head held high - first item of business, caffeine.

Throwing the door open with newly minted confidence she stopped short, staring at what was blocking her path. Sitting outside were bags. Several of them, large totes with logos she didn't recognize. She eyed one warily, poking it with her foot. Was it a body? Drugs? She could get behind the idea of drugs right now. Instead, a light gray sweatshirt tumbled out, followed by a pair of black leggings.

She stared at them, then down the hallway. Cautiously, she pulled one of the bags into the room with the tips of her fingers, dumping the contents inside the doorway. A mess of clothing fell out: shirts, tank tops, sweat pants, cotton shorts, real honest to god underwear made of fully formed fabric. She gaped at the pile, pulling a soft bralette from the mix.

"You need something-"

"Sweet Jesus," Maya yelped, jumping nearly a foot in the air and tripping backwards. Daniel jumped forward, catching her elbow in one hand and raising an eyebrow at her. "Where did you *come* from?"

"My gran always said heaven," Daniel replied with a grin, letting her arm go and she rolled her eyes. He ignored it, gesturing to the pile of clothes. "I took some guesses, went for stuff that's stretchy and comfortable. Let me know if you need something specific and I'll put it on order."

Maya toed at the pile again, glancing between it and the man in front of her. "What's all this for?"

Daniel shrugged and leaned against the door frame. "Well, like we said, the agreement is over. No need to parade you around in-" he waved a hand into the room, "all that."

She rather thought they liked her in the lingerie. Guess she was wrong. "So you bought me real clothes?"

His nostrils flared and even under that beard she could see his jaw clench. Something flashed across his eyes while he seemed to steady himself. After a moment he grinned, "After seeing you in our stuff I decided you look better in more clothes."

Maya glared, throwing what was in her hands at him, instantly regretting it when his large hand closed around the cotton. He examined it curiously, stretching it between his fingers and rubbing the material. "Soft," he commented, raising an eyebrow.

"Comfortable," Maya countered, reaching out and yanking it back.

Daniel studied the pile of clothes. "Didn't realize this stuff would be so touchable."

"Don't even think about it," she warned, narrowing her eyes. Daniel winked at her, backing out of the room.

"You like to be petted, kitten, no shame in that." His voice grew husky, "And I like petting you. You purr so nice."

"Get out," she pointed a finger down the hall and he chuckled as he left.

It took her a few tries to get all the bags in, carrying one at a time and flatly refusing the offer of help from the man stationed five feet from her door. She could do it herself and she *wanted* something to do.

"Well you seem better."

Letting out a yelp, Maya threw a t-shirt at the intruder, groaning when Dr. Paulson ducked it and raised an eyebrow. "Why is everyone scaring me today? You," she pointed at her guard, "why didn't you say something?"

"Sorry ma'am."

"Ma'am," she scoffed, backing up and waving Paulson into the room. "They call me *ma'am*."

"You get used to it," Paulson said as she walked by, watching as Maya hobbled back to the bed. "Diego said you hurt yourself?"

Oh did he? Maya thought but didn't say, lifting the side of her shirt instead. "Banged my hip and it's bleeding again. I don't think he needed to call you though. I expect this will happen regularly."

"It will," Paulson assured her, "but if Diego wants to pay me ten grand to make the house call that's his money to waste."

"Ten grand?" Maya almost yelled the number. "Are you kidding me? I should have been a doctor."

"It's not all rich clients," Paulson smiled as she re-bandaged the wound. "Sometimes you're in a community clinic with some scrappy boys who get into too many fights."

Maya hadn't given much thought to where the Kings had come from. Assumed that, like her, they had grown up in the life. "How long have you known them?"

"Daniel since he was born, the other two since they were around ten? Eleven?" Paulson gave a fond smile, standing up with her bag. "I've fixed more broken bones and wounds on those three than the entire rest of my practice combined."

Laughing, Maya stood, trying not to limp too badly as she walked Paulson to the door. "Well, I'm not sure if I should tell you I hope I don't see you again, or that I hope I do so you can take a trip to Fiji."

Paulson laughed, "See if you can stub your toe or something next week, the new Cartier line is coming out."

Maya continued to chuckle as she shut the door, dumping every shopping bag on the floor with a gleeful smile. *Pants.* There were *pants*. And maybe they didn't have buttons or zippers but they were *pants*. And buried in the bottom of the bag, a few pairs of flats.

Shoes. Without heels. Maya nearly cried.

The only bag that confused her was a small paper sack with what looked like men's briefs. There were a few different styles, but they had no tags and smelled like the same detergent her sheets were washed in. Why would Daniel give her a bag of men's underwear?

Resigning herself to never understanding the unfathomable mind of that man, she giddily pulled on a pair of yoga pants patterned with flowers, then a sky blue sports bra and a soft t-shirt. For the first time in almost two weeks she felt like herself. A person, and not just another decorative object in the house.

The shoes didn't fit with the bandages but she carefully placed them in a spot of honor in the closet, promising them she'd wear them some day soon. She'd have to reorganize the closet, find space for the new clothes.

Why? You're not staying.

She pushed the thought aside. They weren't going to make her leave until she'd healed some, which was at least a few days from now. That was enough reason to get a little organized. Nodding at the guard in the hallway she almost skipped to the kitchen, as much as she could in her condition.

"You look happy," Stefan remarked, cup of coffee in one hand as he sat at the island.

"I have pants!" She was going to tell everyone. Maya turned slightly so he could see them, noting his eyes lingering on her waist. "And they have a *pocket*," she frowned. "Not that I have anything to put in it."

"Here," Stefan reached back and pulled his wallet, thumbing a hundred bucks at her.

Maya blinked. "What is that?"

"Something to put in your pocket."

"Where do you expect me to spend that?" she asked, curious what his answer would be.

"Daniel can be bribed sometimes," Stefan shrugged, setting

the bill down and putting his wallet away. "Never hurts to have it on hand."

Shaking her head, Maya slipped the hundred into the side pocket. As ridiculous as it was, it felt nice to be *carrying* something. She reached for the kettle but Stefan slid a mug her direction, already steaming hot with the bag in it.

"Heard you get up, figured you'd want one."

"Thanks," she wrapped both hands around it to get a grip, sighing at the warm feeling as it slid down her throat.

"This the new stuff Daniel got you?" Stefan gestured at her.

Maya nodded, too engrossed in her tea to make a reply.

Stefan's eyes lingered on the hem of her t-shirt. "You look… cute."

That made her look up. "Cute?"

"A little girl next door-ish," his teeth flashed white when he smiled at her. "I like it."

Maya did too.

13

Things got... *different* after that. Not in a bad way, but in a way Maya couldn't quite put her finger on. It was at least in part because she was wearing clothes, which meant she seemed to move on from 'decorative table lamp' to, well, not quite a *person* but not an inanimate object either.

It had been nearly a week since the attack, and no one had brought up what the next steps were going to be. They hadn't forgotten her, she still ate with whoever was home that night. And she saw them all the time in the hallways or common areas. They were friendlier, occasionally remembering to ask her how her day was even if she didn't ask first. She felt like a roommate, or a pet. A cat that slunk around the edges of their lives.

Right now, she was living up to the thought, basking in the midday sun out on the terrace. She spent more and more time out there, letting the early summer light stave off the chill in the house. No matter how warm it was outside, the apartment always felt like it wasn't hitting fifty.

I wonder if I could get a garden growing?

She'd started cooking more for herself during the day, using what leftovers were in the fridge along with whatever she could dig up from the back of the cabinets, but maybe she could talk them into a couple of plants, or a tomato vine.

Sitting up she considered the area through narrowed eyes. There was room for at least one above ground planter, maybe two, without impinging on most of the space. She could grow squash, anyone could grow squash, and cherry tomatoes. A few small pots for herbs and-

Shaking herself from the day dream she swung her legs off the lounger. There was no way she was going to bring that up. Planting a garden spoke of permanence, and she wasn't going to be in the apartment long enough for any of it to ripen anyway. But she *could* ask for some groceries, couldn't she? Surely that wasn't off the table?

Stepping inside she grabbed her sweater and slipped it on, swiping a piece of paper and starting a list. A small list. Just a few things. Testing the waters, as it were. Finished, she headed for Daniel's door, pressing her ear to it and then knocking softly.

"What?"

Poking her head around she smiled at him, "May I come in?"

He waved a hand and she took it for a yes, crossing to his desk and dropping the list onto the corner.

"What is this?"

Maya took a step back, pulling the sleeves of her sweater down over her hands. "A shopping list."

Daniel frowned at it, then at her hands, eyebrows drawing together. "It's food." He looked at her like it was a question.

"Yes?"

"We have food."

Maya rolled her eyes. "You have condiments, mixers, and one entire shelf of the freezer is alcohol. I don't think any of that could even charitably be called 'food.'"

"I know for a fact there's a bag of peanut butter cups in

there."

"Peanut butter cups are not food," Maya countered. She puffed her lip out, "C'mon, I'm injured and sad and stuck here til I heal up... buy me some gouda."

Daniel snorted and set the list to the side. "Your feminine wiles won't work on me."

She perched on the edge of the desk, swinging one leg. "*Please*?"

"What did I just say?" his eyes remained glued to his screen. She might as well have not been there.

Pouting harder she crossed her arms. An idea occurred and she leaned forward until her lips were barely brushing his ear. "Please Daddy?"

The entire desk shifted when Daniel moved abruptly, his knee catching the underside with a loud thunk. He glared at her and she giggled.

"Fuck you, that's not fair."

Maya snorted, "Well it's the only time you're going to hear it."

"We'll see," he growled ominously, straightening his setup and ducking back into his work. If pouting and cajoling wasn't going to work she'd have to try something else.

Eyes lighting up she patted her pockets, "Aha!" She pulled the hundred Stefan had given her a few days ago, holding it between two fingers. "Didn't think I'd get the opportunity so soon." Sliding it along the desk she waggled her eyebrows at him. "Does *this* make a difference?"

Daniel finally gave her his full attention, eyes darting between the money and her face. "Where the fuck did you get cash?"

"That is my secret," she pushed it further his direction, "so how about it?"

He yanked the bill from under her hand, holding it up in the dim light and studying it. It took Maya a moment to realize what he was doing. "Are you checking if it's real?"

Daniel grunted, folding the bill and holding it between two fingers, staring at her. After several long seconds he huffed a breath. "Leave the list. I'll send someone out for it."

Maya's eyes widened. "I can't believe that worked."

"Go away," he growled.

"Thanks Danny."

"Don't call me Danny."

"What smells so good?"

Maya hid a smile, juggling the bread between her fingertips. It was *hard* to make sandwiches when your hands were wrapped in a hundred feet of bandages but she was doing… *okay*. "Cheese."

"Cheese?" Stefan popped up next to her, leaning over to look at the griddle pan. "Holy fuck you're making grilled cheese? I haven't had one of those in years."

"And tomato soup," Maya pointed at the pot on the back burner. She tried to pick up the spatula, fumbling with it for a second before pinning it between both hands.

"You need some help?"

She wanted to say no, but staring at the utensil sticking straight into the air she decided her pride wasn't worth burnt cheese. "I do, thanks."

Stefan took it deftly, flipping the sandwich in a smooth motion and prodding at the one she set next to it. "How hungry *are* you?"

"That one's for you," Maya said casually, ignoring the way his gaze shot to her.

"Really?"

"Well, since you're helping."

He hummed and slid the first sandwich off, pointing at the one she set down to replace it. "That for me too?"

"Daniel, if he wants it."

"What for? He's not helping. I'm helping, I should get two."

Maya snorted, "You can have two without having Daniel's." Cutting the finished sandwich in half, diagonally of course, she held one wedge out to him with the tips of her fingers. "Good?"

He studied it for a moment before biting in, his face quickly collapsing into pure bliss. "Fuck yes, what the hell is in this?"

"Don't curse at my sandwich," she scolded, hip checking him softly.

He rolled his eyes and took another large bite, talking while he chewed, "No really, what the... what's in this?"

"Gouda, a goat cheddar, few other things."

"Marry me," Stefan asked, eyes wide and looking at her in all seriousness.

Maya smiled, pointing at a sandwich and motioning for him to flip it. "You can't afford me."

"Ouch," he playfully threw a hand over his chest, "shot right in the heart."

"I'm sure you'll survive." She offered him another bite, feeling quiet satisfaction at the pleasure on his face. "It's not like you're lacking for company."

"Oooh," he nudged her shoulder with his, "jealous?"

"Not at all, option's there right?"

Maya paused.

Had she really just said that?

Yeah, yeah she had. Stefan was grinning at her, licking a bit of cheese from the corner of his mouth and a surge of heat shot down to her toes.

"Anytime you want."

Groaning, Maya tried to cover her face with her hands, pressing the padded bandages to her cheeks. "Can we leave the flirting til I'm slightly less injured?"

Stefan hummed noncommittally. "No promises. Where's the other flipper?"

She reeled from the sudden change in topic. "The what?"

"The flippy thing," he made a vague motion with his hands, studying the rack of utensils. "There's a knife missing too."

"Do you mean the spatula?"

He frowned, holding up the one in his hand. "I thought this was a spatula."

"They're both called spatulas and the other is probably in the dishwasher."

"We have a dishwasher?" Stefan seemed genuinely surprised.

Maya poked him in the chest, "How do you think your dishes get washed?"

"I don't know," he glanced around, poking a few cabinet doors. "I leave dishes around and they end up back in the cupboard. We could be throwing them away for all I know."

Maya's jaw dropped, her hand stilling from where she was ladling soup into the line of mugs. "You have to be joking."

"I don't keep track of the dishes," he protested, making a triumphant noise when he found the dishwasher disguised as another cabinet.

"And yet you knew there was a spatula missing."

"That's just situational awareness."

Maya huffed, pointing at a sandwich that needed turning. "How do you guys survive without someone to take care of you?"

"You volunteering?" he gave her a sly look and she elbowed him softly.

"I am *not*."

"Pity," for a moment he seemed serious, looking down at her with an inscrutable expression. Then his eyes lit up with mischief. "I was going to buy you one of those frilly aprons for you to wear with-"

"The fuck is going on in here?" Daniel's voice cut over whatever Stefan was going to end that with and thank God for it.

"Maya is making sandwiches and you can't have one," Stefan responded before Maya could.

"Well that's shitty."

Rolling her eyes, Maya grabbed the one from the pan, still hot and melting, and cut it in half. "Here, there's soup too," she gestured towards the mugs.

Daniel stared at the plate like he'd never seen one before, not taking it. Then he looked at Stefan. "Is the restaurant closed?"

"If you don't want it," Stefan reached out but Daniel snatched the plate first, turning away quickly.

"That's not what I fucking said."

"Language," Maya sing-songed, lifting the pot lid and stirring the soup gently.

Both men gave her matching long-suffering looks and she stifled a laugh. "I'm cooking - therefore my kitchen, my rules."

"Is that how that works?" Stefan asked with a smile.

"Yes," Maya responded definitively, pointing at a sandwich. "Hey, mister situational awareness, you're about to burn that one."

Stefan cursed softly and Maya looked up at Daniel. "Thanks for the grocery run. I appreciate it. There's something about a grilled cheese that feels like home, ya know?"

Something inscrutable passed over his face and he nodded. "With gouda?"

Maya grinned at him "You betcha."

He poked at the sandwich on his plate. Then took a cautious bite. Like Stefan his face changed completely, the first half of the sandwich disappearing in two bites while he waved the second at her. "Why have we been ordering food if you can cook?"

"Because I'm not your employee," Maya answered, debating flipping him off. She decided against it, not sure she could get the point across with her limited mobility. Daniel tilted his head, studying her and she stared back, wondering what that thoughtful look on his face was.

"Well if you're going to stay with us maybe you should consider it," Daniel said after a moment, reaching for a mug of soup and another sandwich.

Maya noted Stefan's expression, the shock on his face, before she offered, "Stay?"

Daniel looked like he regretted the comment, eyes darting around the room. "You said you had nowhere to go. We already got someone to clean but if you want to get back in the panties and cook for us I wouldn't say no."

Mulling that over for a minute Maya snorted at him. "No more sandwiches for you."

"Didn't want one anyway," he grouched, but his eyes stayed on the golden bread as it came off the griddle.

The sound of the front door made them all turn. Everyone was going to be home tonight, apparently. Diego's face was buried in his phone as he snapped. "Who reset the thermostat to fucking seventy?"

"And hello to you too!" Stefan called out, waving the spatula.

Diego finally looked up, stopping in his tracks. "The hell is going on?"

"Grilled cheese," Maya smiled at him. "And don't let Stefan tell you there's none for you, I got a whole stack going."

He looked around like he'd never seen food before. "Are the restaurants closed or something?"

"Jesus," Maya rolled her eyes, "have you guys *never* used

your kitchen?"

"I might have fucked a girl here once," Stefan offered, pointing at a spot next to where Maya was standing.

Slowly, Daniel reached out and shifted the plate of sandwiches off of the spot, giving Maya a commiserating look as he did so.

She shut her eyes, counting to ten. "I did *not* need to know that."

"None of us needed to know that," Diego said sternly, stopping by the island and looking over the food. He shifted the groceries around, examining the wrappers for the cheese, the type of bread it was, a scribbled note Maya had started earlier that day.

"What is this?"

Maya looked up and lunged, trying to snatch the paper out of Diego's hand. "Nothing."

He raised an eyebrow, holding it further away. "Doesn't seem like nothing." He scanned her handwriting, a small frown developing. "Barista, waitress, customer service... what is this?"

Sighing Maya slumped on the island, cradling her elbows on her palms. "I'm trying to figure out what I can do after all of this. I don't exactly have a lot of marketable skills."

"After?"

"Yeah," Maya nodded at him, "you know, when I'm all healed up. I gotta do something. Thanks to you I have some money but it's not *retirement* money or anything."

Diego looked thoughtful, handing the list off to Stefan.

"Why isn't lingerie model on here?" he asked and Maya laughed, snatching the paper and tossing it in the trash.

"Funny."

But Stefan wasn't laughing. "I'm not joking. You'd make a killing."

"I can't imagine there's a market for nearly thirty, plus size lingerie models."

"Offer to be our cook is still open," Daniel pointed out.

"What's this?" Diego looked up from the sandwich he was tentatively examining.

"You *have* a housekeeper and she's very nice," Maya stated firmly.

"We do?" Stefan asked with a frown.

"*How do you think things get cleaned in this*-" she cut herself off when she saw his shoulders shaking. "That's not funny."

His loud guffaw echoed through the apartment, even Diego and Daniel had wry twists to their lips. "Remind me sometime about this bridge I have to sell you, sweetheart."

"I swear to *God* I was smart before I met you three."

Daniel took another sandwich, pulling the crust off and setting it aside before asking, "Then why don't you have better jobs on that list?"

"Because I don't have any training or education to back it up, not any you can put on a resumé anyway." She put a hand on her cocked hip, tilting her head, "Yes Mr. HR person, when I was thirteen I learned how to run a cocaine processing plant so invoicing should be no problem."

"You did?" Diego's eyebrows rose. "Where?"

"Colombia, where do you think," Maya countered. "And it was a long time ago. I doubt it's still relevant."

"So what *do* you want to do?" The question was asked around a mouthful of cheese, Diego looking vaguely embarrassed by how he mumbled.

"I have this idea but - you'd have to be a certain kind of person to do it. And I'm not sure I'm it."

Diego snorted, "Why don't you tell me what it is before you start doubting yourself. What's the market?"

"Money laundering."

The words hit like a brick, Diego's jaw dropping for a second. Then Stefan started laughing, wrapping an arm around her waist and burying his face in her hair.

"You never cease to surprise me, sweetheart."

"Where'd you get the idea, another magazine article?" Daniel's tone was teasing and she stuck her tongue out at him.

"It wasn't a magazine - and using the lack of record keeping for guns dumped in conflict areas to import virtually untraceable stock was a *good idea*."

They stared at her in various stages of shock. "Say that again," Diego's voice was firm, his head tilted thoughtfully.

Maya blinked, suddenly unsure. "When the military pulled out it was cheaper to leave things in war zones than to bring them back. And because it's, you know, a *war zone*, the record keeping has been less than stellar. Millions of dollars in weapons just waiting for someone to scoop them up." Her eyes darted between the three men. "All you'd need is the right contact and I figured chances were good that you had one."

Diego stared at her for so long she began to wonder if he was still alive, his eyes unblinking. Finally he said, "What's your idea?"

"For what?"

"You said you had a money laundering idea, what is it?"

"Do you know anything about event planning?" Daniel barked a laugh and turned away but Diego's eyebrows rose in interest so she powered on. "I used to work for this caterer and we did some really high end events. There are people who spend hundreds of thousands, sometimes *millions* of dollars, for birthdays and vow renewals and all kinds of things. And virtually all of the outgoing business is cash - photographers, caterers, artists... whatever."

Diego didn't say anything and even Daniel looked interested so she powered on. "And the best part is there's no physical business. Unlike a taxi stand or a mattress store, there's no need for a storefront. Just a webpage. Maybe set up a photo shoot for the media portion but your business is *exclusive*, of course, and caters to very private clients so there's no available photos of each event." Maya was on a roll now, pacing back and forth and gesturing into the air with her mitten hands. "The hook is that the product you're selling is transient - I can just say that I threw a party last night and I made a million dollars and who's to say it didn't happen?"

The room was silent as she finished, the men in the room watching her as she wound down and stood there, bandaged hands on her hips. Stefan's smile was encouraging, Daniel looked amused and Diego…

"Talk to me about the financials."

"I don't have numbers," she stumbled, looking to Stefan for help. He nodded at her and she took a breath. "But you could pay people as independent contractors. You keep one accountant on payroll, they can both create the fake invoices and pay your people. So someone might get a check every month for his service as a 'photographer,'" she made air quotes with her fingers. "They're independent so you don't have to worry about most employment laws, and they would just file taxes as self-employed."

"Honey," Diego cut her off with an easy smile, "what makes you think our people *want* to be filing taxes?"

"You know what took down Al Capone?" Maya pushed, catching a small smirk from Daniel in the corner of her eye. "It wasn't murder or theft or any of that, it was *taxes*."

"She's right," Stefan spoke up and Diego turned to look at him. "What? She is."

Diego rubbed his jaw, scratching at his beard and then nodding. "Put together a business plan." His words startled her and she blinked at him owlishly. "What? Pull something together for us to look over."

"I don't-" she glanced around, "I was just spit-balling, I

guess I can do something with paper if you-"

Diego cut her off, "For fuck's sake, Daniel get her a laptop."

Was it that easy? "Are you serious?"

"It's not a bad plan, and the gun-running... it's basically the same idea we came up with - only it took us half the night." He pointed at her, snagging half of a sandwich. "Next time we try to shut you down, don't let us."

Maya felt a warm flush creeping up her spine. She'd had a good idea. *Two* in fact. She'd never had anyone actually listen to one before.

It felt kinda nice.

14

"So, how do you make a business plan?"

Maya was a ball of energy, bounding from bed to shower, full of ideas. She got dressed quickly, scarfing down half a bagel and immediately going to find Stefan in his office, staring at his laptop with a frown.

He looked up when she entered, raising an eyebrow. "The internet exists."

Perching on the edge of his desk she made a face at him. "I don't have my own laptop yet." Drumming her fingers on the wood she huffed at him, "Also, I doubt money laundering fits a traditional template."

"That's true," he said, leaning back in his chair and tucking his hands behind his neck. "Why don't you ask Diego? This is really more his field."

"Diego is who asked me to make the thing," Maya pointed out, "I can't also ask him how to do it."

Stefan hummed, darting his attention between the screen and her and Maya's eyes went wide. "Oh, sorry, did I interrupt something?" She went to stand but he caught her waist, guiding her back to her spot.

"Nothing that can't be ignored," he assured her. He tilted

his head thoughtfully. "I'm not sure about the business plan, Diego's never asked anyone for one before and it's been years since I had to think about it."

"Really?"

He shook his head, "Nah, we usually bat ideas between the three of us til something falls out, then Diego does his magic."

"Oh." She thought about that, tucking the morsel of information away. "Well, what do you *think* would go in it?"

"If I were doing it?" She nodded and he pursed his lips. "I'd start with what it looks like legit. As if you were going to ask him for start-up funding. Give an overview of the market, are there licenses you need, how much can you reasonably clear without it being obvious it's a front?" He ticked the things off on his fingers as he said them. "Then you're going to go into the structure. What's the minimum amount of hires to make it look legit, is there anything else you'd need? Business cards, that kind of thing."

Maya nodded along, grabbing a post-it from his desk and scribbling it all down. "How do you know all this?"

"Dropped out of an M.B.A."

Jaw dropping in shock, Maya's hands fell to her lap. "Wait, what?"

Stefan shrugged like it wasn't a big deal. "Diego had some ideas, needed our help. It was an easy choice."

"You said 'our' help," Maya looked at him quizzically. "Daniel too?"

"Yeah, he was out at some tech firm doing God knows what," Stefan's eyes drifted to his computer again and he held a hand up at her while he typed something.

She waited for him to finish. "I knew you guys were close, I guess I didn't really think about how close."

"They're my brothers," Stefan shrugged nonchalantly. "Lost my family young."

"I'm so sorry," Maya reached out and set a hand on his

shoulder.

"Eh," he gave her a wide smile but his eyes were blank, "I was nine. Not like I really remember it."

Nine is definitely old enough to remember, she wanted to scream. Maya wanted to hug him. Draw him into her arms and pet his hair and coo in his ear. She always was a softy for a sob story, she knew it. Even if Stefan shrugged the whole thing off.

"Anyway, was there something else I could help you with?"

Maya watched the moment slip away with a sigh. "So I just do the research and what? Make a presentation?" She glanced down at the notes in her hands. "I've never done that."

Stefan snorted a laugh, patting her knee. "I would generally recommend *not* putting your criminal endeavors into data like that. Just a suggestion."

"Okay, so not the crime stuff," she made a note of that, writing 'crime' and circling it with a big 'X' across it, feeling joy when he smiled back at her. "But I could make notes of the legit stuff, right?"

"Yeah, sure." He glanced down at his phone, smiling and looking up at her. "Guess what?"

"What?"

"Your laptop is here."

Maya squealed, jumping to her feet and only wincing a little at the jarring motion. "That quick? For real?"

"Yeah, Daniel has it." Maya pulled a face, biting her lower lip. Stefan laughed up at her, patting her waist. "He's not that bad."

"I don't think he likes me very much."

"Daniel doesn't like anybody," Stefan told her. "He tolerates people, and so far he seems to tolerate you fine."

She huffed, grabbing her post-its and standing to leave. Then on impulse turned and hugged him. Bending at the waist and trying not to smash her boobs into his face. She let him go just as quickly, stepping back and waving her notes, feeling a blush crawl up her neck.

"Thanks for this."

Stefan looked a little shell shocked, blinking at her as he said, "Anytime, sweetheart."

"When did you get a couch?"

Daniel barely looked up, something she was coming to expect, and shoved the box on the corner of his desk at her. "Couple days ago."

Maya reached for it, studying the couch from the corner of her eye. It was wide, deep green with huge cushions. It looked like the kind of couch that would eat you alive. A perfect snuggling couch.

"Okay, *why* did you get a couch?"

"Why do you care?"

Why *did* she care? She tucked the box under her arm, pursing her lips. "Can I sit on it?"

A long-suffering sigh from Daniel. "Fine."

Oh it *was* comfortable. Even better than the one in Stefan's office. Stefan's was more for show but this... she moaned as she sank into it, pulling her feet up and tucking them under her. "This is *nice*."

Daniel was watching her over his glasses, a strange look on his face. He shook his head sharply, frowning. "Don't mess it up, it's brand new."

Maya rolled her eyes, attacking the plastic wrapping on her new toy. She fumbled with the box, trying to slide her nail under the stickers holding it closed. She grunted with the effort, considering chewing her way into it.

"Here." A pocket knife, closed thankfully, appeared in front of her face, Daniel raising an eyebrow as he offered it to her.

She took it carefully, shifting slightly as he sat next to her. That was... new. But she didn't have time to think about his behavior, she had a shiny silver laptop, cords tumbling into her lap as she dumped the box out.

"It's so *pretty*," she sighed, petting it with reverent fingers. Next to her Daniel was separating the cords, plugging the power in and handing the other end to her. "Oh, does it need a charge first?"

"Probably," he held his hands out and Maya hesitated, eyeing him suspiciously.

"You're going to give it back?"

"For fuck's sake," he grumbled, snatching it when she dropped it into his grasp. "As though I need another."

Maya hid a smile, peering over his shoulder while he set the computer up, quickly going through screens she would have spent ages thinking about.

"Are you sure I don't want-"

He shushed her, waving a hand in her face. Well, okay then. Fine. It wasn't like it was *her* laptop or anything.

"Password?"

Maya yanked the computer back, tilting it away from him as she typed one in. He hid a smirk and she huffed. "I know you can probably crack it in like ten minutes but I still want it to take you ten minutes."

"Four," he corrected, taking it back. He was on the web now, downloading program after program, windows opening and closing rapidly.

"What are you doing?"

"Getting you on our system and encrypted." He didn't stop what he was doing to answer and Maya shifted closer, her thigh pressing his.

"Ooh, nice." She watched his fingers fly across the keyboard, something graceful and only a little attractive about it. Just a smidge.

"Here," he set the computer back in her lap. "It'll take a while to update everything. In the meantime you can change the desktop picture or whatever."

Maya glared, noting that he didn't get up. In fact his body was turned slightly towards hers, watching to see what she was doing.

"Just for that," she snarked, "I'm going to change it to a photo of you."

He snorted, leaning back and folding his hands on his stomach. "Good luck finding one."

"I'm going to find one," she assured him. "And I'm going to draw horns and a tail on you. No, rosy cheeks and big doe eyes. You're going to look so cute."

"Don't you fucking dare," he warned and Maya tutted.

"Language."

Raising an eyebrow he wagged a finger at her, "Nuh uh, this is *my* kitchen. My rules. One fuck per sentence. Minimum."

Maya pursed her lips and glared, turning her attention back to the computer. She glanced at the news, scrolling through the local section to see if anything big had happened.

"What, no response?"

Lips firmly together, she refused to look at him. There, a picture of a trio of baby rabbits in a basket. Opening up the file she put labels over the bunnies, biting back a giggle. Quickly setting her wallpaper to the disgustingly cute photo, she handed the laptop back to Daniel when the notifications started dinging.

"If I knew it was that easy to shut you up I'd have *oh for fuck's sake*." He glared at her, fingers hovering over the keyboard and scowling at the tiny furry faces on her screen. Each bearing a name, one of which happened to be 'Daniel,' hovering over the ears with a pink arrow pointing down. Maya couldn't help it, bursting out laughing and falling into the arm of the couch, wrapping an arm around her middle as her whole body shook from the force.

"*Your face,*" she gasped, giggles still overcoming her as he continued to glare.

"My *fucking* face," he corrected.

"Your *freaking* face," she grinned back at him, seeing the corner of his eyes crinkle as he fought a smile.

"They aren't going to think it's funny either," he pointed at the two rabbits flanking the one with his name, each with their own text hovering over their heads.

"My computer, I get to decide what's funny - what's *freaking* funny," she corrected before he could. He snorted, eyes on the screen, a small smile tugging his lips under his beard. Maya lounged back into the corner of the couch, watching him work. Without really thinking about it she reached out, lightly running her fingers over a spot behind his ear.

Daniel froze, eyes shutting, and he tilted his head slightly. "What are you doing?"

"You missed a spot," she thumbed the area again, slightly longer than the rest of his close cropped hair. Suddenly realizing what she was doing she yanked her hand back. "Sorry. Jesus, I didn't even think-"

He caught her hand, stopping her wild gestures. Looking at her over his glasses he gently set it back in her lap, mindful of her bandages. "Don't uh, don't worry about it." Looking almost flustered he ran his hand over his head, feeling the spot she'd touched. "I'll have to be sure to catch that next time."

Maya nodded, jumping up and looking anywhere but at him. "I shouldn't bother you. I'm sure you have things," she gestured vaguely, "I'll come back later. Or you can find me. Or just…"

He said something she didn't catch, closing the door firmly behind her and rushing down the hall.

* * *

145

"Doctor Paulson!" Maya crossed the stone floor, only barely stopping herself from hugging the woman. "I am so ready to see another person you don't even know."

The doctor smiled, shifting her bag to her other hand and giving Maya an awkward side hug. "Going a little stir crazy, are we?"

"Stefan finally showed me how to get to the TV, which has helped considerably," Maya chattered as she led Paulson to the back bedroom. "But they are the only people I've talked to in like a week and no one should have to go through that, I don't care how cute they are."

"It sounds like you need enrichment, I can tell Diego to roll a pumpkin in here for you."

"Ha. Ha." Maya said sarcastically. "You are very funny."

"I try," Paulson smirked, patting the bed for Maya to hop up. She made approving sounds at the state of her feet, only covered in band-aids at this point, then checked the bigger cuts on her arms and legs.

"These all look good. Keep taking care of them and the scarring should hopefully be minimal."

Maya held up her hands hopefully, "And the mittens?"

Giving her a half smile, Paulson unwrapped the bandages, taking extra time to examine the right hand and the stitches there. She poked and prodded until Maya was ready to punch her before finally pronouncing, "I think we can leave the wraps off but only if you-"

"Yes!" Maya pumped her fist, "*Finally*." Seeing Paulson's disapproving look she quieted down, sedately laying her hand in her lap. "I'm sorry you were saying?"

"Don't let them soak in water, and I've got some stretching exercises I want you to do."

"Yes ma'am."

Snapping her bag open Paulson handed her a salve that smelled like lavender, making Maya wrinkle her nose. She took out a notepad and started jotting down instructions, complete with little drawings of hands.

"Twice a day for the next week, once a day for the week after." She tore the sheet off and handed it to Maya. "I only need to come back if something goes wrong."

"Yes ma'am."

Rolling her eyes Paulson gave her an assessing look. "Is there anything else we need to talk about?"

Busy setting the items aside, Maya turned back with a confused look. "Like what?"

"Were there any prescriptions you were taking before," the doctor waved a hand, "all of this started?"

"A multi-vitamin." Maya thought about it, "But I can get that over the counter."

"Any birth control?"

Oh. That… made sense. Of course she would ask that. "I've got an IUD," Maya was blushing beet red, she knew it. "The clinic was offering them last year and so I got one. It's still good for a while."

Paulson nodded, "And your last blood screen?"

She didn't say for STDs and Maya was grateful. "Uh, a while ago. I haven't had any... *relations*… in quite a while."

The doctor raised a disbelieving eyebrow and something clicked in Maya's head. "Wait, did they ask you to ask me this? Those *assholes*."

Paulson snorted. "No, they didn't. And even if they had I wouldn't tell them what you said. I'm covering bases for *you*. This is not a normal situation, and I want to be sure you're taking precautions."

"Oh," she was definitely still blushing. "We haven't - I mean we flirt but I don't think they're actually interested."

The woman gave her a long, disappointed look. "I never pegged you for stupid."

"Excuse me?"

"Or hopelessly naïve."

"Now wait a minute-"

Paulson cut her off with a sharp gesture. "I'm not going to have the birds and the bees talk with you. Whatever you're going to do, do it safely. The IUD is a good start but they aren't everything. Do you have condoms?"

Maya wasn't going to argue it, she was blushing so hard she could fry an egg on her cheeks. "Yes."

"Good." Picking up her bag Paulson cocked her head at her. "Maybe I'm off-base, but I don't think so. Keep your head, don't let someone talk you into something you don't want to do."

Maya nodded, barely noticing the woman leave.

Of course she knew they *would,* given half an opportunity. Try to talk her into something. The three men had made no secret of that. But then again she was pretty sure they would take the chance to have sex with *anybody*, given the same opportunity. It didn't mean they actually wanted *her.*

And something had changed, since the night she was attacked. She felt like they saw her as a person, not as some random woman. Stefan and Daniel were helping with her business plan, Diego had asked for her ideas on a negotiation coming up. She wasn't going to ruin that by throwing herself at any of them, or letting them put her back in that box of decorative objects she'd so recently escaped.

It wasn't worth it.

Was it?

"Miss Alvani?"

Maya jerked up, shouting out, "Yes?" The security guard raised an eyebrow and she smiled. "Sorry, feeling a little high strung. It's Ryan, right?"

He nodded, looking pleased she'd remembered. "I'm supposed to tell you the bosses will be out this evening and ask if there is anything you want."

The apartment to herself and anything she wanted?
Maya had some ideas.

15

The music was loud and Maya wasn't wearing pants.

She had started the evening with pants, she was pretty sure of it. Yes, of course she had. She had spilled butter on them, a casualty of the batch of cookies she was pulling from the hot oven. Slipping them onto rack of the double oven she wasn't using, she waved vaguely at them with one hand, admiring her bright orange nails. The first thing she'd done this afternoon upon getting her hands back was give herself a mani-pedi in the brightest color she could find.

Or that Ryan could find. Bless him, she could only imagine him staring at racks of nail polish to find 'the cheeriest color there is.' He'd brought back five, ranging from hot pink to bright green. And a look that screamed 'never ask me to do this again.'

She wondered how much he got paid. Probably not enough.

While she waited for the cookies to cool she got out the icing ingredients, searching through the cabinets before finding a stand mixer tucked above the refrigerator. Whoever had stocked the kitchen originally had had a lot more faith in the men's domesticity than had proven out.

Cheerfully separating egg whites, a dozen ought to do it, she turned on the mixer, coughing slightly when the powdered sugar puffed up in her face. Leaving it to do its thing she reached for her drink. Empty again.

A beat thrummed through the kitchen and Maya swung along, swaying slightly as she squeezed a half a lemon into a jar. She dropped the smushed half onto the counter, fumbling around for another and knocking into her glass.

"Whoops," she lunged forward, righting the glass but sending a lemon over the far side of the island. "Gosh darn it," her grumbles took her around, bending over and scooping the lemon up with a triumphant flourish.

"Well that's a pretty sight."

Shrieking, she tipped a bar stool behind her, darting around the island for cover and scrambling for a weapon. Holding the lemon squeezer in one hand she wound the arm with the lemon back, ready to throw. She halted when she saw the three men, all of them looking at her in various stages of amusement.

"It'd be more dangerous to squeeze it into someone's eye than throw it," Stefan pointed out, crossing to the refrigerator and pulling out a beer.

A blush bloomed over her face and she set the fruit down with a thud, reaching for the knife. "Only if you were close."

She prepared her drink while they floated around her, Daniel and Diego accepting beers and settling onto bar stools across from her while Stefan hovered near her shoulder watching her. Within a minute she was swaying to the music again, mixing the whiskey and lemon with simple syrup from the pot on the stove.

"How many of those have you had?" Diego asked with a raised eyebrow.

"Not many," she protested, holding the glass up. "How many lemons did we have?"

Daniel smirked at her. She liked it when he did that, not that she'd ever tell him. It made her insides flip over and want to do something incredibly ill-advised.

"What's the celebration?" he asked.

Maya grinned, wiggling her fingers his direction. "I got my *hands* back!"

It amused her they hadn't noticed her bandages were gone. She did a little dance move for them, reaching her hands over the counter and making waves in the air. Diego caught one, turning her hand over and running his fingers across her palm. Oh, okay. If Daniel's smirk did something to her this was doing something a hundred times worse. Tingles shot up her arm, making her knees weak and she had to catch herself on the marble.

"You're going to have a scar," he said with a frown, pulling her slightly closer. She went, bending over the counter, following his grasp.

"It's okay." Did her voice usually sound that breathy? "It barely stings."

Diego's frown deepened but he let her go, sharing an inscrutable look with Stefan.

"Anyway," she tried to brush off the low thrum of tension in the room. "I got all my fingers and a reason to party so if you're not here to dance…"

"What's that thing doing?" Daniel pointed.

"What thing?"

"The mixer."

"Oh shit," Maya covered her mouth with one hand, spinning on her toes and catching herself on the counter. "My icing!" Frowning into the mixer she added more sugar, waving a hand at the cloud it produced. "I was going to decorate some cookies."

"What fucking cookies?" Daniel asked with a frown.

"Language," she pointed at him. "Or no cookies for you."

"You just said shit," Stefan pointed out.

Maya gasped, covering her mouth again. "Oh shit I did, didn't I?"

"Five bucks in the swear jar," Diego deadpanned and Maya giggled.

"I still want to know where the cookies are."

"They're cooling," she pointed at the oven, "in there."

Daniel's eyes narrowed as he stood up. "You left them to cool in a hot oven?"

"Of course not," she rolled her eyes. When they continued to stare at her she pointed over he shoulder, "You have a double oven."

Daniel opened the door, the smell of burnt sugar wafting out immediately and a small cloud of smoke. He closed it quickly, turning the oven off and giving her a sardonic look.

"Well *fuck,*" she sighed.

Daniel snorted, waving a dish towel and shaking his head at her. He didn't look mad, he looked almost… fond? A small smile nearly hidden by his beard. "So you're allowed to curse but we're not?"

She stuck her tongue out and he took a step towards her, reaching up and stroking her cheek. "You keep doing that and I'll find a use for it."

"Maya?" Diego interrupted, holding up her medication bottle. "How many of these have you had?"

Maya squinted at him. "Two I think? Maybe three."

"And you've been drinking?"

"I know, I know," she waved him off, frowning at the icing again and adding more sugar. "It's bad to mix but the internet assured me I wouldn't die - it'd just make me feel good, and I feel *great*."

The room was only spinning a *little* bit. And that was normal right? When you danced the world *should* spin. Spin and spin and spin until Stefan caught her with his hands around her waist, his broad shoulders taking up her entire field of vision.

That was the last thing she remembered.

Diego nodded at the guard on the door and pushed through, heading directly for his office. Daniel's voice stopped him, a low greedy growl.

"Well that's a pretty sight."

She was there. Bent over. Long legs completely bare and the crotch of those fucking cotton panties exposed to all three of them. What the *fuck* was she doing? Anyone could have walked in, seen her like that. Could have taken advantage. Could have pushed her over the kitchen island and had those panties around her ankles in a flash. Could be buried in her warm, wet heat that he fucking *knew* would be perfect.

Could have, could have, could have.

The girl screamed, taking cover and finding weapons and he felt a small tug of pride that her instinct was to fight and not run. He ignored Stefan's banter, taking the drink that was offered to him and scanning the mess she'd made of his kitchen, eyes finally falling on a bottle of whiskey and a cocktail shaker.

"How many of those have you had?" He asked, tilting the bottle to check its contents.

"Not many," she insisted. "How many lemons did we have?"

Diego snorted. It was plenty if it made her forget she wasn't wearing pants. He'd like to think that she might dress like this for them. Might dance around half naked and let them take care of the other half. But she wasn't that kind of girl.

God he wished she was.

"What's the celebration?" Daniel asked.

"I got my *hands* back!"

Diego's gaze snapped up, berating himself for missing something so obvious. He caught one of her moving wrists, inspecting her palm, enjoying touching her even as he frowned at the lines he found. Her skin was soft, the angry red streaks a stark contrast to the lighter skin.

"You're going to have a scar." He hated the idea, he didn't want her around but the fact that she'd been hurt under his watch stung. It was an insult, a deliberate one. He expected Stefan to speak up, he was always defending the girl, but Stefan's brain was somewhere else entirely.

Diego's inspection had pulled her over the island, presenting her ass in exactly the way Diego himself had been imagining. He looked at the other man, his brother in ways far deeper than blood, and saw the hunger on his face. The way the man's fingers twitched as he stopped himself from touching. The bare skin of her ass, her thighs; maybe slipping beneath her panties and running a finger along her slit.

Would she be wet? Did she feel the energy in the room too? Fuck, Diego was already half hard and he was barely near her. But thinking of her getting wet from their presence, standing there so close and ready for them.

Fuck he was *more* than half hard.

He distracted himself with his beer, wrinkling his nose at the smell of burning cookies. She was arguing with Daniel, swaying on her feet with a dreamy look on her face. Diego searched the island, finally finding a small orange bottle.

"Maya? How many of these have you had?"

Painkillers and alcohol, potentially deadly but she seemed to be riding a high rather than in danger. He might want to call Paulson just in case.

"This doesn't look right," Daniel frowned into the mixer. "Is it supposed to be this thin?"

"Here," Maya shoved a bag of sugar at him, "add some and turn it up a little."

Diego wasn't sure if it was the 'some' or 'a little' she should have been more accurate about, but what happened next couldn't entirely be blamed on Daniel. He poured what looked like half the bag in, setting the mixer to its highest speed.

The contents exploded.

Stefan blinked, icing dripping from his hair. Diego wiped a smear off his cheek, tasting it with an appreciative hum. Maya looked horrified, hands covering her mouth as she gaped at Daniel, who had gotten the worst of it by far.

"What. The. *Fuck*."

Maya snorted, eyes widening, shoulders shaking. A muffled noise escaped her hands, then another. Daniel glared, turning the mixer off with a flick of his hand.

"Are you *laughing*?"

She shook her head, hands still clamped over her mouth, taking a careful step back. Diego felt a chuckle crawling up his throat. Fuck, when was the last time there had been this much *laughter* in their lives? Had there ever been? His lips twitched as Daniel took a menacing step forward.

Smart girl, she ran.

Not so smart, she ran straight at him.

Diego lifted her onto a barstool, blocking her escape with his body while Daniel caged her other side. She was still laughing, eyes shining brightly and her wide smile drawing him in nearer. She didn't seem to notice how close they were, shoulders brushing as she reached up and wiped a smear of icing from Daniel's cheek.

"You look like a Willy Wonka reject," she giggled and he nipped at her playfully, tongue slipping out to lap the tips of her fingers. Fuck the man was gone for her. She only had to crook a finger and he would be on his knees. He'd reset the house thermostat, locking them out of it, just because she'd said once she was cold. Diego had been there when the fucking couch arrived, Daniel glaring at him and daring him to say something.

"You have pretty eyes."

The words jerked Diego from his thoughts. She was stroking Daniel's beard and the taciturn man was all but purring, nuzzling into her palm. A surge of envy roared through him, his arm going around her waist and pulling her against his chest.

"Sometimes you look at me," she hiccuped softly, then smiled even wider. "You look at me from over your glasses. Like this," she demonstrated, tucking her chin down and staring up at Daniel from under long eyelashes. She bit her lip, letting it go and taking an unsteady breath. It was Daniel's turn to reach out, to cup her cheek and watch her purr for him.

"Yeah, I do," he said simply.

"Why though?" She pulled away from him slightly, turning to look at Stefan and Diego with hazy eyes, brows furrowed. "You *all* look at me sometimes and I think maybe…"

Diego couldn't help it. She was too tempting, too much soft, bare skin. He laid a hand on her upper thigh, caressing his fingers where the flesh pressed together. She gasped, eyes flying to him, mouth parting in a small 'o'.

And then she melted.

Her whole body became loose, a whimper fell from her lips, and Diego had no other words to describe it than that she fucking *melted* for him. Daniel quickly followed his lead, threading his fingers into her hair and dropping his other hand to her thigh.

"We look at you that way because we want you," Diego murmured into her ear, watching the way her breasts rose and fell with unsteady breaths. "We look at you that way because you're always right *fucking* here and so fucking *sweet*." He saw Daniel lean in, saw her shudder with

157

whatever he was doing with his mouth. Diego cupped her chin and turned her to face him.

"We look at you like we want to fuck you, Maya."

She was lost, he could see it on her. Lost in the moment and their touches. Without a word passing between them, he and Daniel pressed her thighs apart, making room for Stefan to step up and between, his hands gripping the skin of her waist and making her shiver. Daniel tightened his hold on her hair, tilting her head back and Diego took advantage, thrusting his tongue into her mouth and tasting the sour burst of lemon and the sweet underlay that was all her.

"I think you want that too," he said as he broke away, panting hot breaths into her mouth. "I think you're sick and tired of being a good girl. I think your sweet little pussy is dripping for us." He shifted his hand up, running the back of his fingers along the damp fabric and groaned. "There she is, we can help with that princess. All you had to do was say something."

Stefan's hands rucked under her sweater, palming her breasts. But Diego wanted it *off*. He could hear the low murmur of Daniel's voice, feel the way she squirmed at whatever filthy things he was pouring into her ear.

Stefan's mouth took hers, his low moan met with an arch of her back. Diego pressed further, stroking her wet pussy through her underwear. "Say it princess, say what you want."

"Do you want it, kitten?" Daniel's low voice rumbled across her, his fingers meeting Diego's between her thighs.

"Tell us you want us," Stefan breathed.

"I do," Maya whined, writhing in the small space they allowed her. "I do. But not…"

Diego froze, Daniel's soft *fuck* falling into the silence of her denial. They wouldn't force her, none of them were that man. Cajole, tempt, tease… they would do a lot of things but never force.

"Why not?' Stefan asked, lips ghosting over her cheek. "Tell me, what's stopping you?"

"It scares me."

Daniel's grin was feral, a flash of teeth and then he was on her again, nibbling her neck and shoulder, his fingers pushing past Diego's to stroke her pussy. "We'll make it good for you, we'll make it *so fucking good*."

Diego turned her face to his. "Open your eyes Maya. Tell me what scares you."

Maya blinked sluggishly back at him. "I want you to like me," she said in a small voice, eyes falling closed again. "Want you to want… me."

She slumped and Stefan caught her as she fell forward. "What the hell?"

"Whiskey and Vicodin," Diego sighed. "Figures that would be our luck."

Stefan shifted his grip, leaning her back against the marble while Daniel pulled her into the crook of his arm. Diego would need to keep an eye on that. Daniel had never been a problem before - but then again he'd never seen him act like this before.

"Does she really think we don't like her?" Daniel asked with a frown.

"Women," Stefan shrugged.

"We'll talk again when she's sober," Diego said with a sly smile. "I can think of a few ways to convince her that will be fun for everyone."

"She won't do it," Daniel pointed out, taking another beer from Stefan. "She's not that kind of girl."

"You so sure about that?" Stefan asked, taking a long swig. "She went from you to me after the party missing a beat."

"She was drunk," Daniel countered.

"Drunk people don't do anything they wouldn't already do."

"Really? So you fucked her then?"

Stefan glared, "Stop being a fucking cunt, you know I didn't."

"But if she was into it either way-"

"Stop it," Diego said softly, watching the two of them jerk their heads his way. "We can't have this *girl* fucking our shit up. Not the way things are."

"So she goes?" Daniel's tone was unreadable.

"We convince her," Stefan said quickly. "She likes us, I think if it was only one she'd be there already. So we convince her three isn't any different."

Diego rubbed the bridge of his nose. "And how do you propose we do that?"

Stefan perched on a barstool, "What was it she said to you? She wanted us to like her?"

Wracking his brain, Diego tried to think back. Daniel got there first, taking his glasses off and polishing them as he said, "A whore we pretended to like."

"That's it," Stefan snapped his fingers. "Well, let's step up our game. I don't think it'll be hard."

Diego thought about it, what it would be like. He'd never really tried to get someone to like him. Stefan had latched on to him at the foster home, and Daniel had fallen in with them for protection originally. Suddenly he remembered waking up with her, the way she snuggled into his arms and how right she'd felt. Maybe it wouldn't be the *worst* thing to play this game, as long as he kept in mind it wasn't permanent.

"I already talk to her more than everyone else combined," Daniel pointed out, "except you two. Not sure how much further I can push myself."

"I'm sure you'll think of something," Stefan rolled his eyes.

16

Lesson learned, don't mix alcohol and prescription medication. A lesson that, upon further research, seemed to be a consensus amongst medical professionals.

Holding her aching head in one hand Maya shuffled into the kitchen, ignoring the man sitting at the island and flipping on the kettle with an unsteady hand. Why did the kitchen smell like burnt sugar?

"How's the head?"

"Mmrph," she replied, pulling down her tea supplies.

"That bad?"

"Mmrph."

Making the tea by muscle memory, she didn't look at him until she had it warm in her hands, Diego's assessing gaze making her blink. "What?"

His eyes narrowed, studying her. "How much do you remember?"

"About what?" her brows pulled together in confusion.

"Last night."

Oh no. What had she done? She shifted on her feet, assessing her body. It didn't feel like she had done *that* at least. Frowning, she stared into her teacup. "There was dancing. And cookies." She tilted her head, thinking. "Something happened to the cookies." Groaning she leaned over the island, stretching her arms in front of her and pressing her face to the cool marble. "God, I didn't make a fool of myself did I?"

"No," he patted her arm absentmindedly. "You were fine."

Maya lifted her head, glaring at him. "You don't ask someone who was 'fine' how much they remember about what they did."

He chuckled, grabbing his mug in one hand and typing something on his phone with the other. "There was a small icing incident but it got cleaned up this morning."

"Icing incident?" Maya called after him, looking around the kitchen. "What icing?"

"Don't worry about it," he called back, the sound of the front door shutting signaling his departure.

Yeah, Maya was going to worry about it. In fact she was going to worry about it a lot. She worried about it as she gathered her laptop and set herself up on the island, carefully laying out her notes and placing her tea just so. And she worried about it as she started going through websites, making notes, and sketching out what a fake event planning company might look like.

In fact, she worried all morning, nearly through lunch, and didn't stop until someone interrupted her with a "Miss Alvani?"

It took Maya a moment to realize that was her, looking up and staring at the hands holding a massive flower arrangement. It could be anyone, their body completely blocked by the petals. "Yes?"

"These came for you, where would you like me to put them?"

"For me?" Maya slid off the stool, crossing over and running her fingers along the blooms. "From who?"

The man shrugged, struggling under the weight, and slid the vase onto the island. The arrangement was huge, at least three feet across, sunflowers mixed with some greenery. The thing had to weigh fifty pounds.

"This is fine," she smiled, finally able to see who it was. "Thanks Ryan."

He nodded, giving her a quick smile, and headed back out to the landing. Maya began to gently pick through the flowers, searching for a card. She was trying to get to the vase when she heard Daniel bark, "Where the fuck did those come from?"

"I don't know." There was no card on the vase either. "Ryan said it was for me but I don't see any-"

Daniel grabbed her arm, jerking her backwards and quickly shoving her behind him as he backed away from it. "Did it occur to you it might be a bomb?"

No, actually, it hadn't. Maya cringed, ducking behind his back, then frowned. "Wait," she tapped his shoulder, "don't your guys scan stuff before they bring it up?"

Daniel stopped in his tracks, arms dropping to his sides. "They're *supposed* to, what if they got lazy?"

Rolling her eyes, Maya stepped around him. "Overreaction much?"

He grunted, crossing his arms and glaring as Maya hesitantly approached the flowers again. He probably *was* wrong, but he'd made her a little skittish.

"Oh, they got here," Stefan's voice made her turn with a questioning look. "I thought you might like them better than roses."

"Are you fucking kidding me?" Daniel bit the words off, glaring at him.

Maya blinked. "They're my favorite."

Grinning, Stefan crossed to her, pressing a kiss to her forehead and moving past them to the refrigerator. What was going on? Stefan was casually kissing her now? And why was he in some sort of staring contest with Daniel?

"I don't-"

"Hey ass-face," Daniel called out. "Checked your messages today?"

Glaring, Stefan set down the bottle of green juice, slipping his phone from his pocket. "I've been busy working on the-"

The two men stared at each other. Maya stared at them. Should she… should she ask? About the flowers? And the messages? And why did she have the feeling that this had something to do with the 'don't worry about it' icing incident from last night?

"Well fuck," Stefan grunted. He frowned and then turned to her with a wide smile, as though a switch was flipped from one moment to the next. "Hope you like them, I just wanted to get you something pretty."

"They're my favorite," she said again dumbly.

Holding his juice up in a silent salute Stefan gave Daniel a look she couldn't place and went to the back of the house without another word.

"Daniel?"

"Yeah kitten?"

"What is going on?"

"Don't worry about it."

She really wished they'd stop saying that.

Someone was trying to get in her room.

Maya struggled to wake up, hand automatically reaching for the carving knife she'd stolen and tucked beneath her pillow. The bench she religiously pulled to block the door slid across the carpet. A muttered voice, footsteps, a door banging open. She crouched, waiting, coiled tight and knuckles white on the knife.

When they opened the door she launched herself forward,

swinging the knife in front of her wildly. Someone cursed, grabbing for her, but she scrambled away. Running for the door, shoving her hair out of her eyes. She could see another person backlit in the hallway and she snarled, waving the knife and feeling her stomach clench. She wasn't going to go down without a fight. Not this time.

They were talking to her but she couldn't hear, blood rushing in her ears. The man in front stepped towards her and she stepped back, directly into a body. They wrapped their arms over hers, pinning them down and lifting her to her tiptoes. Someone had their hands around her wrist, twisting until she cried out in pain and dropped the knife.

"Please, *no*," she was on the verge of tears, kicking her feet out and catching someone's leg. "Let me go."

"*Calm down*," the voice was harsh in her ears, the arms wrapping around her tighter. "Shh, sweetheart, stop. It's just us."

Maya blinked, eyes finally focusing on the room. Daniel stood to her right, the knife he had taken from her loose in his grip. A few feet away Diego had his hands up, one sleeve sliced through.

"Shh, it's okay," Stefan soothed, arms banding around her chest. "It's okay."

"What-?" Maya croaked, swallowing back nausea, "What the hell?"

"Are you done?" Daniel asked, turning and setting the knife on a nearby shelf.

"Done? I don't know what- *Diego*," Maya lurched forward, finally noticing the thin line of blood down his forearm. Stefan didn't let her go, pulling her backwards when she tried to leave.

"It's barely a scratch," Diego reassured her, taking a slow step forward.

"Did I..." Maya shook her head, slumping back into

Stefan's arms. "I'm sorry. Jesus, I didn't mean-"

"What happened?"

"I heard you come in," Maya sighed, "I didn't know… I thought you were…"

Diego's eyes scanned her face, glancing over when Daniel pushed the closet doors wider to reveal the pallet she'd made on the floor. Daniel cursed, turning and kicking the bench hard enough that she flinched. Stefan held her tighter, only releasing her when Diego stepped forward and tilted her chin up to look at him.

"How long have you been sleeping in the closet?"

God, they weren't supposed to find out. She felt so stupid. "Since the break-in - after you left," she admitted, fingers twining together.

He cursed softly, "You know you're safe here right?"

"I know it's just - I can't sleep there. It's never felt comfortable and now all I think about is Michael standing in the doorway and-" she swallowed, trying to catch her breath.

"What do you mean it's never felt comfortable?" Daniel asked with a frown.

That at least made her laugh, "It's not exactly *homey*." The three men blinked at her in confusion, eyes scanning the room as if seeing it for the first time. "The closet is filled with sex toys, every wall has a hook or chains or both, there's a *sex swing* for God's sake." Maya paused, taking a deep breath. "It's your room and I… I know I'm just passing through but it's not an easy room to feel safe in. The whole point of it is…" She didn't finish the sentence. Was pretty sure she didn't need to.

Diego and Stefan exchanged a glance while Daniel asked, "The sex swing is comfortable. Have you tried it?"

"Daniel," she scolded and saw his lips twitch. She huffed a small laugh, "It's fine, really, I just… between the attack and the, uh, *accoutrements* of the room it seemed easier to find somewhere else."

Diego stared at the closet, a frown pulling his features into deep lines. "This is not acceptable."

Maya's shoulders slumped. "I know it's stupid-"

"Not you, princess," he gestured at the blankets. "This. I can't believe you've been living like this and not said anything."

"You've given so much," she pointed out, "and you're helping me so much. I didn't want to push."

Diego grunted, turning and cupping her face in his palm. "We are going to fix this." He jerked his head, and she followed him to the kitchen, sliding onto one of the bar stools and watching Stefan flip the kettle on. Diego looked at Daniel, one eyebrow raised in question. "If I thought I could get her out here right now I would."

"She'd kill you," Daniel pointed out.

Who were they talking about?

"First thing in the morning then," Diego pressed his fist to the marble, watching Stefan slide her a mug. "In the meantime, what are we doing tonight?"

"We could bring in a guard for the door," Stefan mused.

Diego shook his head. "I don't like them in the apartment overnight."

"Seems like maybe you could make an exception."

"I don't-"

"What would make you feel safe?" Daniel asked quietly, his expression neutral.

Maya almost smiled, of course he would be the most direct. Wrapping her hands around the warm mug she stared into the contents, the scent of lemon and mint filling her nose. "I'm not sure." She frowned. "Wait, why was someone coming into the room anyway?"

Stefan flushed, scratching his neck. "I thought I heard something, I was checking on you."

"Oh, thanks. I guess."

"How about if I stayed with you?" he offered, giving her an easygoing smile. "Keep the monsters at bay. Seems the least I can do since this is my fault."

Diego's jaw was clenched and Daniel's mouth was set in a hard line. But Maya didn't have it in her to argue. "Yeah, that'd be nice. You don't mind though?"

"Of course not sweetheart," he stroked her hand. "You deserve to feel safe."

Maya nodded, sighing in relief. "We can move my pallet out in the hall for you, unless you had a cot or something you were planning on-" Diego's laughter pulled her up short, even Daniel had a small smirk on his face she couldn't understand. "What?"

"We'll make sure Stefan is set up all comfy and cozy outside your door princess," Diego assured her, flinging an arm around the man's neck. "Why don't you go to bed and we'll get all that taken care of."

Stefan scowled, shrugging off Diego's embrace. When Maya reached for him he glared at her, quickly turning his expression into a supporting smile when she placed a hand on his arm. "Thank you. I appreciate it."

Without thinking she stood on her tiptoes, brushing a kiss on his cheek. She didn't think about the action until she was almost to the bedroom, missing a step when she realized the casual intimacy it implied.

Maya flipped the light off and closed the door with a loud click. What a weird freaking day. But she *did* feel safer knowing Stefan would be there. And at least she'd stopped worrying about whatever had happened last night with the icing.

Or at least…

Maya groaned, sinking into the bed in an embarrassed heap. She *had* stopped worrying about it.

17

"Maya?" a deep voice called softly. "Maya, I don't want to scare you again. Are you awake?"

Maya groaned, rolling over, scanning the morning light to see if she could determine the time. Not early, but not especially late either. Why did she need to be awake?

"Yeah?" she called out blearily.

The door opened, Stefan poking his head through. "You awake?"

"No," she grumbled, rolling over and pulling the blankets over her head. "I am not."

A rumbling chuckle, and then someone was pulling at the duvet. "Come on sleepyhead."

"*Why*," Maya whined. Weight shifted on the bed and she realized he had sat down on the edge next to her. Her suspicion was confirmed when a hand peeled the sheets back from her face.

"You're cute in the morning," he smiled down at her and she couldn't help but smile back. It was too early to try to keep her face under control.

"You too."

His smile grew warmer, then his eyes scanned down her

neck, to the tank top twisted around her chest. She didn't look, certain that it was showing more than she wanted it to. He leaned down, pressing a soft kiss to her lips before he pulled back slightly, hovering a breath above her.

"What are you doing?" she whispered.

"Isn't this how you wake sleeping beauty?" He arched an eyebrow at her.

Maya snorted. "I'm not asleep."

"Oh, but you said you were." Was he getting in the bed with her? Toeing his shoes off and slipping under the covers. He gathered her close and kissed her softly again. "I promise I will kiss you as many times as it takes to wake you up."

Moaning Maya pushed lightly on his shoulders. "Stefan, I don't want to-"

"Shh," he murmured, nuzzling his nose against hers. "I'm not going to touch you. Even when you *beg* me to. Just kissing."

Well, that was alright then, wasn't it? Maya tangled her fingers into the curls at the back of his head, pulling him closer and opening her mouth for his questing tongue. Deep inside she knew that if she were even the slightest bit more awake she'd be protesting this. But she wasn't. She was drowsy and warm and Stefan felt *really* good.

It was soft, so so soft. He didn't take, didn't force. Nibbles and soft licks and the gentle glide of his lips against hers. She could do this for *hours*.

Knock knock.

Maya's eyes flew open, blinking as Stefan jerked the sheet up and over their heads. "Shh," he warned, pressing a kiss beneath her jaw. "Be quiet."

"Stefan someone is-"

He cut her off, his kiss turning hotter, tongue delving into her mouth. A moan escaped her and she arched into him.

"You know I can hear you right?"

Daniel's voice cut through the sensual haze and Maya blushed to her toes, jerking away from Stefan and covering her mouth in shock.

"Fuck off," Stefan growled, pulling her close again, covering her body with his.

"Stefan, *no*," Maya pushed at his chest and he groaned, burying his face in her neck and rocking his hips against hers. "You said none of that," she pointed out, trying to sound scandalized.

"I changed my mind," he grunted.

"You're the one who said she needed to get up," Daniel pointed out and Maya peeked over the sheets at him. He didn't look angry, just resigned. Arms crossed as he leaned against the doorframe. He gave her a small smile and turned his eyes on Stefan. "And remember what I said?"

Stefan rolled off the bed with a put upon sigh. "Cock-block," he snarled and Maya heard a small huff of laughter from across the room.

"Turnabout and all that shit."

"You're an asshole."

"You just hate that I'm right all the time."

Their bickering made her feel calmer, their voices becoming indistinct mutters as they left. She'd been about five seconds from inviting Daniel to join them - and then what would have happened?

You know what, her body told her, pulsing at the thought.

But we don't want that, she shot back.

Don't we?

Maya wasn't so sure anymore.

The woman sitting on the couch was blonde, slim, well put together in shades of beige and white. As though she'd stepped right out of the pages of a fashion magazine. And young too, at least five years younger than Maya. She tried very hard not to judge. Who knew who this woman was? Probably a business acquaintance of some kind. No reason to be having any kind of feeling about a stranger. And it definitely wasn't jealousy bubbling in Maya's stomach.

But it was jealousy adjacent.

Looking up from the magazine in her lap the woman smiled, bouncing to her feet and tossing it aside. "Hi I'm Jessica! You must be Maya."

Hoping that her smile didn't look as forced as it was, Maya waved, unsure what the protocol was. She noticed Daniel standing in the kitchen and gave him a wide-eyed *'help me'* look.

"Stop being so damned perky, Jess," he grumbled, sipping his coffee. "Give her a chance to wake up and get caffeinated."

Jessica rolled her eyes, coming around the furniture and positively *beaming* at Maya. "Do you want to discuss your ideas or look at the space first?"

Maya tried once again to get guidance from Daniel but he shrugged, hiding a smile. He gave Jessica a curt nod and grabbed a mug before heading back to his office. As he passed Maya he pressed it into her hands, the aroma of her favorite morning blend drifting up. He didn't say anything, continuing on and leaving the two of them alone.

"I don't know what-"

"Let's look at the space then," Jessica chirped, "it'll help me visualize what you're thinking."

Maya blinked at her and the woman continued to smile brightly as she answered hesitantly, "Okay?"

Bouncing over to the couch, in heels no less, Jessica picked up her leather hand bag and marched to the back of the apartment, Maya trailing in her wake. "I'm not sure what we're doing…"

"Oh!" Jessica spun, a look of horror on her face. "They told me that… dumbasses. I'm an interior designer, Diego said you wanted to do some redecorating?"

It was a testament to how little caffeine she'd had that it took Maya a moment to follow. Then it hit her all at once. "The dungeon!"

Jessica reeled back, frowning. "The what?"

Smiling Maya took the lead, "Wait til you see it." Opening the door with a flourish she gestured Jessica inside, snorting when she came to a dead stop just inside the door.

"This is…"

Maya muffled a laugh, watching the woman try to come up with something nice to say. "Salacious?"

"I was going to go with *adult*," Jessica replied, reaching out tentatively and running her fingers across one of the brackets on the wall. Maya noted someone had come through and removed the chains. "You've been *living* here?"

"I'd say you get used to it," Maya grinned, crossing and sitting on the edge of the bed, "but yesterday I found a tube of what I thought was spare toothpaste that ended up being strawberry flavored lube."

"*Ew.*" Jessica shuddered and sat next to her, eyes wide. She stared around the room before seeming to come back to herself, turning and taking Maya's hands in hers. "Honey, we are going to fix this. *Today.*"

"I don't know if-"

The woman waved her off, "I was paid for a rush job and I have never seen a place more in need of one. Let's talk color." She hesitated, glancing around, "Do you *like* red?"

"God no," Maya quickly assured her, "there's nothing in the room I would keep."

Jessica sighed in relief, pulling a swatch book and laptop from her bag. "From scratch. Even better."

They discussed the room for nearly an hour, Maya and her both falling into a fit of giggles over the bathroom fixtures. The closet nearly derailed the whole day, Jessica opening drawer after drawer with increasing incredulity.

"This dresser is my stuff, the rest," Maya gestured, "can go into storage or to some charity shop for adult film props I guess?" Next to her, Jessica rubbed the material of a corset between her fingers. "Or if you wanted to take anything…"

"What? Oh no, I-"

Maya laughed, reaching into the drawer and pulling out a pile of corsets she'd never be able to wear without elective surgery. She dumped them into Jessica's arms, "I insist. You'd be doing me a favor."

"Daniel would *kill* me if he found out I took any of this home," Jessica averred, gently setting the clothes to the side.

Maya took the opening, hardly stumbling as she asked, "How do you two, uh, *know* each other?"

The look on the other woman's face was pure horror. "Not like *that*. Oh my God, ew. No, he's my brother. Well, step-brother."

Daniel had *family*? Daniel was okay with her *meeting* his family? What else didn't she know about them? "Oh, sorry," she mumbled. "They've never mentioned anyone else."

"It's just me and mom," Jessica shifted the racks of costumes. "Stefan and Diego don't have family - *is this a sexy giraffe*?"

Maya snorted, "Do *not* open the dresser in the back. You'll be scarred for life."

Shuddering, Jessica let the clothes go, backing out of the closet. "I will *never* be able to look Daniel in the eye again. What a perv."

You don't know the half of it, Maya thought.

"I hate to ask," Jessica asked, glancing back. "But the clothes, is someone else going to be mad that they're gone? That has to be ten grand in lingerie."

It was petty but Maya took sick pleasure in shaking her head. "If they wanted to keep it they could have moved it out at any time. And if I leave-" the words hit her like a gut punch and she stopped to swallow down the lump in her throat. "*When* I leave they certainly have the money to replace it all."

Jessica nodded, giving her a small smile and Maya hoped the woman was less perceptive than she seemed. She did not need Daniel's stepsister knowing the *salacious* thoughts the bedroom had inspired.

Definitely the bedroom's fault.

Standing in the middle of the room, Jessica stood with her hands on her hips, lips pursed. "Okay. I'll have my guys in to replace the carpet with that high pile gray we talked about. We're going to remove the… *sconces* and repaint to a warm cream. And a dark blue accent wall here."

Maya nodded along, trying to imagine it.

"We'll pick up some plants for the bathroom, you've got good light in there so we've got options. And over there…" Jessica glared at the sex swing. "I've got a hanging chair that could make use of the bracket if you want something. We can move the bed to the other wall and set up a little sitting area by the windows."

"And curtains," Maya added. "I want curtains."

"I've got just the thing." Jessica tapped her lower lip thoughtfully. "Have you thought about art? We could shop but if there's something you have in mind…"

Maya knew what she wanted immediately. "In the front hall there's some photos, they're black and white with these splashes of color? I really like them. I don't know who the artist is but if we could find out…"

Jessica gave her a sly smile, "Oh I know just where to get those. Done and done." Picking up her handbag she looked Maya over. "Why don't you get ready while I make some calls and then we can go."

"Go?" Maya looked around the room. "Go where?"

"Shopping of course."

Maya had never showered so fast in her life. Dressed in leggings and a sweater, she slipped on her flats, sighing in contentment at the idea of wearing shoes. *Outside.* She'd put on a little makeup and even taken the extra time to dry her hair rather than pull it up in a ponytail.

Pony tail, Maya snickered. Daniel had ruined that for her forever.

Checking herself in the mirror Maya smiled. For the first time in ages she felt like a whole person. Not lost or injured, just her. She headed for the door and suddenly realized she didn't have pockets. Hesitating she mentally began going through the closet for something different before it occurred to her she didn't have anything to *carry* in a pocket - she'd used her one bit of cash bribing Daniel for cheese which, in retrospect, was probably unnecessary.

Humming to herself she almost skipped into the kitchen, skirting to the side when she saw Daniel and Stefan in conversation, neither glancing up at her. Jessica held up one finger, motioning to her phone, and so Maya perched on the edge of the couch, watching out the window.

"Ok," Jessica dropped her phone into her handbag. "I've got an appointment with my linen guy and a private showroom uptown to look at furniture. My construction team will be here in an hour or so. Did you hear that?" She shouted the last part, "My construction team will be here in an hour."

Stefan waved a hand at them and Jessica rolled her eyes. "Alrighty then, you ready? Let's blow this joint."

If asked, Maya would have sworn Stefan teleported. One moment he was in the kitchen with Daniel and the next he was standing in the hallway, blocking the front door. "Whoa, where are you two going?"

"Shopping," Jessica crossed her arms and tapped her foot. "We said that."

"No you're not."

Shoulders slumping Maya took a step backwards, but Jessica didn't. Pulling herself up to her full height she shoved Stefan in the shoulder. "Since when do you get to tell me what to do *Stevie*?"

Maya choked, listening to Stefan's exasperated sigh. "You can do whatever you want, I've never been able to stop you. But Maya can't go. It's not safe."

She'd known, deep down, that it was too good to be true. "It's okay Jess," she patted the woman's arm, "you know what we talked about. I trust you to-"

"Oh, jump in a lake," Jessica snapped, quickly smoothing her expression when she saw Maya's shock. "Not you, this jerk. How many people do you have on security? And did you hear me say *private* showrooms?"

Stefan looked cornered. "I don't think it's-"

"You take a full detail," Daniel's voice came from behind her and Maya gave him a grateful smile. "And one of us goes with you."

"Yes," Stefan pointed at him. "Yes that."

Crossing her arms Jessica raised an eyebrow. "Fine, someone's gotta pay for it all anyway. Who's the sacrifice to a day of shopping with the girls?"

"Diego," they said in unison.

"Fucking Christ," Diego grunted, eyeing the racks and racks of linens, "why can't we just order this shit online?"

Jessica gasped, rounding on him in fury. Maya was fifty-fifty on if it was real or not. "You do not get *color* online. You cannot feel the softness or the quality. What is *wrong* with you?" Muttering to herself she marched into the store, calling out to the owner and greeting them like an old friend.

Maya sidled up to Diego. "I agree, so you know."

He snorted, pulling out his phone. "Then why the hell are we here?"

"Jessica wanted to come," Maya pointed out. "And I was open to any opportunity to go somewhere."

He gave her a sidelong glance, following her into the vast space and collapsing into an armchair near the middle of the store. "Fine."

Hiding a smile Maya caught up with Jessica having a heated discussion about sheer versus opaque curtains and the correct way to install them on floor to ceiling windows. Moving on, she wandered into the bedsheets, reaching out and lightly caressing the displays.

"Is there something you like?"

Maya smiled at the man, pulling her hand back. "Sorry, I'm just looking."

"Don't worry about it," he gave her a warm smile. He was a little older than her, handsome but clean-shaven. She paused - since when had clean-shaven fallen off her list of attractive qualities? "We have these out for exactly what you're doing."

Reaching out again, Maya rubbed the soft cotton between her fingers. "I like this one but the color isn't my favorite."

Quickly he pulled a book from a shelf nearby, opening it to show swatch after swatch of fabric. "Take your pick."

"Wow," Maya turned the pages, "this is so many."

"Everything from chartreuse to aubergine, with a few stops in the middle."

Laughing she flipped towards the lighter end, whites and grays. "I like this, the light gray?"

"Silver," he glanced into the book. "Lovely choice. What size?"

"Big," Maya bit her lip. "I don't actually know how big but Jessica probably does."

"What does Jessica do?" the woman asked, popping up nearby.

"Do you know what size the bed is?"

"Queen."

Maya frowned. "That is *not* a queen size bed."

"We're replacing it," Jessica said offhandedly. "The one you have is ridiculous."

She wasn't wrong. "Okay then, queen."

"Fantastic," the salesman snapped the book shut. "Shall we move on to duvets?"

Two hours later Maya stood next to a mountain of fabric. Terry cloth and cotton and sheer gauzy drapes that Jessica assured her would be perfect for the room. Then the salesman gave a number that made Maya's vision go hazy.

"I'm sorry, how much?"

"Eight thousand, two hundred and eighty."

"For *sheets*?" Maya asked in shock. She'd never seen how much the things her mother had bought cost, and they were definitely nice. But not *eight thousand dollars* nice, surely. "Absolutely not."

"What the fuck is the hold-up," Diego grumbled, handing his card over the pile of merchandise. Maya snatched it just as quickly, tucking it behind her back.

"You are not spending eight grand on sheets."

Diego stared at her in confusion, then looked at Jessica. "Are these the best?"

"Yes."

He held out his hand, looking Maya squarely in the eye without saying a word.

"Diego, it's too much," Maya tried to reason. "They're just *sheets*, the new bed would be-"

"What new bed?" He turned suddenly, glaring at Jessica.

"The other is atrocious," Jessica folded her arms.

"Then make it look pretty, but the bed stays."

Maya was in shock and he easily wrapped an arm around her, pulling her flush against him and plucking the card from her fingers. "*You* could afford this, you know," he said softly, still holding her. "With the amount of money we dropped in your account."

Oh God she could, couldn't she? She hadn't looked lately but she'd done the mistress thing a little over two weeks. So that was at least fifty grand.

Taking advantage of her shock he chucked under her chin with his free hand, stepping away and handing the card over. "Have them couriered."

Maya stayed in that state as they drove to the furniture showroom, sitting in the back of the SUV next to a pouting Jessica who refused to let the bed size go. Maya finally had to tell her she *liked* the big bed before the woman moved on to another topic.

Which was, of course, a new bed frame.

"The padded headboards are very in right now," she explained. "But if you want more traditional I could see a nice farmhouse style in white. Or wrought iron."

"Iron," Diego barked from the front seat, not looking up from his phone.

"Is this her room or yours?" Jessica snapped back.

"It *is* his house," Maya pointed out. "I'm just a guest."

Jessica gave her look, one that clearly stated she thought Maya was wrong, but didn't push it. At the showroom they quickly agreed on simple pieces, a dark blue chair big enough to curl up in. New bedside tables and lamps. Maya quickly grew overwhelmed, taking a step back and watching Jessica whirlwind through the store.

"This is a lot," she pointed out to Diego, leaning on a dining table next to him. "Are you sure about all of this? I mean, even just repainting the room would be significantly better."

He grunted, not taking his eyes off his phone as he typed an email. "It was due for a renovation anyway."

That made sense, and with an interior designer in the family they probably did it fairly often. "Did she design the rest of the house as well?"

"Absolutely not." Jesus, the woman had a sixth sense, popping up as soon as she was mentioned. "That ghastly *American Psycho* vibe is all theirs."

Maya snorted. That was *exactly* what it looked like. She didn't bother to be nearby when the total came up for the furniture, standing as far away as possible and examining a gold and glass vase like it held the secrets of the universe.

"We're done," Diego grunted as he walked by her.

"Oh," Maya sighed, trailing him out. "Are we going back?"

"Yeah we-" Diego turned as he opened the door for her, catching her face and frowning. "Is there somewhere else you wanted to go?"

Maya shrugged noncommittally. "Not really. I was just enjoying being out."

Diego didn't say anything, closing the door and climbing in up front. He gave the driver the name of a restaurant uptown and Maya tried to hold back a surge of hope. "Are we picking up?"

"They have a private room upstairs," Diego responded, "if you're interested."

"I am," she was, perhaps, a little too vehement. Diego smiled, catching her eyes in the side mirror and giving her a wink.

"Well, I know better than to stand between you and your food," he teased as the SUV pulled away from the curb. "A man could lose a hand."

Maya poked her tongue out at the back of his head, quickly turning her face neutral when she caught Jessica's assessing look.

"Interesting," the other woman commented with a raised eyebrow. "Very interesting."

Maya had no idea what she was talking about. None at all.

18

Diego's phone was ringing the moment they got to the restaurant and he waved them on with one hand as he stepped to the side. Jessica strode in as though she owned the place, hardly pausing long enough for Ryan to open the door for her.

"Three, the private room," she told the hostess with a smile.

"I'm sorry that room is-"

"Jessie!" A boisterous laugh cut the woman off and Maya took a step back as the blonde was engulfed in a hug by a rail thin man in his fifties. "Are you here to complain about the bar again?"

"I told you steampunk was going to go out of fashion but *no*, you went all-"

"And who is this?" he cut her off, setting her aside and assessing Maya. She waved and immediately felt stupid for it, holding the hand out instead.

"Maya. I'm-"

"Family," Jessica finished for her, raising an eyebrow and giving the man a pointed look.

"Ah," he nodded sagely, returning her expression. "I see."

See what? Maya didn't ask.

"My dear welcome to *The Sage and Grace*. I am Pietro and you are always welcome here, yes?"

"Uh, yes?" Maya responded hesitantly and felt herself instantly swept into a hug.

"Yes," he agreed, setting her aside and glancing at the reservation book. "Dianne, put the one o'clock in the blue room, they won't know the difference." He turned back to Jessica, taking her hand in his and pressing a kiss to the back. "Promise you will not leave without saying goodbye?"

Jessica nodded and as quick as that, the man was gone. Maya couldn't help but gape. "That was... something."

"I helped him with the remodel a while back, when he bought the place," Jessica said, leaning her weight on one hip as the hostess gathered menus. "I wish he'd *listened* to me more, but you know how men are."

Maya nodded, falling in behind her as they wound their way through the tables towards the back.

"The bar is already outdated, which just means he'll be hiring me again soon. I'd be more upset but at least it's more money and *excuse me*."

Jessica stopped short so abruptly Maya ran into her, falling back a step until a large hand caught her arm. She turned to thank her helper and froze, eyes going wide as his grip on her arm tightened.

"Get your hands *off her*," Jessica snapped.

The voice was painfully familiar. "Maya, are you-?"

"I *said*-" Jessica began, moving to step between them but Maya stopped her.

"It's okay. I- Jessica this is my brother, Nico."

Jessica huffed, crossing her arms and raising an eyebrow. "I see you got all the manners in the family."

Pulling himself to his full height, Nico frowned down at her. "And who the fuck are-"

"Nico this is-" Maya hesitated. Her brother and her had

been inseparable growing up, had trusted each other above all else. But that had been a long time ago, more than enough time for their father to make him into a new man. A man who might have a less than noble reaction if he knew who Jessica was.

"Family," she finally finished.

"You *have* a family," Nico snapped back.

"Since when?" Maya raised an eyebrow. "Where have you been the last fourteen years?"

"Doing my duty. Unlike some people I know what family *actually* is." His eyes darted to Jessica and Maya heard the woman growl.

"Well, maybe that's because he didn't kill your first boyfriend. Did he ever tell *you* your only redeeming feature was between your legs? No?" Maya cocked her head at him, folding her arms.

"It wasn't like that," Nico sighed, running a hand through his hair. "He's all talk - you know how he is."

"Fuck you." Maya's hand flew over her mouth, her eyes going wide. "Now you're making me sound like him."

Nico's eyes narrowed on her, his jaw tightening. "What did they do to you?"

"What?"

"Your hand," he gestured curtly, "have they been hurting you?"

"No," Maya corrected quickly. "This wasn't - Jesus this was *dad*."

"Why do you blame him for everything?"

"*Because everything is his fault,*" Maya felt her voice rising in pitch and made special effort to calm herself down.

"It's not his fault you're a fucking *whore*-"

The punch came out of nowhere, rocking Nico back a step and snapping his head to the side.

"That's *enough*," Jessica stated firmly, stepping up beside

Maya and shaking her wrist out. "I'm all for airing out family drama but you do *not* get to talk to her that way."

Chairs screeched along the tile floor as men rose to their feet but Nico held up a staying hand, rubbing his jaw with the other.

"Solid right hook," he complimented. "Well done." His eyes met Maya's and he sighed. "I'm sorry about... Jesus it's your life."

Jessica herded her away before she could reply, mumbling under her breath about overbearing men and brothers thinking they knew what was best.

"You okay?"

Maya shrugged, staring at her shoes. Jessica turned suddenly, grabbing Maya by both shoulders in the shadows of the back hallway.

"Listen to me, your brother is an asshole."

Maya snorted, trying to smile.

"No, he is. Whatever your past is - I'm sure you made the right decision. And as for the guys," she paused, tilting her head to the side. "I don't know what y'all have going on but I've never seen any of them act the way they do around you."

"What do you mean?"

"Diego went *shopping* - do you know the last time he's done that? Never. Never is the last time. I have a tailor sent to the apartment once a quarter so he doesn't have to. Stefan looks at you like you hung the goddamn stars in the sky and Danny..." she trailed off, suddenly hesitant. "You know he's not... a people person, right?"

Maya couldn't help the full laugh this time. *That* was an understatement.

Jessica smiled. "He's always been like that, he just doesn't *get* things like other people do. But that man called me at six in the goddamn morning and offered me anything I wanted to take care of you today."

Raising a hand, Jessica brushed a strand of hair back from Maya's face. "Brothers are the worst, trust me I know. And when I tell you I'm happy to hand over the three I have to you…" They were both laughing now, Maya's shoulders finally beginning to relax. "There's something going on with you guys, something special. Don't let your idiot brother ruin that."

Maya nodded, "Thank you."

"Of course," Jessica said with a bright smile, then winced. "Now I'm going to go back to the apartment and put ice on my hand. I always forget how much hitting someone *hurts*."

"Oh my God," Maya panicked, reaching out, "are you okay?"

"I'm fine," Jessica waved her off, waggling her eyebrows. "Have a nice *romantic* lunch with Diego."

Blushing, Maya followed her gentle shooing motions up the stairs and into the private room. It was huge, big enough for fifteen people at least. But the large tables had been shoved to the side and a smaller four-top centered in the room in their place.

It was also devoid of people.

Maya cautiously took a step inside, peering around to see if there was a corner someone could be hiding in. There were three menus set out, three glasses of water, three place settings… and not a single person.

"Yeah, Lau, you do that and I'll-" Maya spun just in time to be caught by Diego, frowning as he hung up the phone. "What are you doing?"

"Oh thank goodness, I thought I had the wrong room," Maya breathed a sigh of relief.

"Where's Jessica?"

Biting her lip Maya tried to decide how much to tell him. "You didn't see her?"

"If I did I wouldn't be asking you, now would I?" he

responded with a raised eyebrow.

Stepping back, Maya put her hands on her hips and glared. "No need to be snarky, she only just left, I thought you would have passed her. She, uh, she went back to the apartment."

Diego didn't question it, ushering her towards the table and pulling out a chair for her before settling on the opposite side. A waiter came by within seconds.

"The usual, sir?"

The menus were swept away with Diego's nod. A moment later a glass of whiskey was on the table and he was back on his phone, typing out swift messages and grunting occasionally to himself. Maya frowned - so much for a *romantic* lunch.

It was a pretty view at least. Looking out over the water, there was a harbor not too far off and Maya watched the people on the boats going about their business. The day was crisp, probably even colder out where they were. Rolling the ice in her glass, Maya tried to ignore Diego, imagining what it would be like to be sailing instead. She'd never learned but surely she could pick it up. Just get on a boat and go. Go somewhere.

Anywhere.

A steak appeared on the table, a small salad set down in front of her. Diego finally tossed his phone aside, tapping the edge of his glass and a new drink appeared as if by magic. Maya tried to catch the server's eyes but the man purposefully looked away before backing out of the room. Had he heard the fight she'd had with her brother? God, everyone must have heard it. What must they think of her?

"Can I go back to the apartment?" Maya asked quietly, folding her napkin neatly onto the table by her plate.

"I thought you wanted to go out?" Diego finally looked up, giving her a puzzled frown.

"I did," Maya stared out the window, refusing to meet his

eyes. "But this is… I'd just rather be there."

Diego glared, looking around the space, the view, the table. "What's wrong?"

"Nothing," she assured him, wringing her hands in her lap. "It's beautiful. You don't have to come I can just-"

He shifted chairs, slipping into the one on her left, his hand coming up to rest along the back of hers. "Tell me what you don't like," he ordered.

Maya gave a weak laugh, looking down and consciously trying to stop fidgeting. "I thought you were going to have lunch with me. Not just sit near me while the staff ignores me and-" She met his eyes, giving him a forced bright smile, "But it's silly, I know you have work to be doing and you've already wasted half the day on this. It's fine, really."

Those eyes of his - deep brown with the barest flecks of gold - made her feel pinned, unable to move. His expression didn't give anything away, his gaze flitting over her face, her hands in her lap, the salad in front of her.

"You're right," he pulled his drink closer, turning his chair towards her. "I was being rude." Without asking he reached over, pulling the edge of her chair so it faced him more. "And it wasn't wasted."

"You *enjoyed* shopping for towels?" Maya asked incredulously.

"I *enjoyed* seeing you feel comfortable somewhere," he corrected her. A puzzled look crossed his face. "I don't usually get to make people smile."

"Feels nice doesn't it?" Maya said softly.

He grunted, "Don't get used to it." Maya picked at her salad and Diego frowned. "Do you like the food?"

Maya shrugged, "I didn't order it. It's fine, as far as salads go."

His eyes narrowed, one hand lifting and making a sharp gesture. The waiter was at his side in an instant, on alert for whatever he wanted. "Yes sir?"

"Is there a reason you haven't been seeing to my guest?"

The man blanched, from Maya's angle she could see his knuckles go white behind his back. "We have a standing request that-" he trailed off at the look on Diego's face. Giving him an understanding look she placed a hand on Diego's arm.

"It's fine, I'm sure it was a misunderstanding." She gave the waiter a smile, "I would love to see a menu, or if there's a special you recommend I'll take that."

"We had some lovely snapper come in this morning," the waiter quickly assured her. "Fresh off the boat, the chef is doing wonders with it today."

"I'll take that, and an orange soda if you have one."

The waiter nodded and disappeared before Diego could continue his intimidation campaign. Maya pursed her lips, trying not to laugh at his put upon expression. "Sorry, were you enjoying yourself? I can bring him back if you weren't done glaring at him."

Diego laughed, taking a long drink and pushing his steak to the side. Maya frowned at him in concern, "Don't wait for me, your lunch will get cold."

He turned to her with a shrug, his full attention on her for the first time as an orange soda appeared by her elbow. She took a sip to avoid his assessing gaze. She'd asked for his attention, now she didn't know what to do with it.

"How's the business plan going?"

Maya lit up, turning to him and waving a hand. "Great! I've got some questions I'll need to ask a tax lawyer about but it looks really good."

"Tell me about it," he leaned back, resting his arm on the back of her chair.

"What, now?" Maya looked around. "I don't have my notes."

"Do you need them?" he raised an eyebrow.

Thinking about it Maya gave a small shake of her head. "No, I don't think so. But... I made this whole presentation, with pictures and everything."

Diego laughed, a warm, rich sound that Maya felt to her toes. "I promise I'll look at it too, if you want, but pitch me now."

Maya did. Starting with an overview of what would need to be done to look like a legitimate company, and going through pros and cons of using it.

"You would only really need two people, one if the figurehead is also the accountant." Maya held up her hand, two fingers extended. "The great thing about the industry is it's one person managing and then coordinating the 'contracted' people - in this case anyone you want to send money to. No one would bat an eye at a sole proprietor handling millions of dollars because it's flowing through them to an end client."

"Do you have an idea of who that would be?" Diego drummed his fingers on her chair.

"Well, Stefan says he knows an accountant so it just depends on how authentic you want it to seem."

"What about you?"

Maya reeled back. "What?"

Diego looked as calm as ever, taking a sip of his drink. "We set you up as the CEO, founder, whatever it is - and you take a percentage of whatever flows through."

Maya was dumbstruck, mouth gaping open. "That's very generous but-"

"Stop telling me not to do things," Diego said, giving her a playful growl. "It was your idea, and it's a good one. If it works, it's your take for getting it set up for us."

Maya blinked, barely noticing the waiter's return. "What would that look like?"

"Does five percent sound reasonable?" Diego asked, leaning in to study her meal - as if it needed his approval.

Maya did some quick math. They'd talked about moving millions of dollars through, tens of millions even. That'd be a few hundred grand a year easily. But she wasn't her father's daughter for nothing. "Ten."

Diego grinned, pointing his fork at her as he pulled his now cold steak closer. "You went from 'oh nothing' to 'ten percent' very fast. Seven."

Maya shook her head. "Ten."

He gave a mock frown. "I don't think you understand how negotiations work, princess."

"Ten," Maya reiterated. "Ten and I'll set it up for you under my mother's maiden name and info so if it's ever investigated it'll come down on the Alvani's and not you."

The booming laugh that left him echoed in the room, making Maya's eyes shine with joy. Face alight with amusement he gave her a nod. "Ten percent and I'll consider it a bargain for that. Deal." He stuck his hand out and Maya took it, expecting him to shake it. Instead he brought it to his lips, his goatee tickling her skin as he brushed a kiss over her knuckles. "What an absolute idiot he was to drive you away."

Maya's smile froze on her face, eyes suddenly blinking back tears. Diego saw, of course he did. He saw everything. "What is it?" She shook her head and he pulled her closer, pressing his free hand against the side of her neck. "Tell me."

"It's nothing," she forced a carefree smile.

"Tell me or I'll kiss you."

"Is that supposed to make me want to tell you?" Maya blurted out. Wait, had she really just said that? Diego's eyes grew hot, his lips parting as he leaned further into her. She was blushing, her hand clutching his fingers and he gently soothed his thumb over the back as his mouth came down on hers.

It was as direct as he was, tongue plunging inside, a shocking counterpoint to how gentle his hands were on her. Teeth nipping at her lips, a low hum of approval when she did the same. He took and she gave, sinking into the haze of feelings his mouth was creating. He was different from the others, and she had to shove aside the roll of shame as her brother's earlier words echoed in her mind.

She'd been kissing Stefan *this morning* and thinking it was the best thing that had happened to her. Now Diego was making her rethink that.

"Should have had my tongue in you that first day," his voice rumbled over her. "Your mouth, your cunt, fuck I bet you taste good all over."

Maya moaned against him. This was *wrong*. But then why did it make her so *hot*?

"Forget lunch," his tongue slid down her neck, teeth nipping at the neck of her sweater. "Come back to the apartment and let me eat you out, fuck you with my fingers."

If he had been even a hair less crude with his words Maya would have said yes. Would have fallen into his arms and let all her other worries be damned. She was so pent up she was *aching* with it. But the lewd picture he painted made her brain *skritch*. Her eyes flew open and she pushed his shoulders.

"I think that's a bad idea."

"What's stopping you?" His teeth were on her ear and there was no way he expected her to have a coherent thought while he was doing that was there? "You want me and I fucking want you, so what's the problem?"

"I don't want to disappoint anybody," Maya mumbled into his shirt.

"Disappoint who?"

"Daniel. Stefan. Maybe me. Someone is going to get hurt, no matter what happens, aren't they?"

"There's no reason someone has to," he countered, rubbing

his lips along her neck. "We're big boys, we know how to share."

Shock coursed through Maya, she'd never really considered it. "You would?"

"I could fuck you in the car on the way home," Diego growled, "and either of them would jump at the chance to have you when we get back."

Maya shivered. "But what kind of girl would that make me?"

"A lucky one."

It was so simple for him wasn't it? He wanted something and he took it - he never considered the morality of it. Or what people might think. Maya had struggled for years to learn what it meant to not be that way - to have to function in a society where people had to think about the consequences of their actions. Her upbringing hadn't exactly prepared her either - a fact that became apparent the first time she'd tried to do something for herself.

What if that was what happened here? If she took what she wanted and they hated her for it?

You have to go eventually anyway, she told herself. *This isn't permanent.*

"I lost you," his voice was warm on her cheek. "Where did you go off to?"

"Just thinking." She pulled away from him, petting his cheek.

"Oh?" His eyes lit up, "Anything fun?"

Laughing she pushed lightly at him, grateful when he settled back into his chair. She couldn't think straight when he was that close. "Just trying to figure you guys out. And me."

Diego chuckled, slicing into his lunch. "We're simple men. We see a pretty girl and we want her." He frowned, not at her, thinking. "It also turns out you're not too bad to have around.

Why not live a little while you're here?"

Why not, indeed.

Maya steered the conversation to more quiet waters. Proud of herself for managing to not crawl into his lap while they finished their meal. It was tempting, it was *so* tempting, but she refrained, wiping her mouth with the napkin as their plates were carted away. "Can I buy?"

Diego frowned at her, "That's not necessary."

"I know it's not," she laid a hand on his arm, "but you've been so nice it's the least I can do. And like you said, I do have *some* money now." She gave him a wide smile and his lips twitched in response.

"How do you think you're going to pay?"

She hadn't thought about that. It was true she had a flush bank account, but the money might as well be on the moon for all the good it did her in that moment.

"I could go to a bank branch nearby and-"

Rolling his eyes, Diego waved her off. "They'll add it to my tab."

"But-"

Leaning in he was so close she could feel his breath on her lips. "How about you get it next time?"

"Next time?"

He nodded, not pulling away. Her blood thrummed in her chest, her breath speeding up to small, needy pants. With one hand he tilted her chin up, "Yeah princess. Next time."

19

Maya had a problem.

Well, not a problem exactly. Maya had a *conundrum*.

Sitting in the middle of the bed, she tried to sort through her thoughts. The new room was beautiful, shades of blue and gray, swirls of brass and bright yellow dotted about. True to her word, Jessica had shifted things around, adding a low table and a comfortable chair near a corner. And of course the hanging chair.

The room felt brighter, she couldn't even tell where some of the previous things had gone - the brackets for the chains had disappeared under spackle and a new coat of paint. It was nice, and it made her want to spend time there. Someone had moved the bouquet of sunflowers into the room, both it and the hanging vines in the bathroom making it feel lived in rather than transient.

She liked it a lot, it felt like home.

That was the source of her conundrum.

She wanted to stay. She liked it here, liked them. But she knew this wasn't permanent. Whatever this was it was going to end someday, probably soon. She wasn't injured any longer, they had already done whatever it was they'd hired her to distract her father for. There wasn't really any reason for her to still be there, other than they hadn't asked her to leave.

If she took the jump, if she gave in to what they were each tempting her to do, would that be the end of everything? She worried it would. That at this point it was the only thing that kept her there. Their desire. Once it was sated, or they moved on, she would have to too.

But as she looked around the room it made her think maybe they wouldn't. Maybe they liked her there as much as she liked being there. Yeah, there was the whole sex thing but she got the impression they liked her beyond that. At least, Stefan and Daniel did. And after yesterday, she thought maybe Diego did too. A little. She was about to become a *business partner* with them.

Was whatever was there enough to keep her?

And if it wasn't - why would she want to draw this out?

Congratulations on turning thirty, here's your moral quandary.

Crawling off the bed, smiling at the new bench that she knew for a fact no one had ever had sex on, Maya headed to the shower. Hot water and a mug of tea would help her day. And she would cook something, make her favorites. That would be a nice change from... was it Wednesday? A nice change from dumplings.

And maybe over dinner she would talk to them. Figure out what the future looked like. It would be good to *know* instead of *worry*.

Resolved and dressed she went to the kitchen to look through the surprisingly complex spice rack. The men didn't keep bread but they had star anise. She was sure in some world it made sense.

"Hey Daniel," she greeted him as she entered, watching from the corner of her eye as he worked on a tablet. He didn't answer but she didn't expect one, by now used to his strange interactions. Instead she set a bottle of his morning juice blend in front of him, loosening the top and sliding it near his elbow.

He did glance up then, giving her a curt nod and swiping the tablet to a blank screen.

"Will you guys be home tonight?" she asked as Daniel grabbed the bottle.

"Should be," he replied absently, patting his pockets.

"Ok, I was going to make dinner and wanted to talk to you all. Let me know if you'll be late?"

He nodded, finding whatever he was looking for and striding out the front door without a goodbye. She watched him leave, admiring his backside in the gray trousers he wore. She'd feel bad about objectifying him but all things considered she felt it was earned.

Snickering to herself she started opening cabinets, jotting a shopping list down as she failed to find ninety percent of what she would need. Opening the front door she smiled at a man she didn't recognize. "Hi, I'm-"

"Ms. Alvani," he nodded at her. "Was there something you needed?"

She held the paper out, "Some groceries, for tonight. Can that be done? And I'd prefer it if they didn't know. I want to surprise them."

There was no need to say who 'they' were, and the man didn't ask. Taking the paper he glanced at it and nodded. "I can get one of the couriers on it, do you want it now?"

Pursing her lips Maya shook her head. "No, how about six or so?"

He gave her a sharp nod. "Yes ma'am."

The food arrived at six on the dot, someone knocking loudly until she answered the door with a perplexed look. "Since when did people start knocking?"

"Orders, Ms. Alvani," Ryan responded, ducking inside.

"Whenever you're here alone."

"Oh," she gestured for him to set the bags on the island, wondering if she was supposed to tip him. Maybe she was supposed to tip him all the time. He left with just a nod and a smile, so probably not.

She started with the roast, setting the clock and ensuring it would heat up in time. Once that was safely in the oven she started cutting cheeses and meat, laying them out carefully on wooden cutting boards then wrapping them in plastic wrap and tucking them into the fridge. She set the table, arranging flowers on one end.

There wasn't much else she could do until they got back, which usually wasn't til around eight. That left her plenty of time to get ready. Especially since she was going to wear the dress. The Dress. Capital letters. The shimmery blue one from the first dinner. Maya smoothed a hand down the fabric, felt it slip under her fingertips like water. Her choices were the casual loungewear Daniel had bought or lingerie, and she was *not* going to show in the lingerie. No matter *what* discussion they had tonight. But the dress - they liked it, had admired her in it, and the way they looked at her made her feel beautiful. Powerful even.

But she didn't shave *everywhere* this time. She didn't like it and if something that silly ended up being a dealbreaker so be it.

Maybe she should shave.

No, she shook her head sharply, smoothing lotion onto her legs. Her resolve was firm, if they wanted her they were going to get *her*. Not some woman they had dreamed up.

By eight she was a nervous wreck, doing circuits in the kitchen between the table and the oven, boiling potatoes and triple checking everything looked good. Keeping an eye on the timer and wishing she hadn't decided to wear heels.

At nine she took the cheesecake out of the fridge, telling

herself it would be better closer to room temperature. The roast she left in the oven, hoping it would keep warm and not give everyone food poisoning. Her heels sat neatly by the terrace door.

At ten she sliced the roast onto a platter, setting it carefully between the potatoes and the cheeses. She played with the silverware, considering if maybe the living room would be more comfortable. Taking a chance she opened the front door, but the man on the landing didn't have any messages for her.

At eleven she gave in, finally acknowledging that they weren't coming. Sinking into a chair she let her chin settle into the palm of her hand. Absently she stuck a fork into the cheesecake, marring the perfect circle and slipping a bite between her lips. The tangy sweetness burst on her tongue but it didn't taste as good as it should.

Pulling the wine to her side of the table she popped the cork, hesitating before pouring a small glass. The last thing she wanted was to be a sloppy drunk again when they showed. *If* they ever showed. She knew from experience that sometimes they could be out all night, or come in at ungodly hours of the morning.

Should she wait up?

Taking the glass she went out onto the terrace, hoping the night air would keep her from crying. What was the point in spending all day building herself up if she was just going to cry at the slightest setback. Maybe it wasn't that they forgot, maybe something had happened to them. She'd never forgive herself if she was moping while they were hurt.

Then again, if they were surely the guard on the door would know. Would have told her.

It was a warm summer night, the breeze stroking over her face and lifting her hair. She was halfway to a perfume commercial, if someone were around to see it. Taking a sip of the wine she stared out over the city, trying to decide if it was worse for them to be hurt or for them to hurt her.

Yeah, she was definitely going to cry. A block away a church chimed the hour. All twelve bells fading into silence before she let herself give up. She should go to bed, could ask tomorrow what had happened. Rearrange the dates and maybe try again.

"What are you all dressed up for?"

Stefan's voice pulled her from her thoughts. Trying to identify the emotion coursing through her she pulled herself up straighter, willing the tears to stay at bay just a little longer. "Are you all okay?"

"Yeah, why wouldn't we be?"

She set the empty glass down, taking a last look at the sky before turning around. He was leaning against the open terrace door, arms crossed as he gave her a once over. His eyebrows raised in appreciation, his tongue dragging along his lower lip.

"I thought you'd be back tonight," she said quietly.

A crease formed between his brows. "We had some business come up."

She nodded, crossing to the door and scooping her heels up. The smell of cigars and whiskey drifted off of him and she didn't wait for his response, sliding past him and back into the apartment. Daniel was settled at the table, picking through the charcuterie board while Diego stood with his hands resting on the back of one of the chairs.

"What's all this?" he asked, gesturing at the spread.

Maya paused before answering, dragging the bottle of wine towards her and lifting it lightly between her fingertips. "Dinner."

"What's the occasion?" Daniel rolled a piece of meat around a fig and popped it in his mouth.

"It's my birthday." From behind her she heard Stefan curse, saw the way Daniel stopped his perusal of the food to look at her. She ignored them, drifting towards her room. "Good night."

"Wait," Diego caught her arm and she barely glanced down, halting near him and staring off into the kitchen. "You should have said something."

"I did." Eyes ahead she swallowed hard. "I asked if you'd be home. I said," tears caught on the edge of her voice and she took a steadying breath. All that courage she had summoned earlier for nothing. "I said I had something planned."

Diego tried to turn her but she resisted. "You didn't say it to me."

"It was me." Daniel sounded pained. "Fuck, she asked… *fuck*."

"Please let me go," she whispered. Diego gently pulled the wine from her grip, giving up on making her turn and stepping in front of her instead. There was something dark in his gaze, something she wasn't certain she'd seen before.

"You expected us back earlier?"

She nodded.

"And you did all this for us?" he motioned at the table.

She sniffled softly, "And for me. I wanted to celebrate."

His hand slipped under the strap of her dress, the backs of fingers softly stroking her skin. "I thought you hated this dress."

"I do."

Diego hummed thoughtfully. "And yet, you're wearing it."

Maya didn't know what to say to that.

"You got all dolled up." He was close, so close she could feel the warm rush of his breath and she wished she'd had more than a glass of wine. Wished she'd had the whole bottle so she wouldn't be this mess of emotions. She wanted to cry. She wanted to run. She wanted to kiss him. She wanted to press her face against his neck and breathe him in.

"For us?" Stefan asked from behind her and she nodded before she realized what she was doing.

"Really?" Was that Daniel? She could barely tell. It was getting hot, a small bead of sweat working its way down the back of her neck and making her shiver.

"Why would you get dressed up for us?" Diego was focused, relentless as he caged her in with his body. She could move - a step almost any direction would take her away from him.

But she didn't want to move. Whatever was happening had been building since she first woke up in this apartment. Something dark and a little bit sinful. Something she refused to put a name to.

"Were you hoping for a birthday gift, kitten?" Daniel's voice was close, they were all close. Wasn't this what she had wanted? Their attention on her? Diego made a sharp tsk-ing noise but Maya was already nodding.

The air in the room came alive, crackling with tension. Someone, it must be Stefan, brushed the hair off the nape of her neck and laid a gentle, hesitant kiss at the top of her spine.

"How much have you had to drink sweetheart?" Stefan's voice caressed her ear and she bit her lip to stop herself from moaning.

"Just a glass."

"Anything else tonight?" Daniel stood behind Diego, his gaze steady behind his glasses.

"No."

Diego reached out and tilted her chin up, brushing his thumb along her lower lip. "Do you want us?" Without taking her eyes off his she flicked her tongue along his finger, nipping the skin. His eyes grew darker, his jaw twitching. "*All* of us?"

She threw her plans to the wind. Who cared if they kicked

her out afterwards, if this was the end of her time with them. She wanted this, wanted them, wanted to make this night something to remember.

"*Yes.*"

Diego tasted like scotch, his tongue rolling inside her mouth when he covered her lips with his. His hands cupped her face, fingers digging into the hair behind her ears. She couldn't stop the moan this time, or the way she leaned into him. But Stefan's hands stopped her; Stefan's hands spanning her waist and pulling her into his chest. He licked along her shoulder, sliding up her neck. Without warning he bit down, making her cry out and arch further into him.

"I think Daniel owes you an apology," Diego nuzzled her cheek, turning her head so she was looking at the other man, "don't you?"

Daniel's hands were curled into fists at his sides, his chest heaving beneath his black polo as he watched her squirm between his partners. His eyes followed Diego's fingers as the man dipped inside the V of her dress.

"Would you like that princess?" Diego teased, palming her breast and rolling her nipple between his fingers. Jolts of pleasure shot through her and she barely felt Stefan grabbing her skirt in great fistfuls, hiking it up to her waist. "Want Daniel to make it all better?"

Stefan groaned when his questing fingers realized she was bare beneath the dress. Maya groaned with him, spreading her legs wider so he could slip between them with the gentlest touch. "If he doesn't I will," he promised her.

Daniel was there, jerking her head to the side and kissing her roughly. Diego dropped away, pushing the strap of the dress off her shoulder and then his mouth was on her and God they were *everywhere*. Stefan's hot breath panted against her neck while he swirled his fingers through her slick. Diego's teeth nipped at her nipple. And Daniel - Daniel kissed like he was going to swallow her whole. Those long fingers of his gripping her dress so hard she heard it rip.

They broke away at once, looking down at her. Slowly, Daniel adjusted the fabric in his hands and pulled, tearing it wide and then dropping it to the floor. It should have been *cold* - but they were warm around her, heat radiating off of them. With shaky hands she tried to cover herself but Daniel and Diego caught one each, gripping her wrists and holding them away from her body.

"Don't," Diego growled, releasing her and trailing his fingers down her chest. "Let us see."

It would have been embarrassing, it *should* have been embarrassing. But Stefan was still there - still stroking her in confident, sure touches - and Maya couldn't find it in her to be embarrassed.

The sound of dishes hitting the ground nearly snapped her out of her daze, Daniel sweeping an arm across the table and then turning, jerking her towards him and settling her up onto the cool glass.

"Lay down, spread your legs for me," he grunted, just shy of an order, as he sank into one of the dining chairs. She did as she was told, biting her lip and trying to focus on him and not the two men circling her like sharks.

Daniel jerked her hips towards him, settling her legs over his shoulders. "I can see how wet you are, kitten," he moaned, drawing a thumb up her thigh to her slit. He took a deep breath, eyes catching hers over the rim of his glasses. With one hand he reached up, taking her by the wrist and drawing it down. "Can you feel it baby?"

She could. Lord she *could*. He guided her fingers between her thighs, coating them in her own wetness before leaning forward and taking them in his mouth. The curl of his tongue sent shocks through her, back arching straight into Diego's hands.

"Look at you pretty girl," Diego's voice flowed over her, nose running under her breast. "Spread out like a meal just for us."

With deliberate care Daniel took his glasses off, setting them to the side. Stefan turned her face towards his and kissed her just as Daniel released her hand, dipping down to lick every inch of her. Everything was wet, warm - Daniel sliding his tongue inside her with the same rhythm that Stefan was in her mouth. Diego's lips closing around her fingers with a low moan.

"You taste good," he murmured, tongue sliding down to the web of her fingers and making her shudder. "We could have been doing this for weeks."

She reached for his belt but he caught her, pressing a kiss to her knuckles. "It's *your* birthday, let us show you a good time."

Settling back to the table she did, clutching Diego's head as he pulled her nipple between his teeth. The other tangled in Stefan's hair while she made small whimpers and moans against his lips.

And Daniel, Daniel was working her like it was his *job*. Slipping his fingers deep inside her and sucking against her clit in soft pulses of his lips. It was too much. It wasn't enough. She was going to explode, sink into a puddle on the table. Stefan left her mouth to trail hot kisses down her chest and she cried out at the loss, eyes refusing to focus when Diego took his place, his hands cupping her face.

"Look at me Maya," he growled and she tried, she really did. "Look at me."

Taking a shuddering breath, Maya focused on him, feeling the world dissolve into pure light and pleasure. Each pulse of her heart sending sensation to her fingertips.

"There's my girl," he purred. "Come for us, princess."

She couldn't have stopped it if she wanted to, back arching

off the table and her mouth falling open in a silent scream. Dimly she was aware of Daniel's fingers digging deep into the meat of her, her thighs closing around his head. Could he breathe? Could she make herself relax enough to let him go? Stefan whispered words into her ear she didn't understand, the deep treble of his voice sinking down into her bones.

Diego was petting her, running his hands down her body in long strokes, shushing her quietly. "It's okay. I've got you. Fuck look at you."

Humming between her thighs, Daniel continued to stroke his tongue along her folds, gentle caresses that avoided the most sensitive parts, sending shivers through her body. His hands massaged her thighs, turning intermittently to brush kisses there as well.

"Oh my *God*," Maya breathed, barely able to string coherent thought together.

Daniel jerked her upright abruptly, closing his hands around her neck and pulling her face to his. He tasted like her, God he *smelled* like her. He was covered in her, smearing her own slick across her mouth while his tongue thrust inside. He let her face go, wrapping his hands around her hips and pulling her into his lap, pressing his hardness to her center.

"You feel that kitten?" he groaned into her mouth. "Feel how hard I am for you?"

Diego pressed to her back, the bulge of him equally insistent. "What do you want?"

"More," she gasped, reaching an arm behind her while she pressed her forehead to Daniel. "I want more."

The low laughter that rolled through the room should have been frightening, carrying a dark promise with it. She couldn't place the voice that said, "That can be arranged."

20

It was anyone's guess how they got to the bedroom. Maya was pulling clothes, meeting kisses, feeling hands stroke her body. She was honestly surprised they made it that far at all, stumbling into the foot of the bed as Stefan caught her around the waist, pressing his front to her back. One hand slipped down and she spread her legs so he could slip between, shivering when he groaned in her ear.

"You're so fucking wet." He brushed his nose against her shoulder and her breath caught on a soft inhale. "Daniel got you all worked up for us, didn't he?"

She nodded, eyes meeting the man in question, his chest heaving as he watched her. Holding one hand out she beckoned him closer, smiling when he interlocked his fingers with hers. His shirt was hanging off one shoulder, as far as Maya had managed to get it, a fact he seemed oblivious to.

"Think you can come again?" Stefan asked, almost conversationally. Before Maya could respond he pressed his fingers inside of her, making her see stars. "Mmm, maybe we should find you something to come on? A nice cock to fill you up?"

Cock.

Maya wasn't a fan of the word, it felt so *dirty*. Even thinking it felt like an added layer of sin to what they were doing - which was saying a lot, all things considered. She was about to have sex - *fuck* - three men and the thought of saying a *word* was what was leaving her blushing.

Daniel seemed to have ideas about what exactly should fill her up, letting her hand go so he could roughly shrug out of his shirt and quickly pull his pants off. He wasn't as lean as the other two, more stocky. But his thick thighs made her mouth water and she didn't hesitate when Stefan urged her towards him.

Maya took Daniel's face in her hands, tilting his face up to kiss her while he settled onto the bench. She made to straddle his hips but he turned her around, scooting backwards until he was on the bed and settling her into his lap. His hands found her breasts, plucking at her nipples and she ground herself down on him, both of them groaning at the delicious friction.

"Protection?" Maya gasped. Daniel dropped his forehead to her shoulder and groaned.

"Fuck, yes, that." She saw his hand appear in her peripheral vision, making grabby motions and a box fell onto the bed, foil squares spilling out of it.

"We must be out of the extra small ones," Diego snarked, moving into her line of sight. He was naked, gloriously so.

"Go fuck yourself," Daniel snapped back, snatching at a condom and flinging the empty box in his direction.

Diego ignored the projectile, settling a knee onto the bench and leaning into Maya's space. "More?"

She nodded and he kissed her fiercely, nipping at her lower lip before rising, settling his foot on the other side of her legs, spread open across Daniel's thighs, and rising to stand on the bench. Maya had a moment of confusion before his thick length came into view, bobbing in front of her face.

Oh. That is definitely a cock.

She must have made a noise because Diego chuckled, curling a hand around the back of her neck and pulling her forward, his other hand guiding until her mouth pressed to the head of him. Her lips parted willingly, licking the salty slip of precum, giving a pleased hum as she took him into her mouth.

"Ah *fuck*, Maya," Diego groaned, sinking both hands into her hair, "*fuck*."

Beneath her, Daniel was pressing her upwards, positioning her up and then *down* and she groaned as inch after inch of his thick length pushed inside her.

"Jesus fucking *Christ*," he growled, hands kneading the thick flesh at her waist.

"Listen to that," Stefan was at her side, chin resting on her shoulder while he whispered in her ear. "They can't even find words for how good you feel."

Maya laughed, choking slightly when Diego took the opportunity to push forward. Her hand flew to his hips, trying to control his rough movements. She wrapped her fingers around the base of him, using her hand to stroke what she couldn't fit in her mouth.

"You look real hot sucking cock, baby," Stefan groaned.

It was Diego's turn to laugh, shifting one hand to cup her jaw and tilt her face up. "Stefan always was a bit of a perv, princess. Ignore him."

Diego was one to talk, deep in her mouth while Daniel rocked beneath her. She felt full, *surrounded*. Daniel's fingers clutched her ass, his feet planted flat to the bench and suddenly he *thrust* up and she cried out, clenching down and hearing him swear.

"Oh yeah, baby, is that good?" Stefan was going to be the death of her, cooing in her ear and playing with her nipple. "Do it again."

Whether it was his own idea or not, Daniel *fucked* into her and she saw stars, sucking on Diego's cock harder. He grunted, rocking forward until he was brushing the back of her throat with every thrust. Maya struggled to find a rhythm, trying to take them both at once. It was Stefan who eventually helped, gripping the back of her neck and her waist in each hand and guiding her into a slow undulation that had all three of them gasping.

Stefan chuckled to himself, nuzzling her shoulder, "Next time we should film this."

Next time. Maya moaned at the thought, feeling the response of the two men inside of her. Daniel had collapsed back into the sheets, straining against her and mumbling something about her ass.

"Get her off for me, Stefan," he growled. "I've, *fuck*, got my hands full."

Stefan chuckled, swatting her flank and making her yelp. Diego shivered and wrapped her hair into his fist, "You make such pretty noises when you come. Think they'll sound the same with my cock stuffed down your throat?" Maya nodded, staring up into his face, watching his smirk fade into something more tender. "That's our girl."

"You gonna come again for us?" Stefan murmured into her ear, his chest pressed to her side. His cheek scratched against hers, his nose nuzzling into her hairline. But his hand, his hand slipped down to rub firm, tight circles on her clit and she saw stars.

"Oh *God*," she groaned, or at least tried to, the words a garbled mess around Diego.

It was too much, every muscle of her body tightening, her eyes rolling back into her head. It wasn't just how she was being touched, how she was being pleasured. It was the way Daniel's hands smoothed up and down her spine, stroking her almost reverently. It was the tenderness in Diego's eyes as he pushed a strand of hair back from her face. And it was the whispered, "That's a good girl," from Stefan when she began to shake and moan and her eyes rolled back in her head and she came.

Fuck did she come.

The world became an explosion of light and color. Someone was talking to her, hands gripping and pulling at her, but she had no idea who because she was having an out of body experience and how did that even *happen*? Her muscles twitched, her breath coming in shattered gasps. She was floating, no falling, no... hands caught her - a warm body was pressed to hers and she clung to it while her whole world came apart.

Maya dimly heard someone else crying out, a gasp and a clench against her skin and her body rocking with the movement of theirs. A part of her mind recognized it as Daniel, coming underneath her with a strangled shout. But she couldn't worry about that, just added the small surge of joy the thought gave her to the overwhelming pleasure that was threatening to undo her.

"You still with us?" Maya shook her head swiftly and basked in the husky chuckle that followed. "You nearly bit Diego's dick off."

Her eyes flew open and she lifted her eyes to find Diego but he was sitting next to her on the bench, idly moving his hand along his length and giving her a wane grin.

"M'sorry," she slurred, reaching out to him and Stefan let her go. She fell into Diego's arms, nuzzling under his chin in apology.

"It's fine," he grunted, re-situating her, "it was fucking hot until I got worried you were about to choke."

She shivered and he shifted her weight. A small gasp left her when Daniel slipped from between her thighs and she gathered enough energy to bring her knees under her, leaning her weight against Diego's shoulder and looking down at the blissed out man stretched across the bed.

"You okay?"

"I'm fucking *phenomenal*," Daniel moaned, stacking his hands behind his head. "*Fuck*, I don't think I got a drop left in me."

"He's always been a bit of a one trick pony," Diego murmured in her ear, running a hand down her thigh. Daniel glared back and she reached her hand out, watching as he captured it and pressed a kiss to her knuckles. She opened her mouth to reassure him but the slide of two long, thick fingers into her made her head spin.

"Ready for me, princess?"

Nodding, Maya let Diego move her around, leaning over and settling her hands on the bed while he took his place behind her. Lifting her hips so her back arched and his knees settled between hers. A sharp *slap* and she yelped, throwing a glare over her shoulder. Diego grinned, sweeping a condom up in one hand and winking at her.

"You can't blame me," he gripped the cheek, flesh spilling out around his fingers. "This ass *deserves* to be spanked."

Maya wasn't sure how she felt about that, her mind whirling suddenly off into insecurities about her body. Were her thighs jiggling while he touched her? If they were he didn't seem to notice, stroking his hands along her skin in long, reverent motions.

"Promise not to bite?" Stefan asked, laying down next to her, a wide grin splitting his face.

Letting go of her worries she nodded, leaning in to kiss him as Diego sank into her in one smooth thrust. He felt different than Daniel, hitting something further inside her that made her vision go white. Stefan shifted his body until he was partially under her, stroking his fingers on her cheek as he watched her.

"Maya?"

"What?" Her head was spinning, her hips rocking back automatically to meet Diego.

"No biting?"

Laughing softly Maya leaned down and licked along Stefan's hip bone, nipping softly at the skin. "I thought you *liked* the biting."

He groaned, sinking his hands into her hair. "Biting is good, just not my cock."

Cock. Maya could grow to like that word.

Opening her mouth, Maya pulled the head of Stefan's cock into her mouth, sucking lightly before moving down his length until she felt she might choke. He groaned beneath her, holding her head tightly but not trying to guide her as Diego had, just letting her know he was there.

As if she could forget.

Diego took her in hard, fast strokes, one hand pressing down on her back and the other gripping her hip. It felt amazing and Maya moaned, curling her tongue around Stefan's cock. He gasped in return, hips jutting upwards and Maya reared back, taking Diego deeper. It was a dance, a ballet of motion, bodies moving in such harmony that she didn't notice Daniel shift closer until his fingers delved through the patch of curls between her legs and he gave her a smirk when her eyes flew to meet his.

"What's the point of having this pretty little pussy if we're not going to make you come all night?" he asked in all seriousness, fingers slipping through her slick to nudge against her clit. She was too sensitive, her mind rebelling at the thought that she had another orgasm in her. But her body was on board, the sharp sensations quickly morphing into waves of pleasure.

She sucked on Stefan hard, holding him down with one hand when he tried to arch off the bed. Drops of precum were quickly turning into small spurts, his grunts telling her he had to be close.

"Gonna come," he gasped. She nodded, not letting him go, licking and sucking and taking him so deep he brushed the back of her throat. Of course he came then, flooding her mouth while she coughed and reared back. His eyes were closed in bliss, his hands holding her still while warm, sticky liquid hit her cheek. "Jesus *fuck*," he groaned.

Diego pulled her back harshly, thighs slapping against the back of hers. "Give us one more, princess. One for each of us."

Daniel's fingers were nimble, strumming her body like he knew every twitch and shudder. Maya propped her hands on each side of Stefan's hips and tilted her head back, squeezing her eyes shut as her muscles bore down so hard Diego cursed.

"Oh *God*," she whined. "Please, I *can't*-"

"You can," Daniel reassured her, using his free hand to cup her chin, not seeming to care about the mess that was on her face. "You can and you *will*."

Fuck him for always being right. Maya arched her back and screamed, Diego's hips snapping in irregular rhythm as he groaned behind her. Her skin vibrated, her brain a fuzzy mess. Tears sprang to her eyes and someone wiped them away just as quickly. The world shifted around her and she collapsed, feeling someone catch her and lay her down on the soft duvet. Stefan was about as much use as she was, cuddled behind her and holding on to her for dear life.

Something touched her cheek and Maya opened one eye to see Diego, shirt in hand, gently wiping her face with a fond smile.

"You got a little something…"

She giggled and took his wrist, pressing a kiss to the inside. His muscles jerked beneath her touch and his face shifted to something she couldn't recognize. Just as quickly it was gone, replaced by a teasing wink, his wrist snatched back so quickly she didn't have time to react.

"Happy Birthday Maya," he told her softly, shifting off the bed and crossing out of her sight. She watched through one cracked eyelid as he gathered an armful of clothes, balling them in his fist as he left. A blanket fell over her and Maya looked up at Daniel, holding a hand out and hoping he would take it.

"Stay."

She could barely focus on his face, unable to identify the emotions that played across it before he gripped her fingers and pressed a kiss to them.

"Stefan has you."

"But I want you." Behind her Stefan stirred and she snuggled back towards him in silent apology. "Both. I want you both to stay."

"Get in the bed asshole," Stefan grumbled and Maya smiled. Daniel huffed an exasperated laugh and then he was there, his naked chest becoming her perfect pillow.

"I can hear your heart beat," she mumbled into his skin, settling her palm over the steadily thumping organ.

"Didn't know I had one."

"Mmhmm," she assured him.

"Go to sleep you two, or roll over and let me fuck you properly," Stefan grumbled.

"Always knew you had a hard on for me," Daniel snickered.

"I wasn't talking to you."

Maya giggled, curling more firmly into both Daniel and Stefan. "Sleep now. Maybe tomorrow."

If she didn't know better, she'd have thought that Daniel's heart skipped a beat.

21

It wasn't surprising she woke up alone. She'd been shocked that Stefan and Daniel had stayed at all, assuming they'd slip away immediately like Diego had. They were who they were and one night of mind-blowing sexual activities wasn't going to change that.

But it was still a little disappointing.

Maya stretched, instantly regretting it as muscles she wasn't aware she had screamed in protest. What had they done that the back of her *bicep* hurt? She was afraid to go see how her skin looked, if she had less than a dozen marks she'd be surprised.

It was nearly two dozen. That she could find.

"Oh good you're-"

Maya screeched, jerking the sheets up and scrambling for her knife. She stopped when she saw Stefan, towel wrapped low on his hips, raising an eyebrow at her like she'd lost her mind. "You done?"

"You scared the bejeezus out of me," Maya pressed a hand to her chest, feeling her heart race. "I didn't know you were here."

He smirked, leaning against the door jamb. "I gathered."

Feeling suddenly shy, Maya clutched the blankets closer, trying to keep her eyes on his face and not the droplets of water sliding down the lean curve of his body. "You take a shower?" It was a dumb question but she felt a pressing need to keep conversation going.

He nodded, pushing away from the door and stalking towards her. "I did. I imagine you need one as well?"

Giving a short laugh she nodded. "I'm *sticky*."

He hummed thoughtfully, pressing a strand of hair behind her ear then pulling another forward. "You have cum in your hair."

"Oh *ew*," she jerked away, reaching up and grimacing at the clumped tangle.

"Weren't complaining last night," he pointed out.

"Shut up." She searched the bed for the soft blanket she knew had to be somewhere, something easily removed and wouldn't be nine miles long so she could get out of the bed without flashing him.

"What are you doing?"

"Looking for something to wear."

He snorted, "It's not like I didn't see it all."

"That was different, it's *daylight*," she said, as though that would clear things up. He chuckled and before she could say anything whipped his towel off, holding it out to her.

"Here."

Oh Jesus, he was right there. All of him in his naked glory, not an inch of shyness. Not that he had a reason to be. She took the towel on autopilot, trying to figure out where she was supposed to look.

"Have you no *shame*?" she asked, only half kidding. He laughed and pulled her upright, squashing the towel between them and backing her towards the bathroom.

"Not an ounce," his lips swooped down to capture hers, one hand reaching out to turn the shower spray on. "Let me help you get cleaned up."

Maya had doubts about his motives but let the towel go, stepping under the warm spray. A shiver of pleasure drifted through her when his body pressed up behind her, then another when his hands settled on her hips.

"That good?" His voice rolled over her like honey and she nodded. She'd never thought showering together to be particularly sexy. Cramped, people fighting for the water - but in a shower the size of a small sedan, it was easy for them to wrap around each other and feel the steam begin to rise. His fingers gently carded through her hair, tilting her head back into the stream of water. He fisted his hand into the base of her skull and tugged slightly, forcing a moan from between her lips.

"Lean back further," he murmured into her ear, "we gotta get you all wet."

Already there, she thought but did as he said, leaning back into the cradle of his hands. The feeling of his fingers massaging her scalp sent tingles through her body, he felt so *good*. She blushed as he worked the tangled clump of her hair with gentle fingers, soaping the mass and then tilting her head to let it rinse away. Examining the shelf of products he grunted, cupping her breasts from behind and thumbing her nipples in slow circles.

"Which one is next?"

"That one," Maya pointed without looking. He took the bottle she indicated, studying it for a moment before slicking the contents into her hair.

"It's gotta sit for a bit," his hands drifted over her shoulders.

"It's fine," she protested weakly, "we can just-"

He hushed her with a hand around her throat, closing gently and cutting her brain off even as she sucked in oxygen. "Nuh-uh, the bottle says to let it sit and we're going to do as we're told, aren't we?"

"Yes."

"Good," one of his hands trailed down her spine. "Good." He paused, breath hot and heavy on her shoulder. "You know what? I forgot to wash your hair."

"What?"

His hands disappeared and she started to turn but he was back immediately, crowding up against her. "Hands on the wall."

She obeyed, holding her breath until she felt his fingers dip over the curve of her stomach, sliding down until they landed on the cap of short curls between her thighs.

"Promised I'd wash your hair, didn't I?" he groaned, threading his fingers through and massaging in rough swipes of his palm.

"Stefan," she moaned, arching her back, pressing her ass against him. He was hard, tucked tight to her backside.

"Did you get cleaned up here?" His fingers burrowed downwards, brushing her clit and then sinking deeper. "Doesn't feel like it." The hand on her neck fell and groped at her breast, rolling her nipple between his fingers. "Feels like you've made a mess."

It had been over a month of living with them and their touches and their little glances. A month of teasing and touching and being *so good* and suddenly she was ravenous for them. Last night felt like a distant memory already, her body aching for more.

"You gonna let me make you come?" His teeth nipped at her skin. She groaned, spreading her legs wider so he could circle his fingers around her throbbing clit.

Maybe it was her whimpered affirmative that set him off but Stefan growled low in his throat, slipping his hand down to thrust two fingers deep inside her. "Fuck baby, you're so fucking *tight*. Can't wait to have you on my cock."

His words were doing as much for her as his hands. Each one falling into the shell of her ear and winding deep into her core. A soft cry left her and he nipped her earlobe, stroking inside her in sharp thrusts of his fingers and grinding the heel of his palm to her clit. "That's it sweetheart, let go. Let me feel you."

She came with a wail, slumping into his embrace, barely noticing him catch her with an arm around her waist and turn her around. He continued to whisper nonsense into her ear, low quiet praises she barely understood, letting his murmurs of *'good girl'* wash over her while he maneuvered her beneath the stream once more, gently slicking the soap from her hair. The heft of him pressed between her legs, gliding along her lips and she tried to form a protest.

"Stefan, condom," she groaned, sinking her fingers into his hair.

"Not going inside," he grunted, mouthing at her throat. "Just let me, fuck, right there."

He pressed against her clit, sliding back and forth inside the squeeze of her thighs. She held on tight, rocking with him, feeling his body grow taut.

"Please Stefan," she nibbled on his lower lip. "Please come? For me?"

Grunting he clutched her tight, taking her with an open mouthed kiss as he shuddered in her arms. She held him through it, nails scratching along his back and nuzzling his neck until he finally pulled back and looked into her eyes.

"You're a dream, you know that?"

Maya flushed with the praise, hiding her face in his shoulder and hearing him chuckle to himself. He turned her to face the spray once more, pressing a soft kiss to the back of her neck.

"If I don't leave I'm just gonna get you all dirty again," he assured her, his warmth abandoning her as he stepped out of the shower. Maya almost called him back, she really didn't mind and what was the point of having such a conveniently large shower if you weren't going to use it? But she let him go, trying to focus on her own ablutions.

Washed and dressed, in the highest necked shirt she could find, Maya hesitated at the door. What was waiting on the other side? Stefan had already shown that things had changed, but he also hadn't *assumed* she'd be open to anything either. Would the others?

"You are a grown woman," she told herself, shutting her eyes and taking a deep breath. "And they are just incredibly powerful people you happen to be attracted to. You can do this."

It wasn't the best pep talk but it got her to turn the handle. Voices drifted down the hall, low murmurs of indistinct origin. Stopping in the entry to the kitchen she watched in puzzlement as Stefan moved around, arguing with Diego about the correct way to open a bottle of champagne. It was frighteningly domestic, Daniel shifting around silverware at the table until it lined up to his satisfaction made her heart lurch.

"What's going on?"

All three turned to her, but it was Stefan that strode over, taking her hands and sweeping in for a kiss that left her reeling. "We fucked up your dinner," he said by way of explanation. "So I figured, brunch."

"Brunch?" Maya asked, as though she'd never heard of it. Glancing around the kitchen she hesitantly ventured, "Doesn't brunch usually have... you know, food?" At the table, Daniel snorted and Maya shared a small smile with him.

"We didn't want it to get cold, it'll get here soon," Stefan assured her. "In the meantime, come have a mimosa."

"Are you trying to get me drunk at," she checked the clock,

"eleven in the morning?"

"We both know that's not necessary," Diego growled in her ear as she walked by and she blushed.

"Twenty bucks," Daniel called out. Maya raised an eyebrow and he winked at her. "Bet Diego we'd have you blushing before you got to the table."

The table he had given her a mind-blowing orgasm on? *That* table?

"Wow," Daniel tilted his head. "Didn't know you could get that red."

Shooting him a glare she leaned against the island, taking the champagne glass with its rich orange contents when it was offered. "I wasn't expecting to see you all this morning," she said simply. Might as well get it out there, rip the bandage off so to speak.

They exchanged a look while Maya gave her drink the kind of intense scrutiny it did not at all warrant. Let them come to whatever understanding they needed to. But when the seconds stretched on she finally sighed and looked up. "I hate to be that kind of girl," she ventured. "But can we talk?"

Diego heaved a heavy sigh, "About?"

If Maya was prone to cursing she would have leveled one at him. Did he really just ask that? Taking a steadying breath, she resisted the urge to slap him. "I'm a guest here, and I don't want you to think I'm not grateful, because I *am*. But I'm also very aware this isn't permanent."

"You want an apartment?" Diego asked, as though it wasn't a massive offer.

"Jesus, no," Maya quickly shook her head. "I mean, maybe someday, but I'm not asking you to like, get me one." She took a deep breath, "I just - we all know I was on my way out before the attack happened. I just need to know what a timeline looks like so I can plan."

"Well we just remodeled for you, seems a waste to kick you

out and have to undo all that," Stefan mused.

"But you're going to want the dungeon back sooner or later." Daniel snorted behind her and she kicked her foot out, catching his shin lightly. "I just need to know how *much* sooner or later."

Diego looked thoughtful, leaning an elbow on the island and running a hand down his goatee. "Well, we're just starting the company, so it'll be good to have you nearby while that gets off the ground. Saves the trouble of finding each other for check-ins. I can see at least a couple of months for sure. We can always reevaluate."

A couple of months. She could work with that. A weight that she'd only barely realized she was carrying lifted from her shoulders. "Oh, that's good. And when the time comes, I may take you up on the offer to help me *find* an apartment."

She stressed the word, giving him a firm look. She did *not* want to be more indebted to them than she already was. He nodded in acknowledgement, and she thought for a moment she saw relief in his eyes. That he didn't have to get her her own place? That she was staying? She opened her mouth to ask but the moment was broken by a knock on the front door and the delivery of five bags of groceries.

"How much did you plan on us eating?" Maya gaped in astonishment, watching as box after box was pulled from local restaurants.

"You deserve your favorites, it *is* your birthday after all," Stefan pointed out, setting what had to be a pound of bacon on the dining table.

"I wanted to get you diamonds," Diego shrugged. "Stefan talked us into the hash browns."

"I thought I already got my present," Maya blurted out without thinking. When three sets of eyes turned on her she realized what she'd said, both hands coming up to cover her face as she whispered, "Oh my God."

Booming laughter echoed in the kitchen, someone grabbing her hand and pressing a kiss to her palm. It turned out to be Stefan, a wide smile on his face. "An absolute dream."

Trying not to meet anyone's eyes she took her champagne flute to the table, sinking into a chair and busying herself with her plate while the men settled in around her. Stefan checked a contraption on the other side of the table, smiling when he passed a hand over it.

"It's finally heated up, who wants crepes?"

Maya blinked, "You know how to make crepes?"

"He does *not*," Diego sighed.

"How hard can it possibly be?" Stefan retorted.

Very hard, it turned out. Within ten minutes there was batter everywhere, several burnt thin slips of what might have been pastry, and no crepes.

"Fucking thing doesn't work," Stefan grunted, sinking into his chair and tossing the flat utensil to the side.

"I always thought crepes were made in a *pan*," Daniel mused to nobody in particular.

"I think you have an industrial crepe iron," Maya squinted at it. "Like for a restaurant."

"Fuck off," Stefan bit without venom, tossing a strawberry across the table. Maya caught it easily, ducking her head and biting down on the fruit with a smile. Stefan raised an eyebrow in interest. "Oh, you have other skills with your mouth. Who knew?"

Now she was blushing again, pressing her napkin to her mouth in an attempt to hide it. "Nico and I were home-schooled, not a lot of friends. Lots of time to make up games. I can also flick a playing card about twenty feet."

"No you fucking can't," Daniel challenged.

"Language," she said almost absently. "And why would I lie to you?"

"Why wouldn't you?" It was said without thought, a dismissive hand wave before he turned to Stefan to talk about some new shipment coming in - but it made Maya frown. She wanted to reach across the table and take his face in her hands. Assure him in some way.

"Stefan has interviews lined up for you today," Diego told her casually, sipping his coffee.

Maya turned to him, "Interviews?"

"For the accountant. We'll start with the one and go from there."

Oh yeah, *that*. "Are you sure you shouldn't do it? The interviews I mean."

Diego snatched up a piece of bacon, "Everyone has been cleared, they're all ours. This would be a lateral move for them. Find someone you can work with."

"Okay," she murmured. "This is - this just feels like a lot of trust. What if we steal all your money and run?"

Snorting, Diego gave her a sardonic look. "I would find you and cut off your thumbs. To start."

Maya wasn't sure if he was kidding or not. Actually, she was pretty certain he wasn't. Swallowing, she nodded at him. "Noted."

"Use my office," he grunted, pushing his chair back from the table. "I'm never in the damn thing anyway."

"Thanks?" she said to his retreating back.

Diego's abrupt departure broke the spell of ease that had settled over the four of them. Daniel mumbled something about work and Stefan winked at her before disappearing out the front door, loudly announcing he had an appointment. Maya was left alone with enough food to feed an army. Every berry she could think of, a gallon of yoghurt, omelettes, bacon from at least three different kinds of animal... it was overwhelming. And also touching that they'd made the effort. And they'd listened to her, talked to her about the

future.
   The whole morning had gone *much* better than expected.

22

Who knew interviews would be so *hard*?

Maya tried not to throw something at the man across from her. He was older, maybe sixty or so, and had yet to talk to anything but the room at large.

"I've been running the books for the warehouses downtown for the last year," he told one of the windows. "It ain't much to switch over to your little pet project, and if it makes the bosses happy…"

"Mr. Stuart-"

"Please, sweet cheeks, call me Kenny."

"*Mr. Stuart,*" she said more firmly. "I don't think you understand the scale of what I'm hoping to-"

"Yeah yeah," he waved a hand. He was talking to her breasts now which *might* be an improvement. "Money in, money out. It's all numbers, you don't need to worry about it."

"Thank you *so much* for coming," Maya said with a smile, ostentatiously pushing her sleeve back to check a watch she didn't have, quickly jerking it back down before he could see. "But there's someone else coming in…"

"Busy day, eh?" he asked without moving. "I heard the

bosses' been keeping you on your toes. Can't say I blame them."

Maya amused herself thinking of what Stefan would do to the man if he'd heard that. "Actually, Diego needs the room and told me to be sure everyone was gone so-"

He leapt to his feet so fast Maya thought he might fall over. "Of course, of course. Please give Mr. Krol my best."

She waited til the door shut behind him before collapsing onto the desk, banging her head softly to the polished wood. So far she hadn't found *anybody* she wanted to work with. Sure, they all knew what they were doing. They could keep the money moving between offshore and onshore accounts until a Fed's eyes crossed.

Maybe she should tell Diego that all they needed was an accountant. Stefan could take over the supervision, she was just a figurehead anyway.

Another knock made her groan. "Oh God, another-" Maya cut herself off when the man walked in, standing and giving him her nicest smile and offering her hand. "Sorry, it's been a long day."

He smiled, giving her a firm handshake and folding his large frame into one of the chairs. He was clean cut, handsome in a farm boy kind of way, and closer to her age. Blonde, the beginning of lines around his eyes - Maya liked him instantly. "Don't worry about it, I figured I was going to be last today and you might throw me off the balcony in a fit of frustration."

Maya's eyes went wide. "Has that happened?"

"Mr. Contreras threatens to sometimes," the man shrugged and Maya noticed he had a hint of an accent. Australian maybe? "Don't know if he's ever done it."

Nodding, she searched for her notes. "Oh well, I'm Maya and you're..." she rifled through the papers. "I have it here somewhere..."

"Greg," he supplied for her, "Greg Stanton."

"Thank you."

"No problem. You sure you want to do this? We can sit and stare into space and pretend this happened if you want."

Laughing, Maya finally found the paper she was looking for. "No no, let's get this over with. Please tell me how you're going to run everything so I don't have to do any work."

"Is that what you want?" he asked with a raised eyebrow.

"It seems to be the consensus," Maya sighed.

"Well, if that's what you want, sure. I'm currently on accounts for a casino, another laundry as you probably know, so the switch over is more a matter of paperwork than skill."

Maya nodded along, staring blankly down at her notes.

"This is your project, right?" he asked. "Why aren't you taking the lead on the books?"

"Finance isn't my strong suit," Maya sighed then gave him a pointed look. "But other people will be checking on it so don't get any ideas."

He laughed, a rich sound that filled the room. "Wouldn't dream of it. And if you wanted to learn I'd be more than happy to help."

"Really?" Maya sat forward abruptly. "You would?"

"Sure," he shrugged, "it's not that hard, you just have to learn a few rules and know when to look up others."

"Huh," Maya tapped a pen thoughtfully against her lower lip. "I like you."

"Thank you?"

"Wanna come work for Pink Fairy Events Incorporated?"

Greg blanched, eyeing her dubiously. "Is that really the name?"

Maya snorted and tossed her pen down. "No, I'm just messing with you."

Laughing, he closed his eyes for a moment in relief. "I mean, I'd still have joined but my wife would have questions.

Not everyday someone moves from the Golden Asp to Pink Fairy Events."

Maya snorted, a grin stretching her cheeks wide. "I'll send over the business plan. We're trying something new, we're going to account for every penny the company makes."

Greg cocked an eyebrow, "What a novel idea."

Maya stood, walking around the desk and holding her hand out. "I've got a few of them."

"I'm interested in hearing them," he said, shaking her hand again and following her towards the door.

"Oh," she stopped, looking at him sideways. "I know it's silly but I'm not a big fan of swearing. My mom was pretty strict about it and-"

Greg raised his hands, "Are you kidding? My mother would turn in her grave if she knew what kind of language I was exposed to. If you don't like it then done. Nothing worse than a gosh shall pass these lips."

She opened the door, gesturing him through it. "I think a darn would be okay."

"What about dagnabbit?"

She chuckled, waving him away. "A little strong, stick to tarnation."

He nodded, not looking back as he left. He was nice, and respectful - both were important. But out of everyone she'd met that day he was the only one who treated the whole thing like it was a *business* and not a pet project the guys were indulging her in.

Whistling softly she went back to the desk, gathering the information she would need to pass on to Greg when he started. She needed a phone, she'd have to talk to Daniel about that sooner or later. In the meantime, Diego was supposed to be stopping by so she could officially launch the business.

She was about to embark on only the second crime she'd

ever committed. Well, only the second *felony*. Everyone ignored the speed limit.

"So who did you decide on?"

Maya glanced up at Diego, her hands poised over her keyboard. The website was up and running, all of the registration papers were in, the bank accounts were online... she was triple checking everything before the first deposit came in. "What?"

For someone about to commit a felony, Diego looked quite nonchalant, leaning back in a chair across from her with his hands behind his neck. Then again, this was probably one of his lesser criminal enterprises. "For the accountant, who did you decide on?"

"Oh," she turned her attention back to the desk. Did she have all the tax paperwork properly sorted? She'd need to double check that but she was pretty sure there was a grace period for it. "Greg? Greg Stanton."

Diego frowned, staring into space and shaking his head. "I don't know him. Stefan approved?"

"Yeah, he's from the list."

"Then he's fine."

Maya barely heard him. "Okay, so we're squeaky clean. And worst case scenario, we get the money and we end up transferring it all right back. Call it an error. I mean, if we get into this and it doesn't work. But it should work. I've gone over everything three times and so have you and Stefan and-"

A head ducked into her field of vision, Diego's face quickly followed by Diego's lips pressing warmly against hers. She opened immediately, letting him press his tongue inside and lick along hers before he pulled away. Okay, so that was a thing that could randomly happen now. Good to know.

"Transfer the fucking money, Maya."

She did. Head reeling, she sent the official 'invoice' off to one of the Kings' shell companies. A moment later, she was looking at a half a million dollars.

"Oh my God this is really happening," she whispered.

Diego hummed thoughtfully, his fingers playing over her neck, the top of her shirt. "Are you wearing a bra?"

"What?" Her eyes shot up to his and he grinned.

"I think this calls for a celebration."

"What-?" She jerked in place when his hand fell to her waist, slipping under her shirt and roughly palming her breast. "God Diego, I can barely walk from last night."

"So just a blowjob then?" He gave her a seductive smile and she laughed. It quickly turned into a moan when he pinched her nipple. His other hand pulled at his belt, his body turning to settle on the desk in front of her.

Glancing at the door Maya put a hand out to stop him, gently kissing his fingers and standing up. "Go get on the chair," she told him, crossing to the door and ensuring it was locked.

Somewhat surprised by her acquiescence, Diego settled in, hand tucking inside his pants to pull himself free, stroking as she moved closer. "Suddenly shy?"

Leaning over she gave him a soft kiss, shifting so she was straddling his lap in the wide armchair. "Maybe I want you all to myself."

Her fingers worked at his shirt as he cupped a hand behind her head and deepened their kiss, his teeth nipping at her lower lip as she shoved it open. Sliding her palms over his skin she moaned softly, the slight spark of pain as he bit harder making her rock against him.

"Interesting," he gave her a smug look. "Should have known-"

His voice cut off when she licked down his neck, dipping into the smooth skin behind his ear before biting softly at the tendon. Her hands didn't stop exploring, touching every inch of his chest and then pushing his shirt from his shoulders so she could access more. He didn't seem to know what to do with his hands, alternating tangling them in her hair and gripping her waist as she moved lower, sinking to her knees on the floor and nuzzling his stomach.

Giggling, she ignored the hard length brushing her cheek, the trail of sticky liquid it left while she pulled at his pants. "Off," she ordered, looking up at him through long eyelashes.

Diego shifted, shoving his pants and underwear, not bothering with his shoes as he spread his thighs wide. "How are you so bossy on your knees?"

Looking directly into his eyes she pulled the smooth head of his cock between her lips, sucking softly and watching pleasure overtake his face. He swore, reaching out and palming the back of her head, pulling her roughly forward until she choked on the length of him.

"Fuck that's it," he groaned, hips thrusting upwards, "take it."

Maya jerked away, wiping her mouth with the back of her hand and glaring at him. "Stop that."

Diego growled, confusion etched on his features. "Stop what?"

"Using me," she gave him a steady look. "This isn't... I'm doing this because I *want* to be. Let me enjoy it."

He looked perplexed by the idea, his hand loosening as she leaned forward again and slipped him between her lips. His fingers clutched at her hair but he didn't shove, in fact he almost *petted* her as she slowly took more of him into her mouth, using her own hand to steady him until he hit the back of her tongue and then retreating. Swirling her tongue around the head of him she let him slip free, pressing kisses down his length and then back up before repeating the action.

Diego was so tense Maya worried about him. His chest was heaving, the muscles of his stomach pulled taut. With her free hand she scratched lightly into the trail of hair on his lower abdomen, feeling his skin jump and his hand covering hers to hold her still. Humming to herself she intertwined their fingers and took him deeper, pulling softly as she moved her mouth up and down his shaft.

"Jesus fuck," he groaned, holding her hand tighter. "You've got to - *fuck* - I need-"

Maya pulled back, continuing stroking him with one hand, "Let me do this my way? Please?"

He looked lost, his eyes meeting hers and a short nod jerking his head. Taking him in her mouth again she sped up, moaning around the taste of him, the spurts of salty precum.

"Fuck Maya, you-" Back arching, Diego's words became a garbled moan and Maya continued to work him as he came, waiting until the last spasm before shifting her hand to his thigh and just holding him inside her mouth while he softened.

"*Fuck*," he sighed, sinking into the cushions. He pet her hair with his free hand, jerky caresses she wasn't sure he even knew he was doing.

Swallowing one last time Maya shifted so she could rest her head on his thigh, continuing to hold his hand as she nuzzled his skin. "Next time maybe we can try your way," she said softly.

Diego's body shook with laughter, "Your way is fine. Fuck it's..." he trailed off, fingers unlocking from hers to run an unsteady hand through his hair. His head tilted back and he stared at the ceiling for so long Maya thought he might have fallen asleep. When he surged out of the chair and pulled her beneath him she let out a shriek of surprise, her knees clamping against his hips.

"Your turn," he growled, one hand already slipping under the band of her pants.

"I told you-" Maya started to protest but he cut her off with a hand under her jaw, tilting her head back and to the side so he could growl directly into her ear.

"I heard you, you said *barely* able to walk," his fingers slipped through her slick, two dipping down to thrust up inside her. "I want *not* able to walk."

Jesus, she hadn't meant it as a challenge. That was her last clear thought for a long while.

23

Daniel didn't know what to do.

He wasn't sure he was *supposed* to do something. He couldn't remember the last time there'd been a girl in his life he'd seen more than once. Should he check in on her? Surely Diego or Stefan already had. There was no need for *him* to.

But he didn't want to hurt her feelings if he was supposed to, too.

Grunting, he shoved himself away from his computer, rolling backwards and crossing his arms. He hated this. He'd spent half the morning already searching 'what to do the morning after' and it had been absolutely *no* help. Articles written by assholes saying to not contact her for at least a week - obviously impossible in the apartment even if he was willing to do it. Others said to make her breakfast - a task already accomplished with minimal input from him.

He thought about sending her an email but quickly dismissed it as too impersonal, even for him. Similarly, going to *find* her felt like he was trying too hard, he didn't want her thinking he *cared*. He just wanted to see how she was feeling. And if she wanted to go again.

Yeah, he had ulterior motives.

The morning bled into afternoon and he heard people talking, heard Diego and the girl laughing in the hallway at one point. Should he go out there? But if the laughter died, if he was intruding…

"Fuck," he bit off, turning back to his work. He needed to *do* something. A job, a run, hell he could head down to the boxing ring if he wasn't worried about seeing her. They had *slept* together. Had he *ever* done that with someone? Gone to sleep with them cuddled into his side and mumbling things about his fucking *heart*?

Jesus fucking Christ, he needed to get a grip.

A soft knock sounded and he groaned, hoping it would be Stefan with another bank trace to run. "Yeah?"

"Mind if I join?"

He nearly leapt out of his chair, head jerking up to see *her* in the doorway, laptop tucked under one arm and wearing that sweater that was the softest goddamn thing he'd ever felt in his life. A bottle of orange soda hung from her fingertips, a specific request Diego had put into the shopping list.

"Yeah, sure," he mumbled, trying not to study her too hard. Was the mark on her neck new? Or had he given it to her last night? She sank onto his couch with a small sigh, curling her legs under her and settling her computer on her lap - looking for all the world as though she did this all the time.

What was she doing here?

He typed absently, doing a cleanup and file trace, something he could do in his sleep but at least he knew it sounded like he was working. The clack of his keyboard filled the silent room. She didn't say anything, scrolling through what he recognized as the website for the new business front.

The couch looked comfortable, cozy even. And big enough to sleep on as he'd discovered one afternoon. He still wasn't sure why he'd gotten it, an itch had taken hold of him and he'd had it delivered the next day.

She looked good on it.

Suddenly he felt the urge to stretch out, but of course there was no room for him. He grumbled softly to himself, pulling his glasses off and cleaning them in rough motions.

"What is it?"

"Huh?" He jerked his head up, staring at her blurry form before slipping his glasses back on. "What?"

"You sound mad, what is it?"

"I was going to lie down and have a think," he told her, wondering where *that* had come from. "But *someone* is taking up all the space."

She glanced at the wide expanse of cushions and then at him, one eyebrow raised. He met her gaze levelly, daring her to point out the obvious.

"I can go?"

No no no. That wasn't what he wanted at all. Crossing quickly he plopped onto the cushions next to her, stretching his body out and laying across the empty space. By coincidence his head was laying against her thigh, arched upwards at an uncomfortable angle but that was just going to be his cross to bear.

He didn't look up to see what she thought about this development, lacing his fingers across his stomach and closing his eyes.

"Comfortable?" He didn't need to see her to know she was smiling.

"Shh, I'm thinking."

"Well, get your shoes off my couch while you do it."

Daniel cracked one eye open, glaring at her. "It's *my* couch."

"I spend more time on it than you and I don't want to sit in your boot dirt later. Move it."

He grumbled but did as she said, hiding a smile as he toed his boots to the floor with a solid *clunk*. Then he nestled backwards until he was all the way into her space, cheek against her thigh. This was nice, relaxing even. The smell of her soap wrapped around him and he resisted the urge to nuzzle into her stomach.

"There's been several inquiries for weddings." Daniel made a noncommittal noise, not really caring. One of her arms was resting across his chest and she had started scratching his beard. It was taking everything in him not to moan and arch under her like a fucking cat.

"If you wanted you could make an actual business of this."

"Why would we want to do that?" he asked, neck tilting until her fingers stroked the skin lower down. Soft shivers flowed from the back of his skull down his spine.

"I don't know, it was just a thought."

"Let me do the thinking," he chided her, trying to hide a smile. He felt the moment she saw it, the slight dig of her nails into his scalp making him practically purr. She continued her touches, scraping her thumb down the line of his neck and he finally opened his eyes.

"Don't start something you're not going to finish kitten."

"It doesn't have to be all about sex, you know," she pointed out as she continued to make all the blood in his body pool in his cock. "Think of me like a roommate, like Diego or Stefan."

Daniel glared up at her, eyes narrowed. "First of all, I don't want to fuck either of them."

"Really? Neither?"

Squinting slightly he thought it over and shrugged. "Well, maybe Stefan."

Maya's jaw dropped. "Are you serious?"

"Second," he snatched her wrist, pulling it down to press her palm to the bulge in his pants. "Neither of them come in here and stroke me all nice and pretty like you do."

"It was friendly touching," Maya countered, lightly squeezing. "Purely platonic. One might even say professional."

"Professional huh?" He guided her palm beneath the band of his pants, "What kind of meetings are you taking?"

"Daniel…" she started, eyeing her laptop. "I do really need to keep up with this stuff."

"Nuh uh," he pushed her hand deeper. "Here I was having a perfectly productive day when a sexy little kitten came skipping in here and got me all worked up. Now what are you going to do about it?"

She gave him a curious look, cocking her head to the side. "In my defense, I really did just come in here to see you."

His lips parted and he blinked up at her, stunned. Her hair was falling from its messy bun, her lower lip caught between her teeth, and she looked so beautiful he thought his heart might burst with it.

Fuck, you're a sap.

Sitting up quickly he took her laptop, shutting it and tossing it across the floor. She started to protest but he pulled at her ankles, spreading her legs until he could settle between them. "Let's play a game, kitten."

Her eyes narrowed but he could see the rapid rise and fall of her chest, knew she was interested. "What game?"

"Mr. Smith's naughty secretary." He hooked her knees into his elbows, pulling her back against him as he rose above her. "Interrupting his work."

She giggled and his heart flip-flopped. "You're a degenerate, you know that?"

"I do, actually," he countered. "But you like it."

"I like *you*," she corrected softly, one hand reaching up to gently caress his face.

Groaning he dove forward, kissing her so hard their teeth clacked together. His hands ripped at her clothes, tossing them over the side of the couch before he turned her around. He guided her to her knees, curling around her to press her hands to the arm of the couch, forcing her to lean forward before shoving her thighs apart with his own. He scrambled in his pockets for a condom, rolling it on and sinking into her without bothering to check if she was ready.

A small sound escaped her and he slowed his advance, running a hand down her spine. "Okay?"

"Just sore," she mumbled, her cheeks turning red. "Not used to this much *oh*."

He pushed forward as soon as he had the clear, listening to her words turn into a low whimper. "As my secretary I expect you to always be ready for me. Willing, eager even."

Fucking her slow and deep he reached around and pinched her nipple. "Say *Yes Mr. Smith*."

"*Yes*," she gasped, arching her back to take more of him.

"Yes Mr. Smith," he corrected, slapping the back of her thigh with a harsh *smack*. "Or naughty secretaries get punished."

She gasped and turned her head, but he quickly grabbed the back of her neck, pressing her forward until her forehead touched the arm of the couch. Holding her down, bent at the waist in front of him, he could take what he wanted from her, chase the release he needed.

The sound of skin hitting skin filled the room, the rough whimpers he was shoving out of her, the filthy wet squelch of their bodies joining. "What a good little fuck toy you are," he groaned, slapping at her ass with the flat of one hand. "Taking it so well."

"Daniel wait-" she squirmed and he let her neck go, petting a hand down her back.

"You gonna come? Come all over my-"

Maya shoved at the arm of the couch, dislodging him before she turned and held a hand up between them. "*Stop.*"

He froze, eye searching her face. What had he done? She looked upset had he - fuck had he *hurt* her?

"This isn't-" she stumbled over the words, closing her eyes and shaking her head as a fall of hair slipped over her shoulder. He tried not to stare at her breasts but she was making it very difficult. "I don't want this."

How long could he live after his heart stopped? He'd thought... fuck he'd thought she wanted him. When she said she liked him that maybe it meant for *this*. That he wasn't someone she had to put up with to be with better people.

"*Shit*," he bit off, stumbling to his feet. "Shit you should go, I-"

He was nearly knocked off balance when she threw herself into his chest, his arms wrapping around her by instinct. As confused as he was he didn't protest when she kissed him, when she slipped her tongue into his mouth and melted against him.

"I came here to be with *you*, Daniel," she panted when they broke apart. "I missed you today and I know you like all the-" she waved a hand, "but I'm not... I mean I *don't*. I came here to be with *you* and if you don't-"

"Shut up," he said evenly, cutting off her rambling and hiding a smile at her disgruntled frown. They were nearly the same height and he wished for a moment he was taller so he could look down his nose at her. That would really get her riled up.

"If you want something you should ask for it," he scolded softly, running his knuckles down the curve of her spine. "Not buck me off of you like a fucking bronco."

Rolling her eyes she turned him back to the couch, guiding him to sit and then settling in his lap. "You called me a *toy*."

"I think I called you a *fuck* toy," he corrected.

"Daniel..."

"I'm not saying fudge toy."

A giggle escaped her and he felt warmth bloom in his chest. His fingers gently stroked her thighs while he waited for her to decide what she wanted from him.

He wasn't expecting her to lean forward and nuzzle her nose along his, to press a kiss to the corner of his mouth, to gently pull his glasses off and set them to the side.

"Can you still see me?"

"Yeah," he nodded, licking his lips. "Yeah, I can see you."

"Good," she grinned and he felt his lips stretching into one of his own. "Maybe sometime when I'm more used to all-" a blush crawled up her neck to her cheeks. "The, you know, *attention* - we can play a bit more. I'm not *against* it," she quickly assured him. "It's just that it's a lot to take in."

"You took it pretty well last night," he pointed out and grunted when she shoved his shoulder.

"Be nice," she scolded, turning her hand and lightly stroking his neck. "You're the one who told me to ask for what I want."

"I've yet to hear you say anything like that, actually," he pointed out.

"I want you."

He couldn't have moved if the room was on fire. Watching her rise over him and slowly taking his cock back into her warmth.

"I want you," she said again simply, as though the words didn't bludgeon a hole straight through him. "I like you and I just-"

Daniel surged forward, hands grabbing at her hips and mouth crashing into hers. She met his every move, holding him tightly and rocking her body to take every bit of him he was trying to give her.

"Is this what you wanted?" he growled, fisting his hands into her hair and pulling her face a scant millimeter away from him. Their foreheads touched and he stared up at her. "Me?"

"Yes," she panted, reaching for him, nails scraping along

his skin. "How you look at me, how you feel - I want more. I want it all. Please."

Daniel felt lost, his eyes hazy and unfocused as she worked over him. She cupped his face in her palms and slowed the roll of her hips until he only rested inside her. Ever so softly, she kissed the crease between his brows, the tip of his nose, the barest brush against his lips.

"I've wanted you for so long," she whispered, flitting butterfly kisses across his cheek. "It's silly but you always look so *capable*, your hands," the hands in question skimmed up her back and she shivered, "they're always moving and I want them on me all the time."

"Yeah," he sounded dazed, "I can do that." He sank one arm sank between them, his fingers delving to their joined bodies.

"*Daniel*," she whined, back arching as he swirled his thumb over her clit. "I can't, it's too much-"

"Yeah you can," he assured her, never stopping. "Come for me Maya. I want to feel it. *Please*."

He watched her fight for it, lips parted and body straining up towards hers. It wasn't until her body was shuddering, her muscles squeezing down on his in short bursts, that he allowed himself to come. Burying his face in her hair until he was left as much a trembling mess as she was.

She held him after, raking her nails across his scalp and further down his spine. He didn't look up - *couldn't* look up - keeping his face tucked into her shoulder, breathing harshly into her neck. Something had shifted in his world, something he wasn't sure how to get back. He opened his eyes, saw her soft smile - and lost a bit of himself to her.

It terrified him.

Adjusting his weight he started to move her off him, mouth open to tell her it'd been great. To send her on her way. But she cut him off with an almost *tender* gesture, touching her fingertips to his cheek.

"Stay?" she asked quietly. "Just… stay with me for a minute?"

Fuck, he could do that. He could wrap his arms around her and sigh back into the couch while she burrowed into his chest. It didn't mean anything. Just some post-coital cuddling. To keep the peace in the house.

"Fine," he grunted, feeling her smile. "If you fucking insist."

"Language," she said with a muffled yawn and Daniel huffed a laugh.

"My fucking office, my fucking rules."

24

Maya was going to have to lay some new ground rules. While it was all good and fun to be having as many orgasms as a girl could possibly handle, she was seriously worried about what was starting to look like an inevitable UTI.

"Stefan *no*," she was laughing when she said it but her voice was firm. "I need a break."

He pouted, nuzzling into her neck from behind while she tried to fix her morning tea. "But I had all these good ideas last night."

"And I had to take painkillers, *no*."

He let her go with a grunt, backing up a step and frowning at her when she turned around. "Well, when will you be ready?"

"I don't know," she shrugged, reaching for the milk. "Maybe a day or two? Do we have any cranberry juice?"

"Have Daniel order some, what do you mean a day or two? The fuck am I supposed to do til then?"

Maya raised an eyebrow at him, "Are you really telling me you can't wait a *day*?"

"Or two," he pointed out.

"Jesus, you're impossible," she laughed again.

"So..." he waggled his eyebrows and she shook her head sharply.

"Still no."

"What the actual fuck," he seemed genuinely confused and she wondered how many people had told him no in the last few years.

"Cursing at me isn't going to change my mind, put your big boy pants on and deal."

He gave her a disgusted look. Maya considered if she'd just made a mistake. The ground felt precarious beneath her, one wrong move and she'd be out on the curb. But they *had* promised she could stay a couple of months. That had to mean something, didn't it? Even if Stefan was annoyed with her it certainly wasn't something she'd be kicked out for. Worst case he'd find someone else.

Maya didn't interrogate how sick that made her feel.

"Stefan," she said softly, taking a step towards him. "It's not that I don't want to. I genuinely don't think I *can*."

Tension eased off of him and he moved towards her, catching her in a hug and brushing his nose along her temple. "I forget how fragile your little pussy is."

"*Stefan*." She shoved his shoulders and he laughed, wrapping her up tighter. Twisting so she could hug him back she rested her cheek on his shoulder. "It's just been a while. And this was... a lot."

He pressed a kiss to her forehead. "Fine, understandable. My delicate little flower."

"I shouldn't have said anything," she growled, pinching his side.

"My dainty daffodil," he cooed, twisting away. "All sad because her pussy hurts."

"*Stefan*," she warned again, eyes narrowing, but he laughed in her face. Swooping down to give her a long, languid kiss.

"Rest up buttercup," he murmured into her lips. "I've got

plans."

She couldn't help how her body responded to that, the clench and the *ache*.

"I'm sure you do."

He didn't stay for much longer, giving her another teasing kiss before heading out the front door with a small salute and a wink. She watched him leave with a fond smile, turning over the idea of baking muffins. It would be a change from the ordinary morning meals, and there were chocolate chips in one of the cabinets somewhere. A dozen muffins would do it, although... the way Daniel went through sweets she should probably make two to be sure.

Fifteen minutes later Maya finally found a muffin pan, tucked into the top shelf of a cabinet that also contained several bags of rice, a juicer, and a bagel toaster. Nothing in this kitchen made any sense, nothing was where it should be.

Maybe she could do some reorganizing? They probably didn't know what they had, nevertheless where to find it. It was something nice she could do for them, and it would make her life easier. Task in mind she started with the upper cabinets, pulling everything out and organizing like with like. There was absolutely no reason that mixing bowls needed to be spread across four separate spaces.

"Why do they have a pineapple corer?" she muttered to herself, tossing the offending utensil into a pile on the island. "Nevertheless *two*."

"What are you doing?"

Maya spun around, a wide smile taking over her face when she saw Diego standing with a frown on his face.

"I'm re-organizing!" She held up a pair of tongs, clicking them at him. "Your kitchen is a mess and practically impossible to cook in."

His frown deepened. "It hasn't been a problem before."

"That's because you don't *cook*." She clicked the tongs one last time before setting them aside. "If you did you would be in complete agreement with me. I promise, it will make a billion percent more sense when I'm done."

Diego crossed around the island, looking at the pulled out drawers and stacks of glassware. "Who told you this was okay?"

For the first time, Maya second guessed herself. She hadn't exactly *asked* anyone for permission, she'd assumed no one would care. "No one." He grunted and Maya frowned. "I know it looks bad right now but-"

"Put it back."

Maya blinked at him, and the hard look in his eyes. "I beg your pardon?"

"This," he waved a hand, "isn't yours. And you shouldn't be messing with shit that doesn't belong to you. If you've got an itch reorganize your fucking socks or something."

Reeling back, Maya lifted her chin. "I use everything in here one *thousand* percent more than you ever have."

Diego took a step closer, jaw tight. "And when you fucking leave I'll have to put it all back anyway, so *do what I fucking tell you to*."

Maya gaped up at him. He was *mad*. Full of more anger than she had ever seen on him. Taking a cautious step backward she held her hands up in a placating gesture. "I didn't mean to... I'm sorry. I didn't think anyone would mind."

"Now you know," he snapped, turning on his heel and stalking back towards the offices.

What had just happened?

It took a moment for her to get her bearings, slowly sliding a cutting board to the back of a low cabinet. She had a pretty good memory, she could remember where everything went. And he *was* right, she hadn't asked before rearranging *their* kitchen. She should have asked. It was rude for sure and-

"What are you doing?"

Maya jumped back so quickly she stumbled, biting back a scream. Daniel caught her easily, cupping a hand under her elbow and giving her a concerned look.

"What is it?"

"Oh holy - you scared me." Pressing a hand to her chest she felt her heartbeat. "You almost gave me a heart attack."

"Little high-strung today are we?" He smiled, skirting a pile of glass bakeware and opening the fridge.

"It's nothing, I just gotta put all this back," she waved at the mess with a shaking hand.

He caught it in his, rubbing his thumb across her palm. "What *were* you doing?"

"Re-organizing," she shrugged.

"Nice," he leaned in for a quick kiss and she returned it without thinking. "Place could use it."

Were they *trying* to drive her off the deep end?

"Well, Diego wasn't too happy so I'm going to put it all back."

Daniel shrugged, "If that's what he said."

Thinking for a moment Maya narrowed her eyes, "Do *you* mind if I organize?"

"Why would I? Not like I use it."

"That's what I-" she started then held herself back. "It's fine, I'm fine." It didn't look like he believed her but Maya gave him a warm smile, reaching out and fixing the collar of his dark polo. "I left my laptop in your office yesterday, mind if I drop by later? We could do some work."

"Can't," he said quickly. "I gotta focus on some things. I'll put it by the door."

Frowning, Maya tilted her head. "I promise I won't-"

"Gotta go," he juggled the cup in his hands, checking his phone, "be sure to put this back where it goes, Diego's got a good memory."

Left standing in the middle of the kitchen, the mess of pots and pans around her, Maya struggled to get her equilibrium. People said *women* were flighty? The moods in the house changed so fast she could barely keep up.

"Stupid Diego," she muttered, putting a zester into a drawer with a pack of hot cocoa. "Stupid men and their stupid hissy fits."

"You still in here?"

Eyes turning heavenwards and praying for patience, Maya shook herself before turning to Stefan. "You guys are just in and out today, aren't you?"

"It was a quick meeting," Stefan shrugged. He eyed the kitchen critically, "Something happen?"

"It's nothing, I just gotta put all this away."

"Oh," he grabbed an orange from the bowl, gesturing at her with it. "Well, when you're done why don't you hang out with me til lunch?"

"Yeah, sure," she said absently, trying to remember where she'd found the pie pan.

It took more than an hour to put everything back to any degree of certainty. She was cranky by the time she finished, stopping by Daniel's office and glaring when he didn't acknowledge her. By the time she was collapsing onto Stefan's couch she felt like she could spit nails.

"Don't look so grim, sweetheart," Stefan scolded.

I will look how I damn *well please*, Maya thought sharply but forced a wide smile. She was already somehow in both Diego and Daniel's bad books, she didn't need to add Stefan to it. As the afternoon progressed she only had to fend his advances off twice, each time his puppy eyes and pout getting harder to resist. When dinner came she took it to her room, not interested in navigating whatever emotional minefield had erupted since that morning.

Hours later, snuggled under her duvet, she considered if

this was a consequence of sleeping with them. If so, it wasn't a reaction she had expected. Boredom afterwards, maybe, now that she wasn't a novelty. Or that there would be jealousy or hard feelings. Whatever *this* was, she had no experience dealing with it. All she could do was roll with whatever they threw at her and hope she navigated it well.

"Maya?"

Looked like she'd be putting that into practice sooner rather than later. Sitting up, she squinted at the doorway and the figure silhouetted in the low light. "Diego?"

The door shut with a click and she watched him shed his clothes, padding to the bed on steady feet and slipping under the covers with her.

"I'm not-" she started to say but he was by her side in a moment.

"I need you." The hoarse whisper pulled at her heart and she turned into his embrace, pulling him close.

"I'm-" she started and he cut her off with a soft kiss.

"Let me stay the night," he mumbled the words against her lips, fingers stroking down her spine. "Doesn't morning sex sound nice?"

It did but she didn't have a lot of faith that she'd be up for it. She liked his warmth, though, the press of his skin against hers. "Okay."

It wasn't obvious how tense he was until he relaxed, sinking into the bed with her. Maya sighed, lightly scratching at his skin until he shivered. She considered asking him about earlier, but opening that fight up again was the last thing she wanted to do. Instead she took a risk, "Tell me something about you."

He shifted beneath her cheek but didn't let her go, his heavy sigh ruffling her hair. "What do you want to know?"

Maya cast about for a question."What do you do for fun?"

"I used to do photography, before I got too busy," his low

voice rumbled in his chest and Maya tried not to be distracted by the way his fingers were stroking over her hip.

"Really? What kind?"

"I started in black and white and moved to infrared," his fingers paused and he tapped her skin absentmindedly. "The things it lets you see, it's a different way of looking at the world."

Maya mulled that over, "Like how?"

"You know that one in the front hallway? Of the tree?"

She sat up so abruptly her head spun, "You took that?"

Raising an eyebrow he tugged her back down. "Yeah, the ones in here too."

"I didn't know," Maya mumbled into his skin. "I just liked them."

"I know."

Silence hung in the area and Maya absently traced over his ribs, giggling when he sucked his stomach in with a hiss. "Ticklish?"

"Don't you dare," he warned with a low growl, capturing her hand and laying it flat to his skin.

"I would *never*," she lied, feeling a huff of laughter leave him. "What made you take up photography?"

"The high school we went to, it was one of the electives. And there was this girl..." he trailed off and Maya grinned.

"I don't blame you. I tried out for cheerleading for a tight end."

Diego laughed, pressing his nose to her hair. "Funny."

"I try." After a moment's thought she added, "Do *not* tell Daniel."

"What? You don't want to wear a little pleated skirt and shake some pom-poms for him?" he teased. Maya tickled him in retaliation, her smile wide as he pinned her arm to the bed. His playful growl led to a long, slow kiss that left her reeling before he pulled away and tucked her back into his side.

"Anything else?" he asked with a huff.

Maya heard it for the dismissal it was. He was done talking and she was supposed to get the hint. But she couldn't help but push her luck. "How did you guys meet?"

"In school, sixth grade," he said after a long pause. "Stefan and I knew each other from the group home, and Daniel was that weird kid no one liked. Seemed like a good fit."

"Can I ask," she said softly, "what happened to your family?"

"No clue who dad was." His shrug rocked her gently. "Mom left when I was eight. You remember those safe haven laws a while back? You could drop off any kid at a fire station or something, no questions asked?"

She couldn't help the gasp, the way she pulled away to see his face. "You're saying she just *dropped you off*?"

Diego shrugged, tugging her back to him. "Left me with a backpack full of clothes."

"That *bitch*," Maya snarled into his chest. A rumbling laugh left him and she felt him press a kiss to the top of her head. "How could she?"

He shrugged, "Didn't want me around anymore. It's alright."

It was *not* alright. How could someone *abandon* a child like that? Maya knew it was possible there was a good reason, but right that moment she couldn't think of one. Fury roared through her and Diego let out a small grunt. Realizing she'd been digging her fingernails into his skin she let go, soothing the area in light, apologetic touches.

"Diego I-"

"Don't," he said curtly. "It was a long time ago."

Maya nodded slowly, tilting her face up towards his. He wasn't looking at her, staring across the room with a blank expression. Suddenly he blinked and looked down, one eyebrow raised.

"I mean, you know as well as anyone it isn't just blood, right?" he asked. "When was the last time you talked to your family?"

Mulling it over Maya debated how much to tell him. "I was sixteen."

"See? And we both turned out fine."

The laugh burst out of her and Diego joined in, pulling her up his chest and giving her a soft kiss while they chuckled. Maya brushed his nose with hers, "Definitely fine. I make nothing but good decisions."

"You're here aren't you?" he said quietly.

"Yeah, I'm here."

She held him tight as they drifted to sleep, not waking when he slipped out at some point before the morning.

25

Back on good, or at least somewhat solid, footing with Diego - Maya set a mission to figure out what was going on with Daniel. She hadn't seen him during the morning milling around the coffee pot, each of them in and out of the kitchen until they had enough caffeine in their system to make it through the day. It had become a bit of a ritual for her, sitting on one of the barstools and greeting each of them - now with the addition of lingering kisses from Stefan and a hesitant, although quickly enthusiastic, one from Diego.

But no Daniel.

It wasn't unusual to not see him for a while, he often stayed up late doing whatever it was he did on his computer. She'd brought him more than one hot drink in the last few weeks, and on one occasion sat in his lap curled up against his shoulder. She had dozed while he worked, sporadically nuzzling his nose into her hair.

He was odd, she'd known that from the start. That was fine, she could deal with odd. She would just have to make sure he knew how she felt about him. That she cared. Humming to herself, Maya slipped down the hallway to the last office, sweeping through the door with a smile.

"Hey, I," Maya cut herself off stumbling to a stop, staring into the office. Daniel sat in his usual spot, eyes focused on his computer screen. "Where's the couch?"

He didn't answer, although she saw his eye twitch slightly. He *heard* her, even if he was refusing to acknowledge it. Great, he was still in a *mood*. Sighing, she rethought her strategy. Pouting her lower lip out she strolled to his desk, moving to perch on the edge.

"I *liked* that couch, it-" His hand shot out, blocking her from sitting.

"I'm busy, what do you need."

Maya frowned, backing up a step. "Sorry, your door was open. That usually means you're available."

"Yeah, for business," he grunted. His eyes finally darted up to hers. "You here for fun?"

"I… guess?" She stumbled over the words, eyes widening when he tilted his chair slightly, moving his keyboard to account for the adjustment and then unzipping his fly.

"A blow job would be great, kitten."

What the… Maya's brows scrunched, her eyes narrowing. She was in his office, she was allowed to *think* it.

What the *fuck*?

"Just like that?" she folded her arms.

"Why not?" He wasn't watching her at all, his fly still undone. "Look if you're not here to get me off move along. I've got shit to do."

Maya fumed as she stalked away, slamming his door behind her with a satisfying *thunk*. That son of a *turnip*. How dare he? What kind of person did he think she was? That she would just fall to her knees and do *that*?

You did for Diego.

Maya grunted, stalking through the apartment. That was different.

Was it though?

She jerked the refrigerator open, squinting at the contents. It *was* different. Diego had at least made eye contact with her when he asked. Even she had to admit, that was a low bar.

One Daniel *still hadn't managed to clear*.

Snatching a random bottle she twisted the top off, pretending it was his neck. Let him have his pissy mood, she could deal. There was always the company to check in on. Despite the fact that it wasn't a real business, Maya enjoyed making it look as authentic as possible. She had updates to make to the website, brochures and albums to make. It was fun, in its own way. And it would take up most of her morning. At lunch she caught Stefan, motioning towards his office and following him back.

"I was wondering," she started but he had her backed against the door, his hand slipping under her shirt. "Stefan," she scolded softly.

"Can't help it," his lips skimmed her neck, "what do you need?"

What *did* she need? "I wanted to plant some herbs, outside. It feels silly to send someone out just to get some basil."

"Okay." He was on her breast now, fingers playing with the nipple.

"Really?" Her eyes widened and she pushed him away slightly, "I can?"

He shrugged, "What do I care?"

"And Diego won't mind?"

Shaking his head, Stefan rubbed his palms over her back. "I'll talk to him, don't worry about it. Just tell Daniel what you need."

Maya frowned, pursing her lips. "He's not exactly talking to me right now."

Stefan chuckled, stepping away and heading towards his desk. "What did you do?"

"What did *I* do?" she scoffed. "*He's* the one who-"

"Yeah yeah," he waved a hand dismissively, leaning on the edge of his desk. "He's like that sometimes. He'll get over it."

Maya grunted, walking forward when he reached his hand out, stepping between his spread thighs. "Wish he'd do it sooner, I miss him."

Stefan raised an eyebrow, "Getting lonely? Not enough for you?"

Giggling, she ignored the hard look on his face, brushing his lips with hers. "I miss all of you when you're not around."

Suddenly she was spun, perched on the edge of his desk, her legs wrapped around his waist, and she lost all track of why she was in the office in the first place.

Two hours and one hot shower later, Maya stood with arms akimbo, assessing the large terrace.

"I guess over there?" She pointed at a spot, watching the man set down the waist high planter. It was built like a shallow table, high enough she wouldn't have to bend down but not deep enough to grow any fruits or vegetables. Perfect for a herb garden.

She adjusted its placement slightly as the man returned with bags of potting soil, dropping them next to her. His eyes darted to her neck and she blushed, knowing full and well he was seeing the hickey Stefan had given her.

"Thanks, let me know when the plants get here."

The man nodded and left, passing Diego on his way. Maya held her breath as Diego scanned over the pile of items, brow furrowed.

"I asked Stefan," she blurted out quickly, before he could say anything. He blinked at her and nodded.

"He said."

Silence fell over them and she fidgeted from foot to foot. He wasn't wearing a full suit for once, jacket gone and sleeves rolled to his elbows. He was wearing a vest though,

259

like he'd peeked into one of her late night dreams about him.

"Is this okay?" she asked, gesturing at the planter. "I can move it if it's-"

He crossed the stones quickly, stopping in front of her and his hands hovered in the air between them for a moment before resting on her shoulders. "This is fine. Do you need some help?"

Was he really…? "You'll mess up your suit," she pointed out.

Blinking he looked down then back up at her. "I meant one of the men."

"Oh." Of course that's what he meant, why was she suddenly incapable of coherent thought? "No, that's okay. I got it."

Thumbs stroked her collarbone while he studied her. "Do you *want* my help?"

"Of course not!" she burst out, stepping away. "I mean, if you want to, of course, but I wouldn't dream of - you're so busy and look at that white shirt you shouldn't be anywhere near all this-"

He cut her off with a kiss, resting his forehead against hers. "I'll reassign a couple of the guys to help you and check on you before my next meeting."

Maya nodded dumbly, watching him carefully skirt the gardening implements before heading inside. Heavens only knew how long she stood there before the door opened again and Ryan stepped out, followed by a man she vaguely recognized.

"Boss said you needed help, miss?"

Maya gave herself a shake, turning a wide smile on them. "It's not much, just getting all this soil up into the planter."

Ryan nodded and stepped forward immediately, a knife appearing out of thin air. He lifted the bag as if it were nothing and let the contents spill out where she directed. She sent the other man inside with the brand new pitcher, hardly noticing the way he settled his hand on her wrist when she took it from him. Sinking to her knees, Maya studied the planter carefully, leveling the soil, glancing up at the sky and having the two men shift it twice before she was satisfied about the amount of sun and shade it would get.

"Ryan would you go check on the plants please?"

"Of course."

The door no sooner shut behind him that Maya felt a presence looming behind her. Glancing back, she saw the other man had stepped closer, his crotch nearly at eye level.

"Do you mind?" she asked as evenly as possible, turning away quickly.

"You think about my offer?"

Maya's eyes darted to the door but it was just out of sight. She'd had the planter moved so many times she was now blocked from view by the new angle. No one could see what was happening. Trying to laugh it off Maya went to stand, settling a hand on the planter to steady her but freezing when he pressed her back down.

"I don't know what you mean," she stammered, forcing a smile.

The man hummed thoughtfully and Maya finally realized where she knew him from. The night of the party, so long ago now, he was the one who'd propositioned her.

"Brandon? Right?"

He seemed surprised she knew his name, smiling down at her. "I thought you'd noticed me." His eyes roamed over her and he seemed to make some calculation before reaching for her hand and yanking it to the front of his pants. "We've got time, hundred bucks if you get me off before anyone gets back."

"I'm *not*-" she started, jerking away, but he held her firmly by the wrist and she had to put a hand on him to steady herself. "Let *go* of me."

"C'mon, just a quickie," he wheedled. "You're already fucking those three, what's one more?"

"One too many," she snapped back, shoving at his hip. "Now *move*."

Brandon did so with a pout, shoulders slumping as she stood and took a step away from him. "Coulda been nice."

"I doubt it," she bit off.

"Am I interrupting something?"

Maya's head jerked towards the door, Ryan and Stefan standing there with arms full of greenery.

"Nothing at all!" she chirped, noting the assessing gaze Stefan was giving her. She had a sudden memory of the first day they'd met, the menace as he'd calmly threatened the man who worked for him. The blood on his knuckles and ice in his eyes when she'd patched him up a few days later.

He's going to kill him.

The thought came out of nowhere but Maya was suddenly filled with altruism on behalf of the jerk standing next to her. He hadn't said anything that wasn't true and Stefan looked like he was about to fling the guy off the roof.

She took the parsley from Stefan's grip with a wide smile, reaching up with one hand and tilting his face down to hers for a soft kiss. "Thanks for helping, you want to get your hands dirty too?"

He grunted and jerked his head, the two men quickly dropping what they were doing and disappearing back into the apartment. Maya took a hesitant step away as he set the other plant down, taking the one from her with equal care and setting it aside.

"You don't touch anyone else," Stefan growled, his hand suddenly closing on her wrist. "*No one*, do you understand?"

"Stefan," Maya said as calmly as she could. "You're scaring me."

He blinked slowly at her, breathing hard, before all the emotion seemed to flow out of him. Releasing her wrist with a sudden grin and a cocky smile.

"I'm just teasing." He winked as he said it and Maya had never seen anything so unnerving in her life.

"Stefan…"

He stepped into her space, tilting her chin up with one finger. "You look cute with dirt on your nose," he said playfully, nuzzling his against her.

"I do *not*," she countered, reaching a hand up to wipe it away but he caught it in a loose grip, placing a kiss in the center of her palm. This was the Stefan she knew. Whatever had just happened… she must have imagined it.

"You do," he assured her, backing her up against the glass window. "And a little bit right here too." He ducked his head and brushed a kiss under her chin.

"It's dirty work," she tried to explain, humming softly as he fit her body against his.

"I can think of better ways to get all dirty," he murmured, teeth catching at the collar of her shirt.

"Out *here*?" she squeaked.

"Where everyone can see us," he grinned. "Let them watch how good you take me."

She felt the need to point out, "We *just* did this."

"Not outside," he corrected, hand slipping under the edge of her t-shirt. "We've never done it outside."

"And we're not going to." With a shove she slipped from between him and the window, backing away as he stalked towards her. "Stefan…"

"I'm not going to give you a head start."

It was only because the door was open that she made it into the apartment before he caught her, laughing as he wrapped his arms around her from the back and lifted her to her tiptoes.

"*Stefan*," she shrieked, collapsing into giggles as he nipped at her neck.

"Do I need to intervene?"

"No," Stefan grumbled, holding her tighter.

"*Yes*," Maya gasped, holding a pleading hand out to a bemused Diego. He took it and stepped closer, sandwiching her between their bodies.

"You've got dirt on your face," he said with one eyebrow raised.

"Told you."

"I would love to go wash it off but *someone*-"

Diego rubbed her nose with the cuff of his sleeve, lips twitching as he looked down at her. "It seems you've gotten yourself into trouble."

"I did no such-"

A new voice cut her off, flowing through the air like silk. "What a charming sight."

Diego's head jerked around and Stefan froze behind her. "Lau."

Maya vaguely recognized the two men, eldest sons of one of the other local families. Dressed in sharp suits with identical looks of amusement on their faces. Diego moved away from her so fast she nearly fell, only being caught by Stefan's steadying hands before he too stepped to the side.

"I never realized the Kings' castle was so *homey*," the one on the right drawled with a sardonic lift of one brow.

"I'll meet you in my office, Andrew" Diego gritted out, shoulders almost deliberately relaxed.

"Why bother when we could sit here? Maybe have a tea party?" the man on the left asked, eyes studying every detail of the three of them. Maya's eyes darted between the four men, trying to figure out what she was supposed to do.

"In my *office*," Diego reiterated with a curt wave of his hand.

"Of course," the man on the left nodded his head slightly. "But perhaps you might want to clean yourself up first."

Maya's eyes caught on Diego's cuff, the dirt he'd wiped from her face.

"All the money in the world," the other man, Andrew, sighed, turning towards Diego's office. "And you still can't remove a man from the filth he was born in."

A growl rumbled out of Diego and Stefan stepped to his side quickly, taking his bicep in a crushing grip and whispering something into his ear.

"Go to your room."

It took Maya a moment to realize Diego was talking to her, his voice a hollow order.

"Should I-" she started but neither of them turned to her.

"I said *go to your room*," Diego growled more sharply.

The tension could have lit the air on fire. Maya took a hesitant step backwards, wanting to reach out to them but certain it wouldn't go well.

"I'll-" she started, not sure what to say, but Stefan's head finally snapped to hers. He looked cold, distant, his mouth a thin line the mirror image of Diego's quiet rage.

"*Go.*"

She did.

26

It was hard to avoid people in an apartment, even as large as it was, and Maya didn't try. It didn't really seem to matter because the people she would have tried to avoid acted like nothing had happened. She'd woken up to Diego in her bed on more than one occasion lately, his lips catching in her hair as he pressed himself to her back, lifting her thigh so he could slide inside. Stefan invited her back to his office the day after their run in with the Laus, winking when she settled back onto the couch and joining her there within fifteen minutes. And Daniel… well he actually *was* avoiding her. He had to be. There was no other explanation for why she hadn't seen him in days.

They were confusing the hell out of her.

Nevertheless, she was content to wait them out. They had *moods*, she'd known that from the start, but they eventually came around and she'd be there when they finally got their heads back on straight. In the meantime she could focus her attention on the business and be there when they needed her.

"I'm really supposed to cut a check to Mickey the Razor?"

Maya choked on her tea, glancing up to meet Greg's arched eyebrow. "I'm sorry, what?"

"Mickey the Razor, that's how he's listed," Greg frowned at his computer. "I suppose I could sell it as a stage name. Clown?"

Staring off in thought for a moment Maya pursed her lips. "Magician."

It wasn't their first hurdle in starting the 'above board money laundry.' Maya knew that, as a fallback, they could always switch to a cash business, paying their 'vendors' in wads of hundreds. The company was a cash *out* enterprise only, cleaning money to get it back into circulation, not for further uses. That was the whole point.

The issue of course being that the cash out recipients were not quite above board themselves.

They sat at the kitchen island together, shoulder to shoulder, going through the list of employees Stefan had given her as a start. She was going to need to add some expensive people to the payroll soon, she couldn't push money out of the business fast enough to handle the amounts the Kings were dropping in.

"Hey, you think we could backdate a promissory note or two?" Maya asked, tapping her fingers on the marble. "We could use it to make a couple of bigger payouts to our backers."

Greg frowned, "If it ever got audited we won't be able to show the money in our accounts to start with."

Nodding Maya made a note to run it by Stefan and his team. There was probably a way to do it she just couldn't see. "Oh, by the way, you're getting a raise."

"I am?"

"Yeah, check your email. You've been doing a great job."

A pause and then a soft inhale. "Crikey, that's a lot of zeroes."

Maya giggled, wrinkling her nose at him. "Crikey? Did you just say *crikey*?"

He blushed, running a hand through his hair. "Sorry, uh…
tarnation that's a lot of zeroes?"

Collapsing into laughter Maya pressed the back of her
hand to her mouth. "It wasn't - Oh my God I wasn't-" she was
almost crying, finding it hard to breathe. "I just meant I
hadn't heard you use the-"

"This is discrimination, you know," he pointed out with a
smile and she collapsed into giggles again. "I'm going to file a
complaint."

"Oh please," she shoved at his arm and he caught her hand.
"Like you have anything to-"

"*Maya.*"

Turning, she blinked at Stefan. "Hey, you're home! I have a
question about *oof,*" he was on her suddenly, pulling her off
the stool and into his arms, his mouth slanting across hers
and his hands under her thighs. Maya reeled from the sudden
change in position, catching herself on his shoulders as he
lifted her the short distance to the nearby dining table.

"Out," he growled, not bothering to look at Greg who knew
better than to argue. Maya blinked, trying to make sense of
what was happening even as Stefan's tongue slid down her
neck and his hands jerked her t-shirt over her head.

"Stefan, wait," she pushed at him, "what're you-"

He pulled her towards him with a rough motion, pressing
the bulge of him to her core. "What did I tell you?" he
growled, palming her breast through her soft bra. His hands
were rough, tearing her leggings in his rush to pull them
down.

"Oh sweetheart," he sighed, rubbing his fingers up and
down her. "Always so wet for anybody."

Something was off but Maya couldn't think straight. He
was overwhelming her senses, playing every one of her soft
points that turned her into a mess for him.

He pushed her face down over the dining table, the same

spot where she had first opened herself to them. With quick movements he wrapped her bra around her wrists, holding them to the small of her back as he ran a hand through her folds.

"What were you thinking about?" he muttered, sliding two fingers deep inside her. "Hmm? You thinking about getting railed by that blond asshole?"

What was he talking about? Maya tried to ask, turned her head so her cheek laid flat to the table but something much larger than his fingers was there, scattering every thought she had to the wind. All that she had left was his name, uttered in soft panting breaths as he thrust inside her harshly.

"That's right, take it," he moaned, pulling her wrists tighter. Maya had the passing thought he wasn't wearing a condom and she should probably say something about that but his hand pressed the back of her neck to the table and she lost the thought entirely.

"She's got a hole free if you want it."

A hand touched her cheek and her eyelashes fluttered open, her dazed eyes falling on Diego pulling his belt loose. "Right here?" He teased her, running his thumb along her lips, "Letting him fuck you where anyone could see what a slut you are for us?"

Maya's head swam, his words barely registering. Even as he slowly pulled her to the edge of the table and slid his cock into her mouth she couldn't do anything but moan softly, the slap of Stefan's hips jerking her body.

Diego wrapped her ponytail around his hand, using it to hold her mouth still while he fucked her too. Tears welled in Maya's eyes, her heart hammering in her chest. It was all so much and she wanted them, she did, but maybe not like *this*.

It didn't take long for Diego to come, pulling out and jerking off over her neck and cheek. Maya gasped for air, searching for the words she needed.

"Stefan-" she gasped and he wedged a hand beneath her, fingers unerringly finding her aching clit.

"Yeah? What is it?"

She didn't know anymore. She didn't think she wanted this but she didn't want it to stop either. It was the most attention Diego had paid to her in daylight hours - sprawled in a chair nearby, watching her with a blank expression on his face. And Stefan's fingers continued to push her higher until she was whimpering and writhing in his grasp.

"That's it," he leaned forward, pressing his hand to her cheek and pushing Diego's come into her mouth. "That's my dirty little slut."

She wanted to tell him she wasn't, that the woman sucking on his fingers while he came inside her was someone else. The glass was cool under her cheek, Stefan's hand gentle in her hair as he pulled out and guided her mouth to him. "Clean yourself off me."

Unable to consider doing anything but follow his instructions she opened her lips, licking at the tang of their combined release.

"Sorry I left a mess," Stefan smirked and Maya blinked up at him in confusion. Hands cupped her backside. She could see Diego still so it must be Daniel running a finger through the cleft of her and circling the puckered hole.

"Have you ever?" His rough voice rolled over her and Maya shook her head, heart skipping a beat when Daniel slapped one cheek.

"Will you let me?"

Would she... would she *let* him? Her hands were tied behind her back and she was bent over the table being *used* by them and all she could think was that she would give them everything they could ever want.

Stefan pulled himself free, brushing a strand of hair out of her face. "You gonna let Daniel fuck your ass Maya?"

"Yes," she gasped, closing her eyes and trying to pretend she wasn't this person. That she didn't want this so badly. Daniel's hands lifted her up, untangling her wrists from the cloth and closing his fingers around her neck.

"You gonna take us all?"

All? How? She didn't ask, nodding as hands caught her, moved her into the living room, settled her over Diego's lap. He slid inside easily, reaching up with one hand to scrape his come on her face back and into her hair. He jerked, forcing her to arch her back, thrusting her breast towards him.

"Relax for him, princess," he grunted and Maya felt what must be Daniel probing behind her. She didn't know where he had found lube and she was too far gone to ask, shuddering when he slipped two fingers into her and began massaging them back and forth.

"Over here," Stefan turned her head and slipped between her lips, forcing her to gag as he thrust into her mouth. Daniel settled behind her, slowly pushing the head of his cock into her while Diego shallowly rocked inside her.

It was so *much*.

"She loves this, don't you?" Daniel groaned into her ear.

She couldn't speak, propping her hands on Diego's chest as she tried to take them all. Daniel's arms wrapped around her shoulders and pulled her back harshly into him. He grunted and she bit back a soft whine.

"That's it, *fuck* you take me so well." One hand loosened and skimmed down her side, gripping her waist as he slowly rocked inside of her. "It's a crime you've kept this sweet ass to yourself, you were made for this."

"Made to be used," Diego assured her, pinching her nipple.

"Next time I want her ass," Stefan grunted, palming her jaw and encouraging her to take him deeper. He made the statement as though she wasn't there, directing it at Daniel who grunted an affirmative.

It was a sweaty, messy tangle of bodies. Maya could barely concentrate, letting Stefan use her mouth while the other two used her body. It was like the first time and yet so very different. Then she had felt a part of things, like she was with them. Now...

She felt like an object they were slaking their lusts on.

Daniel came first, clutching her hips and pulled her flush to him while he groaned into her neck. Diego was next, slipping out to press the head of his cock to her clit, his thick come dripping off of her. Last was Stefan, pulling her until her nose touched the hair at the base of his cock and he gave her no choice but to swallow him down.

When it finished they each disengaged in their own way. Stefan patting her cheek and giving her a smarmy, hollow grin. Daniel sighing into the back of her neck before carefully withdrawing, and Diego... well, Diego didn't say a word. Zipping his pants and disappearing to his office.

Maya huddled on the couch, her knees pulled to her chest, wondering what the hell had just happened. Before, the sex had always made her feel closer to them, always made her feel wanted. She'd chased that high more than once, telling herself it meant they cared about her.

That wasn't a lie she could tell herself today.

Staring out the window to the rapidly darkening city below she took several long moments before pulling herself together, scooping up her scattered clothing and making her way to the bedroom.

For the first time since it was installed, Maya used the deadbolt on her door.

In later nights, when she lay awake and tried to remember anything but what had happened, she'd wonder if it was a noise that woke her up. Or was it some sixth sense, driving her to head out of her room and into the kitchen, reaching for a drink of water before the voice floated down from above.

"She's a problem."

She froze, hand stilling over the faucet. Her heartbeat thundered in her ears so loudly she thought she might pass out. That was Diego's voice, coming from upstairs.

"If you fucked up my onsite pussy I'll kill you."

Daniel's voice. Were they still talking about her? They had to be, right? Who else could be-? She swallowed at the term, feeling the back of her neck heat up. Should she go up there?

"I wasn't the one railing Susie homemaker in the ass this afternoon." Stefan's voice. "If she shuts down the fuck train I don't think it'll be all my fault."

Maya sat down heavily on the landing, well out of sight. She didn't want to hear this. She should go.

"Jesus fucking Christ," Diego again. "This is the shit I'm talking about. You fuckers are so obsessed with the easy lay you've forgotten there's a thousand other girls in the world just like her." Pressing the back of her hand to her mouth Maya choked back the gasp at his words. "I can appreciate some grade A pussy as much as the next guy, but this has to stop."

"And how do we do that?" Daniel argued. "You gave her her own fucking business."

A business they *trusted* her with, or so she'd thought. Diego quickly disabused her of that notion. "And it served its purpose, got us between her thighs. Stanton can take it over."

Pain welled in her chest. It was all happening again. Her life being dictated by men who didn't care about her. She'd been played, all those nice words, they hadn't been for *her*. Empty prattle to fill the air while they used her for the only thing she was actually good for.

"We'll set her up in the building, you can go fuck her whenever the mood strikes you," they were still talking, Diego answering a question she hadn't heard.

"I still haven't had her blow me, we'll have to wait til after that."

"Fine, when Daniel's finished getting his dick sucked she's gone. Agreed?"

Maya didn't wait to hear the answer, stumbling backwards and catching herself on the banister before she could fall. Bile rose in her throat and she quickly ran towards her bedroom, covering her mouth until she could dry heave into the sink.

It wasn't... she *knew* what she was to them. She *knew* it. They had never pretended otherwise. Even in their nicer moments it was always obvious why she was there, why they kept her around, why they allowed her to take up room in their lives.

What the *hell* had happened to her? When had she become this woman? Waiting around for some man - *men* she corrected herself, choking on a dark laugh as she looked in the mirror. Letting *men* use her like she was nothing to them.

She'd thought she was *special*. And there was something so intoxicating about being special to men like them. She lived with them, hung out with them, slept with them - not just *fucked* them.

Maya faced the truth of it. She was *easy* for them. Convenient. They'd never lied to her about it either, been upfront from the start that they wanted to fuck her and she... she'd wanted it too. She *was* a whore. And a slut. A toy for them and everything else they'd ever called her. A piece of ass they kept around for when they were bored.

The counter was cold against her back as she slid to the floor, staring at the tiles. Turned out there was something worse than being abandoned.

Being nothing.

She didn't know how long she cried. Knocked her head against the cabinet behind her and muffled her wails into a towel so they wouldn't hear her. There was no way she could face them. Not like this.

Not ever.

Pulling herself together she stumbled to the closet, wiping tears away with one hand. There wasn't much in the way of 'real' clothes. No jeans - hell there weren't even pants with a *zipper*. But there were some simple, lined leggings and she pulled a black pair and an oversized sweater down in rough movements. She considered leaving everything else. The idea of wearing things *they* had bought for her was anathema. Her more practical side won out and she half-filled a cloth bag with underwear and a couple of changes of clothes.

Then she waited.

It was important to get the timing right. Late enough that Daniel was asleep, but not so late that Diego was already moving about. There was a window there, around four or five in the morning. Setting her laptop up she ignored the notifications and watched the clock, sitting in the middle of the floor as it slowly ticked away the minutes until it was time.

Taking a deep breath she slung the bag over her shoulder, pasting a wide smile on as she opened the front door.

"Good morning Ryan," she said cheerily, grateful it was him, crossing and hitting the elevator button as though this was something she did every day.

"Good morning, ma'am," he responded, a furrow forming between his eyebrows. "Are you going out alone?"

"Bagels!" she chirped, holding the bag up as though it might answer his questions. "I heard it's Diego's birthday and I wanted to surprise him."

Ryan still looked worried, darting his eyes between her and the door. "Are you sure you're supposed to be going out?"

Maya gave him her most confused look. "Am I a prisoner?"

"No no no," the man quickly backtracked, holding his

hands up as the elevator dinged its arrival. "It's just- we were told to be sure you were safe."

"Then come with me," she shrugged, stepping inside. "Or have someone meet me downstairs. It's just around the corner."

Ryan seemed to like this compromise, speaking in low tones into a radio on his shoulder and then giving her a nod as the doors shut. Maya resisted slumping in relief. Someone was probably watching the cameras and she pretended to sway to unseen music as the elevator dinged its way down the floors. In the lobby, a man met her with an aggrieved frown.

"I'm sorry miss, it'll be just a minute, we're trying to find someone to go with you."

Maya made small talk, trying not to look as scared as she was. A thought occurred to her and she suppressed an evil smile. "Is Brandon here? We were having a conversation earlier and I was hoping we might continue it."

"He just got here, let me see."

A few minutes later he was there, giving her a smug leer and gesturing her out the door. He dipped down as she passed, taking a long whiff of her hair.

"So what back alley you wanna do this in?"

Biting the inside of her cheek Maya took a steadying breath. "I have to get the bagels first or they'll be suspicious. Come on."

He followed like a shadow - her own personal stalker as she walked the short block to the bagel place. It was packed, as she had hoped, at least a dozen people crowded into the tiny shop trying to get fresh orders in.

"Wait here," she told him, hoping her smile looked warm and not forced. "I'll be right back."

He looked like he might argue but one glance into the packed shop and he nodded, leaning against the wall with folded arms. She felt a brief moment of pity for him - he was going to have a very rough day after she disappeared.

Maya smiled as she entered, staying in his eye line for a minute before shifting closer to the counter - and into the mass of people. When she was out of his sight she ducked further back, into the employee area. Ignoring the bustle around her she searched for the back door, the one she knew they took deliveries from.

It was less than five minutes from entering the shop that she was stepping out into a wide alley, truly alone for the first time in months. She had almost three hours to kill before her bank would be open and she needed to get as far away from where she was as humanly possible.

It was time to move on.

27

"She's a problem."

Stefan sighed, sinking further into the leather, whiskey dangling from three fingers. "What is it now?"

Diego snorted, gesturing with a cigar his direction. "You telling me this afternoon wasn't a clusterfuck?"

Shutting his eyes Stefan leaned his head back, staring up at the ceiling. When he'd come back and seen her, her hand on another man, his vision had gone red. Her laughter and smiles were for them, for *him* if she gave them. All he could think of was making her remember that, fill her with him. He'd never been jealous a day in his life, shared everything with his brothers - but in that moment he could have ripped that fucking blond Australian apart with his bare hands.

Had it shown? He didn't remember how it started, it was all hazy moans and her desperate pleas. Desperate for more… right? God… her face when they'd finished. Had she even come? He didn't know for sure and that bothered him. She wasn't… she wasn't the kind of girl you just fucked.

And yet they had.

"It's fine, buy her something pretty," he waved a hand vaguely, sighing when Diego shot him a glare with a raised eyebrow. Yeah, that wasn't going to work.

"If you fucked up my onsite pussy I'll kill you."

Stefan could barely see Daniel in the shadows, sunk into an armchair and staring into the fire. "I wasn't the one railing Susie Homemaker in the ass this afternoon," he pointed out. "If she shuts down the fuck train I don't think it'll be all my fault."

"Jesus fucking Christ," Diego groaned. "This is the shit I'm talking about. You fuckers are so obsessed with the easy lay you've forgotten there's a thousand other girls in the world just like her."

"Not like her," Daniel mumbled, almost too low for Stefan to catch.

"I can appreciate some grade A pussy as much as the next guy, but this has to stop," Diego continued.

"And how do we do that?" Daniel grunted. "You gave her her own fucking business."

Making a dismissive gesture, Diego grunted. "And it served its purpose, got us between her thighs. Stanton can take it over."

"Not Stanton," Stefan snapped.

"Who the fuck ever," Diego snapped back.

"Where does she go?" Stefan asked with a frown.

"We'll set her up in the building, you can go fuck her whenever the mood strikes you," Diego said, as though he wasn't going to do the exact same thing. As though Stefan would never walk in to find Diego balls deep in her.

Hypocrite.

"I still haven't had her blow me," Daniel pointed out, the barest hint of panic on his face. "We'll have to wait til after that."

Stefan snorted. As soon as that happened Daniel would come up with something else. That she hadn't held his hands or licked his toes or whatever would drag her time out longer. As much as he'd tried to push Maya away, Daniel was in too deep - just like Stefan was. Only difference was Stefan *knew* it.

Diego rolled his eyes. "Fine, when Daniel's finished getting his dick sucked she's gone. Agreed?"

He hated it. Hated the idea of it. But it was for the best. And it wasn't like she'd be *gone*. Just out of their hair, their lives. Somewhere she could go be Maya for them - and they wouldn't have to worry about it.

"It's better for *her*," Diego offered, watching the other two. That was what tilted the scales for Stefan. She needed distance from them. Fuck she was way too good for their bullshit, and as soon as she had a moment to think about it she'd be gone. It was better for them to make that decision first, not drag it out and ruin her more than they already had.

"Fuck."

Daniel really did say it best.

The yelling was not his favorite thing in the morning.

It wasn't entirely out of the ordinary and he ignored it as he stacked his hands behind his head, closing his eyes and trying to drift off to sleep again, mind filled with what he might be able to get up to before they showed Maya the exit.

The banging on his door cut off his musings and he threw it open with a scowl, shrugging into a shirt. "What?"

"She's gone."

Stefan almost asked *who*. But Daniel's face was carefully blank. Downstairs he could hear Diego giving orders.

"What happened?" He scooped his shoes up in one hand, not bothering with any niceties like socks.

"We don't know. She went out for bagels this morning and disappeared."

"Bagels?" Stefan scoffed, taking the stairs quickly behind Daniel. "Who the fuck let her leave for bagels?"

"Told Ryan it was Diego's birthday and she wanted to surprise him."

Stefan paused, slipping a loafer on with one hand, "Is it?"

"Is it what?"

"His birthday?"

"How the fuck would I know?" Daniel snapped, sliding into a chair and pulling his laptop out.

Stefan stalked to the living room, Diego had three men lined up in front of him, each sweating bullets. Stefan smiled, rolling up his sleeves, stepping up beside his friend.

"We keep her in here for her protection," Diego stated in a deadly calm voice. It wasn't a question and the men didn't treat it like one, shifting from foot to foot. "At what point did it occur to you that letting her leave alone was a fucking stupid idea?"

Their nighttime chief of security, Jackson, flinched. "I sent a detail with her. It was just a block - and she was..." His eyes got big and he bit his tongue.

Stefan smiled wider, stepping into his space and tipping the man's chin up. "No, no. Finish that thought."

"Sweet," Jackson stuttered. "She said your favorite was blueberry, wanted to know if I wanted one. I just - how do you tell a woman she can't do something for her man?"

A choked sound came from behind him and Stefan blinked back a swell of emotion. Gesturing Jackson to the side he pointed at Ryan. "Same story?"

"Yes, sir," the man answered quickly. "Said she was getting bagels. I asked her if she was sure it was okay and she said she wasn't - uh, wasn't a prisoner."

"Maybe she should have been," Daniel mumbled.

Stefan waved Ryan aside as well. Yes, he spent most of his days with the accountants, pouring over the books. But this? This was why Diego had him. He crooked a finger, gesturing the last man forward.

"And we come to you," he said with a friendly head tilt. "These two I can almost excuse, but she was left in *your* care. Explain to me how that happened. How she's *not* here and you *are*."

Brandon gulped air, eyes darting around the room. "She told me to wait outside. The shop was small, and she said…" his eye twitched and Stefan noted it. "She said she was meeting someone and I should keep an eye out."

"*What*?" Diego roared and Stefan held up a hand. Slipping his knife from his pocket he flicked it open, pressing the blade behind the man's ear.

"You're very twitchy for someone telling the truth," he pressed harder, watching blood swell up. "Do you want to try that again?"

"It's true," Brandon assured him. "I think it was another guy. She… I mean… she's a bit of a whore…"

Stefan moved so casually he might have been swatting a fly, pulling the knife forward and catching the man's ear in his other hand. Brandon screamed, hands coming up to the wound, and Stefan swept his feet out from under him.

"*You* don't get to talk about her like that," he said congenially, pulling at the thighs of his pants so he could squat next to him. "Understand?"

"Yes sir."

Standing, Stefan wiped the blade on his leg, barely looking up when Diego asked, "Who do we think it is?"

"I know who it is," he said without emotion. "Stanton."

"Her accountant?" Diego frowned. Turning to Jackson he snapped his fingers, "Bring him. Now." He curtly dismissed the other two, leaving the three Kings to brood alone.

"What if she left on her own?" Daniel broke the silence. He was the only one who was willing to voice the question lingering on the air.

"Then we get her back," Diego growled.

"Weren't we kicking her out today?" Stefan pointed out.

"She doesn't get to leave us," Diego snapped back.

So Diego was just as gone as they were. Interesting. He hid it better than Daniel.

"Boss?"

Stefan jerked his head up, a snarl starting as the blonde Aussie walked in the room. "I was just getting in, is something-"

Stefan's hand on his throat cut him off, lifting him off his feet. "*Where is she?*"

Stanton's reply was garbled, hands clawing at the arm that held him. Diego laid a hand on Stefan's shoulder, catching his attention. "He'll need *some* air to answer."

Stefan loosened his grip, but only slightly, letting the man get his feet under him. "Start talking."

"I don't know what you're talking about," Stanton wheezed.

"Maya left with someone, convince me it wasn't you," Stefan snarled in return.

"She wouldn't have," Stanton's eyes widened, fear in them. "Not like - not like that."

"What do you mean," Stefan dropped him, not bothering to feel sorry when Stanton collapsed to the floor.

"Christ, she's head over heels for you, she'd only leave if you forced her," Stanton gasped, rubbing his throat. "How did you not notice?"

"Notice what?"

"The way she lit up," Stanton got to his feet, swaying slightly. "Same way my wife looks at me, you lucky bastards." He shook his head sharply, "There's no way she left of her own free will - not as long as you were here."

A brief thought flitted through Stefan's brain - did she know, somehow, they were getting rid of her? But that was impossible, they'd only made the decision last night. Long after she'd gone to bed.

"He was nowhere near here til about thirty minutes ago," Daniel called out. "Before that he was commuting in, before that at home. With the wife I presume?"

"Sam, yeah," Stanton was getting his bearings back. "She's eight months pregnant, can't sleep through the night. We walk around the house together."

Stefan refused to like this man.

"Go back to your work," he snapped. "Do your job. Tell us if you think of anything."

Stanton nodded, backing away while lightly fingering his neck. He'd have bruises there, Stefan would have to see to it Daniel gave him a raise. For the new baby of course.

"Now what?"

"I'm pulling cameras but it's going to take a while, most aren't going to upload to the cloud until midnight."

"*Fuck*," Diego bit off.

Stefan pulled a mug down from the shelf, slowly pouring himself a cup of coffee. It would help, and he needed to think. "I want to talk to the entire team again. Brandon first."

"I'll have them set up in the rooms," Diego replied absentmindedly. "Who do we think took her? Alvani?"

"If it was Alvani we'd have found her dead in an alley," Daniel snapped, not looking up from his laptop.

Stefan didn't point out that there were more ways to deliver a body with far greater impact. That didn't stop his brain from supplying the images though. A hand delivered via courier, her face left at one of their warehouses, fragments of her body scattered across their lives as they tried to put the pieces back together.

The mug in his hand shattered.

"We'll find them," he said with deadly calm. "And then I'm going to kill them."

28

"Have a good night Chris!" Maya called out, reaching out to flip the bookshop sign to closed. She scooped up Mo, tucking him inside her coat with practiced ease and zipping it up halfway. "You good?" The tortoiseshell cat gave a soft rumbling purr in response, paws kneading against her breast. "Typical man," she scolded with a smile, locking the door and pulling it shut. She'd drop the keys off at the coffee shop next door before heading home.

Lincoln Creek was a quiet town, only about ten thousand people in the winter. A resort destination that made its money on off-roading vehicles, hikers, and mountain bikers. Too low to get decent snowfall. Maya liked it, liked the small town vibe. Everyone didn't know everyone, and with the resort turnover new faces weren't out of the ordinary. But it was easy to get to know people, to settle into the community.

She'd gotten lucky when she first arrived, nearly six months ago, toting a duffel bag full of cash in a beat up Camaro she'd bought from a guy at a gas station. Pulling up on Main Street, *The Written Word* had a sign in their window looking for help, and a quick inquiry had netted her not only a trial shift but a line on a local furnished apartment as well.

It wasn't big, barely larger than her bedroom back home.

No. Not home. Just larger than her last bedroom had been.

Shaking herself she crossed the street, cuddling her hands beneath the solid weight of the cat. "You're getting heavy Mo, is this winter weight or have you been cheating on me with someone else's tuna?"

Home was not back there, in the city, with three men who had broken her heart. Home was here, behind a small grocery store and up a set of rickety wooden stairs behind the building. It wasn't much, but it was *hers*. And she didn't want to draw attention to herself with anything bigger. People would wonder how she could afford it on her hourly.

They didn't need to know about the nearly seventy thousand dollars stuffed under her bed.

No one had been more surprised than her when she'd checked her bank balance the morning she left. There were enough zeroes she wondered if there was an error, abandoning the ATM to go inside and check for certain. But a review of the transactions showed it was all hers. The money from the original agreement, plus her own 'salary' from the events company.

She'd pulled as much as the bank could give her in cash, just under a hundred grand. Barely putting a dent in the astronomical sum in her account. Then she'd tucked the card safely away and left town. It wasn't a certainty that she could be tracked by someone other than her bank, but it wasn't worth the risk. She'd seen Daniel work wonders on his laptop, she wouldn't put it past him to track her by her bank activity somehow.

Regardless, she was several hundred miles from there now.

The first couple of weeks had been the hardest. She'd cried herself to sleep nearly every night, feeling like her heart was breaking. Was it possible for it to break three times? Once for each of them? She'd known she was in deep but hadn't realized how much.

She missed them.

Part of her wanted to go back, confront them about what they had said. Maybe with time they'd realize they had feelings for her too, or that they wanted her as much as she wanted them.

Maybe they'd repainted the place pink.

If she was going to wish for impossible things, might as well dream big.

She kept those dreams to the nights now, lying in her bed with Mo and wishing things were different. By day she was moving on, working, reading, cooking... it was slow going but it was *something*. And somewhere in all of that she was finally starting to get a sense of who she might be.

Who *Maya* might be, on her own.

Glancing up the stairs she sighed. She'd left the lights on again, something her landlord endlessly scolded her about even though she paid her own electric bills. The old man seemed to have a personal vendetta around the idea of wasting electricity.

Maya paused.

No, actually, she *hadn't*. In fact she'd been talking to Mr. Potter when she'd gone to work, and had made a point to ensure all of the lights were turned off before she left for the day. It was probably nothing but... she wasn't up the stairs yet. No one inside could see her. She kept an emergency bag in the car just in case something like this happened. Should she just... go?

Backing down a step she kept her eyes trained upwards, wary of any sign from her apartment. She took another step and bit back a shriek when she stumbled into something.

"Going somewhere, sweetheart?"

He didn't grab her, didn't toss her over his shoulder and carry her off. Stefan crowded close to her until she couldn't do anything but mount the stairs, closing her eyes and trying to think of what she could do to get out of this.

The door was unlocked and once inside she sidestepped quickly, planting her back to the wall. Diego was in her kitchen, rummaging in her cabinets. Daniel stretched out on her couch, muddy boots on the cushion while he thumbed through a magazine. Stefan closed the door softly, leaning against it and blocking her exit.

All three stared at her.

Not at her, her *stomach*. The rounded bulge she cradled protectively as she looked them over.

"How far along?" Diego asked quietly.

"Is it ours?" Daniel swung his feet down, leaning his elbows on his knees.

"Oh for-" Maya rolled her eyes, unzipping her coat and scooping Mo out, setting him gently to the side next to his bowl of dry food. "It's a cat you idiots. The apartment gets cold so I've been bringing him with me to work. I'm not…" she paused, pulling her gloves off. "Is that why you're here? You thought I might be pregnant?"

"We're here," Daniel said quietly, "because you ran from us."

"I *thought*," she retorted, "I wasn't kidnapped."

"You weren't," Diego responded, coming around to lean against her table. "But that doesn't mean you could just leave."

Maya glared at him. "I think you don't know what kidnapping is."

"We thought someone had *taken* you," Daniel snarled.

"And you… what? Were angry someone else was playing with your toy?" Maya heard the anger in her voice and she made no effort to rein it in. "Well, they're not. I left on purpose. So if you don't mind…" she gestured at the door but no one moved towards it. She hadn't thought they would.

"Why did you leave?" Stefan had the audacity to look hurt.
"It's none of your business."

Diego snorted, crossing his arms. "Beg to differ, princess."

A growl bubbled its way to the surface and Maya gritted her teeth against it. "Don't call me that."

"You like it," he pointed out, daring her to say otherwise.

"I liked it when I thought it meant something," she snapped back. "Not just that you couldn't be bothered to remember my name." Taking a deep breath she pointed at the door. "Go home and find some other pathetic, desperate girl to play with."

"Kitten," Daniel started, apparently not listening to a word she'd just said.

"I'm not your kitten!" she yelled, hands balled into fists at her side. "Or your princess or your sweetheart, I'm *me*. Maya."

"We know who you-" Stefan started but she swung on him, fist catching him in the shoulder and forcing him to take a step back.

"No, you *don't*. I was never anything more to you than a distraction and that's *fine*. But don't pretend like you know me. Like you cared about *me*. Don't pretend I *meant* something to you."

"You *did*," he insisted.

"My *grade A pussy* did," she threw back, watching him blink in surprise. "But it could have been attached to a meerkat for all you cared."

"A meerkat?" Daniel asked blandly.

"Sorry, a vacuum so it could suck your dick for you too," she retorted with a sneer. All three were looking at her like they'd never seen her before. Good. Hopefully they didn't like this Maya, she certainly didn't.

Diego reeled away from her, his expression morphing to one of hurt. How *dare* he? How dare he come to her home and pretend *he* was the hurt one? "What kind of men do you think we are?"

"The kind to tuck their pathetic side piece into an apartment so they could visit her whenever was convenient," she growled. "The kind of men to lie just to get between her legs."

"What are you talking about?" Stefan asked, arms folded tight on his chest. But Daniel looked sick.

"Shit."

She lifted her chin at him. "Too bad you never got that BJ - I guess only they can tell you if it was worth the effort you all went through."

"Ah *fuck*," Diego took a step towards her and Mo hissed, arching his back. He stopped, staring down at the cat. "It's not-"

"Were you going to make me leave? That day - you were going to get rid of me, right?" All three were silent and Maya took it as her answer. "Then what does it matter if I walked out or you made me - I'm gone. It's done."

"It's not done," Diego gritted out. Daniel and Stefan were walking towards her, boxing her in against the wall. "We spent months worrying about you, searching for you. You owe us."

"I don't owe you *shit*," she answered, ignoring Daniel's raised eyebrow at the curse. "Get out of my apartment or I'm calling the cops."

"No you won't," Stefan shook his head.

"And why not?"

"Because I'll tie you up in legal matters for the next fifty years," Daniel said calmly. "Or do you have a better explanation for the seventy grand under your mattress than that you stole it from us?"

"You wouldn't *dare*," Maya gritted out. "It came out of *my* bank account."

"And how did it get in there?" he shot back. "Payments from us, while you were under our roof. While we extended our *home* to you Maya. Our *hospitality*."

"I hate you," she spit out.

"Who doesn't?"

God, how could her heart still break a little for him? She shook herself, "Fine, then just get out."

"You're coming back with us, we need to talk about restitution."

Maya scowled, taking a step back. She didn't have time to contemplate her answer or the sharp prick of a needle into the back of her arm. The world was going dark around the edges and she was suddenly overwhelmed with the urge to sleep.

29

At least they hadn't put the sex swing back.

Maya groaned as she sat up, rubbing the back of her arm and glaring at the bright sunlight. They'd drugged her. Those jerks... no, those *assholes*, had actually drugged her. *Again*. They had drugged her and brought her back to the apartment they'd been twelve hours from kicking her out of.

"Son of a-" she gritted out, swinging her legs over the bed and holding out a hand to steady herself. She opened the bedside drawer, rifling through it, but her knife was gone. No problem, she would kill them with her bare hands.

Maya paused, thinking. Killing them was *an* option, but probably not her best one. Not least of which she'd be unlikely to get all three at once - or even bring herself to commit that much violence. She could try to run, but that hadn't turned out so well the last time. Reasoning was probably off the table, they weren't inclined to be logical about the situation.

She had hurt their *feelings*.

What did it matter that they had done it to her first? That they were ten seconds from doing the same thing she had done. She had moved first and it was too much for their precious little egos to handle. Couldn't stand the thought that she wasn't going to be there for their every little whim.

Throwing open the closet doors with a bang, she strode inside like a woman on a mission. They wanted her back? Fine. They could have *exactly* what they asked for. She passed the racks of undisturbed clothes, grabbing for the items stuffed into the far end. The stuff they'd bought she swore she'd never wear.

Teeth gritted, a tic developing in her jaw, Maya dug into the *very* back.

Stefan saw her first, choking on his coffee with a loud noise that startled the other two.

"What the-?" Daniel started, then broke off when she entered the kitchen. She ignored them, crossing to the island. Stefan pushed a mug her direction with a stunned look. She took it, glancing inside at the milky contents. Of course it was exactly how she took it.

"The fuck are you wearing?" Diego snapped.

The outfit was carefully picked, thigh-high fishnet stockings and a pair of stilettos she could barely walk in. Black garter belt and lacy, see-through panties. The bra barely deserved the name, the straps only serving to provide a framework for the bows that tied over her nipples.

"You wanted me back," she said casually, holding the mug out over the sink and looking Stefan directly in the eye. "I can only assume it was to provide the same services." Without blinking she turned the mug over, spilling the contents before letting it fall, the ceramic clattering against the stainless steel.

Stefan blinked at her. She stared stone-faced back.

"Go change." Diego sounded tired, "This isn't you."

"Of course not," she gave him a brittle smile. "What use would *Maya* be to you?" Looking down she assessed the front of his trousers, saw the bulge there. "Looks like someone is interested though."

He pushed himself away from her, cursing under his breath and staring at her like he'd never seen her before. She hated this, hated *them*. How dare they bring her back here like this.

"So who's first?" she asked brightly, perching a hand on her hip and cocking it out.

Diego glared at her.

"Or is it going to be all three again? The table I assume? That's the usual spot." She moved toward it but Daniel grabbed her arm as she passed, pulling her up short.

"We've got people coming over, put on some damn clothes."

"Aren't these the clothes *you* bought for me?" she bit back. "I thought you liked everyone knowing I'm your whore. Liked knowing I was always ready to take you?"

"Don't be a child," he snarled in return.

"But I thought you *liked* that," she goaded him, reaching out and running a finger down the buttons of his shirt. "Does *daddy* not want to play anymore?"

He swatted her hand away, grabbing his coffee and stalking towards the offices. Maya didn't bother watching him leave, turning to the other two men with a large, fake smile. "Two's easier to handle anyway. Do you want to flip a coin for my mouth or-"

Diego moved so fast she didn't see him, cutting her off when he crowded into her space and forced her back against the cabinets.

"You've made your point."

"What point?" Maya mocked his tone, pressing her body against his. "You looked for me for how long? Went how far? Well, here I am. What are you going to do about it?"

A squeak escaped her when Diego lifted her by her thighs onto the counter, stepping between her legs and holding her gently by the throat. "Stop acting like a whore."

"Why?" She wrapped her legs around his waist, crossing her ankles behind his back. "If I'm not here to be *fucked* at your beck and call then what's the point?"

Diego didn't answer, wrenching himself away and leaving with a curse, the front door slamming after him. Maya looked at Stefan and he tilted his head thoughtfully at her.

"What are you doing?"

"I'm giving you what you wanted," she spat, sliding off the counter. "What else?"

Tears were threatening and she dashed her hand over her cheeks, trying to stave them off. She couldn't stand the empathetic look Stefan was giving her, strutting past him with her head held high.

"Maya," Stefan called after her. He looked like he regretted it when she turned around, arching an eyebrow at him and waiting. "You're here because you belong here. With us."

"I'm here because I have no choice," she corrected him. "You made sure of that."

He looked pained and she turned away, unable to bear the thought that she'd hurt him. God, what was *wrong* with her?

So much. So so much.

Maya ached for something to do. Her laptop was nowhere to be found. They probably assumed that with access to the internet she would call for help, contrive an escape.

They were correct.

She tried the front door first, the man on the landing a stranger. His eyes widened when he saw her outfit, gaze snapping to the wall over her left shoulder. "Ma'am?"

"I want to leave, call the elevator."

"May I ask who is going with you?"

Her eyes narrowed on him. "You are. Call the elevator."

Eyes resolutely over her shoulder he shook his head. "No ma'am. You're only supposed to leave with one of the bosses."

Muttering to herself she slammed the door, leaning against it and folding her arms. She knew it wasn't going to work but it still irked her to hear it. Taking a shaky breath, she blinked at the photos across from her. Urging the swirling blacks and whites to come into focus. She wasn't going to break down, she *wasn't*. She was Maya *fucking* Alvani - she was stronger than this.

A hiccup escaped her and she laughed. No, she wasn't, actually. Because no matter what was happening, all she wanted was to walk down the hall to the first person she could find. Sit in their lap and have them hug her and tell her everything would be okay. That wasn't strength.

Was it?

Also, she wanted *tea* damn it. It had felt incredibly good to pour the mug out earlier, spite making her blood boil, but now she was low on caffeine and the world felt more off kilter than it had any right to.

Flipping the kettle on she settled into a dining chair, hissing as the cool leather stuck to the backs of her thighs. She'd forgotten how inhospitable the apartment really was, even if it did seem to be warmer than she remembered.

"Lunch will be here soon," Stefan said from behind her. She watched his reflection in the windows, not turning around. He stared at her, a frown pulling his full mouth down into a pout. "Do you want to come read in my office this afternoon?"

"No."

Shoulders slumped, he turned away, leaning over the island and busying himself with his phone. Diego came in next, from the front door, his steps clipped and steady.

"You tried to leave?"

"Yes."

"In *that*?"

Maya kept her eyes forward, back to them. "Yes."

"Jesus Christ," he muttered, running a hand through his hair. "Running won't work."

A mug appeared by her elbow and she ignored it, blinking back emotion as Stefan took a step away. Why did they have to be nice - so *good* - in all the wrong ways?

It felt petulant to toss it again so she slid it closer, wrapping her hands tight around it as she took a sip. She didn't respond to Diego, watching him and Stefan exchange looks she couldn't process.

"Any better?" Daniel asked. Stefan shrugged and Daniel shoved his hands in his pockets with a sigh. "Fuck I thought we'd be past this by now."

"She's being a brat," Diego responded, his eyes on her. "Let her get her little tantrum out."

Closing her eyes, Maya counted to ten. Then did it backwards. Blowing over the warm drink she busied herself with thoughts of murder.

"Are you giving us the silent treatment?" Daniel scoffed.

"I haven't heard you say anything to me," Maya responded levelly. "Is there anything else?" She asked, standing and moving towards them.

"Jesus," Daniel groaned, pressing his thumb and finger to his temples. "No."

"Then may I go to the room?"

"You don't have to ask permission," Diego sighed. "It's not like you ever did before."

"*Before* I was a guest - at least I had thought I was," she bit off. "*Now* I'm your prisoner. I'd hate to make my captors upset."

"For fuck's-" Diego lept to his feet, stalking over and towering over her, even in the heels. "Stop this *act*. We need to talk about this."

"Fine," she swallowed. "Let me go. You were going to do it anyway, I don't understand what has changed."

"Whether we would have or not is irrelevant," Daniel snapped. "You belong *here*."

"You didn't *want* me," Maya shot back. "Why are you doing this?"

Diego slid closer, holding a hand out that she batted away. "The problem was never wanting you Maya."

"I can't..." her voice cracked and she hated herself for it. "Just let me go. *Please*." Looking into their faces she gave up any pretense that she was strong. "Please, Stefan... Daniel..." she turned her eyes on each of them in turn, "Diego - I can't keep doing this, I *can't*. Let me go home."

"Give us a chance to convince you *this* is home," Diego said quietly.

Maya barely heard him, wrapping her arms around herself and squeezing her eyes closed to stop the tears. "I want *my* bed, and *my* couch. I want Molasses and my stupid cookie jar." She knew she sounded pitiful but she couldn't help it. "I don't want this. I don't want to be here."

"Just stay with us," Diego gently touched her arm. "We can all be happy again. We *need* you."

Maya felt dizzy. Had they not heard a *word* she had been saying to them? Rage clouded her mind, a twitch developing in one eye. If she could have set the apartment on fire with her thoughts she would have.

"It's all still about *you*," she took a step forward, feeling a surge of power when he stepped back. "What *you* want and what *you* need. If you were so eager to be near me again why not move to Lincoln Creek? Did it even occur to you?" Diego's brows drew together in confusion. "Of course not, because then *you* would have had to do the uncomfortable, make the change. And God forbid any of *you* had to do something you didn't like."

"We can't just leave our lives, you know that," Stefan said evenly, as though he was speaking to a child. Maya could have strangled him.

"But I could leave mine? I could leave my life to come back here?"

"It's not the same," Diego tried but she cut him off with a sharp wave of her hand.

"That's the problem," there were the tears again, choking the back of her throat and making her vision go fuzzy. "It is, and you can't see that. You think I am *less than*-"

"Fuck that," Daniel cut her off. "We have *never* thought of you as less than anyone."

"As long as my life, and my dreams, and the things *I* want can be tossed aside for what *you* want, I will *always* be less than you." Taking a shaking step back she lifted her chin. "I spent half my life being an afterthought, an accessory to someone else's story. I won't do it again."

Someone called her name as she left but she was crying too hard to identify who it was. Stumbling, she caught herself on the wall, jerking her heels off and tossing them aside before shutting the door to her room firmly. Stripping the lingerie off she turned the shower on to as hot a temperature as she could stand, sliding down the wall until she hugged her knees to her chest and set her forehead to them.

What was she going to do?

30

Staring into the drawer, Maya considered it longer than she should have. It was right there, shiny and sleek, mocking her. Then again, violating herself like that to prove a point seemed silly.

So no pony tail.

She found rabbit ears instead, a pastel bustier and g-string set that she attached the fluffy bunny tail to, and thigh high white boots. She looked like she'd stepped right off the pages of plus-sized *Playboy*.

Was *Playboy* even a thing anymore?

Keeping her chin high she strutted into the kitchen, bending at the waist to retrieve absolutely nothing from the floor but enjoying the way Daniel choked on air when her tail twitched.

"Fucking hell," he breathed. "*Now* you wear the costumes?"

Ignoring him, she went through her morning routine, finding a yogurt parfait in the fridge and perching daintily on a kitchen stool. Daniel glared at her over the rim of his glasses.

"If you're trying to prove we don't want you, you're doing a piss poor job of it."

"You don't," she responded, licking along her spoon.

"Come over here and I'll show you just how much."

Finally glancing up at him she gave him a slow blink. "You're proving my point."

"Fuck," he breathed, shoving his coffee away. "When did you stop making sense?"

"When you stopped listening to me," she said without emotion.

"I listen," he grunted. "You think you're giving us what we want, kitten, trying to prove a point."

God, how was he so fucking *dense*?

He continued without seeming to realize the hole was digging. "But we wanted you even in those dumb sweaters and leggings that were impossible to get down your thighs."

Was he really going to bring her thighs into this? What a jerk.

"The night I found out you wore my briefs I could have come in my fucking pants. *Shit*."

It definitely wasn't getting hot in the kitchen. Maya fought to keep from squirming. Being angry didn't stop her body from responding to his words. But it did help her tilt her chin his direction and ask, "And what am I doing in these little fantasies of yours?"

"What?"

"You know, when you fuck me on the couch or bend me over the table in your mind, what am I doing?"

"Taking it," he growled, hand clenching on his cup.

"Yeah," she sighed, turning away. "That's what I thought."

Daniel was silent, she could feel him over her shoulder, feel his eyes studying her. She was a puzzle, a line of code he couldn't figure out, and it bothered him. Good. Let it.

She didn't look up when he left, stirring her parfait and keeping her breathing even. It felt a little silly, playing this game with them, when she could just come right out and say what the problem was.

Except she *had*.

She had poured every one of her hurts at their feet and they refused to look at them - convinced that they *knew* what the problem was. That they knew better than her. And she didn't know how to overcome that, or even if she wanted to. How many times could she tell them, and how many times could they brush it all aside, before she finally broke down completely?

Standing, she crossed into the kitchen proper, pulling the drawer with the trash can hidden inside and dropping the plastic container into it. She was sliding it back when a small jar appeared in front of her. It had a yellow label with a drawing of a rabbit on it. Stefan was on the other side of it, one eyebrow raised.

"How apropos," she said, turning it around with one finger. "Why is this here?"

Stefan crossed his arms. "You said you wanted it. So I got it."

Maya stared at the jar, pursing her lips. "Molasses is my *cat*," she pointed out. Opening the drawer next to her again, she dropped the jar into the trash below. "You know, the one you abandoned in my apartment to slowly starve to death?"

"Fucking hell," Stefan groaned tilting his head back and staring at the ceiling before something caught his eye. Maya turned to follow his gaze, seeing Daniel holding an armful of silk and lace.

"What are you doing?" Stefan asked, frowning at him.

"I'm getting rid of this nonsense," Daniel bit back, tossing the lingerie in a pile on the floor. "She thinks this is all about sex so I'm going to prove it's not." He disappeared in the back again and Maya gaped, tears pricking her eyes.

"It's because he cares," Stefan said softly. "We all do. We just want what's best for you Maya."

Maya jerked upright, jaw clicking shut. She marched towards the hall, intercepting Daniel with the next round of lingerie and jerking as much as she could out of his hands.

"How *dare* you?"

"What?" Daniel's brows drew together. "You hate this stuff, you hate wearing it like this, and I *know* you hate wearing it right now. So I'm fucking getting rid of it. You're welcome."

If Maya had been prone to violence she would have slapped him. In fact her arm tensed and only the barest shred of control held her back. "I didn't ask you for this."

"I'm doing you a favor," he snapped back.

"These are *mine*," she yanked a wad of lace out of his hands. "You bought them for me. You *gave* them to me. And now you are throwing *my things* away without even talking to me." Her chest heaved, she was on the verge of a breakdown. "You went into that room you told me was *mine.* My *safe* place and you decided unilaterally that I don't get to have my things anymore." Dropping the lace at her feet she took a step back, sniffling.

"You know we'd give you anything you ever wanted," Daniel tried to reason, his expression worried.

"Until you decide I don't get to have it anymore."

He jerked as though she *had* slapped him, looking at the pile of clothes with wide eyes. "Maya…"

"Do what you want," she turned away, catching Stefan's eye as she shrugged. "You all always do." With one hand she drug the ears off her head, dropping them into the clothes. She wasn't even going to be able to protest the way she wanted. What a joke.

"Ha ha," she whispered, not bothering to shut the bedroom door. It obviously wouldn't stop them anyway. The deadbolt was a false promise, a keyhole on the outside - one she had certainly never been offered a key to - a mocking indictment that she could ever keep them out.

Pacing near the window, Maya curled and uncurled her hands, squeezing her fists until her nails dug into her skin. The pain was sharp, stinging through her. Her heartbeat was so strong she was sure she could hear it, blood roaring. She wasn't going to cry, she *refused* to cry.

"Maya?" Shutting her eyes Maya dropped her chin, not turning around at the sound of Daniel's voice. Her breath shuddered as she struggled not to let him see how much she was hurting.

"What?"

"I, uh, I brought your…" Movement behind her and a soft *whump*. Neither of them spoke, Maya listening to him shifting from foot to foot. Finally he let out a loud exhale. "Fuck, I'm… I'm *sorry*. I wanted to - *shit* - I don't know how to do this. Make someone happy."

A tear escaped and Maya fought the urge to dash it away.

"Are you going to look at me?" Daniel's tone was incredulous. "I'm trying to apologize here. The least you could do is meet my eyes."

Lifting her chin, Maya looked towards the ceiling as though she could see straight into heaven and ask God for help. Turning only her head she did as he asked, not bothering to hide how glassy she was with tears.

"I accept your apology."

His eyes narrowed on hers, as though he suspected a trap. "So I'm forgiven?"

Maya shrugged. "Sure, if that's what you want."

"Fucking-" Daniel cut himself off, rubbing the back of his neck and grumbling. "That's not what I meant."

"What *did* you mean Daniel?" She turned fully around, folding her arms over her stomach and cupping her elbows with her fingers.

"I just wanted…" he searched for words. "I felt bad. About before. And I wanted to fix that."

"You want me to forgive you so you can stop feeling bad?"

"Well... *yeah*."

With all the strength she could muster Maya looked him dead on, steeling her spine. "It's not my responsibility to make you feel better, Daniel. You're upset because you hurt me, and now you're asking me to take on the additional burden of absolving you. Of telling you it's going to be okay. I'm not going to do it."

"But what can I *do*?" His voice had a pleading edge to it, his eyes wild.

"That's not my responsibility either." She dropped her eyes, slumping into an exhausted posture. "Would you please leave? I'd like to be alone."

Daniel hesitated, shifting from foot to foot. "Maya..."

"*Go...*" The word was whispered, her voice catching in her throat. It was the only one she could push out, everything else stinging behind her eyes. He left and she sank to the ground, back pressed to the cool glass window. She felt hollow, the tears that had previously threatened disappearing, only to be replaced with cold numbness.

31

Maya had never considered herself a particularly spiteful person. When words were said and feelings hurt, she was always the one to give first. To reach out and apologize and hope the other person would meet her halfway. Nor did she hold grudges, life was too short to be mad for that long.

So it was with some surprise when a dark, ugly emotion began to build over the next few hours. Staring at the photographs hanging on the wall she felt resentment begin to take root inside of her. And when that turned to a sense of furious resolve she embraced it. Changing out of the ridiculous outfit into something more comfortable while she plotted. Jotting notes on the back of a magazine as she sat in the small sitting area in her room - *not* in the new swinging chair although she had to admit she liked it.

By the time the sun had gone down she was ready.

She closed her eyes and took a deep breath, opening the door and venturing out into the apartment. There was no one in the large common areas so she went straight to step one.

Groceries.

The man on the landing was new, leaning back in a chair and fiddling with his phone when she opened the front door.

He dropped it with a clatter, cursing softly as he debated between picking it up and standing up to greet her. He eventually chose the latter.

"I'm sorry ma'am you can't-"

"I have a shopping list," she cut him off, holding the paper out to him.

"Oh, yeah, sure. I'll pass them on and they'll be here in the morning."

"No," Maya raised an eyebrow, keeping her face expressionless. "I want them within the hour."

"But it's nine o'clock-"

"Are you telling me that no where in this entire city there exists a twenty-four hour market?" He hesitated and she stepped back into the apartment. "An hour," she reiterated and shut the door before he could protest further.

Step two wasn't her favorite but it was important: Find out who was home.

She checked the offices first, cautiously poking her head into each. They were all empty and Maya carefully stole the items she wanted. Pads of paper, pens, books, even a set of keys that made her eyes light up. She stacked each into her arms and took them back to her room, dumping them on a the low table. She called their names up the stairs, progressively louder, before venturing up and delicately opening each bedroom to call again.

Satisfied she was alone she hit the kitchen, opening every cabinet and drawer, pulling mixing bowls, dining ware, cutlery, and an assortment of cooking tools. And, of course, the kettle and mugs. Those she set on the bed, cocking her head and eyeing the room. On her next trip she took the long console table that was behind the couch, setting it against one wall and moving the kitchen items onto it. The small toolbox she'd found under the sink she set by the door, tucking a screwdriver into her pocket.

She flung the front door open again. "When are they expected back?"

"Ma'am?" The man jumped to his feet.

"Your bosses, when are they expected back?"

"Um, they're at the casino…"

"When they get back can you please tell them I'd like for them to knock?"

He blanched, "I don't know…"

"They'll be upset with me, not you. Just do it."

Okay, that was good, she had some real time and could probably do this all in one go. Reviewing her list she prioritized, going upstairs first and disconnecting the small wine fridge in the corner. It was tucked into a fancy cabinet which she made no effort to be kind to, setting the bottles to the side, and hefted the appliance into her arms. It was heavy, easily forty pounds empty, and she was careful as she carried it downstairs and set it in the corner of her room next to the console table.

She had to use the screwdriver to detach the built in microwave, pulling the stove vent hood down to find where the cord was going. But it too went to her room. The TV was more difficult, the cords were hidden behind the wall and it took Maya a good fifteen minutes to find the access point and pull everything free. The TV itself was about as heavy as the fridge and she carried it carefully to the bedroom and set it in the middle of the bed.

Finished, she set her hands on her hips, blowing a strand of hair out of her face and surveying what she had done. Snapping her fingers she went to the cleaning room, tucked in the back, and took every towel she could find, a bottle of detergent, and an armful of paper products. She stopped in the kitchen and stole the dish soap as well.

What next? Someone knocked at the door and Maya froze. If they were home…

"Ms. Alvani? It's Dereck, I have your shopping?"

She was smiling so widely when she opened the door it startled the man. She thanked him profusely and shut the door firmly in his face, waving off his offer to help. The shopping went to the bedroom too.

Whistling to herself she hefted the bags of lingerie Daniel had dropped off and took the stairs, setting them in the middle of the coffee table at the center of the room. There was no hesitation as she walked into the first bedroom and stripped the sheets, throwing the pillowcases into the lounge. The bedding she tossed in the shower, along with as many clothes as she could easily find. She turned the water to hot and shut the glass door with a whimsical tap of her foot.

She did the same thing to the other two rooms. Collecting any scrap of cloth she could get her hands on - including several very nice leather jackets - and tossing them into the shower to soak under the hot spray. In the lounge she cleaned them out of every liquor bottle, collecting a particularly nice set of tumblers. She cleared the shelves of books too, stuffing them into the pillowcases and then dropping them to the floor below.

A song came to her and she sang it softly to herself, feeling much like a Dr. Seuss character stealing the holiday spirit as she examined what was left of the apartment. Cabinet doors were open, the contents spilled out onto the floor. Every throw pillow was gone, every book or indeed every piece of entertainment at all. She did leave one gift for them, however - four framed photographs she had pulled from the bedroom wall and left neatly stacked by the fireplace.

As a last precaution, Maya took the keys she had found and tried them on her door lock. They weren't a fit, which was better than she could have hoped. Leaving one sitting in the lock, she found the hammer in the toolbox and opened the door as wide as it could go, bracing it with a wedge. It would need one quick hit to be the most successful but Maya had faith.

It took two. Maya frowned as she picked up the head of the key that had just snapped off, tossing it into the room. With a few careful whacks she mangled the keyhole beyond recognition. It would take a blowtorch to get it free, which suited her perfectly.

Surveying her treasures she set her hands on her hips, going through her checklist one last time. Then she smiled.

And locked the door behind her.

"We fucked up."

Diego looked up as Daniel plopped into the leather arm chair across from him. "Oh? What was your clue? The crying or the yelling?"

"Both," Daniel said in all seriousness, pouring himself a glass of scotch. "Fuck if I have to see her cry one more time…"

"What the fuck are we doing?" Diego asked, eyes steady on his friend. "Since when do we kidnap people like this?"

"Well, this is - I believe - the second time…"

"Fuck off," he grunted, taking a drink of his own whiskey. "You know what I mean. She's *pissed* and she has every fucking right to be. We *fucked up*."

"Yeah," Daniel groaned, leaning his head back. "Not sure how we fix it."

"I'm not sure we *can*," Stefan's voice floated over from the third chair. "You should have seen her - she thinks we killed her fucking cat."

"What cat?" Daniel asked with a confused look.

"The brownish one, back at the - you know, the *cat*," Stefan tried to explain.

"Oh," Daniel's brow furrowed. "What *did* we do to the cat?"

"It ran out the door as we were leaving," Diego grunted. "No clue after that."

"Is it possible we're bad people?" Stefan asked blandly and Diego snorted.

"I think it's likely. For other reasons, but also for this."

They sat in silence, listening to the sounds of the casino bustle below them. They were not going to run the risk of being overheard again - of being taken out of context - by sitting in the apartment.

You weren't taken out of context and you fucking know it.

Yeah, he could own up to that.

"I ask again," Daniel said, "how do we fix this?"

"Can we, I don't know, *orchestrate* a return to normal?" Diego mused. "The lingerie is really throwing me off." Stefan barked a laugh and Daniel glared. "What?"

"Daniel tried that," Stefan chuckled. "It did *not* go well."

"What did you do?"

"I was going to fucking get rid of it!" Daniel insisted. "She hates the shit, always has. But then... *fuck* she was so fucking *mad.*"

Diego blinked, confused. "If she hates it, why would she care?"

"Because it's *hers,*" Daniel explained. "And I was, apparently, doing whatever the fuck I wanted with her."

"Think of it this way," Stefan pointed out, "if I went into your office and tossed your server rack would you be mad?"

"I'd fucking kick your ass."

"You'd *try,*" Stefan said blandly.

Daniel took his glasses off, pinching the bridge of his nose. "Okay, okay. *Fuck.* I get it. Jesus fucking Christ women are complicated."

In context, it sounded pretty straightforward to Diego but this was the most emotional growth he'd seen from Daniel in years so he bit his tongue. Daniel stared into space, the way he did when he was working through a puzzle.

"I mean, is there any value in just *asking* her what she

wants and *giving* it to her?"

Diego and Stefan both blinked at him. When it was put that way it sounded kind of stupid that they hadn't tried it. "We've done that," Diego pointed out. "We gave her those clothes she actually likes."

"I just bought them for her, I didn't exactly ask her opinion," Daniel corrected.

"What about the business? She wanted to do something different and maybe we could get her onboard with something else. She seems to like it-" Stefan started but Diego shook his head.

"No. Actually she tried to turn me down. I insisted she be a part of it."

All three men fell silent, thinking back over their time with Maya. Diego tried to think of something he'd actually asked her about before just doing it, but to his chagrin the only things he could think of were sexual. And even those were few and far between.

"I *think*," Diego sighed. "We *might* be assholes."

"Well, we knew that already," Stefan tacked on. "I just... I thought we were being nice."

"You are really fucking bad at this," Daniel grunted, ignoring the looks they both gave him.

"And you're better?" Stefan snorted incredulously.

"I didn't give her a fucking bottle of maple syrup," Daniel snapped back.

"Molasses," Stefan corrected. "It was fucking molasses and you know what? Forget it."

"We let her pick out her own room stuff," Diego offered. "I mean, we kind of insisted on the remodel but she did get to choose all of that." A thought occurred and he sighed. "Okay, maybe not *all*."

"What did you do?" Stefan growled.

"I insisted she keep the bed." He held his hands up

defensively, "It's comfortable and perfect for all of us!"

"It's a wonder she didn't kill us in our sleep," Stefan sighed.

"Yet again I say," Daniel spoke up. "Have we tried just asking her what she wants?"

"And when she says she wants to leave?" Stefan whispered quietly.

None of them wanted to think of that, falling into silence as they swirled their drinks and watched ice melt. They didn't say another word to each other, staring into space and lost in their own thoughts. When the waitress came back with new glasses Diego waved her off, noticing how both Stefan and Daniel were rising to their feet. There was only so long they could avoid the inevitable.

The ride back was quiet, Diego stared out the window and thought about what next steps could be. They could start with meals, he couldn't recall if they'd ever asked her what she felt like - other than the times she'd requested stuff to cook. After that maybe some new clothes. He leaned against the elevator door, watching the counter click up.

"Fair warning, she's probably still pissed about earlier," Stefan said blandly.

"I did put all the lingerie back."

"Jesus," Diego sighed, "why am I always fixing shit you two fuck up?"

"Fuck you," Stefan snapped. "We all fucked this up."

"Yeah, but I knew better than to try to fix it," Diego said smugly, stepping out of the elevator. "You two made it worse." Nodding at the man on the landing Diego crossed the hall swiftly, reaching for the door.

"Sir, wait!"

Frowning, Diego turned, watching the new guy fumble behind him.

"*What*?"

"The Miss - Miss Alvani asked me to tell you to knock before you went in."

Stefan arched an eyebrow. "She did, did she?"

Terrance nodded, looking sick. "Yes sir. Sirs."

"Did she say anything else," Diego leaned a shoulder against the wall, folding his arms and watching with interest.

"She uh, she asked for some shopping. Mostly groceries. She was pretty insistent they get here tonight."

Diego mulled that over, watching his friends do the same. Daniel had a skeptical look on his face, "Was there cheese on it? Bread?"

"Yes sir."

Daniel's eyebrows rose and he turned to Stefan. "Think she's making those sandwiches again?"

It seemed too much to hope for, and definitely too much to hope she'd made anything for *them*, but then again she'd been surprising them for the better part of eight months. Anything was possible.

Diego knocked sharply on the door, waiting with his head cocked. When he didn't hear anything he knocked again, the corners of his mouth pulling down. On the third knock he turned to Stefan, "How many fucking times am I supposed to knock on my own door?"

"One more?"

When no one answered again Diego tried the lock, somewhat surprised when it opened. "Well we tried you can't-" His eyes cut to the left, on the sliver of the kitchen he could see. "*Fuck.*"

"What?" Stefan shouldered past him, charging into the kitchen and swearing. "Fucking hell *again*?"

Diego rounded on the guard. "Who came in here?"

"No one," Terrance held his hands up, "I swear, Dereck dropped the shopping off but he didn't go inside."

Daniel shouldered past him but Diego stayed, menacing

the guard. "When was the last time you saw her?"

"About three, maybe four hours ago?"

"Get everyone mobile up here," he snapped. "*Now*."

Daniel's heart was in his throat, his eyes taking in the kitchen, the TV missing from the wall, the... lack of pillows? Who the fuck came in and stole pillows?

"Maya," Stefan pounded on the door in the back of the house and Daniel followed the noise, stopping a few feet behind him. "Maya I know you're going to be mad but I'm coming in. Something's happened out here and we need to know you're safe. *Maya*."

Stefan turned the handle, jerking back in surprise that it was locked. "What the fuck?" Stepping past him Daniel examined the door for any signs someone had tried to force their way in.

"Get out of my way," Stefan ordered, "I'm going to knock it down."

"Wait," Daniel bent to peer at the door, squinting through his glasses. "The lock's been sabotaged."

"What? Let me look."

Daniel stepped back and studied the door. It looked pristine, no signs anyone had assaulted it other than the mangled lock. A thought flitted across his mind and he grabbed at it, examining it from all angles.

"Stefan, don't try to break the door down til I get back, okay?" Stefan gave him a curt nod and Daniel walked back to the kitchen, noting the open drawers and the gap where the microwave used to be. Diego shut the front door and Daniel waved him over.

"What do you see missing?"

"What do you mean? Where's Maya?"

"In a second," Daniel gestured at the mess. "What's missing?"

"Microwave, kettle, some plates maybe? Looks like the silverware drawer is just gone."

Humming Daniel walked back down the hall, pushing Stefan out of the way before knocking softly. "Maya, are you in there?" When no one answered he sighed. "Are you going to talk to us?"

A flash of white at his feet caught his eye and Daniel bent, retrieving the folded piece of paper and opening it to reveal a single word.

No.

He laughed, he couldn't help it, handing the paper back to Stefan and leaning against the door. Stefan held it up to show Diego, giving Daniel a befuddled look. "What the fuck does this mean?"

"Maya has moved out."

"Out?" Diego pushed Stefan aside. "Where the fuck did she go?"

Daniel pointed at the room. "I believe she has made herself a place to live without needing to interact with us."

"She *what*?" Stefan was fuming and Daniel stepped in his way when he made a lunging move for the door.

"No." Stefan looked nut-punched so Daniel explained, "I already went through the 'invading her space' argument, you don't need to too. She's in there, she's safe, and she wants to be there. Right Maya?" When no answer came he snorted. "The silent treatment *is* a little childish, don't you think?"

"*Fuck you.*"

Daniel choked back a laugh. "Yeah, no one is going through that door without her permission."

"Since when are you like this?" Diego asked with a raised eyebrow and Daniel shrugged.

"Since today I suppose."

Stefan stormed away, to do God only knew what, and Diego gave him a curious look before following behind.

Suppressing a smile, Daniel made himself comfortable, leaning into the wall by the door and shoving his hands in his pockets.

"If you're listening... I don't think they would have. I mean, maybe if they didn't know you were okay, but not..." He rubbed the back of his neck. "I uh, I need to - *fuck* - I was an ass earlier. About the clothes. I shouldn't have touched them."

The room beyond was silent and Daniel let his breath whoosh out. Was she even still listening? It would be real fucking stupid to be apologizing to no one. Although, maybe easier too. A loud sound from upstairs caught his attention and he turned his head, listening to the cursing and shouting between Stefan and Diego.

"Do I even want to know?" he asked the door before pushing off and sauntering towards the apartment proper, hands still stuffed in his pockets and taking the stairs at a steady pace. On the floor above he raised an eyebrow at the mess, poking his foot at what was left of the wine cabinet. She'd gotten herself a refrigerator, good for her.

"Jesus fucking-" a knock came from downstairs and Diego pushed past him, muttering to himself about water. Out of curiosity, Daniel went into his own room, pausing as he stared at the bare mattress and scattered pillows.

"Huh."

His walk-in closet was empty, drawers pulled out and strewn in a path to the bathroom. Why was the shower...?

His laughter echoed in the tiled space, a grin splitting his face as he stared into the glass cubicle with all of his clothes in it. All of his *thoroughly soaked* clothes in it. He contemplated opening it, studying the amount of water and deciding against it. Back in the common area Stefan was looking through the bags on the coffee table.

"Did she get all your stuff too?" Stefan asked.

"Yeah, Diego?"

Stefan nodded. "He opened his shower, flooded the place."

Daniel snickered and peered into the bags, biting back another laugh when he saw the lacy contents. "Well at least she left us something to wear."

"You're taking this *very* well," Stefan snipped, collapsing onto one of the chairs. "One might think you were involved."

Daniel held his hands up and sat down, searching for something to drink. "Just impressed." His usual decanter was gone and he frowned, scanning the room. "Where is the-"

"She took it. Or threw it away. Either way..."

Daniel did laugh out loud then, rubbing his hands down his face. "Clever."

"I'd think it was funnier if I hadn't just bought that bottle of '61 Balvenie."

"You can buy another," Daniel pointed out.

"It's the *principle*."

Diego stomped up the stairs, throwing himself across the end of the couch and glaring at the ceiling. "The guys are getting a cleaning crew, I've got someone getting our spare shit from the safe house. I assume she hit you too?" Daniel nodded and Diego grimaced. "What the fuck happened?"

Stefan started laughing, meeting Daniel's eyes with a raised eyebrow. "It *is* impressive."

"What the fuck is wrong with you two?"

"We were just discussing how to fix this, right?" Stefan snickered. "Well, I think Maya has proposed her solution."

Diego blinked, face blank, and then he snorted, reaching a hand to flip the cabinet next to him open. "This is such bullshit."

"She took the liquor," Daniel smiled.

"Son of a-" Slamming the door closed Diego slid until he was fully horizontal on the couch. "Tell me again why we worked so hard to bring her back?"

"This actually makes me like her *more*," Daniel commented.

"It would," Diego sighed. "So what do we do?"

"Tonight?" Stefan asked. "Nothing. Tomorrow we should try and talk to her. And get her cat."

"The one we left in the mountains?" Daniel asked incredulously.

"Look, I don't know about you, but I was actually paying attention this afternoon. She thinks we've been selfish which - you know what? Fair. The way I see it," Stefan held up a hand, "there's three options. One, we keep going like we have been and hope she breaks."

"Not an option," Daniel cut him off. "I like it when she's feisty."

"Two, we stop being selfish and let her make an informed choice."

"And three?" Diego asked.

"We let her go."

Put that way it didn't seem like a choice at all.

32

Mreow.

"Is there some reason we had to be the ones to make this trip?"

Stefan focused on the road, trying to ignore Daniel in the seat next to him. They were only a few miles from the apartment and if he made it that far without murdering the man it would be a miracle.

"Because I needed someone else to confirm what the thing looked like."

Mreow.

It was supposed to be easy. Go back to that shithole town, find the cat, go home. But everything that could go wrong did. The cat wasn't in the apartment, or anywhere nearby. A visit to the local shelter had turned up nothing concrete, although a cat matching his description had been brought in and then adopted out recently. Daniel had to hack into the shelter's system to get the information - a system, he scoffed and told him, that even *Stefan* could get into. However, the new owner of the cat was not inclined to give Fluffernutter up.

"Fluffernutter?" Daniel had snorted. "Who names a fucking

cat Fluffernutter?"

That had earned him banishment to the car before the woman slammed the door in their faces. It took nearly five grand and a promise that they would send regular updates on Fluffernutter's life before they could leave.

Mreow.

"You would make an excellent coat," Stefan called back, knuckles white on the steering wheel. The damn thing hadn't shut up the entire trip. And he was pretty sure it had thrown up in the backseat of his Jag, purposefully aiming through the mesh in the soft sided carrier.

Mreow.

"How certain are we that that's the right cat?"

Stefan sighed, "About eighty percent?"

"If we paid five grand for just some cat Diego is gonna kill us."

"Fuck that, his last watch cost at least three times that, he can fucking relax."

Mreow.

"Shut up," they both snapped at once.

Mreow.

"A fucking cat skin coat," Stefan mumbled to himself again. Twenty minutes they'd be back, assuming no traffic. It was fine.

"The fuck took you guys so long?"

Daniel dropped the cat on the kitchen island, hissing back at it when it hissed at him. "Do not fucking start. Did the shit arrive?"

"Yeah," Diego jutted his chin towards a mess of boxes on the table. "What kind of pet needs that much stuff?"

"Hers," Stefan stated flatly, staring him down. "Have you seen her? Has she-?"

Diego shook his head and Stefan's shoulders slumped. He hated that she was still locked away but absurdly happy no one had gotten to see her while he was gone.

"This is the cat?" Diego asked, bending his head to peer into the career.

"Yeah," Daniel answered from the refrigerator, handing a beer to Stefan. "We're pretty sure."

"*Pretty* sure?"

Stefan used the edge of the counter to pop the top, taking a long swig before gesturing at the growling bag. "Around eighty-five percent."

Diego's eyes turned heavenward and Stefan would have bet everything he owned the other man was praying. "I've moved forward with worse odds," he finally muttered.

Leaning against the island, Daniel gestured towards the fireplace, drawing Stefan's attention to the stack of frames there. "Did you have art printed while we were gone?"

Diego growled, tossing back nearly half his beer in one go. "They're the ones from her room."

"I thought you said she hadn't talked to you?" Daniel asked incredulously.

"She left them when she raided the house," Diego corrected.

"Why would she-" the words cut off abruptly as Stefan shook his head sharply at him. Daniels's eyes narrowed, his head cocking to one side in confusion.

Diego answered anyway. "Presumably because they reminded her of me."

Silence hung over the kitchen island, all three men staring into the distance. The glass of the bottle made a sharp noise when Stefan set it down abruptly.

"We need a plan," Stefan settled his elbows on the marble, leaning forward and clasping his hands. "Something more than this fucking cat."

Mreow.

Daniel flushed, taking his glasses off with one hand and

cleaning them with the edge of his shirt. "I did some research in the car and a lot of it is bullshit but some of it made sense. We've got to let her know that we know what we did wrong. And give her assurance it won't happen again."

Diego snorted. "That sounds like real weak shit."

"I don't hear you volunteering anything better, asshole," Daniel snapped.

"You know much it pains me to say it but Daniel's probably on the right track," Stefan butted in before the two could come to blows. "We've tried telling her what we want, and we've tried telling her what *she* wants. Neither have worked all that well. Apologizing is the next logical step."

"She's not talking to us," Diego pointed out. "Are we supposed to stand in the hallway and hope she's listening?"

"Could we use the cat as bait?" Daniel asked with a poke at the carrier. Another hiss came from inside and he glared.

Stefan hummed thoughtfully, moving the cat away from Daniel. "I don't think that would go over well."

"A peace offering?" Diego mused. "Offer the cat free and clear and then see if she'll come out?"

"It's worth a shot," Stefan responded with a shrug, picking up the carrier and motioning for the other two to gather the assorted cat accoutrements. He waited for them to set the items outside the door and then carefully set the cat on top of the pile.

"Maya? Are you... I know you're not going to answer me but we…" Stefan stumbled over the words, glancing back at the other two. "Shit we went and got the cat. And cat shit. I'm going to go to the other end of the hall, I promise no one is going to try to force your door open but he's right outside."

It was quiet on the other side and Stefan backed away, as promised, standing shoulder to shoulder with Daniel and Diego and staring intently at the door.

A full minute passed before the sound of the deadbolt

broke the silence and Stefan held his breath. The door opened a crack, then slightly wider. An arm reached out and grabbed the strap of the bag before yanking it inside. Another thirty seconds or so passed before the door opened wider and he caught a glimpse of her head as she took the box, turning the lock behind it.

A whoosh of breath left Diego and Stefan echoed it. "Well that went better than I expected."

"And now?" Diego asked with a raised eyebrow, shoving his hands in his pockets and leaning against the wall.

"I did the cat thing," Stefan pointed out. "Someone else can do the next part."

"*Son of a* ..." Diego grumbled before moving away from them and knocking softly on the door. "We would like to talk with you, would you come out here?"

Stefan held his breath as they waited. He swore he could hear the tick of Diego's watch from six feet away. There was no sound from the other side, not even that awful *mreowing* noise from the cat.

Shoulders slumping Diego turned back around, sighing and giving them a defeated look. "I guess-"

All three of them jumped to attention when the door opened, drinking in Maya's form filling the doorway with the cat cuddled over one shoulder.

"What do you want to talk about?"

Daniel's mouth gaped open and Stefan was in no better state. He hadn't actually thought she'd open the door. Diego recovered first, taking a step away from her and a deep breath.

"About you. About us."

"I want to go home," she said firmly, lips pursed together.

"Okay."

She blinked, narrowing her eyes. "Okay?"

"If that's what you want, I'll have a car brought around

right now. If you really want to leave, we won't stop you."

Maya's eyes flew to Diego's, then to Stefan and Daniel in turn. "You'll just... let me walk out?"

"We'd like to know you're safe," Diego said softly. "But if you don't want us to know I won't blame you."

Silence fell heavily between them as Maya thought that over. It took everything in Stefan not to step forward and touch her. Reassure himself she was there.

"Okay."

Something inside Stefan broke and he turned away, catching the look of pain on Daniel's face before he hid it. He heard the waver in Diego's voice as he said, "Take anything you want. It's all - take it all. I'll call down and-"

"No." Stefan glanced back and saw her shake her head, her hand trembling as she reached up and shoved a lock of hair back from her face. "You said you wanted to talk. About us. Talk."

"Here?"

Maya cracked a small smile at Daniel's question and Stefan could have hugged him.

"The living room is fine."

It was almost a dance to move, none of them wanting to turn their back on Maya. For her part she drifted through them like a wraith, gently setting the cat on the couch next to her and sitting up straight. None of them dared try to sit next to her, settling into a row across from her instead.

"We fu- *fudged* up," Daniel broke the silence. "Bringing you back here, it was a mistake." He glanced over at the two other men and continued, "We panicked - when you left us it was... *shit* - I mean, *shucks* - *fuck*..." He grimaced and Maya gave a small, genuine smile at his faltering attempts to censor himself.

Diego came to his rescue, "What Daniel's trying to say is that we want to include you. In all of this. And we want to make that as easy as possible."

"Let us try," Stefan said softly. "I know it's all messed up but I can - *we* can be better. Give us another chance."

"Another chance for *what*?" Maya asked and Diego jumped in quickly.

"To be with us. To be a part of us. We had that for while before we fucked it up," Diego held a hand up and tilted his head. "I'm not censoring that one, we fucked up. We don't - we've never had that kind of life. Girlfriends or wives and all of that." He waved his hand, "I don't know what it looks like but it's *with* us. We're brothers and you're-"

"A sister?" Maya offered with a skeptical eyebrow.

Daniel barked a laugh and Stefan bit back a smile. "Absolutely not, I don't think any of us have brotherly feelings for you. But maybe a family? If you'll have us?"

"I won't be less than you," she said in a small voice, eyes falling to where Mo was kneading the couch cushion.

"You never were," Diego responded just as softly. "And I'm fucking sorry we ever made you feel that way."

"Four Kings," Daniel said quickly. "A partnership to start. And then we can see where to go from there."

"Four Kings," she murmured, staring past them.

"This can be your home if you want it," Diego ventured carefully. "Or if you want to live somewhere else that's okay too. Just… we're trying to make this right. Give us an opportunity to make this all right."

The room went silent and Stefan held his breath as he studied her face. Was she really thinking about it or just planning how to let them down easily. The cat leapt down from the couch and sauntered over to their side, studying each of them with yellow eyes.

"It's a lot," she finally said and he jumped to his feet.

"You don't have to decide right now, we can go." He gave Diego a pleading look and the other man rose with more grace, shaking his cuffs free of his sleeves.

"Of course, we don't want to pressure you. We can go out, give you time to think. If you decide to stay we can talk more later and if not…" He hesitated, swallowing hard. "Like I said before. Take anything you want. Take everything. Just let Ryan know where you want to go and it's done."

She nodded again and Stefan led the way to the door, giving one more longing look at her sitting on their couch before shutting it firmly behind them.

Left alone in the apartment, Maya took a deep breath and let it out slowly. She waited a few minutes, heart in her throat, before crossing to the front door and slowly poking her head out.

"Ryan?"

"Yes Ms. Alvani?"

"I'd like a car please."

"Of course." He reached to his hip for a radio and Maya quickly held up a hand.

"No no, never mind, just… checking."

She shut the door, walking back to the apartment in a haze. They really were going to let her go.

Maya sank onto the couch, staring into space. That was what she wanted, wasn't it? To be able to make her way in the world, to not be caught up in this life with three men who confused the hell out of her?

Or was it only the choice she wanted?

"What would you do?" she asked Mo, raising an eyebrow as he dug his claws into the leather of the chair near her. She smirked as thin lines of stuffing began to show through. "Good kitty."

Sitting wasn't doing her brain any good so she got up and paced, looping through the kitchen and the living room. "They already said they don't know how to be with someone," she told Mo. "Which, *obviously*."

Mo let out a plaintive *meow* and Maya gave him a smile, fetching the cat carrier from her room and tipping it to the floor before dropping it on the couch. "I'm not opening a brand new bag of treats for you, you monster. Eat what's already open."

Tail straight in the air, Mo turned his back on her, stalking into the kitchen.

"Yeah that's about right," she sighed, settling her elbows on the island. Half the cabinets were still open, evidence of her raid. Some were bare while others, like the shelf with the baking pans in it, were relatively intact.

Tilting her head Maya studied the shelf. That wasn't where the baking stuff had been before. The cake pans used to live next to the sink while the majority of the baking sheets were above the double oven. How had she not noticed that yesterday?

Taking a step around around the marble island she pulled open the first drawer she saw, expecting to see a mix of wooden spoons, measuring cups, and a set of whiskey tumblers. Instead, a neat set of whisks, spoons, and spatulas sat in a caddy made for the space. The drawer next to it was similarly tidy, except where she'd absconded with half the contents. The cabinet below looked the same, and the one next to that.

They'd re-organized the entire kitchen.

It wasn't how she would have done it, but it actually made a little bit of sense now. Mo jumped on the island and Maya pet him from nose to tail. "You don't think... you think they did this for me?"

Mo didn't answer but there was no reason they would reorganize for themselves. A sudden thought occurred to her and she stepped out onto the terrace, a small smile blooming on her face.

Her herb garden was still alive. In fact, someone had installed a watering system on it with several different timers. She rubbed a basil leaf between her fingers, smiling wider as the rich smell drifted up to her. A flash of brown caught her eye and she scooped Mo up, going back inside and nudging the door closed behind her.

"You know what," she told him, "I think today was the first time I've ever heard Diego say he was sorry. That's progress."

Daniel was right, they *were* trying. They were *really really* bad at it - but they were trying. The kitchen and the garden and Mo... if she left she'd always wonder what could have been. But if she stayed...

What if it all happened again? What if they decided they didn't want her, or had their fill of her? She couldn't do that again, she hadn't yet recovered from the first time. Maya wasn't the type of person to hold her affection back, to play it safe. If she stayed she'd be all in - and she wasn't sure they even understood what that *meant*.

"If I stay," she cautioned Mo firmly, "there would have to be ground rules." Mo gave her a curious look and she held up her hand. "One, a safety net for me - and you of course." A low purr emanated from him and she took it as agreement.

"Two, they're going to have to learn to talk about things, that one is very important. No more silent treatments and avoidance." Dropping the two fingers she pursed her lips. "They've at least made a start on that."

She sighed and slumped into the couch again. "What do you say, Mo? Think we can make this place a home?"

Because that was what Maya really wanted, a home. Was that even *possible* in this life? All she knew was her father and his friends, men with mistresses and more illegitimate children than they could keep track of. It wasn't a life she wanted for herself. Then again, she couldn't imagine any of them being as close as her Kings were. The mutual respect...

how fluidly they worked together. She had been a part of that for a minute, had seen what it could be like, and if she stayed she wanted it all.

They were *family*.

Maya wanted a family.

33

"What do you think she'll do?"

Diego stared into his whiskey, swirling the liquid around the perfect sphere of ice in the glass. "I don't know."

He didn't, and he *hated* it. Diego's life was based around knowing things. Who was up and coming and who was falling. What products would sell and which were more trouble than they were worth. He knew how to read people, to tell in a moment if he could trust them and…

Maya threw him.

Months ago he'd assumed they were getting a spoiled cartel brat, getting by on daddy's money. But it quickly became apparent that she was something else entirely. She never asked for anything they couldn't provide with pocket change, and even those things were intended to be shared. On her birthday, a perfect opportunity to wheedle something out of them, she'd made *them* dinner. When she'd left she'd taken nothing with her but a change of clothes.

He couldn't wrap his head around it.

People *always* wanted something from him, except his brothers. Power or money or whatever was on the table, people didn't keep his company just for the sake of it. And he didn't want theirs either - took his comfort in those he knew were with him to the end.

"She has *never* done what we've expected her to," Daniel huffed a soft laugh. "So whatever we think is probably wrong."

Diego felt a spark of hope at that. He was pretty sure she was going to leave - he would. After all the shit they'd put her through, no one in their right mind would stay.

"We had to do it," he said to no one in particular.

"We did," Stefan agreed with a sigh.

"Do you think we explained it well enough," Daniel asked with a frown. "We didn't even talk about the last time, what happened. She's probably still mad about that. Maybe we should send a note back to the apartment to-"

Diego shook his head sharply and Daniel slumped in his chair. "We told her she could make her mind up. We've got to give her that time."

He checked his watch. It was nearly midnight, they'd been at the casino for half the day. But no one wanted to bring up the idea of going back, no one wanted to know for sure what she'd decided.

Cowards.

Snorting, he shifted in his chair. Yeah, they were. But he knew what it had been like the last time she left. The fear and the anger, the short tempers and the yelling. He wasn't in any hurry to get back to that.

"If we wait too much longer we'll have to wake her up," Daniel pointed out softly and Diego sighed.

"Are we ready for this?"

They nodded at him and he stood slowly, straightening his cuffs. "And we're all agreed, if she's gone we let her go. No one goes after her."

Daniel nodded and Stefan followed suit, though more slowly. They rode back to the apartment in silence, standing stiff in the elevator as it beeped its way upwards. When the doors opened he blinked at the waiting guard, for a moment he'd forgotten the man would be there.

"Has..." Stefan flinched slightly and shook his head. "Have you seen Maya?"

Ryan nodded, "Yes sir, she came out and asked for a car."

Diego's shoulders dropped, his heart sinking with them. "How long ago?"

"Not long after you left."

She hadn't even thought it over, had run from them at the first chance. A knot formed in his throat and he gave Ryan a curt nod, pushing the apartment door open and striding inside. Daniel paused in the hallway, looking unsure about what to do, while Stefan immediately strode to the back of the apartment, calling Maya's name.

Diego wasn't surprised when he returned alone. Of course she'd left, that's what everyone did. There was a fucking *reason* he only trusted two people.

"I don't believe it," Stefan muttered, eyes scanning the space as though he might conjure her. "I just... I don't believe it."

"Fuck off," Daniel snarled. "Have you *met* us? I'd be surprised if she took ten minutes to think about it."

"Maybe *you're* an irredeemable ass - but some of us have things to offer the world."

"Like mooning over a woman who wants nothing to do with you?"

Diego groaned and sank onto the couch. Eyeing the cat carrier across from him he considered his next course of action. He should go away for a while, maybe somewhere tropical - or Berlin. There were some great clubs in Berlin where he could forget his troubles in an avalanche of available women.

"Maybe if you hadn't tried to throw away her shit she'd

have stayed," Stefan shouted.

"I think it was the *second kidnapping* that did us in," Daniel shouted back.

"*You were on board with that.*"

"Shut. Up," Diego growled. Coming to his feet and using his height to his advantage. "She's gone and we're not going to do this. Get a fucking grip."

Daniel crossed his arms, glaring from behind his glasses. Diego had lost track of how many times he'd offered the man corrective surgery but he kept refusing. "I think we're allowed to take a fucking minute."

"Christ," Diego bit off, heading for the stairs. "You two have your pity party, I've got to get back to work."

"Don't act like you're not wrecked," Stefan's voice followed him. "Like you're better than this."

"I *am*," Diego snapped back, rounding on them. "Of fucking course she left. When will you two realize that people don't *stay*? It's just us, no one else."

"She really did a number on you, didn't she?" Daniel said softly.

"Fuck off, she was just another girl." Diego straightened his jacket, pulling at the sleeves.

"Not her, your mom," Daniel clarified. "Always knew you were a bit fucked up but never realized how much."

"That was years ago," Diego replied. "It has nothing to do with-"

"You had dinner at my place every Sunday for years," Daniel continued. "You took my sister to her senior prom. You *know* the world isn't like that. Why are you so committed to the idea now?"

"*Because she left*," Diego roared. "We asked her to stay and *she left* and-"

Stefan cautiously put a hand on his shoulder, and Diego held himself upright with sheer force of will. These men had been with him through some of the worst years of his life - and the best. If there was anyone he could break down in front of it was them, there'd be no judgment.

"How the fuck could she just leave?" he nearly whispered the words.

Daniel's reply was just as soft, "Wouldn't you?"

There it was. They hadn't been good enough for her and she knew it. He sighed as Daniel slumped his way to the back, probably to lose himself into his screens. Diego rubbed a hand over his face, letting Stefan sit him back onto the couch and nodding along to the offer of a beer. He took it a moment later, watching Stefan shove the cat carrier to the side as he sat across from him.

The cat carrier.

Diego sat bolt upright, nearly throwing his beer in his urgency to set it down. Stefan said she'd thrown a fit over the damn cat, he couldn't imagine her hand carrying the thing out.

"*What the fuck*?" Daniel's voice called from the back. Stefan leaned to see around the corner but Diego's eyes were glued to the bag, trying to make it make sense. "The fuck is this demon spawn still doing here?"

Diego spun, eyes catching on the cat held at arm's length in front of Daniel. It looked content there, swinging from the man's grip.

"Why would she leave the cat?"

If Diego hadn't already been racing down the path he was on he would have been as confused, but he was and so he said, "She wouldn't."

"What do you-" Stefan's eyes grew impossibly wide and he suddenly darted for the door, throwing it open with Diego hot on his heels. "Maya, when she took the car did someone go with her?"

"She didn't take it," Ryan gave them a strange look, eyeing

the cat with trepidation. "She asked for the car but went back inside. Only time I saw her."

Diego resisted the urge to strangle him. "Did anyone else go in?"

"Not that I saw."

He didn't like that answer, filing it away as he pointed at the man. "I need everyone. Security, any runners in the building, *everyone*. Have them meet me in the conference room downstairs."

Ryan nodded and Diego strode inside, rushing to the back bedroom to look for any clues. Daniel followed behind, using an underarm swing to toss the cat onto the bed. The cat seemed to enjoy it, bouncing slightly before strutting across and claiming a pillow.

"She wouldn't have left the fucking cat," Diego mumbled. "So she's got to be here somewhere or-"

"She was taken against her will," Daniel finished for him. His face hardened, the tendons of his neck becoming stiff ridges. "*Fuck that*."

Daniel spun on his foot, stalking to the back of the apartment and the bevy of servers he kept back there. Diego only had the vaguest idea what the man did, all he knew was that when he needed to know something, needed to get into something, Daniel always came through.

He'd find her.

Stefan had their head of security against the wall when Diego came back out, the man's throat held tightly in Stefan's fist. "Stefan, if you strangle him we can't talk to him."

Stefan let him go, watching the body crumple. "This is the *second* time you've let something happen to her. Tell me why I shouldn't skin you alive."

Jackson blubbered and Diego sighed, watching as a guard approached with a printed list. "Everyone who has been in and out of the building," he held the paper out and Diego took it, scanning the names. It was sectioned off, other apartment owners in their own section, each verified and background checked before they moved in. Businesses on the lower floors, all employees accounted for. Their own men, each tried and true and-

"Brandon Fountain?" He arched an eyebrow, "He was let go after the last time. What the hell was he doing here?"

Jackson finally drew himself up, face clouding. "He shouldn't have been, let me... let me see what happened."

"Do that." Stefan's face looked congenial, almost friendly - if you didn't notice his eyes. "Do that and come back and we will continue this conversation. Ryan? Go with him. If he tries to run, shoot him in the leg."

Jackson and Ryan both nodded. As pissed as he was, Diego knew he'd need to rein Stefan in. Killing your men indiscriminately was a good way to get someone to put a knife in your back.

"We'll find her," he reassured his friend. "And when we do you can tear whoever took her limb from limb. I promise."

"It was Alvani," Daniel's voice came, rounding the hall with a laptop tucked under his arm. "I had a hunch so went straight to the security feeds we've got outside his complex. Took her in about an hour ago, no sign yet if she came out but I got my guys skimming the data."

"Alvani," Diego's eyes narrowed.

"Can we fucking kill him *now*?" Stefan snarled.

Diego nodded slowly. "We're going to need more power than we have. It's time to call in some favors."

"That's going to take too long," Stefan protested. "He sent someone to fucking kill her last time."

"If he's going to kill her she's dead by now," Daniel pointed out calmly. "If she's not, we can buy time to get our resources together."

Stefan growled but didn't say another word, stalking out of

the apartment to presumably find someone else to assault.

"Send out the call," Diego told Daniel, "I want anyone we've ever helped get out of so much as a parking ticket here by tomorrow evening. And get a message to Alvani."

Daniel raised an eyebrow. "What's the message?"

"The Kings are coming for their Queen."

34

Shaking her head, Maya stumbled from the SUV and put out a hand to steady herself. She wasn't entirely sure what had happened. Having made the decision to stay she'd had a shower, taking time with her hair and putting on a comfortable pair of leggings and a sweater she knew Daniel liked. She'd been going back to the kitchen when a hand grabbed her, covering her mouth, and the world went dark.

Again.

Maya was really going to need to talk to someone about possible brain damage from all the times she'd been knocked out this year.

She'd come to being pulled out of an SUV, groggy and discombobulated, hardly knowing where she was. Looking up at the glass and stone villa she swallowed back a surge of nostalgia, and an upswell of fear.

"Oh great, home sweet home."

The guards didn't say anything as they led her inside and her feet moved on autopilot to the wide sunken entertaining room that overlooked her mother's garden. A handful of people sat inside. Her brother, slouching in an armchair near the bar. A man she didn't recognize, probably her father's new sergeant at arms, pacing by the far doors. The broad back of Eric Alvani was silhouetted against the large bay windows, his face in profile to her as he stared out into the dark night.

He looked older, more lines on his face, a new scar on his cheek. But his eyes were the same, cold and dark, a shark waiting for her to get in the water.

"What? No hugs for your father?" he asked with a cocked eyebrow.

"If you wanted to see me you could have asked," Maya replied, crossing her arms.

He huffed a laugh, stepping from the window and crossing towards Nico, pouring a whiskey and holding it lightly in his hand. "Would you have come?"

Maya didn't bother answering, concentrating on controlling her breathing instead. In two three four, out two three four. Eric laughed, a hollow noise, and gestured at her.

"I presume you know why you're here?"

"I mean, you tried to have me killed once. Possibly raped and killed?" She tilted her head and stared at the ceiling. "I'm not sure if it's immediate murder or long torture you're after though. Regardless, I'm guessing I'm not long for this world."

"I considered ransoming you back to them," Eric mused. "The irony of it amuses me. But I neither need their money, nor could I stand the thought of you continuing to be their whore."

"Slut, technically," Maya pointed out. "I didn't get paid to sleep with them."

"So you are a bad businesswoman as *well* as a whore," Eric tutted. "It's like I taught you nothing."

"You did *what*," Nico whispered, turning his head up to stare at his father.

"Oh, you really didn't know? He tried to have me killed." Maya couldn't help the wave of relief that washed over her.

"It wasn't relevant to your work," Eric snapped down at his son, placing a hand on his shoulder and squeezing it harshly. "I didn't need you distracted by some false sense of sentimentality."

"He sent Michael," Maya informed her brother. "I told you what happened, you just didn't believe me."

"He said he was killed on a job, didn't say what it was," Nico stared into space, a look of concern painted over his features.

"As I said, it doesn't matter," Eric snapped.

"They're going to come for me," Maya told him levelly. "Are you prepared for that?"

"I'm counting on it," Eric poured himself another drink. "Leave it to my daughter to have a cunt that brings down an empire."

"They're going to-" Maya cut herself off, realization dawning on her. She was wrong, they *wouldn't* come. The last conversation they'd had… they would assume she had left them again. Her heart lurched in her chest, her mind conjuring images of them coming back to find her gone. They wouldn't look for either, had sworn to her they wouldn't.

God, she hoped, just this once, they would break their promise one more time.

Maya's eyes narrowed, "What have you done?"

"They've been wanting to move against me and I've given them the excuse they needed. They call their little meeting and I can take them off at the head - a coup d'etat if you will." He laughed at his own joke and Maya shivered.

"It doesn't matter, we're here now and I've got you for bait if I need you, in the meantime…" Eric gestured and the man next to her grabbed her arm, shoving her towards the back of the house. Maya didn't fight him, there was no point and this wasn't the time anyway. Instead she made note of the changes in the house, the furniture moves, the new paintings.

The room he took her to used to be an office, somewhere people could take meetings onsite when necessary but not her father's private spaces. It was a small bedroom now, sturdy bars on the windows and a heavy deadbolt that thudded when he locked her in.

To think, she'd recently been lamenting her lack of functional locks on doors.

Pacing by the window Maya tried to think, tried to reason. They had seemed so serious, so dead set on leaving this to her decision - they *weren't* going to come. Not for her anyway. Maybe for the insult, as her father had said, but not for her.

Collapsing across the lumpy bed she blinked back tears. They would think she left them again, that she didn't care. That she hadn't *chosen* them. Her earlier decision cemented more firmly in her mind. Her place was with them and they needed to know that, be reassured of it. Even if this was the end of her story, she *had* to get a message to them somehow so they'd know.

She fell asleep with tears on her eyelashes, curled into a tight ball on the comforter.

A pounding on the door jolted her awake some time later and she blinked against the sharp morning sun. The door opened without warning and she scrambled back, hands held up defensively. Someone else she didn't recognize stood there, beckoning her forward impatiently.

"Come on, take a piss so I can put you back."

Oh, yeah, now that he mentioned it she *did* have to go. Badly. Maya scrambled for the door, all but elbowing the man out of the way. He grunted and reached for her but she dodged him.

"I lived here for ten years, I know the way."

He grumbled something to himself and trailed behind her as she made the turn, reaching for the door handle just as a hand settled over hers. Turning in annoyance she startled back when she saw who it was.

"Nico? What are you-?"

Nico shushed her, waving a hand over her shoulder imperiously and the guard took a few steps back. Turning back to her he slipped something into the band of her legging in the guise of turning her to face him.

"I just wanted to let you know, those bastards you like so much, they won't be much longer for this world," he smirked as he said it, eyes boring into hers. "They've called a meeting for tonight and Eric's got a mole and he's going to take the whole pack out at once."

He squeezed her wrist and Maya let out a theatrical gasp, eyes searching his face. "You *jerks*," she hissed and Nico's lips twitched. He nodded at her and stepped back, letting her by to rush into the bathroom and slam the door behind her, turning the flimsy lock. She pulled the object out, staring down at the phone screen and thinking.

She didn't know anyone's number.

There had never been a reason to call them, if she needed them she asked someone and suddenly she was *incensed* that they had never offered their numbers, even if she was unlikely to have remembered them. Could she call the building manager? That would be a public number, right?

She didn't know the address.

"Oh my God," she whispered, "what the hell?"

All that time and she'd never gotten the address. She might be able to guess, bring up the maps and try to match the view to the building, but that would take ages and she wasn't sure it would work.

"Hurry the fuck up, I gotta get lunch," the man barked from outside.

"It's *that time*," Maya yelled back and he sighed, shifting outside the door.

"Fucking women."

Wait… lunch. Lunch meant food. *Food deliveries.* There were *always* deliveries to the place, and Daniel put in the orders himself. He'd told her that once as she looked over his avocado bowl with açaí. He didn't trust anyone else to put the orders in right.

Maya rifled through her memories, trying to pick out a restaurant name and one leapt to the front immediately. A quick search pulled up the number and she held her breath as the phone rang, hoping they'd be open.

"Taco Tony's, what can I get ya?"

"*Fuck yes,*" Maya breathed, fumbling with the phone, "I - I'm a friend of Daniel Norwood and I need to get a message to him."

There was a pregnant pause before Tony coughed, "I don't know who you're-"

"Please," Maya begged, "I can't get ahold of him. I ate your tacos every Tuesday night for weeks. I know you deliver there. He's in danger."

The line stayed silent for a beat before he said, "Not saying I do know him but if you tell me what the message is I can't say it won't find its way that direction."

"Oh God, thank you." Maya nearly dropped the phone in her haste, "Tell him dad's going to hit the meeting tonight. I don't know with what but he's got someone on the inside."

A soft hum vibrated through the other end and Maya could almost feel his wheels turning. "And who's the message from?"

"Ma-" she froze. If he knew who she was, if he recognized the name, he might think it was a trick. "Kitten. Tell him his kitten told you that."

"Kitten huh? This a sex thing?"

Maya laughed despite herself, "I wish. Just please get it to him?

"Not saying one way or the other, but I appreciate you

calling in." His voice switched back to the one he'd had at the start, "Remember we have two for one fish tacos Fridays," and he hung up.

Maya stared at the phone, trying to decide what to do next. If she kept it and it was found… but how sure was she that the message would get through? Hesitating one last moment she opened a drawer, tucking the phone in the very back and using a box of cotton swabs to cover it.

Having taken care of her business she opened the door and smiled at the frowning man outside. "All done."

He grumbled again and took her back to the room, shoving her inside and leaving her staring at the walls looking for what she was going to do with her day. A warmth surged through her and she smiled, for real this time. Nico had helped her. He definitely *didn't* know about what their father had been doing. She hadn't realized how much it had bothered her to think he would.

With nothing else to do, Maya sat cross-legged on the bed and began to plan the meal she would make when this was all over. She'd bet Diego liked mac and cheese, and she could try her hand at cookies again for Daniel. Stefan was a human garbage disposal, he'd eat anything.

Content with her fantasies, Maya let the day slip by.

35

There was a blood stain on Stefan's sleeve.

Examining the spot with a critical eye he sighed, unbuttoning the cuffs and rolling them back to cover the dark red splotch. There was blood under his fingernails as well but he was less concerned about that.

"You've been more than steadfast," he told the man hanging from a hook in the middle of the room. "No one could fault you for that. I could only wish you had been as loyal to us." He reached out and tipped the man's head up with one finger. "But I'm getting bored with this. Tell me why she was taken or I'll hand you over to the guys and they're going to be so much worse. I at least need something from you - they'll be having fun."

"I don't *know*," Brandon whined, toes kicking against the floor. "They told me to get them in the building. If I knew anything I would *tell you*."

Stefan sighed and stepped back, idly kicking one of the man's fingernails across the floor with the toe of his shoe. "Pity."

He left him hanging there, ignoring the frightened pleas as he called for the elevator and idly rubbed his hands on a cloth. There was a blood trail that led to him, he'd need to have someone take care of it. The elevator dinged its way up while he mulled things over and he strode out without a word, ignoring the men milling about and zeroing in on Diego.

"Nothing. Just confirmation it was Alvani who did it," he announced, flipping the tap on and rubbing at the edges of his nails. When they got Maya back he wanted clean hands, didn't want to worry about sullying her with what he had done.

"Same up here, Daniel confirmed she's still in the house, we've got a spotter that saw her in the hallway. But I can't get a read on what his plans are." Diego rested his fists on the dining table, glaring at the house schematics and security blueprints he'd bribed and threatened out of a local architect.

"It's got to be about us, right?" Stefan asked, glancing over the papers. It was a mess to him but seemed to make sense to Diego.

"I don't know," Diego grunted, looking up. "I don't know enough about why... did she ever tell you what happened? Why she left home when she was a kid?"

Stefan shook his head, "No, we never... she didn't want to talk about it and I never pressed."

"Me neither." Sighing, Diego sank into a chair, running a hand through his hair. "He's tried to have her killed, and now kidnapped her right out from under us. I feel a little self-centered insisting it's about us but..."

"All the signs point to it," Stefan offered, leaving to fetch a bottle of water. "If it was just about her he'd have done something before all of this. He has to want something from us too." Stefan paused and turned, catching Diego's eye. "You're worried if it's not, aren't you?"

"Fuck yes," his fist pounded the table and Diego pushed the papers aside. "If it's not I don't have any fucking leverage.

She's just *there* and I can't do fuck all about it."

"It doesn't matter," Stefan said softly, waving a hand when Diego started to speak. "It doesn't. He *made* it about us. The others will see that. This move, it broke every boundary, every rule. They'll take your side."

There was an unwritten code in their life, a series of norms that kept things from all out war. If you were going to hit someone directly, go after the head of an association, you did it hard and fast and you *finished it*. No loose ends, no dangling retaliations. You swallowed them whole or not at all. If the Alvanis had broken that the Kings might be able to get the other less than lawful businessmen to not only look the other way - but support as well.

Without it…

"We're doing this no matter what, right?" Stefan asked with the calmest face he had. If Diego said no he'd walk out the door, go get her by himself if necessary. Daniel would probably help.

"Of course we fucking are," Diego snapped back. "If we have to go in there and get her out bare handed we will."

Breathing a soft sigh of relief Stefan sat across from Diego again. "Just keep Daniel away from me, he's a shit shot."

"I heard that," Daniel grunted, settling at the table as well. "We have a plan?"

"Two." Diego pointed at a map of the area near the compound. "Technically three. One if we get actual support, one if we don't, and one if all we get is approval. Our chances obviously go up with the first option, and with the third we don't have to leave town after."

"I like the first one," Stefan told him with a smile and Diego rolled his eyes.

"I figured. Do you have the force numbers?"

"I do," he tapped his temple.

"And Daniel, you got the insights on the security footage?"

"Ready to go," Daniel cracked his knuckles.

There was a knock on the door and Diego looked up, settling his face into the one Stefan knew best. The face that said Diego meant fucking *business*.

"Here we go."

Daniel hated these meetings. He never knew what to do with himself. Diego had the talking covered and Stefan was always onhand to bolster with whatever little drops of info might be needed. But Daniel just sat there, or more often paced around trying to sneak away. He would have too, if Diego didn't always insist he come.

This time, though, he was invested. Standing near the back of the room and listening intently as Diego laid out their case. This was about *Maya*, and if she was hurt or something happened to her he didn't know what he was going to do.

"To be clear," the head of the Lau family said, leaning forward in his chair. "You expect us to not only sanction this war but to aid you in it? Over the man's own *daughter*?"

"She's ours, not his. *Our* family. And she was taken from us," Diego said evenly and Daniel bit back the urge to curse. He'd have ripped the guy's head off by now.

"So you say," someone else said, Daniel hadn't bothered to learn their name. "But all we have is your word. Alvani is saying she ran from *you*."

"The fuck she did," Daniel bit out and Diego shot him a cold look. With a grunt, Daniel pushed off the wall, striding into the hallway beyond and shutting the door behind him. If he couldn't keep his shit together he didn't belong in there but fuck he was ready to be *doing* something.

"Mr. Norwood?"

Daniel lifted his head, eyeing the messenger down. Joe something, a newer guy. "What?"

"There's a Tony here? He said he needed to speak with

you."

Frowning, Daniel shifted through his mental notes. "I don't know a Tony," a thought struck him and he frowned. "*Taco Tony?*"

"I think so?" The man grimaced and Daniel tried not to look quite so imposing.

"Tell him it can fucking wait," he waved a hand dismissively and turned back to the door.

"Mr. Norwood," the young man sounded like he was going to faint, "I'm sorry but - he said it was urgent."

Urgent? What could possibly be fucking urgent from the goddamn *taco* place? But, at least it was something to get his mind off things for a moment, maybe clear his head a little. "Fine, send him up."

A minute later Daniel was face to face with a man old enough to be his father, jet black hair with graying temples and more than a little paunch on him. "You Tony?"

"Yeah, you Norwood?" Daniel nodded and the man gave him a dubious look. "What's your Tuesday order?"

"What?"

"I wanna know it's you, I don't trust these guys."

Daniel frowned. "Eight carne asada tacos, eight el pastor, two super quesadillas, nine super burritos - surprise me - and extra on all the salsas. Now what the fuck is going on?"

Tony relaxed, pulling at the edge of his shirt. "Thank fuck. I got a message."

"From who?"

"Didn't say, said she was your, uh, your kitten?"

Daniel had the man's coat in his hands before he could think, nearly nose to nose with him. "*What did she say?*"

"Said her dad had someone on the inside. At a meeting. Was going to hit it."

Someone at a... Daniel turned with wide eyes, shoving the man away from him and darting back to the conference room.

He ignored the angry looks from the others in the room, shoving his way to Diego.

"The fuck are you-" Diego started but Daniel cut him off.

"We got a message from Maya. Her dad's going to hit the meeting, there's a mole."

Diego choked when he heard Maya's name and stood to his full height when Daniel finished. "My apologies, we will need to cut this short gentlemen, I've just been informed that Alvani has taken exception to this meeting tonight."

Garcia guffawed, rolling his eyes and leaning back in his chair. "Ah yes, wouldn't that be convenient."

"You misunderstand," Diego gave him a tight smile. "He's going to hit *all* of us."

The men in the room bolted upright, at attention. "When?" someone asked.

"I don't know," Daniel told him. "But we need to go. *Now*."

There was a scramble for the door, Stefan crossing to the front of the room to stand with them. "What happened?"

"You know where we get - never mind. Maya got a message through," Daniel explained, pushing through a side door and into the office beyond. "We need to regroup. Figure out what the threat actually is."

"What are you thinking?" Stefan asked Diego.

"To take out the whole group. Probably a-"

An explosion rocked the building and Daniel held a hand out, steadying Diego.

"Jesus fucking Christ he's crazy," Stefan yelled over the sound of the ringing in his ears, stumbling through a door and into the smokey hallway beyond.

"Did us a favor," Diego laughed, eyes a little wild. "They're definitely on our side now, come on."

Daniel followed him to the back of the building, pushing through an emergency exit and flying down the steps below. Diego had the right of it, Alvani had to be insane to go after everyone, but then again, it had quite nearly worked. Who knew how many Alvani had just killed, even with the warning. Without it there could have been -

Daniel skidded to a stop, barely noticing Stefan running into his back. "*Fuck.*"

He turned and took the stairs two at a time going up, ignoring the calls of the men behind him. He glanced through the glass window on the door for only a moment before tumbling into the service hallway.

"What are you *doing,*" Diego grabbed his arm, stopping him before he could go through into the cleaning room at the back of the apartment.

"Her fucking cat is in there," Daniel shouted, shoving Diego away. "I'm not going to let her fucking cat die under our watch."

Diego reared back, eyebrows snapping together. Behind him Stefan gave Daniel a nod. He understood at least. After a moment Diego nodded as well. "We go in with a plan, I'm not losing either of you over a fucking *cat.*"

Daniel nodded, reaching out and grasping the hot doorknob. They'd go in together, as they always did.

36

It made the news, of course it did. An explosion in a downtown high rise was bound to be reported on.

"*Authorities do not have leads on what caused the incident at 435 Riverview but so far they are not ruling out arson.*"

Maya choked on her laugh; at least she knew their address now.

Across the room her father held up a glass of champagne. "To the Kings, who were nice enough to gather all my enemies in one spot."

Maya glared at him, chest heaving. Had her message gotten through? Judging from the news footage it didn't look like *anyone* could have survived but if they'd been warned maybe they hadn't been there.

Hope kindled in her chest and she nurtured it quietly. Next to her, Nico patted her hand, giving her a soft look. "People got out," he whispered. "We don't know who yet but people did get out."

"Thank you," she whispered back, jerking away when their father's eyes darted their way. Nico didn't flinch, standing and walking across the room to face the man toe to toe. Nico had the advantage however, with a good three inches of height to stare down from.

"This was stupid," he said without preamble. "You've changed the game, opened up us to all kinds of retaliation."

"By who?" Eric crowed, gesturing with his champagne flute. "There's no one *left,* my boy. I have secured our *future.* You should be *thanking* me."

Nico glared, plucking the glass away. "Every two bit asshole with a grudge is going to be on our tail now. Every lowlife with a dream of hitting it big. It's open season on the Alvanis."

Eric grunted and brushed past his son, pouring himself whiskey instead. "By *who*? There's no one who could take us." His eyes narrowed and he pointed a stubby finger at Nico, "I don't need this from you, *brat*, I got enough of it from *her*."

Maya tried not to look interested, examining her nails and trying to drag her remaining moments out as long as possible. She knew she'd been insurance, but they were well past the need for that.

"Leave her out of this," Nico snapped. "She's your fucking daughter, and if you think for a minute I'm going to let you-"

"*What*?" Eric's eyes snapped, his back going ramrod straight. "Tell me what I can or cannot do in *my home*. Fucking do it."

There was a sound, loud and sharp and rumbling, and Maya couldn't help but turn to where it came from. The front gate maybe? Not loud enough to be the door.

"What the-" her father started but he'd heard the same thing Maya had.

Gunfire.

Nico smirked, folding his arms. "I guess someone was left to retaliate after all."

Eric cursed again, grabbing the man nearest him and pulling the Colt from his belt. "When this is done..." he warned, checking the clip and chambering a round.

Nico casually moved in front of Maya, pulling her up with one hand and tucking her behind his back. "It's already done."

"Get out of my way," Eric aimed the gun directly at his son and Maya flinched.

"No."

"I said-"

A shot rang through the room and Eric turned to face it. Nico grabbed Maya by the waist and shoved her to the side, putting a heavy couch between her and her father.

"Stay here," he ordered, reaching behind him and pulling a gun from the waistband of his pants. "Try not to get shot."

"Nico-" Maya yelled after him plaintively but he was already gone. More gunfire and Maya covered her head, counting her breaths and waiting for it all to end. It took sixty seven breaths for the last shot to be fired. For her to hear a voice she thought she might never again.

"Where is she?"

Maya leapt to her feet, zeroing in on Stefan with a gun in one hand, a bloody knife in the other. He rounded on her quickly, immediately shifting the gun to a new target when he saw it was her.

"Maya, thank fuck, are you okay?"

"I am," happiness suffused her and she couldn't help the wide smile on her face. "Are you? Is-?"

"We all got out," he reassured her. "We got a little beat up but we're fine."

"Oh thank god," Maya started to cross to him but he motioned for her to stop and she did, focusing all her attention on him and ignoring her father.

"Came for your whore did you?" Eric asked calmly. "Gotta say, never thought she had it in her."

Stefan growled and Maya's heart nearly burst when Diego appeared behind him, the sleeves of one arm of his shirt burnt through. He whispered something and Stefan relaxed, dropping the gun to his side.

"So this is how the Alvanis end," Diego said conversationally, walking into the living room and looking around with interest. "Not with a bang, but a whimper."

"It should have worked," Eric snarled. "It should have fucking worked. You were too fucking cocky with - it should have fucking worked."

"You didn't count on your daughter's resourcefulness," Diego gave her a smile and crossed to her, holding a hand out which she took in a firm grip, reassuring herself he was real. He drew her in close, pressing a kiss to her forehead before turning back to Eric.

"I knew that little cunt couldn't be trusted," Eric grimaced.

A knife appeared in his thigh as if by magic, Maya never saw it leave Stefan's hand. One moment it was there and the next it was across the room. "*Language*," he chided and Maya could have kissed him. But she had to clear something up first, before things got out of her control.

"It wasn't me, well not *just* me," she told Diego, petting his arm. "Nico told me, helped me get to you."

"Really?" Diego raised an eyebrow. "Interesting."

Eric was furious, losing all control of his English abilities as he began to rant and rave, alternating between cursing a blue streak and whining about the knife in his leg. Maya ignored him.

"Please, I don't know what you're... be kind to my brother? Would you?" Diego nodded and she stepped away, turning to Nico. "Can you promise... if this all... it's not my decision but if you make it through tonight can you swear not to harm me or my family? Ever?"

Nico snorted, "As if I would."

"Nico..." she chided and he smiled.

"On a stack of *Mr. Popper's Penguins*, as long as I get to see my nieces and nephews I'll never touch a hair on your heads."

A wave of warmth rushed over and she dashed forward, catching him in a hug. "Thank you. I love you."

"Love you too," he whispered into her hair, patting her back. "Now get out of here unless you want to see the messy part."

Maya nodded and stepped back, moving to leave. She went via Stefan, stroking his cheek for a moment and smiling when he caught her hand and pressed a kiss into it.

"What do you want us to do about your father?"

Maya looked back at the man who had overshadowed her entire life, saw the hatred in his eyes, and shrugged. "I don't care what you do, just don't do it for me."

Stefan nodded and she left, passing a few security guards she recognized and giving Ryan a warm smile as he gave her a tight nod. The front doors were wide open and she took the front steps slowly, eyes scanning for the one person she was missing. She spotted him near the back, pacing near a black SUV.

"What are you doing out here?" Maya asked, crossing over to him. He looked rough, face streaked with soot and a cut along one cheek.

"Maya!" Daniel took a step towards her and flinched, clutching near his stomach. She raised an eyebrow, studying him.

"What's wrong?"

"Your cat is an asshole," he grumbled, unzipping his leather jacket and showing her the top of Mo's fluffy head. Maya gasped, reaching out and Daniel hissed, jerking away.

"What is it?"

"He's got his fucking - *fudging* claws in me." He hissed again and glared at his middle. "Why don't you go bother her, you cuntnugget?"

Maya couldn't help but laugh at Daniel censoring 'fuck' but not 'cuntnugget.' "I guess he likes you," she reached a hand out and scratched the cat under his chin, feeling the rumbling purr. "Thanks for getting him out."

"Of course," Daniel tried to look nonchalant, cradling a cat with one hand. "He's yours."

Maya switched from stroking the cat to stroking Daniel, cradling his jaw in her hand and pulling him forward so she could lean his forehead against hers.

"I'm glad you're okay."

Daniel nodded, swallowing and taking a shuddering breath. "I thought we'd lost you."

"I thought I'd lost you too," she whispered back.

Unspoken words hung in the air between them but Maya didn't reach for them. It wasn't the time, they should all be together when it happened. Yet Maya let herself bask in it a little, nuzzling her nose to his.

"Can we get out of here?"

Daniel jerked upright, eyes wild. "Shit, fuck, *fudge* of course. Get in."

He held the door open for her and climbed in after, giving the driver an address for a hotel downtown. Maya leaned into Daniel's shoulder while they traveled, petting a purring Mo and trying to keep her eyes open as the adrenaline wore off.

"C'mon," Daniel nudged her gently, "we're here."

He caught her as she stumbled from the car, keeping one hand cupped under Mo and the other around her waist. A brief argument ensued at the front desk when they saw the cat but Daniel began to throw out numbers that eventually netted a room key.

It took Daniel three tries to get the door open, Maya no use as she leaned into his back and nuzzled the soft leather of his jacket. Once inside Daniel immediately took it off, settling Mo onto the couch in the center of the penthouse suite with a stern look and shove. Mo, being Mo, ignored it, butting up against Daniel's hand with a loud purr.

Maya smiled to herself, kicking her flats off and heading towards what she hoped was the bedroom, climbing into the center of the large bed and groaning when her head hit the pillow. She shut her eyes for a moment, relishing the feeling of peace that overcame her.

"I'll be out here," Daniel said and she pushed herself up on one hand. "Let me know if you need anything."

Maya shook her head, holding her other hand out. "I need you, come here."

He came without question, crawling into the bed with her and letting her pull him into her arms. His head rested against her chest, his hands clutching at her waist. A shudder wracked his body and she lightly scratched her nails over his scalp, making a soft soothing noise.

"It's okay, we're here. Together."

Daniel nodded and held her tighter. As she was debating what else she could say she heard the door to the suite open, and the voices of the two men she most wanted to see in the world.

"Maya? Daniel?"

"In here," Maya called back, not moving from her position with Daniel when he acted like he might roll away. He took the embrace willingly, sinking back into it and burying his face into the soft fabric of her sweater.

Stefan paused when he saw them and Maya held a beckoning hand out. He didn't need to be prompted twice, sliding in behind her and sandwiching her firmly between his body and Daniel's. She felt his lips on the back of her neck, a soft kiss as he settled in with a sigh.

Diego hesitated, standing by the open door. Maya knew this wasn't something he was comfortable with. He didn't show his emotions that way, but she reached beneath Daniel and gestured Diego over, watching as he laid down away from Daniel's back and took her hand in his, pressing a kiss to her fingers.

Maya shut her eyes, letting herself sink into the warm feeling of having them again. Letting her boys hold her as they sank into a dreamless sleep.

37

It was warm. Maya sighed as her eyelashes fluttered open, flexing her fingers and toes and smiling when she felt someone squeeze back. It was Diego, still there even though the morning sun was brightening the suite by the moment. There was a shift behind her and a soft hum, Stefan cuddling closer and she felt his half hard length press against her back.

"Morning," he slurred, nuzzling behind her ear.

"Morning," she whispered, glancing down and catching Daniel looking up at her. His glasses were askew and he looked incredibly uncomfortable. She took them off him gently, passing them to Stefan who set them aside.

Daniel leaned up and pressed his forehead to hers and she smiled, moving so she could brush his lips with her own. He groaned and behind her Stefan shifted, pressing harder.

"We shouldn't," Daniel warned, his palm sliding under her shirt. "We need to talk about things first."

Maya nodded, "We do." Sitting up slightly she pulled her shirt off, tossing her bralette after it immediately and laying back between them. "Probably. But not yet."

Daniel groaned and kissed her fully, tongue flicking into her mouth and teasing her own. Stefan's hands were between them, shoving her leggings and underwear down her hips until they lay in a tangled heap at the foot of the bed. He pressed her thigh and she lifted her leg, setting her foot behind his knee and opening herself wide to his exploring fingers.

"I missed you Maya," he whispered into her ear, gliding his fingers through her slick. "I missed your laugh, your smile… and this absolutely perfect *cunt*."

Maya gasped and arched her back, gasping again when Daniel ducked his head to pull her nipple into his mouth. She met Diego's eyes, his fond look as he propped himself on one arm and watched them. She could barely think, shivers of pleasure wracking through her as Stefan petted her and Daniel nibbled at her breast.

Pulling her further up, Stefan pressed inside her an inch at a time, slowly impaling her while she squirmed against him. Daniel replaced Stefan's hand with his own, rubbing tight circles on her clit while Stefan used his hand to hold her hips steady while he rocked into her.

"That's it Maya, let it… ah *fuck* you feel good."

Maya moaned, pulling Daniel's face to hers and tasting his lips, nipping at his jaw while Stefan teased her with long, full strokes. It didn't take long, Maya was so wound up she exploded after barely a minute, clenching on Stefan while he groaned into her ear.

As she came down she felt Stefan slip from her and her brow furrowed in concern. She was pretty sure he hadn't - but then Daniel was there, pressing inside and rational thought flew out the window. Stefan reached down and played his fingertips over her. He was more teasing, lighter touches that just skimmed where she needed him to be. Chuckling as she writhed against Daniel's body and he thrust into her sharp and fast.

"*Please*," she whined and Daniel shushed her.

"Be a good girl and come for us again. Can you do that for us, Maya?"

She groaned and Stefan finally gave her what she needed, pressing the heel of his palm high on her sex and grinding it down as she screamed, nails digging into Daniel's shoulders and his breath hot in her mouth.

Behind her Stefan shifted, letting her fall limply onto her back, Daniel's still hard length slipping out of her. He didn't seem to care that he hadn't come, turning towards her and pressing his face to her breasts, licking slow circles around her nipple. Stefan propped himself on his elbow, grinning at her and tracing his fingers over her lips.

"That good?"

Maya nodded and jerked in shock, glancing down to see Diego gently stroking her ankle. He didn't pull her towards him, as she thought he might, but rather prowled up the bed until she was caged between his arms. "Mind if I join?"

With a laugh she held her arms out, letting him come over her and give her a bruising kiss before he moved down and spread her thighs wide. She blushed as he stared at her, spreading her lips with his thumbs before giving a satisfied groan and licking a broad stripe through her. God he felt so *good*, long soothing strokes that sent tingles through her body, his hands splayed across her inner thighs to hold her even wider.

"That's it," Stefan smiled down at her. "That's our girl. You can do it."

Maya arched her back, feeling Daniel's lips skim over her collarbone before settling on her ear, nibbling the sensitive flesh while Diego's tongue slipped over her clit.

"I can't," she whined, blinking up at him through watery eyes.

"You can," Diego assured her, hooking her knees over his shoulders and slipping two fingers inside her. She cried out, clenching down hard on him. "Yeah, I can feel that. You fucking *can* Maya. Wanna feel you come for me."

Maya didn't know up from down anymore. There were hands everywhere, mouth sucking on her skin, words she barely knew the meaning of washing over her while they praised and cajoled and in the end ordered her to come for them again.

Who was she to say no?

Lights burst behind her eyes and her throat felt raw from the noises she was making. She felt encased by them, their warmth surrounding her and she let herself go completely, shuddering and writhing and barely feeling them hold her close as she slowly lost her sanity.

It took her a long time to come back to herself, looking down to see Diego propping his chin on her stomach, grinning when her eyelashes fluttered open.

"Good morning."

Maya barked a laugh, raising her hands to cover her face. "Oh my God."

Someone gently pulled one away, Stefan pressing a kiss to her fingertips as he smiled at her. "That was pretty hot."

She blushed, suddenly conscious of her nakedness, and that the fully clothed men around her were still hard as rocks.

"Come here," she reached for Stefan's face, one hand slipping down to find Daniel but they both shushed her, Diego going so far as to pressing his teeth to her stomach with a low growl.

"Stop it," he told her without venom, "let us do this for you."

Maya frowned. "But I don't want that." Diego's expression shifted to one of horror and she quickly rephrased. "I mean that - I don't want this to be about *me*, it should be about *us*."

She wasn't sure what she was trying to say, only that she wanted to give back to them, *be* with them. Daniel seemed to understand first, letting her hand resume its journey downward and groaning when she took his length in her palm.

"You're fucking perfect you know that?"

"Language," Maya giggled but he cut her off with a laughing kiss, rolling her on top of him and pressing her hips back so she straddled his waist.

"So what word should I use when I want to fuck you?"

Diego pressed against her back, rocking her hips so she slid against both him and Daniel. Maya tried to focus, staring down at Daniel through a haze of emotions.

"Making love?"

There was a heartbeat of pause in the room and then Daniel surged upwards, only missing out on kissing her when Diego turned her head to his, pressing against her so harshly she saw stars. Daniel wasn't dissuaded, sucking a bruising kiss into the side of her neck instead. She shoved at his shoulders, urging him up the bed and his clothes from his body, arching her back when she finally got his underwear off and could bend over and pull him deep into her mouth.

"Jesus *Christ*," he groaned, hands fisting into her hair. She didn't mind, letting him guide her up and down, tonguing against his sensitive flesh and sucking on the head. Diego moved behind her, the sound of his clothes hitting the floor, and then his hands pulling her hips higher and groaning as he sank inside her. The sharp strokes made her whine, humming around Daniel who cursed in response.

"Fuck Maya, I'm gonna..." he tried to warn her and she sank down further onto him, digging her fingers into his hips and licking every drop he gave her when he arched and came deep in her mouth. Diego followed soon after, cursing as he tried to shift position to rub between her legs. Maya didn't mind, clenching her muscles down until he grunted and pounded into her harder, the warm rush of liquid between her thighs making her feel more than a little smug.

They collapsed next to each other, Maya sitting up on her knees and wiping one hand across her mouth. The two looked *wrecked*, Diego's hair was mussed and Daniel had a dazed expression on his face. Both were breathing heavily and Maya could feel her own chest rising and falling with her own rapid breaths.

"I got you," Stefan whispered into her ear and she let herself melt against his bare skin, shifting when he lifted her slightly so he could settle her on his thighs. Sighing as he molded her hips into his hands and arched her back and slipped inside of her. A shuddering gasp escaped her and Stefan chuckled, nuzzling beneath her ear.

"Look at them Maya," he ordered and she did, watching them watch her. Daniel looked stunned, eyes glued to her face and the expression she made as Stefan took her. There was a hint of adoration there, as though she had only to beckon a finger and he would be with her a second. And Diego... his eyes roamed over her possessively, lingering on the marks their hands and mouths had made. He looked smug, self-satisfied, like a cat that had finally caught the canary. But then he met her eyes and she saw something else - pride. Pride for *her*.

Stefan guided her arms up, pulling her hands behind her head and into his hair. Her body was stretched out, exposed, one of his hands cupping her breasts like an offering while the other played between her thighs.

"Love you," he groaned into the shell of her ear. "So fucking much. You're ours, aren't you? Please say you're ours."

His tone had a pleading edge and her heart lurched, words spilling from her without thought. "Yes, yours. All yours. Always."

She came, body aching, nerves so sensitive she almost hurt. Stefan sank his teeth into her shoulder and shuddered behind her. Maya had to grab his wrist to stop him from touching her, tears springing to her eyes and he whispered apologies into her ear, wrapping his arms tightly around her body and pressing her forward into the waiting arms of Daniel and Diego. It was his turn to rest between her legs, his head rising and falling with each breath she took.

Maya didn't know how long she lay there. No one said a word, bodies pressed together in an awkward pile. Diego was the one who eventually broke it, stroking a finger down her nose and pressing a kiss to the tip.

"Now we *really* have to talk."

Maya giggled, laughing harder when Stefan frowned at how the action made his head rock back and forth from its place on her lower stomach.

"C'mon," Diego shifted quickly, pulling her upright by one hand and smacking Stefan's bare ass. Stefan yelped and Diego kept pulling, holding her as she stumbled on weak legs. "Go take a shower, we'll get some new clothes sent up."

Mreow.

Maya laughed, pressing her forehead to his shoulder. "And cat food. Or Mo might eat one of your dangly bits."

"Do cats do that?" she heard Daniel ask as she stumbled towards the bathroom and she pressed a hand to her mouth to cover the laugh.

One long hot shower later and Maya felt like a new woman, thanking Stefan when he slipped inside with a pile of new clothes and dodging his kisses when he tried to back her into the shower again.

"Diego will kill us," she murmured, nipping his lower lip.

"I can take him," Stefan assured her, pulling at the towel wrapped around her.

She guided him out with a shove, closing the door firmly and waggling a finger in his face. He pouted theatrically before turning away, answering a question from Diego she hadn't heard. The pile of clothes held options, more leggings and t-shirts, but also a cute summer dress in dark green. She slipped it on out of curiosity, examining herself in the mirror. It looked *good* and maybe it would distract the men again and she could put off the conversation that was about to happen. Adjusting the thin straps on her shoulders and fluffing her hair, she all but skipped out of the bathroom.

"Shower's free," she singsonged, grinning when Daniel let his laptop slip off his knees at the sight of her.

"I'm next," Stefan jumped in, patting her ass and murmuring, *"Minx,"* as he passed by. Diego raised an eyebrow, scanning her appreciatively and then turning back to the window and his phone conversation. That left Daniel and the plate of croissants in front of him which seemed like an *amazing* idea.

"That thing should be illegal," Daniel grumbled as she settled in next to him, tucking her feet under her and leaning on his shoulder.

"*You* bought it," she pointed out, flicking a flake of pastry from her chest.

"I just sent down your measurements, someone else did the shopping."

Humming happily and nibbling at the chocolate filling, Maya barely paid him any attention, only noticing when he shifted slightly so she could settle more comfortably into his side. It took three croissants to slake her, Daniel giving her a disbelieving look when she polished off the third and she said defensively, "I didn't eat yesterday!"

His eyes narrowed and he reached for his phone, immediately ordering half the room service menu before giving his place up to Stefan with a mutter about women never saying what they want.

Stefan worked on his phone with one hand while he sat with her, the other around her shoulder and stroking his fingers along her arm. Mo came searching then, hopping onto the couch and into her lap and she stroked him under the chin how he liked.

"So the apartment is just *gone*?" she asked after a while.

Stefan nodded, "We might be able to salvage a few things but they blew out all the windows and half the twenty-eighth floor along with our conference room."

"Wow." She scrunched her face, twisting her lips into a moue of concentration. "Can't say I'll miss the furniture."

"Don't worry," Daniel assured her, "the sex swing was in storage. I'm sure it survived."

"Oh screw you." She kicked his thigh and he grunted, squeezing her ankle.

"Wait, so screw is acceptable but fuck isn't? I need some guidance on these rules."

Maya blushed, biting her lower lip. "Screw is *also* bad."

Gasping theatrically, Stefan tickled her side. "Did little Maya just *cuss*?"

Squirming away from the Maya flounced to the other couch, dropping onto it and glaring at them. "Jerks."

Pounding one fist to his chest Stefan scrunched his face up like he might cry. "Oh, a shot right to the heart."

Maya stuck her tongue out just in time for Diego to round the wall and blink at her. Feeling childish Maya quickly tucked her skirt around her thighs, patting the seat next to her and then frowned when he took a chair to the side instead.

"We need to talk," was all he said and Daniel and Stefan both immediately set aside what they were doing, shifting to move across to the other couch.

Maya sighed, "Okay."

No one said a word.

As the silence stretched Maya had to fight to hold back a smile. The men kept looking at each other, each one trying to get the other to be the first to speak. After what felt like a full five minutes Maya took pity on them.

"I was going to stay."

All the tension seemed to leave the room in an instant.

"With conditions."

"Anything," Daniel and Diego said in unison, Stefan nodding along.

"I want a room with you guys, not a million miles away. And my own office." She laid the condition out with precision, testing the waters.

"You can have as many rooms as you want wherever you want," Stefan responded quickly.

"And I want my own guys that work for me that I pay with my own money." Daniel frowned and Maya continued, "At least for a while."

Daniel still looked conflicted but Diego nodded, "You want to be sure there are people around loyal to you."

Maya met his eyes with a level look, "Until we know that this is going to work-"

"I get it," he cut her off. "We can figure that out but I don't see why we can't."

She'd expected more pushback about that and his quick acceptance made her hesitate.

"What is it?" Stefan asked softly.

"I'm not a mind-reader," she finally said after a long pause. "And I'm not going to spend all my time trying to figure out what you guys are thinking - I'll drive myself crazy. If something is bothering you, you have to *tell me*. Not just avoid me," she shot Daniel a look and he blushed, biting his lower lip. "Or yell at me," Diego didn't wait for her eyes to fall on him, already nodding, and she moved straight to Stefan. "Or fuck me over a table."

"What about making love to you over a table?" he asked with a sly grin.

"Maybe," she conceded. "Occasionally. But because it's fun not because you're all bent out of shape."

"Promise," he held up two fingers. "Scout's honor."

"Still the wrong hand," Daniel sighed.

"Is there anything else?" Diego asked softly, eyes steady on her face.

"I want you," Maya shrugged. "And if we can make it work… I think we could all be happy."

"All of us?"

Daniel's murmur was almost too soft to hear, his eyes boring into hers from behind his glasses.

"*All* of you. You're a package deal, right?" She pointed at them and then made a circle, "Well, now *we're* a package deal."

"This feels too simple," Diego shook his head.

"Shut *up*," Stefan snapped at him.

With a laugh Maya moved off the couch, sitting on the edge of the coffee table so they were all together. "It's not simple at all, of course it's not. We're going to have to feel our way through a lot of things. But I love you," she looked each of them in the eyes as she said it, "and family isn't just blood, right? Sometimes it's people finding each other."

"I'm glad we found you," Daniel told her solemnly.

Maya smiled, feeling her chest fill with warmth. "I'm glad I found you too."

Suddenly she frowned, glaring at them. "But I swear to God if you knock me out *one more time*-"

About the Author

BRANDY JONES began stealing her grandmother's romance novels at ten years old, smuggling them home and dreaming of a hero to sweep her off her feet. Decades later, she's expanded her requirements to all genders but still dreams of romance. She lives in California with her dog and three houseplants she hasn't yet killed.

Printed in Great Britain
by Amazon